Praise from *New York Times* Bestselling Authors

"Jacquelyn Frank is a fresh new voice, a stunning new talent. I look forward to the next book."

—Sherrilyn Kenyon

"Jacki Frank's NIGHTWALKER series depicts an engrossing alternate world, drawn in prose that is lush and lyrical."

—Linda Howard

"Jacki Frank's JACOB is mesmerizing, breath-taking, scorching sex and filled with unforgettable characters."

—Christine Feehan

"JACOB: THE NIGHTWALKERS is the page-turning beginning of a fresh, original, new series. Readers will devour Jacob's story and camp out at the bookstore demanding more. Jacquelyn Frank knows how to write an intense, rip-roaring good read!"

—Cathy Maxwell

"An astounding, fresh, captivating new voice—paranormal fans will devour this book!"

—Lori Foster

"Like the most delicious chocolate, JACOB: THE NIGHT-WALKERS is rich, dark, and satisfies every craving."

—JoAnn Ross

THE NIGHTWALKERS

JACOB

JACQUELYN FRANK

ZEBRA BOOKS
Kensington Publishing Corp.
www.kensingtonbooks.com

For Laura,
my proofreader, my editor, my cheerleader,
my critic who keeps me from looking silly,
my very most loyal fan and one of my best friends.

For Tanya,
who believed in me just as much as Laura has
and in all the same ways.
Thank goodness for the internet!

And . . .
for Pat,
who gave me my very first typewriter
and made me put my money where my mouth was
at the tender age of thirteen.
I finally did it!!!

With special thanks to:
Kate, Robin, Sulay and Diana.
Thanks for all you have done
and for putting up with all my . . . eccentricities!

Extra special thanks to Lori Foster
for holding a very fated contest
and all the authors who helped her run it.
It changed my life into what I always wanted it to be—
the life of a published author!

CHAPTER ONE

How ridiculously simple it would be to cause them harm.

From far above, he watched with unwavering dark eyes as they walked down the shadowy street. The human male was so absorbed in his flirtation with his female, he would have no chance of protecting her from harm should they be surprised by a threat, What if he were to drop onto them from his current height?

Although in that instance, "surprised" wouldn't be an adequate descriptive. The debate of defense would be futile as well. A human versus one of his ilk?

Jacob the Enforcer exhaled a sardonic laugh.

The redheaded woman had chosen poorly, in his opinion. No respectable male would have encouraged his partner to venture out on such a forbidding night. Mystical portents aside, the street they walked was notoriously disreputable. Menacing shadows shifted with threats unknown to simple human senses as clouds skimmed over the fickle light of the moon.

The couple walked beneath him, oblivious to his camouflaged presence.

Not to mention the coming of the other.

Jacob cocked his head, taking careful note of the other's distant movements. Though the man-made features of a glass-and-concrete city numbed the Enforcer's favored senses, he could still follow the comer's progress easily. The younger, less experienced Demon was being careless, his focus riveted to his objective.

The human female.

Jacob recognized the younger Demon's hunger, feeling it as it eddied into him, oppressive and pungent with the musk of unrestrained lust. The young Demon, Kane by common name, was stepping in and out of solid existence as he progressed toward the redhead. Kane's fixation was making him uncharacteristically single-minded. He had no idea that the Enforcer had pursued him, that he was now lying in resolute wait for him.

Kane abruptly appeared on the pavement below in a burst of roiling smoke and the distinctive odor of sulfur. He was several yards behind the unknowing couple, his teleportation going completely unnoticed despite its display.

Jacob waited, the tension stretching his nerves taut. Although it pressed on him to interfere, it was his duty to let the other Demon commit to his course. Only then would he have justification for bringing the laws of their people down on him. All the while, he prayed to Destiny that Kane would regain control and walk away.

As Jacob gave the other Demon his chance to change his mind, he sat as still as a stone, watching Kane step into the recently trod path of the couple. When he passed beneath the Enforcer's unseen perch up on the light pole to gain on his prey, Jacob launched upward into the air in a light, airy leap from one lamppost to the next several yards down the sidewalk. There was no sound as his feet touched the cool metal, no rustle of the clothing he wore as he crouched down once more in perfect balance. The only telltale sign of his presence was the sudden flickering twitch of the light. It only took him a moment to compensate, making the others below him perceive all as normal, though in actuality the light continued to flash with increasing spasms of protest.

He kept his thoughts hidden behind this projected camouflage as well. He knew that even in the grip of these basest of instincts, Kane would sense him if he did not. And yet, a whisper in the back of his mind was begging the Enforcer within him to just once, only this once, make an error. *One small error*, it murmured, *and Kane, who is so dear to you, will sense your presence and your thoughts. Let him have the chance that you have denied so many others.*

No one would ever know what Jacob sacrificed to deny that insidious whispering. Regardless of the voice's entreaty, he could not forswear his duty.

So instead, he watched as Kane sent out his summons to the vulnerable couple. Abruptly, the male human turned and walked away from the female, abandoning her without reason or the awareness that he was doing so. The redhead turned completely around, facing the approaching Demon. She was quite beautiful, Jacob noted as she faced the lamplight, with a lush, long body and auburn curls hanging in lengthy coils down her back. It was clear why she had attracted Kane. It wasn't the Enforcer in Jacob that allowed a small, quirking smile to play at the corner of his otherwise grim lips.

Kane sauntered up to her, completely confident of his power over her, and reached to touch her face. Jacob could see the thrall in her eyes, the manipulation of her mind making her soft and pliant, making her turn her cheek into his affectionate caress.

The affection was a lie. What would start with this gentility could not possibly end with it. It was the nature of the creatures that they were, and it was inevitable. This was why he could never have allowed Kane any more warning than he had already given hundreds . . . no . . . thousands of times before this.

Jacob had seen enough.

He leapt lightly into the air, his long body tumbling gracefully in a backflip until he came full around and landed soundlessly behind the redheaded woman. He discarded his camouflage so abruptly that Kane sucked in a loud, startled breath. He froze when he saw Jacob, and the Elder was easily aware of what the young Demon's thoughts must be.

The Enforcer had come to punish him.

It was enough to make Kane swallow visibly in apprehension. His hand jerked away from the redhead's cheek as if she'd burned him, and his concentration broke from her. She blinked, suddenly becoming aware that she was sandwiched between two strange men and had no idea how she had gotten there.

"Take hold of her mind, Kane. Do not make this worse by frightening her."

Kane obeyed instantaneously and the lovely woman relaxed, smiling softly as if she were in the easy company of old friends, now completely at peace.

"Jacob, what brings you out on a night like this?"

Jacob wasn't deterred by Kane's casual quip or his attempt at saving face through levity. The Enforcer already knew the other male was not wicked at heart. Kane was still relatively untrained and, considering the conditions of the night, it was easy for him to be led astray by his own baser nature.

That did not change the stark facts of the moment. Kane had literally been caught with his hand in the cookie jar. His knee-jerk reaction, understandably, was to bargain his way out of the punishment he knew was impending. He would start with humor and continue on to every other tool in his arsenal.

"You know why I am here," the Enforcer said, nipping those tools right in the bud with a chill, disciplined tone that warned Kane not to test his mettle.

"So maybe I do," Kane relented, his dark blue eyes lowering as he shoved his hands deep into his pockets. "I wasn't going to do anything. I was just . . . restless."

"I see. So you thought to seduce this woman to appease your restlessness?" Jacob asked bluntly as he folded his arms across his chest. His entire manner radiated the image of a parent scolding a wayward child. It could be an amusing thought, considering Kane was just about to enter his second century of life, but the matter was too serious by far.

"I wasn't going to hurt her," Kane protested.

Jacob realized that Kane actually thought that was true. "No?" he countered. "Just what *were* you going to do? Ask politely if you could visit the savageness of your present nature on her? How does one word that, exactly?"

Kane fell stubbornly silent. He knew that the Enforcer had read his intentions from the moment he'd decided to stalk prey. Arguments and denials would just worsen the situation. Besides, the incriminating evidence of his transgression was standing between them.

For a brief, passionate moment, Kane's thoughts filled with vivid mental imaginings of what could have been more incriminating. He suppressed a shudder of sinful response, his eyes falling covetously on the woman standing so beautifully serene before him. Had Jacob been even slightly off his irritatingly perfect game and come into the picture a half hour later . . .

"Kane, this is a difficult time for our people. You are as susceptible to these base cravings as any other Demon," the Enforcer said with implacable resolve. It was as though Jacob were the one who could read Kane's mind, rather than the other way around. "Still, you are a mere two years from becoming adult. I cannot believe you have me chasing you down like a green fledgling. Think of what I could be accomplishing if I were not standing here saving you from yourself."

Kane's rugged features flushed red with the shame Jacob intentionally laid at his feet. It relieved the Enforcer to see the reaction. It told him that Kane's conscience was once again functioning, his usually smart sense of morality closer to restoration.

"I'm sorry, Jacob, I really am," he said at last, this time with sincerity rather than as another ploy to try to disarm the Enforcer. Jacob could tell he was sincere because he finally stopped staring at the redhead as if she were due to be served to him on the proverbial silver platter.

As the Enforcer's dynamic presence stabilized his principles, Kane was realizing that he'd placed Jacob in an untenable position, perhaps in a way that might forever mar their relationship. Kane's throat closed with the sharp sense of remorse that knifed through him.

It was as overpowering as the dread that was welling up within him. He'd betrayed the sanctity of their laws, and there was punishment for that—a punishment that made an entire species catch their breath and back away whenever the Enforcer entered the vicinity. Kane could suddenly feel the weight of Jacob's position, and it sharpened his regret to a point of pain in his chest.

"You will send this woman home safely by reuniting her with her escort and making sure she remembers nothing of your misbehavior," Jacob instructed softly as he watched the tumult of emotion that swam across Kane's face. "Then you will go home. Your punishment will come later."

"But I didn't do anything," Kane protested, a swift rise of inescapable fear fueling the objection.

"You would have, Kane. Do not make this worse by lying to yourself about that. You will only convince yourself that I am the villain others like to make me out to be. That will only cause us both pain."

Kane realized that truth with another upsurge of guilt. Sighing resolutely, he closed his eyes and concentrated for all of a second. Moments later, the redhead's escort loped back across the street with a smile and a call to her.

"Hey! Where'd ya go? I turned the corner and suddenly you weren't there!"

"I'm sorry. I was distracted by something and didn't realize you'd gone, Charlie."

Charlie linked his arm with his date's and, completely oblivious to the two Demons barely a breath away, drew her off.

"Good," Jacob commended Kane. It was simple and to the point. The younger Demon was becoming quite efficient as he matured.

Kane sighed, sounding gravely bereft.

"She's so beautiful. Did you see that smile? All I could think about was how much I wanted her to smile when . . ." Kane flushed as he looked at the Enforcer. Jacob was well aware that her smile hadn't been his only motivation. "I never thought this would happen to me, Jacob. You have to believe that."

"I do." Jacob hesitated for a moment, for the first time making it obvious to Kane that this had been a terrible struggle for him, no matter how well he projected otherwise. "Do not worry, Kane. I know who you really are. I know that this curse is hard for us to fight. Now," he said, his tone back to business, "please return home. You will find Abram there awaiting you."

This time, Kane brushed away the welling trepidation within himself. He did this for Jacob's sake, knowing how deeply this cut the Elder Demon, even though his thoughts were too carefully guarded for Kane to read. "You do your duty as you would with anyone. I understand that, Jacob."

Kane then gave the Enforcer a short nod of kinship. After glancing around to make sure they were unobserved, he exploded into a burst of sulfur and smoke as he teleported away.

Jacob stood for long moments on the sidewalk, his senses attentive until he was confident Kane was truly returning home. It wasn't unprecedented for a Demon to try running away and hiding for fear of impending punishment. Nevertheless, Kane was on the proper path, in more ways than one, once again.

Jacob turned and glanced up the street in the direction the human couple had taken. It never ceased to amaze him how lacking in instincts humans were. For all their civilization and technological advances, they had truly lost something valuable in trading away their animalist intuitions. That woman would be forever ignorant of how close she had come to danger. Meeting a wayward Demon in the shadow of a cursed moon was something no mortal wanted to be a part of.

Jacob released himself from the hold of gravity and rose into the air, barely causing a displacing breeze as he did so. His long, athletic body cut through the night like a beautifully honed blade. He soared past high-rises, some of the lights in the nearest occupied windows flickering in complaint at his passing. He burst up into the clear night sky.

Here, Jacob hesitated. He paused to study the bright, waxing moon with a frown he could not suppress. This was the way it was the weeks before and after the full moon of Beltane in spring and Samhain in autumn. These holidays were held Hallowed by Demons, but at the same time, they were the center of their curse. Restlessness amongst his people would only grow worse this coming week, peaking at the fullest moon. There would be more straying in the fledgling and adult generations. Even Elders would find their control sorely tempted.

Jacob had been chosen as Enforcer for a reason. His was a control beyond measure. Even the Demon monarch was considered more susceptible to this madness than he, and that was saying a lot considering that in all his four hundred years as Enforcer, Jacob had never been called to pull Noah, the Demon King, into check.

Jacob was grateful for that. Noah's powers were not something he would relish going up against. Their King hadn't earned his position by mere bloodlines like those in human histories did. Noah had earned his place based solely on his leadership and superiority of power.

As Jacob flew onward, his thoughts turned philosophical. Was it harder to be Enforcer or to be the King who must choose the Enforcer, as Noah had chosen Jacob? When making the choice, Noah would have been forced to acknowledge that there was an equal chance that he might one day find himself face-to-face with the Enforcer.

It was a brave leader who could still make the best choice knowing that one day he might live to regret it.

Noah looked up from his reading, the eddying energy of Jacob's approach reaching him long before the Enforcer himself drifted in through a high window in the form of a soft shower of dust. The Demon King understood that Jacob had allowed him to be aware of his coming, as he always did, out of respect. If he had wished, the Enforcer could have camouflaged his presence right up until the moment the dust coalesced into his normal athletic form, as it was doing now.

Noah watched the other Elder, who was now floating above the floor in solid form. Jacob returned his relationship with gravity to normal, touching down with the fluid grace that was always present in his natural movements.

The King sat back, his impressive build filling the oaken frame of his high-backed chair. Where Jacob was shaped for quick, agile power, Noah was bolder in his musculature and build. This was easily seen in the snug fit of his buff riding breeches and a silk shirt specifically tailored to the wide breadth of his shoulders. Still, Noah had his own style of elegance, and it showed as he casually hooked a black-booted ankle over his opposite knee. He sat silently for several beats, taking the Enforcer's measure thoroughly.

"I take it you found your youngest brother in time to stop him from causing any chaos?"

"Of course," Jacob replied in dismissive tones, instantly

striking Kane's enforcement off the list of topics he was willing to discuss at present.

Noah got the message loud and clear and graciously accepted the terms. He watched as Jacob moved to pour himself a drink, paused to sniff the contents of the glass, and raised a questioning brow in Noah's direction.

"Milk," Noah offered.

"I know that," Jacob said impatiently. "From where?"

"A cow. But imported from Canada, nonpasteurized, and unprocessed."

"Hmm. I expected better on your table, Noah."

"The children were here. Anything better would have been too potent for them. They would have gotten tanked up and you would have been hunting down six of my sister's drunken little troublemakers. You recall what trouble she was when she was their various ages, do you not?" the King asked. "Imagine the spunk of her progeny."

Jacob actually grinned at that, tipping the glass up to his lips and taking a tentative sip. Judging the milk to be refreshing enough, he downed half the glass. "Your sister Hannah," he recalled, "barely drew breath before she began to cause trouble. For that matter, I am not likely to turn my back on any of your relations anytime soon." He toasted the King with an impudent tilt of his glass. "I am, of course, excluding Legna from the notorious side of your genetics," Jacob added generously.

"Of course," Noah replied dryly.

"So, how are the children anyway? Your sister must be going crazy trying to keep all of them under control, given the circumstances," Jacob remarked. He glanced upward out of habit, indicating the moon neither of them could see.

"Why do you think Hannah brought them here? I

think she was hoping the foreboding presence of their royal uncle would help control them." Noah reached up to rub a knot in his neck. "I could have used your help. Imagine how well behaved they would have been if the Enforcer had walked in the door."

Jacob knew Noah was teasing him, but he didn't see as much humor in the statement. The Enforcer, in the Demon world, was what mothers used to scare their children into good behavior. It was a necessary evil, considering the powerful mischief young Demons were capable of, but that didn't mean it sat well with Jacob. It made for a pretty solitary existence, actually. Those Demon children grew up into adults and Elders who never quite shook off their fear of the Enforcer.

Then again, that made his job all the easier. It was a rather nice perk when all it took was his appearance to quell even the most powerful stomachs, making actual battles for control less likely. He was surprised it had worked so well on his brother. Kane was notorious for claiming that, having been raised by the Enforcer, he wasn't at all intimidated. That obviously wasn't true, and Jacob wasn't sure how he felt about it. Grateful he hadn't had to fight his baby brother? Of course. But happy that his brother was as terrified of him as all others were? No, not really.

"So, have you learned anything useful?" Jacob indicated the large, dusty tome sitting half read on Noah's table.

"Not really." He paused for a beat, narrowing a pair of jade and gray eyes on Jacob, his irises so pale in contrast to his tanned complexion that they seemed to glow in the firelight. Noah's inspection made it clear that he hadn't missed the artful change of subject. "As archaic as we tend to be in culture and customs, these books prove how modernized we really are. It is like reading another language."

"Language is a living thing. As a scholar, surely you must appreciate that even a language as old as ours evolves over time."

"Well, that does not help me much now. We are in the midst of an intensifying crisis, and I am no closer to finding a solution than I ever was."

"Then we will just have to maintain, as we always have," Jacob said quietly, his modulated tone meant to settle Noah's piqued frustration. Noah's temper was ten times more famous than his sister Hannah's, though he usually exhibited ten times more control over it as well. Noah firmly believed that no individual could rule over others if he could not control his emotions. "I have faced everything imaginable and persevered, Noah. No one will be harmed, or be allowed to do harm, for as long as I draw breath."

"But it is getting harder, is it not?" Noah looked up and met Jacob's eyes sharply. "Every year I watch you become busier and more disheartened. Every year I see more of the most highly accomplished Elders lose control as if they were in their first hundred years all over again. Tell me I am mistaken."

"I cannot tell you that," Jacob said, sighing heavily as he ran a long-fingered hand through thick, brown-black hair. "Noah, I had to enforce Gideon just under a decade ago. Of the handful of Demons I thought to be impervious to this madness, Gideon the Ancient was highest among them. *Gideon!*" Jacob shook his head, mute with his disturbed emotions and the chilling memories of that dreadful encounter.

"And he is still wound-licking. Gideon has not come out of his stronghold for these past eight years."

"Well, he certainly will not come about while this is continuing to grow worse." Jacob frowned dourly as he sank into a chair across from Noah. "His seat at the Council table gathers dust and leaves us . . . incomplete."

Noah was aware of Jacob's personal angst over that fact but refused to let him wallow in it. "It is for the best, at the moment," Noah remarked. "I do not think you relish the idea of having to rein him in twice."

"No. I do not. But I am positive that locking himself away alone is the worst choice—the choice that will be far more likely to lead me and Gideon once more into a devastating conflict."

The bitterness in Jacob's voice was not lost on the King. Noah had never known another man with the Enforcer's sense of responsibility, loyalty, and morality. Death was the only thing that would ever convince Jacob to step down. This Enforcer would never retire so long as he breathed.

But something had not been right with Jacob for a while now. Year after year he was forced to bring the Elders he most respected to heel as madness briefly overcame them. It was clearly dragging Jacob down in both mind and spirit.

The worst, Noah supposed, had been the aforementioned confrontation with Gideon. Previously, Jacob had been the only Demon who could claim an actual form of friendship with that great Ancient. It had lasted up until the Enforcer had been forced to choose between that friendship and upholding the law. There had been no choice, really. Not for Jacob. The law was like lifeblood to him. An Enforcer with Jacob's level of dedication and sense of obligation would psychologically destroy himself if he defied the law.

Noah was aware that if he himself lost control of his

faculties during one of these Hallowed full moons and
Jacob were forced to snap him back like a recalcitrant
child, it would be hard for him not to resent the Enforcer for it. Sure, it would be for his own good, for the
good of the entire Demon race, and definitely for the
good of the defenseless humans they coexisted with,
but Elder Demons were a mightily proud lot and Noah
was no exception. Falling prey to weakness was bad
enough; having Jacob witness it was worse. Having the
Enforcer punish them brutally, as the law demanded,
was unbearable.

Noah did not envy Jacob his position in the least.

Just then, the man of Noah's concerned thoughts
raised his dark head from its brooding bent, tilting it
to one side as his semirelaxed frame rapidly grew
tense. Noah felt the hairs on the back of his neck stir
as the other man's sensory powers filled the room.
Every Demon had his own particular abilities in which
he excelled, and Jacob's hunter's perceptions were
among his keenest.

"Myrrh-Ann comes," Jacob said, putting his glass
down on Noah's desk as he rose to his feet. "She is extremely agitated."

Just then, the two large doors at the end of the room
burst open violently. A swirl of dark dust and wind spun
into the room, whirling like a small tornado, crossing
toward the two males in the blink of an eye. It abruptly
settled with a final twist into the figure of a beautiful
woman with hair as soft and silvery white as the clouds,
her normally blue eyes nearly obscured by the domi-
nating black width of her pupils as unspeakable fear
pulsed behind them.

"Noah!" she gasped, reaching blindly for the King as
her panic caused a shudder to ripple through the air,

bending every flame in the room. "He has been taken! You must help me! I cannot lose him! He is everything to me!"

"Hush, now," Noah soothed softly, coming around his desk to pull her into a comforting embrace. "Calm down, Myrrh-Ann," he said quietly. "I assume you are talking about Saul?"

"It was horrible!" the young beauty sobbed, clutching at Noah's shirtfront. "He disintegrated beneath my very hands! Noah, you must help us!"

Noah and Jacob both went very still, their eyes meeting over Myrrh-Ann's bright head. They didn't need to speak to know the other's thoughts, to sense the quickened breath of alarm in one another.

"What do you mean, 'he disintegrated'?" Jacob asked carefully.

"I mean he has been Summoned! Enslaved!" Myrrh-Ann screeched, whirling in Noah's hold to glare at the Enforcer with all of her terror and outrage. "One moment he was with me, touching me, cradling our unborn child in his hands as it moved within me." Her hands went reflexively to her rounded belly, as if she were afraid it would be the next thing to be taken from her. "The next moment his face was contorting in such unimaginable pain. Dear, merciful Destiny! He began to fade, feet first, in a swirl of the most acrid and vile smoke I have ever known." She turned back to the King, clutching the silk of his shirt in her despair, her nails scoring the fabric. "He screamed! Oh, Noah, how he screamed!"

"Myrrh-Ann, please sit," Noah said, using a soft, comforting turn of voice to soothe her. "You need to calm down before you drop your babe too early. You have done the right thing by coming to us. Jacob and I will get to the bottom of this."

"But if he is enslaved . . ." Myrrh-Ann shuddered violently from head to toe. "Noah, how is this possible? Why? Why my Saul?" Myrrh-Ann lowered her voice to a rapid, breathless whisper of panicked, babbling words. The two others in the room could barely follow all the implications of her shattering thoughts as she rambled.

Could this be accurate? There hadn't been a Summoning of a Demon in almost a century. It was possible she was mistaken. Demons had once been threatened to near extinction from this horrific act of enslavement. It had been a necromancer's trick, a black sorcery that had faded in frequency as Christianity, science, and technology had come to reign. With the demise of such magics, peace had come.

The exceptions to that peace were obvious—the uncontrollable periods of madness that plagued them during the Hallowed moons, dodging relentless human hunters, and the occasional skirmish with other Nightwalker races.

As long as there has been the world, there have been Nightwalkers: the races of the night who breathed the nighttime air best, felt refreshment in the moonlight, and used the sun as a heavenly orb meant to be slept by. Demons, Vampires, Lycanthropes, and more shared these traits, if not always the same moralities and beliefs.

For as long as there have been Nightwalkers, there were those who sought to hunt them, humans armed with ignorance and folklore who stumbled about trying to murder them. These humans, fearing what they didn't understand, were fanatical in their quest to rid the world of the so-called creatures of pure evil. While normal human hunters did not faze the Demon race much, human magic-users known as necromancers were another issue entirely. In their spells lay a fate far worse than death for any Demon captured.

Myrrh-Ann's accusations could mean a crashing disruption in the balance of their world. It would mean that this ultimate magical threat had somehow become reborn. Some would say such a thing was inevitable as the recent human fascination with cults and dark magic had intensified, but the speculation was a far cry from the actual occurrence. A human magic-user? After all this time? Myrrh-Ann's story made it frighteningly possible.

"Noah, take care of Myrrh-Ann. I will track Saul."

"No! Oh, please!" Myrrh-Ann screamed. She made a mad leap for Jacob, who easily floated out of her reach and began to rise slowly into the air, intent on getting on with his grim duty. He felt wind suddenly swirl about in a room where there should be none, felt her tempestuous outrage rising, a reflex to her fear.

"Myrrh-Ann, time is short," Jacob said, his voice curt and reverberating against the high ceiling as he neared it. It froze her hysteria within her laboring chest. The air condensed and went still as he got her attention. "If I can find him in time, I can try to save him. If I cannot, then you know what my duty is. Believe me when I tell you I would rather bring him back to you and the babe."

With that said, the Enforcer disappeared in a streak of arrowed dust.

"He will kill him! He will murder my Saul!" Myrrh-Ann wailed, sobs ripping from her body.

"If it comes to that, Myrrh-Ann," Noah murmured softly, "it will mean the Saul we have loved is long gone already."

* * *

Isabella turned from the window when her sister's key sounded in the door.

"Hey, Corr, have fun?" she greeted while turning back to her stargazing.

"It was okay," her sister replied, dropping her keys on the table and shrugging out of her jacket. "He's a nice guy. Maybe too nice."

Isabella rolled her eyes, seeking guidance from the stars.

"How can a guy be 'too nice' in this day and age?"

"So speaks the great dating expert," Corrine rejoined tartly. She couldn't recall Isabella ever going out on a date, not even in high school. Corrine shrugged, clearly lacking understanding of her sister's antisocialism.

Isabella turned from her contemplation of the moon.

"So explain to me what 'too nice' means."

"Well, let's see . . ." Corrine mused, moving to stand next to Isabella, joining her in looking out at the October night. "He's very nice, very polite, and very predictable. I guess that's what I'm saying. He's nice, but not very exciting. Maybe you should go out with him."

Isabella laughed, her eyes widening in humor. "Did you just insult me?"

"No, not at all." Corrine chuckled, draping an arm over Isabella's shoulders and hugging her tightly. "I just would like to see you meet a nice guy. Even if he is 'too nice.' Although I don't think this one would easily adjust to the stuff that comes out of your mouth on occasion. Oh, and perhaps I should warn him that even though I am the redheaded sister, you are the one with the scary temper."

"Ha! It wasn't me who plagued Mom with the rebellious adolescence from hell."

Corrine laughed. "And it wasn't either of us who plagued Daddy with Mom's temper."

The sisters giggled in commiseration. Each knew exactly where they had earned their outspoken ways and stubbornness from, genetically speaking.

"Well, thanks for the offer of your hand-me-down boyfriend," Isabella said with a smile, "but I think I'll decline."

"Suit yourself." Corrine shrugged, leaving her sister and crossing into the kitchen. She peeked into the refrigerator.

Isabella turned back to the window and studied the moon a while longer. There was always something about it that got her juices flowing. Lately, she was restless, craving . . . something. She didn't know what. Being cooped up in the house was driving her mad, though. What she really wanted was to be out and walking around. Or running.

She mentally shook her head. Running after midnight in the less savory parts of the Bronx? No wonder people used to think the full moon made people crazy. If anyone could read her thoughts right now, they wouldn't recognize her as the calm, bookish Isabella they all knew and loved. That and they would probably nail her to the floor for her own safety.

In fact, Isabella had frequently wondered if the people who knew and loved her actually knew her at all. How could others know her, when she was beginning to doubt she even knew herself?

She lived a comfortable, quiet life, rather pathetically stereotypical for a single librarian. She even had the requisite pair of cats. She loved her books. There was such a wealth of information to be had, so much to learn, so many stories being told. Her appetite for it all had never once wavered since the day she had learned to read. She had probably forgotten more information than most people ever read.

However, where books had always been key to her contentment before, Isabella was now somehow . . . dissatisfied.

Isabella reached for the window and opened it swiftly, leaning out past the unscreened frame and into the cool, bright night. Everything always looked so different when the moon shone as brightly as the sun. Unlike the sun and its golden glow, the moon turned everything pale or silver. Shadows were long and mysterious, the boring black asphalt becoming a highway of incandescent gray.

"If you fall out onto your head, it will serve you right," Corrine remarked sarcastically from behind her. "I thought you were putting that screen back."

"Did you say you were going to bed?" Isabella asked, not bothering to look away.

She heard her sister blow an undignified raspberry at her, Corr's answer to everything when she couldn't think of a snappy enough response. "Yes, I'm going to bed. Make sure you lock the door before you go to sleep. Don't stargaze too long, you said you had to work early tomorrow."

"I know. Good night," Isabella said, waving behind herself without looking. She didn't see Corrine roll her eyes at her before heading down the hall to her bedroom.

Isabella leaned farther out of the window, bracing herself on the arms folded beneath her breasts as she looked down five stories to the sidewalk just below. Her hair drifted slowly over her shoulder, sliding like a silky black snake down her breast until it hung suspended in the night air.

Her eyes drifted around until she spied a man, dressed dark and dignified, coming toward her building. His footsteps were clicking softly through the night, his stride long and assured. She didn't know how, but even from her awkward height she could tell that his casual walk was a pretense. There was something in that lithe male figure that was very much on guard, and very . . . ruthless.

She judged him to be quite tall, comparing his height to the doors he passed. His hair was exceptionally dark despite the moonlight shimmering off it, probably black or a dark brown. She wasn't sure, but she thought it was caught back in a ponytail. He wore a long gray coat, unbelted and unbuttoned, with his hands tucked casually into the pockets. It shifted around his legs as he moved, gaping now and again, revealing a bluish gray shirt and black slacks. Expensive, sophisticated, and radiating even from a distance.

This was hardly an upscale neighborhood, and aristocratic, well-dressed men were not a common sight. In these parts they were more likely to be labeled as a meal ticket. Somewhere in the warehouse alleys up ahead, the dinner bell would be a-ringing.

The thought was no sooner completed than the man abruptly stopped. She saw something flash in the moon-scattered darkness around his face and she had the strangest notion that he'd just smiled. He was looking around, obviously in search of something.

Then he looked up.

Isabella gasped softly as he looked directly at her, her heart making an inexplicable jump beneath her breast. This time he clearly smiled, a sudden dash of white in light and shadow. He took a step, glanced both ways up and down the street, then leaned casually against a telephone pole as he looked up at her again.

"You are going to fall out."

Isabella blinked as the resonant voice drifted up and around her. He wasn't shouting. His voice had just floated up five stories and effortlessly spoken into her ear.

"You sound like my sister."

She didn't shout either, somehow knowing she didn't need to. Why didn't she find that strange? Well, she did find it strange. She just wasn't bothered by it.

"Then that would make two of us who think you should not be leaning out of a window like that."

"I'll make a note of your concerns," she responded dryly.

He laughed. The deeply male, inviting sound seemed to swirl around her, wrapping her up in the sensation of his amusement. It made her smile and hug her arms tighter around herself.

"Besides," she continued, "look who's talking. What are you doing wandering around these parts in the middle of the night? Have much of a death wish?"

"I can take care of myself. I would not worry."

"Okay. But you didn't answer my first question."

"I will," he countered, "if you tell me why you are dangling out of a window."

"This isn't dangling. It's *leaning*. I'm just looking around."

"Being nosy?"

"No. If you must know, I was looking at the moon."

She watched as he glanced over his shoulder at the moon, the act so casual that she got the feeling he wasn't so very impressed by it as she was.

"During your stargazing, did you happen to see anything unusual around here?" He framed the question in a very offhand way, but something told Isabella that he was far more concerned with her answer than he was trying to let on.

"The unusual is usual these days. Did you have something specific in mind?"

She felt him hesitate, knew he was debating within himself about something. He released a short, heavy breath.

"Never mind, sorry to have bothered you."

"No, wait!"

Isabella jerked, thrusting out a hand in a staying motion. The movement unsettled her precarious perch and she was suddenly struck with the odd sensation of her body shifting and gaining momentum. Her socks slid, the wooden floor providing zero traction, and her feet flew up off the floor as most of her body weight came over the windowsill. A strangled sound of surprise escaped her lips as she fell headfirst into the black and silver night. The sensation of falling yanked her stomach around and she figured that she would probably have thrown up if she were not about to die.

But instead of smashing into unforgiving concrete, she landed against something solid but giving. There was a sensation of whiplash as her body caught up with the sudden break in her speed, and bright stars swam around her eyes behind the lids she had squeezed tightly shut.

Isabella was rasping for breath, her adrenaline catching up with her as she clutched at whatever solid thing was within her reach.

"It is all right. You can open your eyes."

That voice. That deep, masculine, sexy, alive-and-not-splattered-on-the-ground voice.

Isabella popped one eye open and focused on her

grasping hands. They were curled around the gray fabric of the lapels of his coat.

"Holy crap," she gasped, both eyes flying open and looking up into the face of the man who had apparently saved her from cracking her skull open. "Holy—" She broke off, finally getting a good look at his features and getting yet one more shock to her system.

He was incredibly and unbearably beautiful.

There was no other way for her to adequately describe it to herself. It was beyond being just handsome. Handsome was a common masculine adjective, limited in its scope. This man was honestly beautiful. His facial features were so very elegant, taking the term *noble* to the extreme. Dark brows winged up over dark eyes, both of indeterminate color in the shadows of the night. So dramatic, but then so belied by the ridiculous childlike length of lush lashes. His magnificent eyes were lit with a soft, smoldering light of amusement as his sensual mouth was lifting up at the corner in a smile she could only call sinful.

"How did you . . . but that's . . . you couldn't possibly!" she spluttered, her hands opening and closing reflexively on his lapels.

"I did. It is not. And apparently, I could." He was smiling broadly now, and Isabella was certain she was the cause of some unseen bit of amusement. She glowered at him, completely forgetting he'd just saved her neck. Literally.

"I'm so glad you find this so entertaining!"

Jacob couldn't help his growing smile. She was so focused on him that she hadn't realized they were still a good ten feet off the ground and floating at the exact spot where he'd met her precipitous fall. That was for the best, he thought, sinking down to the pavement while she was distracted by the taunt of his amusement. He was going to have enough trouble as it was explaining how he'd managed to catch a woman hurtling to her death from five stories up. Let's see . . . five stories times . . . oh, about 125 pounds . . . times gravity . . .

"I do not find your situation entertaining," he responded honestly, very carefully keeping her attention as he brought his weight back to human standards. "I am actually just pleased to see you are not hurt."

Isabella blinked a couple of times, suddenly realizing just what this stranger had done for her.

Jacob watched the pixieish beauty's expression change from peevish indignation to utter horror. He mentally kicked himself for reminding her of her close call, even though logically there was no avoiding it. He watched as she pulled her full bottom lip between her teeth to keep it from trembling. The simple vulnerability sent a wrenching sensation through his chest, leaving him inexplicably breathless. Awareness and emotion exploding all around him, Jacob found himself staring at each and every nuance of the woman in his arms.

She was a compact and curvaceous little thing, her petite frame feminine and soft in all the places males liked a female to be abundantly soft. The moonlight enhanced a flawless complexion, pale like the near transparency of some Nightwalkers he'd seen in his extensive lifetime. She had sinuous black hair, ludicrously thick and long, and he could feel the weight of it as it pooled against his chest and clung to his biceps. Her features were small and delicate, her mouth lush, her eyes as large as an innocent child's. A pixie with eyes of violet, turned lavender in the moonlight. It was amazing how the moonlight enhanced her beauty. As he cradled her against his chest, he also marveled at how warm she was. He hadn't realized how enticing human warmth could be.

Jacob caught himself in the borderline-illicit thought, and reality returned in an explosion of shock. He nearly dropped her in his haste to put her away from himself. Flicking an acidic glare at the moon over his shoulder, he shoved his hands deep in his pants pockets and resisted a bizarre urge to pull her close again.

Finding herself back on her feet all of a sudden, Isabella was a little dizzy and bewildered. The man had abruptly put himself at a distance, as if he'd just realized she was some sort of a plague carrier. Then again, most men were likely to be uncomfortable when a woman showed any signs of distressed emotions. Still, he stayed close enough to reach for her if she needed him, but it took only a breath or two before she was clear and steady again.

Jacob watched her guardedly as she shoved a huge handful of hair back behind an ear nowhere near large enough to keep it pinned in place. The thick, silky cloud drifted forward again the moment she released it. He found himself besieged with the urge to push it back for her, just so he could discover the texture of it. He swallowed hard, cursing to himself in his own language, his jaw clenching rigidly.

"I don't know how to thank you, Mister . . . uh . . ."

"Jacob," he supplied, his growling tone making her start and back up a step.

"Mr. Jacob," she said uneasily.

"No, just Jacob," he corrected, forcing himself to speak more evenly, hating the idea of her fearing him just like everyone else. She was human. She had no cause to fear him.

"Well, Jacob," she said, her lavender eyes studying him

cautiously. Yet, an instant later, she was bold. "I'm Isabella Russ, and I'm extremely grateful to you for . . . for what you did. I can't believe you didn't break your neck."

"I am much stronger than I look," he offered in explanation.

Bella found that hard to believe. He looked every inch as powerful as he must be to catch her like that. He wasn't built brutishly, but he was nicely broad chested, large shouldered, and definitely hiding nothing of his physical fitness under his clothes. His was a lean, athletic build, taut and tight in all the right places from what little she could see and had felt beyond the gray coat. But beyond his dark good looks, great body, and the piratical ponytail, Jacob had an air of power to him that was like nothing she'd encountered before. Yes, he was definitely stronger than he looked, and not just physically.

It was enough to make even a lukewarm librarian shiver. A total package, complete with a European accent that was rich and elegant, just like the rest of him—Hungarian or Croatian, perhaps. He was quiet, graceful, and controlled, reeking a self-assurance that was piercing and an underlying dangerousness that sent that shiver up her spine after all. A total, enticing package for certain.

One that was probably married with six kids.

Isabella sighed as she reacquainted herself with reality, the release of her breath stirring up the hair on her forehead. "Well, anyway, thanks for . . . well . . . you know." She gestured lamely up to the window she'd fallen from. Her brows knitted together in puzzlement for a moment. How exactly had he been able to catch her without breaking his back? It looked impossible.

Suddenly Isabella felt the hair on the back of her neck rise up.

Jacob watched the little pixie's head jerk around sharply, her pretty eyes narrowing warily. It was enough to trigger Jacob's own instincts, and he felt out into the night for whatever it was that had disturbed her. To his shock, she had apparently picked up on the very thing he had been looking for.

Malevolence. Terror. Saul's utter terror. Jacob could smell the fear. He could taste the acrid stain of black magic. He was nearby, just as Jacob had suspected he would be when his trail had ended abruptly in this area. Whatever had pulled Saul kicking and screaming through the miasma of the darkness was once more invoking, poisoning, and tormenting the imprisoned Demon.

Yet Jacob's hunting senses caught no trail, found no direction.

Perplexed, Jacob's head came back around and his gaze pinpointed the small human woman who still stood with her head cocked toward the unknown beyond. Was it possible? Could this female have retained those instincts that, a couple of hours earlier, he had been accusing her race of having bred out of themselves, sensing what even he could not seem to get a fix on? He'd never heard of such a thing.

But Jacob felt her disturbance, smelled the change in her body chemistry as her adrenaline kicked up in a classic flight-or-fight reaction. Oh, yes, she definitely had a sense of the evil nearby.

"We better get off the street," she said quickly, reaching to take his arm.

"Why?" he countered, standing his ground against her tug.

"Because it's not safe," she said as if explaining to a two-year-old. "Now quit being macho and do as I say."

Do as she says? Is this tiny little woman actually trying to protect me? The concept floored him. "I am not being *macho*," he retorted, being purposely obtuse now as he watched her anxiety and reactions build to a crest. It was mesmerizing to watch color flush her face, her pulse flashing madly in her delicate throat and her full breasts swelling with her increasing breaths.

"Oy!" Isabella rolled her eyes. "Fine! Whatever. Just get off the street!"

"Why?" he persisted.

He watched in fascination as she once again blew back her hair with an exasperated sigh and planted her fists onto her round hips, her feet bracing stubbornly apart.

"Look, there're just some places where it isn't a wise idea to stand in the middle of the street arguing, and this is one of them! If you're bent on staying here, that's fine. I'm going—"

She stopped on a sharp gasp, her hand flying up to her throat and a faint gurgle of sound bubbling up. Jacob instinctively reached out to help her, not liking the wide and wild look of her startled lavender eyes.

"Isabella? What is it?" he demanded, pulling her protectively into his hold.

"Someone . . . oh, God, can't you smell it?"

He could. It was all around him, faint but unmistakable. The scent of burning flesh. Sulfur as well. But he had the honed hunting senses of any predatory species he wished, and it was none of those senses that brought the scent to him. There was no trail, no path. It was obscured from him. He was perplexed, but only spent a moment being so. This was a human woman with no such abilities as his, and yet here she was, gasping for breath, behaving as if she were breathing in thick clouds of smoke and sulfur when clearly she wasn't. Not physically.

Someone else was.

Saul.

A type of clarity burned in the back of Jacob's brain, although he was more mystified than ever. The Enforcer didn't pause to mull over the whys, hows, and impossibilities of what was happening. He only wanted to know one thing.

"Where? Can you tell me, Isabella? Where is he?"

"Close! Inside of me!" Her hands grasped at the fabric of her shirt across her chest, as if she wanted to tear the presence out. Her eyes were tearing, fat droplets flowing down her face as they tried to wash away smoke that wasn't even there.

"No. Listen to me." He reached to cup her face between his hands, instantly aware of how small she was between them, how delicate, as he tilted her face up to his. "It is near but not within. Where? Look and tell me where!"

Isabella whirled out of his hold and began to run, coughing and choking on phantom smoke as she lurched and sprinted. Jacob was fast behind her as they rounded a corner and crossed the street. She took one more corner and brought them face-to-face with an imposing set of rusty corrugated steel doors.

A warehouse. Long abandoned, and yet, in an upper window there was light flashing violently. Unnatural, cold light Jacob had foolishly thought he would never see again in his lifetime. He seized his tiny guide by her shoulders, drawing her back against his body as he bent toward her ear. Despite the disparity in their heights, she came to fit against him flawlessly.

"Listen," he murmured soothingly as she continued

to struggle for her breath. "This is not your agony, Bella. Do not own it like this." He glanced up at the ominous glow in the window, his heart pounding with the pressure to act, but he couldn't leave her there to suffocate. If her mind believed enough to react with tears and a hoarse voice, then she could believe herself into asphyxiation. "You can see there is no smoke. Are you listening to me, Isabella?"

She was. Though she didn't speak, she drew in her first clear, deep breath in what had felt like ages to them both.

"Good," he whispered, his warm breath skittering down her sensitive neck. "Now stay here, out of sight, and just breathe."

Jacob reached for the seam between the doors and wrenched them open as if he were tearing paper and not enormous pounds of steel, camouflaging the sound as a matter of second nature. Anyone inside would perceive it as merely metal creaking in the wind.

Instinctively, Isabella followed him into the dimness beyond the doors, giving no thought to his instructions. She was afraid of what was happening, but she was more afraid to be alone. She trailed him, her hands clinging to his flapping coat as he strode through the pitch and shadow. There were flares of light and then blackness, the combination blinding her painfully. Jacob walked on without hesitation, as if it were broad daylight, moving toward the light with a sense of menace that was palpable to her. Unexpectedly, she felt him rising up before her, apparently climbing a ladder. He slipped out of her grasp and she was left fumbling for the ladder on her own.

She couldn't find it. No matter how much she felt around, she couldn't find the means he had used to bring himself up to the loft level of the warehouse. All she could do was turn toward the light that now back-lit his figure as he slowly, stealthily crept up on the source of it. Her harsh breath seemed to make too much noise as she struggled for oxygen. Jacob moved closer and closer.

Suddenly, he leapt.

Really leapt.

Isabella might have been seeing things in all that haze of gloom and light, but she could've sworn the man made a lithe twenty-five-foot leap from a standing position into the fray of whatever it was that was up there.

Hell promptly broke loose.

Without warning, the smoke she'd smelled roiled out of the sickly light, spilling off the edge of the loft like a foul waterfall in green, rust, and black clouds. Then there was a massive explosion, debris and bodies hurtling out of the loft like missiles, forcing Isabella to duck and cover, her eyes burning with the flare of light.

Unbelievably, it was raining men.

Jacob crashed to the floor about ten feet to Isabella's left with a bone-jarring thud that kicked up an enormous cloud of dust. Another body slammed into some boxes not too much farther away. A third struck the floor near the open doors, actually landing on its feet. The man absorbed the shock of his landing like a cat. Then, with a swirl of the fabric of his coat—or was it a cloak?—he turned and ran out of the open doors.

Ignoring everything else, Isabella reached for the broad shoulders of the man heaving heavily for breath on the floor.

"Jacob!"

"Isabella, get the hell out of here!" Jacob roared the command as he lurched awkwardly to his feet, grabbing her and thrusting her back and away from himself so hard that she fell over backward and landed on her bottom. She sputtered for a moment, cursed at the embarrassing and bruising pain, and had every intention of telling Mr. Jacob Macho to go to hell.

The words froze in her throat as the man who had landed in the boxes rapidly rose up above them.

Literally, rose up.

Floated right up into the air.

Isabella gasped as she witnessed this and as she realized several extremely important things. The man who was hovering above her and Jacob was not a man at all. Although bipedal and relatively humanoid, it was actually some kind of enormous creature with hellish green eyes glowing fiercely out of its misshapen head. It had long, enormous ears that pulled up and back into points, fanning out like webbing or fins rather than ears.

It had fangs.

Oh, and very, very big wings.

Isabella had a strange, hysterical urge to giggle.

Okay, when exactly, she wondered, *did I fall asleep?* Of course people didn't just catch people who fell out of windows. She absolutely would never follow some strange man into an abandoned warehouse. And there were no such things as fanged, bat-faced creatures *flying* around the Bronx.

Then the creature focused directly on her.

Okay, time to wake up, she thought as panic rose in her throat.

The winged thing began to make a dive for her.

Like flashing lightning, Jacob flew off the floor in another incredible leap, connecting with the monster midair. Their collision was a sickening sound of flesh and bone impacting, and Isabella flinched. Jacob's momentum sent the tangle of their bodies hurtling into more boxes well across the room.

Frantically, Isabella scanned around herself, looking for some kind of protection. The first thing she found was a heavy rod, rust flaking off in her hands and scratching at her palms as she picked it up. She scrambled to her feet, hoisting it like a Louisville Slugger, waving it threateningly in case Jacob hadn't quite finished the job.

He hadn't.

Suddenly the two struggling bodies leapt out of the boxes in a burst of flying cardboard. This time the slimy beast had the upper hand, its enormous wings building up speed as it hurtled Jacob helplessly upward, finally slamming him full bore into the ceiling. The sound of long metal plates buckling pinged through the shadows and Isabella watched in horror as Jacob plummeted to the ground like a weighted stone.

He hit at bone-breaking speed, the appalling impact kicking up another cloud of dust. Isabella choked, horrified as she watched a dark puddle ooze out from beneath the darkly beautiful head of her would-be savior.

She stood, frozen in place, as the creature circled above her once, twice, drifting down like an anticipating vulture until it lightly came to rest on the balls of its clawed feet just in front of her. She got a good look at it, taking in the slimy russet skin, protruding chest, and concave belly. Its lips were thin and pulled back to expose two rows of fangs, as well as the two that tusked out in a terrible snarl. The hands were the worst, tipped with greenish claws about six inches in length, dripping a dark liquid that looked suspiciously like the puddle forming under Jacob.

"Pretty," it hissed.

Okay, so the voice is worse than the hands, Isabella amended mentally.

"Yeah, well, you could use a facial or something." Isabella slapped a rust-covered hand over her own mouth. *Oh, great, Bella, antagonize the big bad creature, why don't you?*

"Pretty meat," the creepy thing elaborated.

Well, that didn't sound good at all, she determined.

"Um . . . you know, I hear vegan is the way to go these days," she offered, her voice pitching higher as the fiend advanced on her with a step, forcing her to backpedal.

"Warm meat. Hot meat." Then the thing made a crude speculation about the meat of a particular part of her female anatomy.

"Hey! Watch your mouth, buddy! And stay where you are, or . . . or . . ." Isabella raised the rod threateningly, trying to think of the best way to intimidate a gargoyle. "Or you are going to get whacked in your meat!"

Well, it was a male after all, and some things just had to be universal.

Then again, she thought as it smiled wickedly and reached to fondle itself between the legs, *maybe not.* The look it was giving her was positively lascivious, its eyes rolling around in its head, drool dribbling down its chin.

Now if that wasn't universal, she didn't know what was.

Suddenly, it grew tired of toying with her and leapt forward. Isabella squealed in alarm, instinctively falling to the floor and somersaulting right out from underneath its target area. She scrambled to her feet much more easily than she would have imagined a bookworm like herself would have been able to. She turned, her heart pounding violently, just in time to see the thing regroup and lunge angrily toward her once more. This time all she could do was swing out at it with the rod in her hands, praying she made hard enough contact.

She didn't.

Instead, she spun around, 360 degrees. She promptly fell onto her backside.

All at once the creature was falling on her, laughing and slobbering with glee one minute . . .

. . . screaming a terrible scream of pain the next as it landed right on the rod she still held, impaling itself through the chest. Isabella blinked, momentarily shocked at how easily it seemed to slide into the creature, hardly any pressure or counterforce from her hands needed. She was next aware of powerful hands jerking her out from under the writhing monster just in time to save her from being at flashpoint as the thing burst into a conflagration of flames.

After a hot, wild burn, the creature disintegrated in a puff of smoke and ash. The overpowering stench of sulfur made Isabella gag even as she was pulled under the protection of a now-familiar overcoat and taken swiftly outside. Once she had a few gasps of fresh air and could wipe away the tears streaming down her face, she looked up into those dark, troubled eyes she had just begun to know.

"Jacob! I thought you were dead!"

"Hardly," he assured her, reaching out to brush away the rust and tears streaking willy-nilly across her cheeks. "Just had the wind knocked out of me."

"I should think so! You're bleeding!"

She reached for his wounded head, but he caught her wrist in a sturdy hand before she could touch him.

"I am fine," he insisted. "I am the one who should be

worried about you. How did you manage to keep him away from you?"

"I don't know. I grabbed the first thing I could."

She opened her hand, realizing she still had the rusty rod clutched tightly within it. It was covered in a goo she didn't think she wanted to identify. She held it toward Jacob, but he jerked back away from her as if she were going to set him on fire. He grasped her wrist, turned it away from himself, and gave it a little shake until the offensive rod clattered to the ground.

"Iron," he said, his quiet tone clearly bemused. "How on earth did you know to use iron?"

"I didn't. It was the only thing there. Just lucky, I guess."

Somehow, Jacob doubted that. But he kept his counsel. Clearly, this chance meeting was turning into something much more complex.

"Jacob, what was that thing? I mean, was it real? Wait. Don't answer that. Of course it was real. But how? Was it some sort of experiment gone bad? I've never seen anything like it!"

"That . . ." Jacob hesitated, sighing once. "That used to be one of my friends."

CHAPTER TWO

Jacob paced his parlor, tunneling the fingers of both hands through hair that already wore deep impressions from previous passes. Though he had not relished telling Myrrh-Ann that her husband was dead, Jacob had done his duty to completion. She had known the implications of Saul's capture and Noah had tried to prepare her for the worst, but Myrrh-Ann had understandably reacted with a mixture of grief and fury. She had attacked Jacob with both her power and the more personal contact of her fists.

She'd had no time to cause him physical pain. Noah had reached out to touch her, draining the energy from her violent, flailing body. She had fainted into the hands of the Enforcer. Jacob had been unable to bear holding her. As her weight rested against him, he could feel the rustle of new life moving against him through her swollen belly. It had felt like a betrayal to know that sort of intimacy when the mother would never have allowed it had she been given a choice.

Myrrh-Ann did not need to know that a human had killed Saul. It was better that she cursed Jacob, hated the one justified by their laws to deliver such a sentence, rather than a vulnerable woman who barely knew what she'd done. Noah had sensed he was holding back information. The Enforcer was aware of his monarch's perceptions, but he hadn't seen fit to elaborate just yet. He needed time to think first. He needed to sort through the night's implications before anyone else learned what had truly happened in that warehouse.

First and foremost was proof of the existence of a true necromancer, one born with power and skilled enough in black arts to Summon a Demon. This he had seen with his own eyes, though it shamed and infuriated him to admit it because then he also had to admit that he had allowed that stained being to escape unchecked into the world. The sudden appearance of a magic-user did not bode well for Jacob's race. Indeed, it did not bode well for any of the Nightwalker clans. Where there was one, there was bound to be others, and Demons were not always their only victims.

And then there was . . .

He stopped in his tracks, looking up at the ceiling where Isabella now slept in a room above him. He had broken an herb capsule under her nose, the combination inducing sleep, allowing him to make off with her to his home in England unawares.

The woman had done the impossible. She had slain a Demon. Even more impossible, before the slaying had even taken place, she had sensed him, empathized with him, and tracked him. A human able to slay a Demon was unheard of. Not unless the human was a necromancer.

Isabella was not a magic-user. Jacob would have known instantly. There was an unnatural aura, a vile stench that clung to magic-users. The bastard who had captured Saul had reeked of it up in the loft. The putrescence still singed Jacob's sensitive nostrils. Isabella's scent was soft, clean, and delightfully pure. Even under all the filth of that warehouse, Jacob had still been able to smell the enticing wholesomeness of her scent. No perfumes or lotions, no dissolute habits, not even the territorial musk of a male marred her bouquet.

Nor was she any of the other immortals that walked the night. Nightwalkers who chose to walk amongst humans were nearly indistinguishable from them. However, breeds could identify each other's "tells," those little differences that gave them away. There was no doubt in Jacob's mind that Isabella was human.

But a human who could kill a Demon? Even Demons had a hell of a time killing one another. That was why being the Enforcer was such a lethal job. Only the eldest of their kind were powerful enough to do mortal harm, and only Jacob was unreservedly sanctioned to do so. Capital punishment was terribly rare, and it was no easy task accomplishing such a sentence.

As was evidenced this evening.

Isabella had merely picked up a rod of iron and plunged it into Saul's heart. Jacob couldn't do this. No Demon could bear touching iron. Contact with it was like violent acid on the skin. If the wound was penetrating, it was excruciating agony. If it penetrated the heart or brain, it was death. Jacob looked down at his hands, his thumbs slightly burned from the rust that had mingled with Isabella's tears. He'd not taken note of the contact until it began to act the irritant against his skin.

Regardless, the Demon skeleton was like steel, nearly impervious. How had a little thing like her pushed that rod through ribs and breastbone on the way to the heart? Besides, unlike the Lycanthrope's vulnerability to silver, which was widely known in fiction, a Demon's weakness to iron was not at the forefront of human knowledge. Had she somehow known this obscure detail? To assume that would be to assume she had known what Saul was, although, after transformation, Saul had appeared the epitome of a human's ideal demon. Or had it been exactly as it seemed, a fortunate happenstance?

Jacob remembered coming to, finding himself on the warehouse floor, and shaking his hair and blood out of his eyes. This just in time to see the monstrous Saul bearing down on the small woman and to realize he could never reach her in time. His head had been ringing so badly that he couldn't even concentrate to use his power. He'd never known such a feeling of frustration and helplessness before. He'd made unforgivable mistakes in the encounter and it had almost cost them their lives. Providence should never have needed to enter the situation. A hundred years between encounters or not, he should have remembered what dealing with the Transformed would be like.

Jacob had known what Saul's demented brain and body were focused on when advancing on the striking little female. A Demon as far gone as Saul was in that moment had only two basic, urgent demands, The first was self-preservation. This was why it was a formidable advantage to have a Demon enslaved. Once its civilization was stripped away by the acidic spells that bound it, the captured creature would do anything for its master if it were promised life or eventual freedom, including using its elemental powers in service.

After self-preservation was satisfied, the Transformed Demon's next thought was, of course, satisfying its rampant lust, a state especially magnified during this full moon of Samhain. It was a similar form of what Jacob enforced and punished his brethren for. It was what the red-haired woman would have experienced if he hadn't kept Kane in check. But Kane's treatment of that woman would have very much paled in comparison to the way Saul, Transformed and perverted as he was, would have violated Isabella. The thought of it sent revulsion crawling down his neck, stuttering his heart into a painful, rapid beat. Jacob had seen Saul's distended phallus as he climbed on top of Isabella. Now he closed his eyes against the vile pictures stirring in his imagination, curling his hands into fierce fists as he shook the images away.

It was forbidden for a Demon to harm an innocent human being in any way. It was their golden rule, and it was the law Jacob was sworn to uphold above all else. Above even Noah's desires, should they run contrary to it. It was especially taboo to attempt to mate with a human. They would be far too frail for such a volatile ordeal. Jacob once more thought of Isabella, so delicate and so much smaller than their species. Lovemaking between Demons was laced with an elemental ferocity that often surpassed excessive aggression. Isabella would snap like fragile little twigs under the onslaught of such passion.

This did not mean that Kane or Gideon or the many others whom Jacob had been forced to enforce over the centuries were deviants of the worst kind. They were merely victims of the curse of their race. Demons spent the entire waxing and waning of the Hallowed Samhain and Beltane moons struggling for control. Every minute of those two potent holidays was an exercise in torment as their bodies and spirits cried to the maddening moon. Somewhere in their genetic codes it was written that during these phases, the urge to mate would supersede all else. Like an animal going into heat, they suffered an all-consuming urge that even the most polished and civilized of their kind had to struggle to control. Usually, Demons would satisfy themselves with each other, but living in tandem with humans as they did, it was far too easy for the mating instinct to be misdirected.

Every year he found himself hunting down the most respected of Elders who were falling prey to this condition. It pained him terribly to see madness on those faces he held esteem for. Or, as in Kane's case, held love for.

Jacob had never fallen victim to madness himself. Even as a fledgling he'd never weakened to the point of craving a human female. But he had been fledged hundreds of years ago, and there had not been more than six billion humans crowded onto the planet then. Even so, he'd always had a hard time figuring out what the attraction was. Though they looked alike, Demon and humankind were very different on chemical, mental, and intellectual levels. Still, asking a Demon to reason out why he'd be attracted to a weaker being while he or she was in the throes of the impulse was futile. And if he were going to be completely honest with himself, there had been a moment earlier when even he had felt the powerful draw of a soft, warm body and big, beautiful moon-lavender eyes.

Jacob swore softly, running his hand through his hair again as he moved to pour himself a drink. It wasn't mortal alcohol he reached for, however, it was animal milk—at body warmth, preferably, but room temperature sufficed. Goat's milk, sheep's milk, and even other more exotic kinds of milk produced for the

young of more unusual animals were intoxicating to
Demons somewhat like alcohol was to mortals; the
average pasteurized homogenized milk in stores was
about as potent as a cup of grape juice, where something like giraffe's milk would be the equivalent of a
strong, exotic brandy. The rest were stronger and
weaker depending on the animal and where it was
raised, much as a particular winemaker or grape
grower could produce something indigenous only to
its breed of grapes and its region of growth.

Jacob poured himself a glass of Himalayan goat's
milk and sank down into the depths of an easy chair.
He rolled his head around, trying to ease some of the
kinks in his neck, mulling over all the same thoughts
again, knowing that soon, whether he made sense of
things or not, he was going to have to talk to Noah.

"Hello?"

Jacob started at the soft, unsure greeting, lurching to
his feet and turning sharply to see Isabella rubbing
sleep out of her eyes as she walked heavily down from
one step to the next.

Impossible!

He was not able to cast sleep inducements into a
person's mind like Kane could or force them into sleep
by draining them of all their energy as Noah could, but
he sure as hell knew how to blend potent enough herbs
to do the trick. She should have been out for hours!

"Oh, hello," she said, smiling at him sleepily when
she spied him gaping at her from below. "Jacob, right?"

"Right," he agreed, at a loss to do anything other
than respond.

His eyes raked over her as he tried to puzzle a solution, but he only succeeded in reminding himself what
a fabulously luscious figure she had. She'd soiled her

clothes at the warehouse, so he had stripped her of her jeans, T-shirt, and socks and had clothed her in one of his own shirts. Somehow, seeing her in it, breathing, awake, and vital, made for an alluring visual stimulus. She carried herself in a kittenish sort of way, slow and vulnerable and irresistibly inviting. Her long, black boa of silken hair dipped both outside of and within the collar spread wide over her small shoulders. The deep vee of the shirt beneath her throat, caused by neglected buttons in his earlier haste, allowed space for one long lock of midnight to snake down her breastbone and into the enticing hollow between her breasts. Hers was a breathtaking shape, boasting ample curves for so slight a frame. Gorgeous, full breasts, a drawn-in waist, the curves at her sides set just deep enough to settle both hands within them, fingers spreading out over soft belly or tempting hips or . . .

Jacob felt his blood surging in hot response to his imagination, his body hardening so unexpectedly and so swiftly that it took his breath away. He turned his head away quickly, tearing his eyes off her and muttering a fiery expletive under his breath. His glass slammed down on the table in front of him and he pressed his hands atop the furniture, as if the feel of the wood could somehow ground him. His hearing, always sensitive, picked up the sound of her body and clothing as she completed her descent into the parlor. Even though she was half a room away, he could track her scent. That clean fragrance had altered, heated by sleep and perfumed by the freshly laundered sheets of his guest room. It reminded him of a sultry summer night, filled with flowers still warmed by daylight, clean damp grasses, and the sweet, delicate musk of a being clearly of the opposite sex.

Fresh, pure, warmly tempting.

And coming closer with every step.

"You should be sleeping," he said abruptly, feeling her start when he broke the heavy silence of the room.

"I woke up."

He heard her shrug. It made perfect sense to her and made none to him. She took another step, and another. Jacob was suddenly overwhelmed with the urge to call out to Noah. It was such an absurd impulse that he almost laughed at it. Such a summons was unprecedented, and it would very likely bring the King down on them with both proverbial barrels blazing since Jacob was not the type to ever need help, never mind call for it. *But who,* he wondered in a moment's panic as her nearing heat began to assault him, *who enforces the Enforcer?*

No! Damn it! You are stronger than some slip of a human female! She is not even doing anything! Jacob would not let the madness of that accursed moon get the better of him. He had never lost control in his life, and he was not about to start now. He had set a staid example for over four hundred years and he wasn't going to tarnish such a superlative reputation, not when Demons like Kane so desperately needed his guidance and censure.

With a grim set of his jaw, he turned to face her.

"What am I doing here?" she asked, her long fingers absently reaching to touch one of the many antique knickknacks on the table, softly shaping it, exploring its textures and craftsmanship until she smiled with a delight that lit her eyes an electric purple. She moved on to another, one of his personal favorites in his expansive, lifelong collection. Her eager fingers swept it with fascination and a specificity of touch that enthralled him. "I'm assuming this is your home?"

"Yes, it is."

"I don't even remember coming here. It's quite lovely," she complimented, her enormous eyes taking in the expansive room and all its rich appointments. "I see you have a thing for antiques."

He nodded, knowing full well that what she called antiques had been brand new when he had purchased them so many years ago. Of course, there was no sense in telling her that, so he remained silent.

"You don't talk much, do you?" she asked offhandedly as she reached for a tiny wooden figurine that she would never realize had been carved by a woman in a long-extinct African tribe hundreds of years ago, shined and mellowed with the woman's spittle and painstaking rubbing. "Though after what happened earlier, I can understand not feeling chatty."

Isabella put down the little wooden figure, moving her light, caressing touch to the next thing and then the next, her sensory curiosity devouring all the curves and textures of his belongings. Her gentle fingers skimmed the high tabletop, heading close to his left hand where it lay slightly curled atop it.

Jacob moved away awkwardly, all of his usual grace evaporating as he took a clumsy backward step to escape the nearness of her. *Hell*, he thought vehemently, *the woman ought to have the sense not to get too close to a male she hardly even knows!* Especially a human woman. She had no power, nothing innate to protect herself with, yet here she was, wandering trustingly into his reach.

Then again, she'd just killed one of his kind only a few hours ago.

"I do not mean to come off unfriendly," he managed with politesse in spite of his turmoil of thoughts. "I am not used to having the company of others is all."

Well, at least that was the truth.

Isabella tilted her head, causing more of her raven black hair to skid forward, settling like black silk against her breast as she took his measure. The touch of her eyes was akin to physical contact. The exquisite glitter of violet curiosity began with a light dance across his face, a gentle glide over his shoulders, and then a slow drifting across the expanse of his chest. Everywhere that gaze fell, Jacob felt his skin begin to burn, the muscles beneath jumping tensely to attention, his clothing insignificant beneath her visual investigation. His abdomen flexed, the sinew of his thighs twitching unbearably as she inspected him relentlessly. She couldn't possibly miss the raging hard-on he had.

The muscle in his jaw clenched as he felt her thorough examination like a brand. Did she realize what she looked like as she did this? Had no one ever warned her of how the half-mast sweep of the thick lashes framing her candid eyes was nothing short of natural sensuality at its most potent?

"A loner," she said at last. It was a statement, and she nodded to herself in agreement. "I can tell you don't have six kids running around. Not with all this price-less stuff within reach. By the way"—she met his eyes directly, and Jacob felt his breath stutter to a stop— "did you undress me?"

It was that moment that Jacob became convinced she could not be human. No mere human female could put so much influence into such a simple question. No sane mortal woman would have even dared ask such a thing while standing half naked inches away from an obviously aroused male stranger.

Isabella didn't even see him move. One minute he was standing away from her, the next his hands were on her. His commanding grip encircled her upper arms and she was yanked up off her feet and against his chest. She let out a sound of surprise as her breath rushed out. Before she could inhale, his mouth was seizing hers with barely checked ferocity.

Her hands came up reflexively, clutching at the front of his shirt for balance and for a potential protest. That protest barely germinated as his hard, athletic physique burned its masculine strength into the curves of her softer, more pliant one. He was impossibly fit, every muscle blending perfectly into the next, and she could feel him positively vibrating with life. Male and potent, it was everywhere. His hands were arresting and sure as they moved to draw her more securely against the power of his body.

Jacob's mouth scorched against hers with a cunning sensuality that was part art form and part natural talent. It was nothing like the awkward kisses she'd tried in the past, and there was nothing platonic or re-motely giggle-worthy about the sensations he inspired, whether it had been invited initially or not. He kissed her aggressively, his hot mouth and the flick of his tongue touching her lips, both coaxing and demand-ing all at once, as if he knew something about her that she'd never discovered. There was dizziness and rushes of heat and the pounding pulses of her blood. She tin-gled across her breasts and lower until she blushed. She felt a surge of adrenaline, then the wash of a sen-sual desire she'd never conceived existed. She relaxed her lips against his, her heart fluttering like a wild bird caught in an unexpected snare.

Jacob felt the inherent invitation keenly. He'd been waiting for it. He accepted it with an invading sweep of his tongue, moving deeply beyond her lips and seeking the momentarily withheld mate she kept shyly hidden. It was the only thought in his head—making this contact, tasting her in a specific way, dragging her flavor into dimensions rich enough to drive a saint insane. All following thoughts were focused within the haven of a hot, sweet kiss. There was nothing else.

Isabella felt a wave of heat erupting up from deep within the core of her body, the splash of it oozing outward into every single vein and vessel. The feeling was extraordinary. Until she'd felt it for herself, she'd been honestly oblivious to her effect on him. Now, warmth slid like liquid fire along the underside of her skin, and she wondered if it felt the same for him. Her tongue touched his of its own volition. She grew braver and undeniably curious.

His mouth ravaged across hers with desperation and a primal need she had no hope of comprehending in her naïveté. It was as if she were the last woman on earth, the only woman worth kissing. She felt the misting heat of his breath as it rushed over her face and into her mouth. His fingers swept up the pronounced curve of her lower spine.

Jacob growled low in his chest as her mouth welcomed him further. She tasted sweet, unbelievably sweet, like the heavy delicacy of a forbidden candy. Her skin temperature was increasing exponentially, nothing like the cooler skin of a Demon female, and he could feel every degree like a taunting touch. Even his own naturally cool body was flung into extremes of heat not normal in his kind. A cacophony of urges washed through him, so many of them that his thoughts became a haze. Instinct took the reins as his hands skimmed over the curves of that unbelievably hot skin, from her shoulder to the bend of her waist and down low over the swell of her enticing backside.

She was exceedingly soft, fitting his touch with exquisite perfection. His fingers flexed strongly on her bottom, pulling her farther up off her feet and deeper into the bend of his body.

He released her mouth suddenly, his breath coming so hard that they swayed to the rhythm of it as they stood entangled together. His eyes searched her face restlessly, studying her as if she were some sort of complex puzzle. Isabella could do little more than cling to him, trapped as she was against his demanding, dominant body. She watched his nostrils flare as he took a deep, purposeful breath, as if he was drawing in a fragrance. But she wore no perfume. Then he leaned in and nuzzled her neck, inhaling deeply against her skin. It was an erotic sort of thing to do, and Isabella felt her belly constrict in response. His tongue touched her skin over her pulse, his teeth scraping over the sensitive area, and she shivered under the stimulation.

Jacob felt her body tremble. He made an appreciative sound low in his throat as he sought her mouth once more, branding her with his taste, bleeding his own scent onto her fragrant body. She made a soft, sexy little noise and it burned over his raw senses.

Their melded bodies jerked as his arm swung out, sweeping across the top of the table just behind Isabella, sending a cascade of priceless trinkets spilling to the floor. She was lifted up and her bottom contacted the wood tabletop under the guidance of his urgent hands, the sitting position naturally drawing up her thighs. Her knees bracketed his hips, her ankles hooking around his legs as if she'd done the action a hundred times before. She gave little thought to the fact that she hadn't. She felt the thunderous beat of his heart against her breasts, the vibration throbbing right through her entire body. Jacob's palms cradled her head, his urgent fingers grasping at the fine tendrils of her hair. It was supple, heavy silk, filled with the fragrance of a flowery shampoo. The heat of the skin it grew from was divine.

He was acting purely on impulse, every wild twist of his mouth against hers a reflection of that mindless need for gratification. Jacob's hands dropped, his long, urgent fingers wrapping around her hips and dragging her forward to the very edge of the table, holding her steady as he pushed himself deeper toward the juncture of her thighs. She gasped at the strength he used to command her pliant body, and then moaned beneath his demanding lips when she realized she could feel his impressive arousal against the very center of herself. His body was hard, hot, and straining against barriers of fabric for the mate so close within reach. She made an abandoned sound of pleasure, wriggling up toward his aggressive frame instinctively. Her hands glided down his back, over his waist, and onto his taut buttocks, where she could feel every muscle straining toward her.

Jacob groaned with coarse satisfaction at her eager response. He made savage use of her mouth, kissing her until she was bruised, gasping for breath and practically chanting a sound of encouragement that scraped over his already raw senses. He was bombarded by her natural perfume, her aroused sex, and her blood as it pooled and heated in her erogenous zones. The mixture was heady, and he felt as if he were swimming in it.

Isabella was drowning in his fierce passion, hypnotized by the rock of his body as he used her mouth with wicked skill. He moved against her as if he needed urgently to caress all of her at once. Then she felt fingers thrusting hungrily under the shirt she wore, burning back up over her hips and belly until he'd caught her breasts in impatient palms. His touch was aching skill, an assured manipulation that molded her supple weight as he rubbed his palms against her. Then he drew an already peaked nipple between thumb and forefinger and rolled it into a deft pinch. Isabella gasped, her torso bucking forward into him. She moaned when he toyed with the opposite breast in a similar fashion, melting liquid down the center of her body until she was soaked with it.

She became aware of his personal scent, musky and darkly spiced, and ripped away from his mouth so she could burrow her face into his neck and drag him deep into her lungs, just as he had done to her. Her tongue licked along his carotid pulse and he whispered a fast, foreign phrase through clenched teeth as he shuddered in response.

"Tell me," she demanded mindlessly. She let go of him suddenly, reaching for her shirtfront and ripping it open, not even pausing to think about what a wanton gesture it was. She looked down, stirred by the contrast of his dark skin against her pale breasts as he fondled her. She placed her palms on the backs of his hands, urging him on, tightening his touch. "Tell me," she repeated in a low, coaxing voice.

Jacob's senses roared, every nerve ending in his body broadcasting her heat, her sultry perspiration as it dampened their clothing and her deliciously lithe skin. His fingernails lengthened slightly, reflexively, and he felt the bristling of the fine hairs on the back of his neck. The animal within was so close to the surface now that he could hear it howling in the recesses of his mind. This woman, with this impossibly tempting body, was his.

"Mine," he growled, low and dangerously.

The urge to mate with her rode over him in torrid waves. He could slice the remainder of their clothes from their bodies with his bare nails. He could be buried deep inside her a second later.

"Yes," she panted softly, as if reading his mind. Her hands swept through his hair, fingers curving until her nails were running over the sensitive back of his neck, erotically taunting those alert hairs and making him even harder than he already was. She scraped her nails through the fabric of the shirt covering his back, around and up to his chest, simultaneously drawing him deeper into the tender trap of her locked legs.

"Isabella."

Her name rumbled out of him roughly, the aroused sound of his voice brutal in its honesty. His primitive need was to dominate her, to feel her writhe in pleasure, to make her his mate. He launched back and away from her for all of a second, grabbed her roughly by the shoulders, and in a rush of vertigo and harsh manhandling, she was thrown to the ground on her hands and knees. He was behind her immediately, his muscled arm like a band of steel as it crossed her lower abdomen from hip to hip, his other hand grasping through her hair until he had firm hold of the back of her neck. He jerked her back hard against himself, her bottom snuggling deep into the well of his hips as his thighs pushed hers apart.

Isabella cried out, a gasp of stuttered shock and carnal awareness. Something in her mind tried telling her she should be afraid, but she wasn't. Quite the opposite. Her body was eager, damp and welcoming, and becoming more so with every erotic rub of his suggestive burrowing against her. She didn't know that he could smell that heady increase in her aroused scent and that it was putting her in escalating danger. All she knew was that, for the first time, she wanted to know what it would be like to be taken by a man.

That was when the room exploded.

Isabella was crushed into the floor by the initial force of it. Violent winds suddenly ripped at her body, lifting her and throwing her through the air like a limp doll even as single-minded hands tried to hold on to her, the lingering grip bruising her flesh as she was torn from its hold. Isabella landed with a grunt on soft furniture. She sat up and shook away the whipping tendrils of her hair, the haze of passion, and her disorientation. Her vision cleared in time to see Jacob hurtling across the room, slamming forcefully into a wall, driven into the plaster by hurricane-force winds.

That was when she noticed there was another man in the room.

Perceiving the blond stranger instinctively as a threat and hearing Jacob roar in outrage, Isabella scrambled off the couch and hurled herself at the intruder. Unfortunately, he was built like a brick fort, and she felt rather like a dust mote bouncing ineffectually against him. He turned his head, a lazy, unconcerned movement, and cocked a gold brow at her in surprise and . . . amusement? He flicked a hand in her direction and once again she was swept into a maelstrom of wind that stole her breath away.

A second later she felt all of her weight suddenly disappear, her body becoming the consistency of dust, causing the confining wind to pass right through her. She watched in awe as debris caught in the slipstream rushed through her as well. She heard the newcomer swear bitingly, and Isabella instinctively knew the golden-haired visitor was going to do something to injure Jacob further as he focused all of his attention on him. She felt a force of power explode out from the giant and could see the eddy of air currents as they hit Jacob like a nuclear blast. About the time the side of the house blew out and sent Jacob flying outside, Isabella became solid again. Her touchdown onto her feet was abrupt and awkward.

By now, she was working purely on instinct. Jacob had saved her life and was in terrible danger, and she had to do something. Before another millisecond could pass, she was once more hurtling through the air. As if Bruce Lee had suddenly invaded her, Isabella found herself nearly kicking the man's head off his body. She whirled and struck again, his surprised grunt giving her satisfaction as she swung her leg up and around high enough to force her heel into his Romanesque nose.

The intruder flew backward at the impact, landing hard on his back with a stunned cough. Before he had a chance to regroup, she was on him, straddling his massive chest and grabbing up the nearest thing she could find to threaten him with. It happened to be a heavy potted plant, the planter made of some kind of pewter. It wasn't an iron bar, but she was sure it would hurt. She wielded it over his head with the confidence of that fact radiating out of her every pore.

"No, wait!" He threw up his hands in a protective gesture, and in spite of herself, Isabella hesitated. "I was protecting you!"

"Like hell!" she barked out, aiming the planter with intent.

"I swear! Listen to me, please. He would have hurt you! Don't you understand that, you foolish woman?"

"Tsk . . . it's not wise to insult a 'foolish woman' with the upper hand," she threatened, jiggling the pot in her hands until the leaves of the plant within shook.

"What in hell is going on here?"

Isabella and the stranger looked at each other, both taking a moment to realize that neither of them had spoken, even though that had been the sentence on the tip of each of their tongues. They turned their heads in unison to see yet another stranger, this one with dark reddish black hair and an imperious aura that, in a way, reminded Isabella of Jacob. This new stranger stood reeking of power and authority on the threshold of Jacob's home.

"Noah!" the one stranger said to the other, a mixture of relief and embarrassment in his voice. "Get this hellion off me."

"Come one step closer and I'll bash his tiny brain in," Isabella warned.

Noah didn't move, but he didn't look very concerned either. Instead, he looked as though he were just this side of laughing his head off. Isabella was aware of his eyes traveling leisurely over her, and that was when she realized the torn shirt she wore was gaping wide, exposing a great deal of her breasts.

With a cry, Isabella dropped her burden and grabbed her shirt, clutching the material closed. Unfortunately, she forgot she'd been holding the pot over blondie's head. With a yelp of shock, he jerked his head aside, avoiding the brunt of the would-be weapon's strike but getting a face full of planting soil when the pot burst and spilled its guts all over him.

Isabella was aghast as the man spluttered and spat out words that sounded suspiciously like swearing in a foreign language. She scrambled off his chest, not wanting to be within reach when he regained his eye-sight. The blond giant sat up and shook off mounds of soil with a couple of jerks of his head. Isabella was backing off from the two strangers, her wary eyes glued to them, her hands still grasping at her shirt.

Noah watched the ebony-haired female take in her surroundings with the sharp eye of a hunter. The King was full of questions, but he didn't think he was going to get much satisfaction out of her. He turned instead to the other man in the room. "Elijah, would you care to tell me what is going on?"

The huge male surged to his feet, dusting dirt out of his hair with a disgruntled sound as he turned a grim expression to his King. "I was passing by and there was a massive change in the atmosphere. It was so strong it literally jerked me out of the sky. I investigated and it turned out it was a change in gravitational force. A side effect of . . . well . . . Jacob was out of control. He was . . . I found Jacob . . . um . . ." Elijah shifted his weight in discomfort. "He was consorting with this female . . . or about to. I stopped him just in time."

"Jacob?" Noah gasped, his shock so resounding that Isabella felt instantly insulted.

"No one asked you to stop him," she said sharply, her eyes shooting fiery daggers at the one called Elijah. "What the hell business is it of yours if Jacob . . . uh . . . consorts with me?"

"That would require a lengthy explanation," Noah offered in answer.

"I have time," she shot back.

Noah stepped forward, made eye contact with her, and raised his hand in a graceful sweep of his fingers. "You look tired," he remarked.

Isabella blinked, was overcome by a wash of

exhaustion, and yawned against her will. Her chin lifted stubbornly as she swayed on her feet.

Noah went very still and Elijah's jaw fell open.

Noah manipulated her personal energy further, literally sucking the strength out of her with such force that Elijah could feel it tingling across his skin. Isabella stepped back hard as if hit physically. Helpless against Noah's awesome power, she crumpled to the floor, curled up into a fetal position, and promptly fell into an exhausted sleep.

Jacob opened his eyes and instantly regretted it. His head was a gymnasium of jumping, dashing pain. With a groan, he forced himself into an upright position, trying to shake the fog out of his skull. He looked up, focusing on two blurs before him, one darklike shadow, the other decidedly more like gold.

Noah and . . .

"What in hell are you doing here?" he demanded upon recognizing Elijah, indulging in the knee-jerk reaction of hostility even though he wasn't at all sure why he wanted to.

"Saving your ass," Elijah quipped, smiling with a flash of teeth that was a combination of boyishness and outright feral pleasure.

"The hell you are!" Jacob barked, his pride bent at the very idea. He might be in a fog, but he knew he could take care of himself and needed no one to save him from anything.

"I am sorry to say it, my friend, but he is telling the truth."

Jacob swung his gaze to the Demon King. Noah's sea

green and gray eyes were a serious match to the grim press of his mouth.

"Look, Jacob." Noah indicated to something lying curled up on the couch next to his hip.

Isabella.

Beautiful Isabella. Curled up like a sweet kitten and breathing so deeply that she made a noise in the back of her throat with every exhale. Sound asleep, looking like an ethereal angel, and . . .

Bruised.

He stared in horror as he realized those were *his* fingerprints pressed deeply into her neck and throat, as well as the bare curve of her upper thigh. Everything came rushing back to him, the implications hitting him like a gut punch, stealing his breath away as his face burned in appalled shame.

"Oh, no," he rasped, his dismay and devastation grinding into those two simple words.

"Easy, Jacob," Noah said quickly. "Elijah arrived in time to keep you from harming her any further."

Barely, Jacob recalled. He remembered the lust, the craving for Isabella that had so overwhelmed him. He remembered how close he had come to taking her, mating with her, damn the consequences. In fact, the consequences had never once entered his mind. Even now, though he was full of despair over his lack of control, he couldn't shake the urge he had to get closer to her, to touch her, to drag that delicate body in a crush against him and taste her again. It rode him heavily, rooted in his gut and groin, and he was filled with the dreadful conviction that he would never be able to remove that need from his soul. Ever.

"I never meant to hurt her," Jacob said quietly. The irony of speaking the exact words Kane had used gutted him with anger—anger at himself and frustrated outrage that those he highly respected had been witness to his humiliation.

"We know that," Noah said evenly, hoping to be some kind of comfort to him. "What we do not know is how she came to be in your home." Noah leaned forward. "What in the world would possess you to bring a temptation such as this onto your territory?" the Demon King demanded of his champion. "You are not infallible, Jacob, even if you are the Enforcer. You are Demon. You too can fall to the madness of the Hallowed moon."

"I know that!"

"Then why," Elijah asked, "did you bring her to your home?"

"Because she . . . because I needed to figure something out about her. She is not usual for a human female."

"You're telling me," Elijah said wryly, gingerly touching his bruised nose.

"What made you think she was unusual?" Noah asked.

Jacob took a deep breath before dropping the bomb. "She killed Saul."

The two Demons across from him sucked in air as if they were suddenly drowning for it. Jacob instinctively got to his feet and sat on the arm of the couch beside Isabella's head, crossing an arm to the back of the sofa in a clearly protective gesture.

"That is impossible," Noah said quietly.

"I saw it with my own eyes. Saul had completely Transformed. I miscalculated his power . . . his strength. It has been too long since I have fought an altered Demon. He severely injured me, but *she* stopped him."

"This little human creature killed one of us? One of the Transformed?" Elijah snorted in disbelief. "He must have been unconscious. Incapacitated."

"That same little creature broke your nose not twenty minutes ago, Elijah," Noah reminded him dryly. "Were you unconscious or incapacitated?" The King was frowning, worry lines etching deeply across his broad forehead. "I have never heard of such a thing," Noah informed them. "You were right to detain her, but it was wrong of you not to be forthcoming about it sooner. I do not understand why you put both of your lives in danger, Jacob. What would have kept her from possibly killing you? And then the way Elijah found you with her . . ."

"I cannot explain it. Any of it. I just . . . I just knew she was not a danger to me. Even in spite of knowing how she has affected me, I still do not look at her as a threat or at myself as a threat to her. I cannot explain it, Noah. I have been the Enforcer for four hundred years. Never in all that time have I strayed. Never once have I entertained the slightest craving to do so. And yet, with her, there is no conscience in me. No sense of my cultural mores. She . . ." Jacob paused to move a wisp of hair off her cheek. "It feels as though there is no wrong in what I did. Everything I have come to believe in my lifetime tells me that it is very wrong, but it does not *feel* like it."

"That's the madness talking," Elijah scoffed with disgust. "You were like an animal when I arrived, Jacob. You would have torn her to pieces."

"No!" Jacob's fury was punctuated as he snarled at Elijah. "The urge to mate with her was not entirely that of a beast who would use any female without discrimination. It was different. I . . ." He was at a loss, looking away from the stunned expressions of the other two males. "It was primitive, yes, but not just lustful instinct. It was more . . . deeper . . . something I could not resist. No, not even I."

Noah stood up then, suddenly feeling like it would be a good idea not to be sitting so close to this woman who had somehow managed to become the fixation of the unbendable, unshakable Jacob. Jacob's moral code was what made him the best Enforcer they'd ever had. It was what protected him. If he had succumbed to madness, there had to be something more to it than met the eye.

Who was this woman who could kill a Demon, who had beat down Elijah, the Captain of Noah's fighting forces? Enchanting Jacob, the implacable Enforcer? And what of the way she had resisted his drain on her energy? Yes, Noah thought heavily, there was definitely more to be discovered here.

He could only hope that it was not the bad tidings he thought it was.

CHAPTER THREE

Isabella opened her eyes, blinking rapidly to clear away sleep and gain focus.

She sat up suddenly, the quick movement belied by the sensation that she was dredging her body through heavy water. She groaned, her head throbbing, the urge to fall back onto the couch and sleep almost irresistible.

Then she remembered. Everything. In a sudden panic, she looked around for Jacob, terrified that she had let him down and allowed the two intruders to harm him. She spotted him the length of an enormous stone room away, his tall figure standing beside a fireplace that threw him into a myriad of golden lights and dark shadows. She sighed, relieved that he seemed as healthy as ever.

Jacob felt something slither warmly up the back of his neck and into his mind. The sensation of relief was so strong he could have easily mistaken it for his own, except there was something softer about it than he was capable of. He turned his head and saw her sitting up, looking at him.

He was less shocked this time that she had shaken

off another attempt at putting her to sleep, but it still impacted him, especially knowing Noah had been behind this last effort. Jacob slipped his hands into his pockets, closing them tightly. He began to walk toward her, knowing he had to face her having hurt her, regret dragging at his heart with harsh sorrow. His steps never faltered, though. He was ashamed, but he was strong enough to admit when he had erred and to face the consequences.

Isabella watched him approach, his powerful, catlike grace emanating purpose. She felt her heart leap, remembering how he had touched her, the command of his embrace and the drugging sensuality of his kisses. She recalled how shockingly easy it had been for him to hold her body in thrall, how his masculine hands had felt running the curves of her figure, and the skill of elegant fingers that had demanded a blueprint of her.

Jacob came to a halt, still half the room away from her but inexplicably besieged by her thoughts as she remembered what he had done to her. Her vivid memory cast image after image into him, everything down to sensation and scent, so real in the remembering that it was as if he held her that very instant. His entire body rippled hard in response, his pulse pounding in his throat as she recollected that primitive, aroused feel of him.

Jacob was not a telepath or an empath, so how he was receiving her thoughts was lost on him. What was more, he sensed she was equally close to his mind, making it a profoundly intimate exchange. He should have been disconcerted by that idea, but something else had caught his attention instead.

He discovered no fear in her memories. Even as she wondered at her own abandon, thought about how out of character it all had been, there was no trepidation or regret. In fact, she was frighteningly accepting. Actually, she was curious, intrigued, and entertaining thoughts of what it would be like to be touched by him again, to kiss and taste his mouth. Jacob shuddered, his entire being tuning in to that siren call of her thoughts and body.

"Jacob."

His name was used as a warning, and it dragged him out of Isabella's enchantment of him, bringing his attention around to the three who had entered the room. Isabella looked also, recognizing the two males as the invaders of Jacob's house. She lurched to her feet, bristling defensively as she moved to place herself between them and Jacob.

The newest stranger was a woman. Isabella felt positive that she had never seen anyone so beautiful in all of her life. She was quite tall, wickedly long-legged, and had coffee-colored hair curling down in a beautiful cascade the entire length of her body. The white togalike gown she wore was light and flowing, except where it was bound snug beneath and between her breasts in a crisscrossed pattern with thick bands of intricate brocade. This flattered her flawless, tanned complexion and enhanced the green-gray color of her eyes. She held herself with a serene poise that reminded Isabella of a goddess, but the compassionate smile that warmed her refined features made her seem far more approachable than any of the men. She stood out like an angel amongst brooding devils.

"On behalf of my brother and myself, I welcome you to our home, Isabella," she said, her voice captivating with its exotic accent and sophisticated modulation. "Do not be afraid," the goddess continued, "no one here will harm you or allow you to be harmed. My name is

Magdelegna. My friends call my Legna, and you may also if you wish."

"Where am I? Who are all you people?" Then, more strongly, her voice full of warning, "Why did you attack Jacob?"

The three other Demons watched with interest as the tiny human woman took yet another protective step back toward Jacob. The idea of such a fragile creature defending the Enforcer made their mouths twitch with amusement.

"It was not so much an attack against Jacob as it was an act of protecting you. When Elijah came upon you, he feared Jacob would unwittingly hurt you," Legna explained.

"Well," Isabella snorted, thrusting her fists onto her hips and jutting out her chin in irritation, "I'd call that presumptive, wouldn't you? He was just . . ." She realized exactly how they'd been caught and promptly blushed to the roots of her hair. "I mean . . ." She stamped her foot in frustration as they began to let their grins spread over their faces. She even heard Jacob chuckle softly behind her. "Well, what should it matter to any of you what we were doing?" she demanded belligerently.

"It does matter. It will matter to you as well once you know everything."

Isabella was instantly washed with dread and a heart-fluttering panic. A hundred things rushed through her head as she tried to fit a logical explanation to their disquiet. She latched on to the most likely. "You're married!" she declared, whirling around to confront Jacob.

"No. I am not married," he countered, his dark eyes radiating no humor at this point. "Isabella, do you not find anything the least bit odd about *how*, exactly, I was attacked?"

The prompt made her hesitate. She remembered the wind, the vortex of power that had thrown them both about like dried leaves instead of human beings. She recollected the one called Noah stepping up to her one moment, and the next she was waking up here. She recalled being caught by Jacob after a five-story fall and fighting a horrible creature he claimed had once been a friend.

"Okay, what the hell is going on here?" she demanded. She actually wasn't afraid. She had been born with an insatiable need for information that overrode any fear she might have felt about being caught up in these peculiarities. She was realizing that she had been completely ignoring some very odd occurrences and, if she'd had one of those huge cartoon mallets right then, she ought to be bonking herself on the head with it and saying "duh!"

"First, we wish you to remember that you are in no danger from us," the one called Noah said, his smoky voice reaching out to reassure her.

"Hey, I broke Arnold Schwarzenegger's nose over there, don't forget. I'm not afraid of any of you." Isabella indicated Elijah with a jerk of her head. Elijah's face colored with embarrassment. She smiled inwardly. At least she had the blond's number. Besides, she was very certain that although he was maintaining a distance, Jacob wouldn't let a single one of them touch her.

"Isabella," Legna said, still gentle, still reassuring. "Though we may look a lot like you and others of your species, we are . . . different."

"Species? What are you, like, aliens or something?"

"No, we are indigenous to Earth," Jacob said.

Isabella turned at the sound of his voice, suddenly feeling that whatever she was about to hear, she wanted to hear from him. "Then please explain. I'm not an idiot and I won't freak out like some serial heroine. Stop coddling me and just give me some answers."

"Very well." Jacob stepped closer to her, wishing he could be touching her as he told her what he knew was going to be nearly impossible for her, with her human convictions, to comprehend. The impulse frustrated him because it came even when he was consciously trying to control it. "Human folklore is full of myths and legends about creatures that walk the night. You call them monsters. To us, they are just other species. To us they exist, just as we exist, alongside the human race. The Nightwalkers. The Dark Cultures. We who live best during the dark cycles of the Earth."

Isabella tilted her head, seemingly taking in that bit of knowledge. He could feel her rapid thoughts as she tried to fit certain pieces of information together, discarded them, and then began anew. She was so intelligent, so sharp, and he marveled at the working of her practical mind.

"So, what are you telling me? That you guys are vampires?" The idea gave all-new implications to the encounter she'd had with Jacob, making her shiver with a feeling she blushingly refused to identify. It could explain why the others thought she would be in danger from him. Then again, weren't these people a little too perfectly tanned to be keeping out of the sun?

"No. We are not those, though they do exist," Legna said.

"They do? You're pulling my leg!" Isabella snorted with disbelieving humor.

"There is much more in the universe than can be known to man."

"Yes, but blood-sucking, undead monsters?"

Jacob chuckled softly, stepping up to her and reaching to touch gentle fingers to her face, the pads at the tips of them so clearly reverent as they glided over the soft curve of her cheek.

"Vampires take offense to those descriptions. Outside of some special abilities, weaknesses, and the need for blood, most Vampires are not too unlike anyone else you might know. You might know one or two and not even realize it."

"Oookay! Next you'll be telling me there is an Easter Bunny and werewolves!" Isabella exclaimed.

"Well, I cannot vouch for the Easter Bunny, but Lycanthropes are definitely to be found, though not always as wolves."

Isabella stared at Jacob as if he had sprouted canines and fur himself. "So," she murmured numbly, "if you aren't any of those things, then what are you saying that you are?"

"I will tell you, Isabella," Jacob said softly, his fingers stroking her cheek once more, soothing her frayed nerves, "but remember, just because a word has terrible implications in your mythos does not mean that is really the way it is."

"Just tell me," she whispered, her large eyes pleading with him.

"We are called Demons. We are a race of elementals, immortal and gifted with nature-oriented powers. We are a highly civilized species with a strict code of honor, morals, and beliefs. We desire to peacefully coexist with your species, to protect our human friends from whatever baser sides there are to our natures. That was why

Elijah drove me away from you, Bella. It is forbidden for a Demon to harm a human and, therefore, it is taboo for a Demon to . . . to try and mate with a human. It has always been that way."

"But . . ." Isabella shook her head, trying to clear it of a rush of implications and confusions. "Is that what that thing was in the warehouse? One of you? A . . . Demon?"

"Yes and no. Demons, for the most part, look as you see us now. We behave as civilized as you see us behaving now, the exception being occasional moments of primitive behavior which we try to monitor very closely. Saul, the creature you destroyed, was a perverted, corrupted Demon. It takes a very specific set of circumstances for that extreme transformation to happen, and it has not happened in over a century. Until tonight."

"What's more," Legna spoke up, drawing Isabella's attention, "tonight has been the first time that we know of that a human has been able to kill one of our kind. Attempted, yes. Succeeded, never."

"Also, on this night of firsts," Noah added, "is the first time Jacob, one of the most controlled and disciplined among us, has ever lost control with a human female. You may not see it, but that has a tremendous significance to us."

"Believe me, it was tremendously significant to me as well," she said dryly. "So you mean to tell me that you all can't be killed? Is that what you mean by immortal? Because if that's the case, that was one pretty dead immortal in that warehouse."

"We can be killed. By one another, by other powerful Nightwalkers, and . . . magic-users," Noah edited gingerly. "Immortal means that we are long lived, many of us centuries old."

"Centuries?" Isabella swallowed visibly. "How many centuries?" she asked Jacob.

"A little over six."

"*Six hundred years?*" Isabella found herself suppressing another one of those hysterical giggles she was prone to since meeting Jacob. "Talk about your older man. Oh, wait, you aren't even a man." Isabella's eyes grew huge as the implications of that particular realization hit her. "What . . . um . . . what would have happened if . . . I mean . . . if . . . uh . . . you know . . ."

This time everyone in the room shifted uncomfortably.

"Actually, we do not really know," Noah said. "It has never happened before. At least, not with uncorrupted Demons. The Transformed . . . well, there have been tragic instances where women and men have been found . . ."

"Torn apart," Jacob said bluntly. He had seen the stark reality of this. They were vicious and brutal fatalities. This was what compelled his vigilance and drove him to make no mistakes. His failures simply took too expensive a toll.

"However," Legna continued quickly, her compassionate eyes on Jacob's face, "we have always felt that such a mating would be too much for a human to survive, even with an uncorrupted Demon."

Isabella could believe that. Jacob's primal dominance had been consuming. She didn't want to think about what would have happened if Elijah and Noah had not shown up when they had. It was clear by the expression on Jacob's face that he was having a similar thought.

"I never wanted to hurt you. You must believe me, Bella," he said quietly.

"Jacob is telling you the truth. Something happens

to our people at this time of year that makes our instinctive urge to mate very difficult to control," Noah explained. "We police ourselves strictly, but sometimes it gets the better of us."

"Wait. Wait a minute." Isabella threw up staying hands, shaking her head as everything she was learning tumbled around inside of it. "This is a very imaginative story, but how am I supposed to believe any of it? I mean . . . you all look so normal. Disgustingly good-looking, but normal."

Jacob felt his lips twitch. This woman constantly made him want to laugh out loud. At himself, at their habitual solemnity, at everything he felt he had been taking far too seriously for far too long. Instead, he reached down and took both of her little hands in his, enjoying the way she curled her fingertips between his fingers, trusting him regardless of all she had learned.

"Do not be afraid," he murmured.

Isabella opened her mouth to ask him why she should be afraid, but a sudden sensation of lightness washed over her and took her breath away. She watched his strange eyes as her feet lifted effortlessly from the floor, her body following his lead as he drew them up into the air together. She threw her arms around his neck, her heart pounding with disquiet and adrenaline as they went higher. He felt her entire body tremble, like the quick flicks of a cat's tail.

"Destiny has made me of the Earth, Bella," he whispered softly in her ear. "I can manipulate gravity, communicate with all living things, and move tectonic plates against one another if I so choose. I can grow a seed to maturity with a thought and cause it to wither and die with another. I am able to feel the life forces of every living thing born of the Earth. I can hunt anything that travels the paths of this world with all the heightened senses of the most accomplished predators. I am Nature, and She is me."

Isabella exhaled a soft "Oh," watching now as they climbed higher away from the others who watched them, until they reached the rafters. It wasn't until she was looking down on everything that she realized they must be in a castle. It was the only thing they could be in that would match the walls, floors, and ceilings of the enormous room they were in.

After a moment, Jacob slowly lowered them back to the marble flooring, holding her protectively against himself as their bodies grew weighty once more. She saw worry in his eyes and his urge to be her protector. Even more, she felt it. She realized that she was developing an attunement with Jacob's emotions and thoughts. She didn't know how it was happening, but how could she ask that in the face of the fact that she had just flown around the room in his arms?

As she tested this newfound ability, she felt something telling her that his desire for her was merely curbed and controlled, not gone as she had begun to suspect. For some reason it gave her a sense of relief. Reckless though it might be, there was a very powerful part of her that did not want to be just a passing primal urge to him.

She stepped out of the circle of his arms and looked at Elijah.

"The wind?" she asked.

"Destiny has chosen me for the Wind," he said in resonant tones as he swept out his hands in a showman's gesture, even while he winked at her. "Atmospheres, temperature, air, these are mine to beckon." And he did, sweeping a breeze through the room just strong enough to make Legna's gown ruffle. Suddenly, without even a flash of light or warning, Elijah's form dissipated into thin air, becoming the air. His voice swirled all around her as he playfully lifted her hair up from her shoulders, drawing it into a banner that fluttered high above her head, making her laugh. "The weather sways to my will, the tempests and pressures of it mine to manipulate. I can infuse a place with life-giving oxygen or remove it completely. The Wind is the breath of life, and She breathes through me."

"Elijah," Jacob snapped out, a dark glare of disapproval tinged by a perceptible gravitational shift meant to add to his warning. He didn't like Elijah playing with her, and he was making it very clear.

"Destiny has chosen Fire for me," Noah injected as Elijah's form faded back in and the breeze died down, shifting focus back to the disclosures. The way they spoke, with such pride and reverence—Isabella was thrilled by the energy of it. She gasped when Noah's powerful body turned hazy and then swirled into a column of smoke. He lingered in this form for a moment before becoming solid once more. "I am the lava that pulses deep in the Earth's core, the conflagration that burns away the old so that the new might be born in its wake. I am that which boils and seethes and is volatile and explosive. I am the warmth of the sun, the manipulator of all energies. Fire burns in me and for me, and She is all that I am."

"Fire and Earth Demons are among the rarest of our breed, the most powerful of our kind," Jacob said. "Noah is King. Our leader."

"But fire cannot live without air," Elijah remarked, an impudent gleam in his green eyes.

"Air cannot be purified without the Earth," Jacob countered.

"Gentlemen, please." Legna spoke up, sighing in exasperation. "Shall Bella and I leave the room so you can measure each other on the tabletop?"

Isabella laughed outrageously. Legna had dared to say such a thing to these men of phenomenal power! Then it occurred to her that males of the species might not be the only ones with abilities of such magnitude.

"What about you, Legna?"

"Destiny gifted me with the Mind," she admitted quietly. "I am illusion, that which is created and real only in the Mind. I am the embodiment of empathy, logic and reason, impulse and desire. I desire to be somewhere, and there I will appear." She gave an example of that by exploding into a cloud of smoke heavily scented with sulfur. A second explosion brought her reappearance behind a gasping Bella. Unable to help herself, Isabella laughed and applauded the feat. "I am seduction, charisma, and pacification," Magdelegna finished. "These are the true powers of the Mind, and She shares them with me."

"Wait a minute, Fire, Earth, Wind, and . . . Mind? What happened to Water?"

"Not in this room, but I shall call for a Water Demon if you desire," Noah offered graciously.

"So that means there are five different kinds of Demons? One for each element? Although the Mind element is new to me."

"Actually"—Jacob smiled kindly—"it is true, humans only believe there are four elements. Currently we have six. Earth, Wind, Fire, Water, Mind, and Body."

"Currently?"

"You never know what the future holds. Mind

Demons only appeared about four hundred years ago. It is evolutionary."

"I see." She glanced at Legna, her brow knitting in thought.

"You are curious about something?" Legna prompted.

"Yes. I'm sorry, but it seems like they can come into a room and blast things away, but what you have is more . . . benign?"

"Female Demons are very different than their male counterparts. Our abilities tend toward, shall we say, the more insidious nature of our elements. Those parts of all elements that have potent effect but are not noticed outright until it is too late. For instance, a female Fire Demon. She can manipulate temperature to a small degree when held in comparison to a male like Noah, but temperament is where her true Fire is found. Fire burns in all of us, in our rages, our passions, our jealousies, and so forth. Imagine the ability to manipulate such things. Passion alone has changed the face of the world."

"Luckily, we only have three Fire Demons in existence," Elijah joked, elbowing Noah in the ribs in amusement.

"One of which is Noah and Legna's sister, Hannah," Jacob explained sotto voce.

"Also," Legna continued, clearly warmed to her topic, "there are shared abilities, ones that cross not only sexes but elements as well. For instance, Elijah can become the fog, a weather condition, but so can a Water Demon, because that is what fog is. Both male and female Mind Demons can teleport, but only males are telepaths and only females are empaths."

"I get it."

And she did. Somehow, it all made sense. To have

such power at one's fingertips, she thought, was a daunting prospect. It had the potential to corrupt so absolutely, as the saying went. Yet not this proud, self-censuring race. There was comfort for her in that, because she needed something to counteract the unnerving understanding that things like werewolves and vampires were actually real. She also saw very clearly why they kept themselves a secret from her race. If humans ever found a means to entrap Demons, they could be used and perverted in the extreme.

That was when the last piece of the puzzle fell into place.

"What happened to Saul? You said he was Transformed. How? You were hunting him," she added, turning to look at Jacob. "That's why you asked me if I had seen anything. And when we found him, that bluish light . . . the other man . . . tell me, Jacob. What happened?"

"He was captured. We call it Summoning. There are certain humans, known to us as necromancers, who long ago learned a secret method of Summoning a Demon, entrapping him, and bringing his powers under their domination for a period of time." Jacob's jaw tightened grimly. "With every command the magic-user makes, a transformation begins, advances, and eventually, a Demon becomes what you saw—a mindless creature without control or a sense of right and wrong. It is our worst nightmare."

"Oh my God." Isabella brought a hand to her mouth, her eyes expressing her horror. "You mean that could happen to any of you?"

They all nodded in grim unison and Isabella felt her stomach turn over in protest. These beautiful creatures? Their grace, vigor, and determined sense of right and wrong, destroyed? Perverted into one of those drooling, mindless gargoyles?

"Why are you telling me this? Aren't you afraid I'll somehow endanger you? Why do you trust me? I mean, for heaven's sake, I've killed one of you. Oh!" She gasped in horror. "I didn't mean to! I swear!" Tears leapt into her large violet eyes and Jacob could not resist the urge to enfold her in his arms. He drew her to his chest, cradling her head in one large hand, soothing her with soft sounds as she shuddered in revulsion.

Noah was fascinated by Jacob's tender gestures with her. These were not the actions of a Demon bent solely on an act of lust. The more he watched, the more the Demon King saw that something was connecting Jacob to the little human, something he couldn't quite fathom yet. "Isabella," Noah addressed her, "we look on what you did as an act of mercy. Saul was far beyond our help. If you did not destroy him, Jacob would have been forced to."

"It would have been worse for Saul to survive as a monster, harming anyone of any race he came across," Legna pointed out gently. "Isabella, if you had evil intent, if you meant to harm any of us, I would know. I would feel it in your emotions. As it is, all I feel is honesty and remarkable courage."

"We are telling you all of this because it is our belief that you are somehow a part of our future." *My future.* Jacob fought the urge to personalize it. "You displayed some uncanny abilities last night, Bella. I believe that Destiny chose to cross our paths, even to the point of throwing you out of the window." She laughed shakily at that as he rubbed warm hands gently over her shoulders and arms and explained himself. "Being creatures of the elements, we believe in Destiny and all things inevitable.

The change of the tide, the altering face of the Earth, life and death. These are natural destinies. Individuals have special destinies, things we will do that Destiny has designed for us to do. You have joined our destiny for a reason, and we wish to find out what it is."

"Why?" she asked, her voice hitching sensitively in the query as she tried valiantly to push back her tears. "I mean, so far all I have done to your people is kill one, beat the tar out of another, and drive you to—" She broke off, flushing. "Why the hell would you want anything to do with me after all that?"

"I wouldn't say you beat the tar out of anyone," Elijah spoke up, his chin jutting out belligerently.

The comment compelled Isabella to laugh through her tears. She cast a sideways look at Legna. "I see some things are a constant between the males of both our races."

Legna chuckled and nodded in response. Elijah grumbled under his breath.

"So what do we do now? I mean, how do we find out how I fit into the whole destiny thing?"

"History inevitably repeats itself, becoming the template for the future," Noah said. "Perhaps I am wrong when I say no human has ever killed a Demon before. Researching history may shed some light on this unique situation. Since it has been a century since we last saw a necromancer, we ought to reexamine the components of a Summoning and the recorded details of a transformation. Perhaps it will lend us a clue as to why at the same time as these magics are renewed, so did you appear. We will go to our library. It is quite vast and contains a complete history of our people."

Isabella's head came up sharply, her eyes gleaming with sudden avarice.

"Did you say *library*?"

* * *

It was a few days later when Isabella climbed the
stairs from the library slowly, leaving the cool, dry en-
vironment and rubbing at the ache in the lee of her
shoulders. Sunlight was pouring in through the windows set high in the stone walls of the enormous hall
she found herself in as soon as she stepped out of the
door leading to the underground vault of books.

Her surroundings were eerily quiet, bereft of activity
and life. She wasn't wearing a watch, but she suspected
it was close to ten or eleven in the morning. It was so
strange to be in full daylight in a castle that was re-
puted to be the center of a culture, and yet there was
not even a hint of activity. Her breaths seemed to echo
in the rafters of Noah's home. Stone loomed all
around, and while there were pieces of fine furniture
in the Great Hall, everything was very simplistic in its
way. It was the sparseness in so much space that gave
the feeling of stepping back in time. That and the fact
that there was no electricity. However, the important
stuff was compensated for in one way or another.
There was gas lighting, fairly modern facilities, and
every amenity she could think of—except a phone.

The library itself was a database, most of it sectioned
into its own fascinating logic of reference. The system
was impressive, as was the sheer antiquity of the
recorded data itself. The Demons were dedicated historians, and there were thousands and thousands of
books and scrolls for every century, every era. Noah,
she had discovered, was a scholar like herself. He was
unspeakably proud of his library, eager to share it with
someone new who appreciated its value as much as he
did. The labyrinth of books, shelves, tables, and cases

stretched beneath the entire foundation of the enormous castle—beyond that, even, Noah had confessed
to her. There were vaults that continued on at all four
compass points. These, he had told her, held the very
oldest and most delicate works. There were things in
those vaults, the King had told her, that even the
longest-lived Demons had never seen or heard of. The
library, he promised, was so vast that it would take far
more than even a Demon lifetime to ever know everything it held. In the present, Demon scholars were
recording as faithfully as their predecessors had done
before them. The world was growing by leaps and
bounds, and they were scrambling to keep up with it.

But the King, the scholars, and all other Demons were
in their beds. The business of their lives hung suspended
until the shadows of dusk began to fall. Isabella looked
up and around herself. There were windows everywhere
and the Great Hall was full of light, except none of it was
plain. Every inch of glass was stained. The pictures were
breathtaking, an artistry like nothing Isabella had seen
before, depictions of everything from mythology to a
clever reproduction of Monet's *Water Lilies*. The effect
was light, but in brilliant rainfalls of color.

Isabella stood in the center of the room, splashed
with a kaleidoscope of warm daylight. From what she
had been told, and what she had even more recently
read, this was what made daylight most bearable for
Demons. The direct onslaught of the sun acted like a
fast-acting narcotic. Unconsciousness would come with
overwhelming speed to the unprotected Demon who
found himself caught out in pure daylight. Even these
sprays of muted color were so powerful in effect that a
Demon could do little more than curl up for a con-
tented sleep within it. The sun, Noah had told her, did

not harm them as it did most other Nightwalker species. It made them vulnerable to harm. It was nearly impossible to resist the pull to sleep, making it difficult for all but the most powerful Demons to master any semblance of function during the cycle of the sun. Isabella was pleased the sun did not actually cause harm to Demons. At least they could see the sunrise, provided they had that level of power. From her understanding, most other Nightwalker breeds would burn to a crisp if they even thought about attempting it.

Isabella suddenly sensed she was no longer alone. Jacob watched as she turned her head quickly, her fall of hair fanning out like a black, fringed shawl for a moment before settling with a silken swish against her back and shoulders. She moved her body into the turn as well, the flexible lean of her figure all curves and shapeliness, her back and waist arching as she tried to find him. He felt the throb of his own pulse, deep down the center of his body, the innate response just from watching her move.

She was a mimic, he was realizing. She picked up scents wherever she went and either made them a part of herself or became in sync with them. Mixing with her own clean scent was the odor of books and dust from the library and the soft aroma of ash from the fireplace that remained always burning in Noah's Great Hall. She smelled enticingly of home and wisdom, earth and familiarity, and an innocence of sensuality that was deeply tantalizing. It was, he realized, the essence of nature that she wore. These were Earth's trademarks, and to Jacob, a Demon of Earth, it was ambrosia. It tugged at him, beckoning, whispering of how very much it suited him, until every fine hair on his body was stirring with electric interest.

Jacob stepped out of the shadows of one corner of the Great Hall, his long, lean body filling the vast hall with its quiet but commanding presence. Isabella nervously rubbed her hands along the denim on her thighs, erasing the sudden moisture that coated them at the simple sight of him. Her heart doubled in beat, lurching against her ribs as if it were frustrated to be imprisoned away from him. Even knowing all that she knew, even though he himself had warned her she should have a healthy fear of him, her body practically sang for him when he entered the room. Everything about him beckoned her interest. His assured and authoritative aura was a palpable thing, his dark clothes wrapping around his fit body with sexy sophistication and telling tales about the physique they concealed. He wore expensive slacks, the material a brushed silk that matched his shirt in quality and color. The black dress shirt was worn in a relaxed manner, the first couple of buttons undone beneath his tanned throat, the cuffed sleeves rolled halfway up his fit forearms, exposing the dark dusting of hair on them. No watch or adornment of any kind, the simple silver buckle to his slim leather belt the only hint of decoration. He stood a room away, his legs braced apart as if he were rooted to that place in the marble floor, but still she felt his energy and his warmth. It was as if he stood at her back, close enough to exchange body heat, his head bowing so his breath stirred her hair.

Isabella shivered and licked her suddenly parched lips, unaware that his keen hunter's eyesight became riveted on the action. "I need to speak with my sister," she said after what felt like ages of silence. "I know Noah sent a male Mind Demon back to New York to 'implant' her with the impression that I would be gone for several days so she wouldn't wonder where I disappeared to, but I want to talk to her on the phone just the same."

"There is no phone here," he replied.

Then he was moving toward her, his ground-eating stride like the stalking of a grand jaguar, graceful and calculated and a rippling symphony of muscle. It made the large room seem suddenly very small. His dark eyes were restless for the whole of the journey, moving quickly and succinctly, yet all of this rapt observation remained focused forward, limited only to the space in which she stood. When she realized that those black, bottomless eyes were fixated on her and her alone, when she could feel the rough, possessive urges behind them that he was struggling to hold in check, her heart insisted on pounding hard enough to burst her rib cage. She was practically panting for breath by the time he reached her.

Jacob stood toe-to-toe with her, disregarding all sense of personal space. He reached out, hesitating briefly as he searched her eyes. Satisfied with whatever it was he saw, he brought his fingertips to the rise of her cheek. She could feel them vibrating with his intensity. He caressed her, drifting like her own hair against her, shaping her face with a soft reverence that made her throat ache with response.

"I will take you to a phone. You can even go home if you like. I do not want you to feel that we expect you to neglect your life."

The sentiment was in earnest, Jacob reflected, but it was followed quickly by the sensation that he should not allow her out of his sight. He could not understand this grasping need he had to keep her close, especially when he was so aware of how dangerous it could be.

He was obsessed with the craving to touch her, even if it was just this simple caress he was indulging in now, the tracing and learning of her lovely pixie features. It made him feel sublimely grounded, a singular relief after the oppressive tension that he suffered whenever he was kept too far away from her.

He watched her constantly, day and night, even while the sun dragged at him and demanded his obedience in sleep. He was exhausted, yet here he was again, midday, sitting in the shadows above the library just so his senses could feel her movement below his feet and listen to the soft litany of her mind as she studied and reasoned out the information she was absorbing.

"*We* will take you to a phone, Isabella."

Legna, who seemed to have materialized out of nowhere, delivered the correction. Isabella felt Jacob bristle instantly, a sensation of prickling discomfort skipping down the nape of her neck as she absorbed it from him. He took a slow, decided step back from her, giving her room to breathe, but somehow her breath seemed to strangle in her chest at the separation. She shook her head and glanced from one to the other. Legna's countenance was as serene as always, though it was very obvious that she had been disturbed from her day's rest. Jacob's features, however, were a dark storm of energy and emotion. His forehead creased with frown lines and his brown-black eyes radiated something bordering on hostility. Isabella's entire chest tingled with the rush of it, his prickling emotions popping like fireworks in her brain.

"Thank you, but I am sure I can manage on my own," Isabella insisted, her feelings torn between her upset that Legna had been disturbed from her rest and that Jacob was just plain disturbed. All she wanted was for everyone to be calm and to go about their normal routines.

"Isabella." Legna spoke again in that soft, compelling voice of a diplomat, which Bella had discovered was Legna's role in her brother's court. "Though we do not wish to curb your freedom, Noah has expressed great concern at the thought of you leaving our circle of protection. Please consider, knowing all that you do now, the dangers that might present themselves to you. Until we know the nature of your significance to us, and ours to you, we would feel much safer if you were to remain here or remain protected by allowing for a Demon escort when you travel."

"Legna . . ." Jacob warned, the threat in his voice coming through with sheer masculine authority. "We have no right to ask such a thing of her."

"Actually," Isabella spoke up, cutting off the female Demon's retort, "I wasn't planning on leaving. I just wanted to talk to my sister, touch base, say hi. You know, boring stuff like that. It's a pretty mundane task and certainly not worth all this concern. Honestly," she said, looking down at her dust-covered hands and rubbing them together, "you'll have a pretty hard time getting me out of that library of yours. It's like nothing I've ever seen before. So complex, so . . ." She looked at Jacob, meeting his eyes even though their intensity so overwhelmed her. "Your culture is fascinating. I can't even begin to fathom how far back these records go. The dedication it must have taken to build that archive is incomprehensible. You couldn't drag me away if you tried."

Isabella took her eyes away from the compelling depth of the black gaze he had fixed on her so raptly. She was a conundrum to him, and she knew it. She could sense that his reaction to her mere presence was an overriding confusion and a moral storm within him. She felt the urge to retreat back to the library, to place herself at a safe distance from him. Not that she was afraid of him—actually, to be honest, her surprising lack of fear in the face of such fearful prospects was what disturbed her. She was not using discretion in her thoughts or the impulsive reactions of her physiology when he was near. Like all things, wisdom came with experience. She had nothing to draw on for guidance when it came to the way she felt around Jacob.

"You do not owe us so much of your time, Bella," Jacob said, extracting her from the circle of her thoughts. "In fact, we are the ones who owe you. Why do you make our trouble your own so willingly?"

"You said it yourself," she replied quietly, not even realizing that her feet were taking her toward him, closing the gap between them of their own volition. "I'm somehow a part of all this. Somehow my destiny has become linked with yours."

Legna might as well have not been there for all they were aware of her in that moment. The King's sister was overcome by a sensation of connection, an electric joining between the two of them that was blatant as well as ignorant of the forbidden borders it toyed with. As an empath, Legna was a conduit for the sexual and emotional tension in the room. She was flushed with it, her skin misting with warmth. These were permissible feelings, in spite of the fact that they were the most intoxicating collection of desires she had ever felt as an empath.

Noah had made her duty clear. She was to monitor the Enforcer. At the slightest hint of uncontrolled behavior, she was to summon the King with all due haste. But she sensed no threat, no rampant moon-fed lust.

She had felt it in the past in men and women brought to face Noah by Jacob's hand of justice. It was a wild, ferocious thing. It clawed away at common sense and respect, shredding away even the smallest thought of consideration or control. Control was the key here. The Enforcer's emotions surged like a wild, dark tide within him, yet there was still control. Jacob practically vibrated with it, clearly using every resource he owned to manage his impulses and desires. She would not call out to Noah until she felt the first crack in that formidable mental fortress. Jacob was a proud creature. If she called for interference without cause, he would be hurt and embarrassed, and she could not bear the idea of causing him that pain.

"Believe me," Isabella was saying softly to the Enforcer, who was paying rapt attention to her every word and movement, "I want to know the answers to these questions much as any of you do. I can feel . . ." She hesitated, and Jacob watched as she clutched a small fist over her breastbone. "There is something inside of me. I can't explain it, but it's not all me. I mean, it's not familiar to me. It's as if something alien has sprung to life inside of me and this . . . this new life comes with a seeking sensation that overwhelms even my voracious curiosity. Can't you feel that?"

"I can feel that," Jacob responded sympathetically. His soulful black eyes brushed down Isabella's small body, lingering on the way back up to her gaze. "I can feel your hunger to know. It effervesces in my brain like sparkling water. Though I did not know you before this, I know there are new places in your mind that were not there before, coming alive."

Legna felt her heart slam still with shock. Jacob was Earth. Only a Demon of Mind could read such thoughts, feel such finely tuned empathy. Jacob's knowledge was far too personal . . . too intimate. It was also more than what Legna herself could sense. It seemed as though with every progressive hour, it was harder and harder for her to sense from Isabella. She was becoming like a blank place. Jacob should have no empathic abilities whatsoever, except perhaps with his prey during a hunt, yet it was clear that the Earth Demon knew more about the workings of Bella's mind than she did.

Jacob's lashes lowered slowly as he took an obvious deep breath through his nose, the slight movement of his head and the concentration in his expression telling that he was analyzing the sense he was using. It was such a basic, animalistic thing to do, so clearly predatory and aggressive.

"And senses." Jacob and Isabella spoke together, their voices pitched together perfectly. "Everything is so much more than it was before."

The recital rattled Magdelegna to her very core. She had never seen anything like this before. Her senses were awash with emotionally charged information, forcing her to recoil and draw up her hardest defenses. Legna's knee-jerk response to this was to call for Noah with all of her mental capabilities.

Isabella was so startled by the flash of bursting flames so close to her that she nearly fell over. Jacob reached out instinctively to steady her, but his broad wrist was caught in an iron grasp before he could touch her. Jacob jerked, his eyes slicing across Noah's reach with vicious irritation until he met the King's implacable gaze.

"Do not touch her, Jacob."

"Let go of me," the Enforcer commanded, his low voice full of volumes of outrage and threat.

"I know you would not intend to harm her, Enforcer,

but we both know that intentions will be for naught the moment you touch her. She has proven to be a dangerous lure. Do not torture yourself further with her nearness."

Isabella flushed at the Demon King's high-handed behavior and his insulting references to her. "Uh, excuse me? I resent being treated like Typhoid Mary!"

Noah ignored her, his full attention on Jacob. The King had evidently been roused from his bed on abrupt notice, his black hair tousled with sleep, causing the reddish highlights within to stand out in the sunlight. He was matched with Jacob in height, but it was clear by the muscles laced tightly over the whole of his broad body that he had weight and basic physical strength over the Enforcer. Isabella could see this very clearly because he wore nothing but a pair of gray shorts made of a soft cotton material that was far too revealing.

The unexpected awareness made Isabella jerk her eyes to neutral territory, and red splotches burned over her face and chest. Jacob felt the reaction sparkle across his skin like fire, felt her embarrassment and its causes like a splash of acid in his brain.

Noah heard the low predatory sound rumble up from Jacob like a fast-rising storm. The King instinctively braced himself, knowing he might be forced to deal with Jacob at his moon-fed worst. He made the mistake of thinking Jacob was going to attack him.

Jacob used his breathtaking speed to spin past the other male, breaking Noah's hold on him at the same time he was snatching Isabella up from the floor and sweeping her a good ten feet from the other male. He swung her around to his back, placing himself between her and her line of sight to the Demon King.

Noah's fists clenched, his body rippling in preparation as he turned to face his wild friend. Jacob greeted his clearly visible aggression with another territorial snarl. Isabella's heart was pounding with fear and dismay. She knew what had set Jacob off. She could feel it radiating through their shared psyche. Possession, protection . . . and outrage. Around all of this was wrapped a sheer animalistic territoriality. Jacob was of the Earth, of nature and all of her creatures. Isabella realized then that there was no separating that from him, no matter how civilized and intelligent a man he became. With morals and instinct combining, Jacob saw Noah as an insult and a threat to his feelings of possession for her.

Stuffed back away from Noah as she was, Isabella could only find one other person to appeal to. She looked to Legna, her wide violet eyes begging the female Demon to do something, praying that the empath would understand what was happening. Legna's gray-misted eyes, such a perfect duplicate of her elder brother's, were averted. Because the room was filled with so much volatility, she had barricaded her mind against the storm around her. Yet the moment Isabella broadcasted her need, her desperation of emotion, the empath looked up at her quickly.

Why can't you feel Jacob? Why can't you understand what is happening? Isabella wondered desperately. Was she misinformed about the beautiful diplomat's power? She was so new to this; perhaps her concept of their power was mostly imagination.

This thought was easily discarded when a billow of heat radiated off Noah, the burst hitting them like a suffocating desert wind. The Demon King's fist uncurled, opening with an outward flicker of fingers, and a ball of fire erupted into his palm.

"Legna, get your charge to safety," the Demon King

commanded, his smoky voice rough and reeking of his threatening power.

There was an awesome rumbling sound and Isabella felt the earth shudder beneath her feet. She reached out to grab Jacob's shirt, clutching it for balance even as the protective arm he held behind himself tightened to draw her closer.

"Noah, wait!"

The cry came from Legna, who braved the intense heat surrounding her antagonistic brother and grabbed the arm that he had loaded with fiery ammunition. Noah's first reaction was to reabsorb the fireball so he would not burn her.

"Oh, thank God," Isabella uttered on a low, relieved sigh. She buried her face into Jacob's back as she continued to cling to him for support.

"Legna!" Noah castigated his sister with a rough growl of temper.

"Noah, it is not what you think. Stop!" She pulled harder when he tried to shake her off. Legna was well aware of how difficult it was to draw her brother back from confrontation and anger once something lit the match. It was the essence of Fire, and it wasn't his fault. She felt his justification, felt his turbulent upset that he was being forced to face down a friend. He was angry. Angry at the Hallowed moon, which he thought was brutalizing Jacob, brutalizing all of his people and beating their honorable spirits down into shame and low beastly behavior. "Noah, listen to me," the empath said, her voice pitching low and soft, the tone musical and sweet. Isabella felt a change go through Jacob, minor but detectable. The low rumble of sound that had been boiling up from his throat quieted to just an occasional crackle of warning. "Jacob is not maddened

JACOB   101

by the moon," she continued, that velvet softness of words flowing over both tense men and Isabella. "Hear me, my beloved brother. I feel what he feels. I know. Trust me to know."

"Jacob would never threaten me if he were sane," the King argued, but he had finally looked away from his target, meeting his youngest sister's imploring gaze.

"Unless," she replied softly, "you did something he felt threatened Isabella. Noah, you must remember that there is something that connects them, something that draws them to each other."

"That accursed moon is the cause," Noah bit out.

"An amplification. It is true, and we all know it. The Hallowed moon amplifies everything we feel. In Jacob's heart, in the very core of his being, he is a protector of innocents. Usually human innocents. That is what he will always do first and foremost. Even against you. Also, this is his greatest fear, that he would have to battle you one day for the sake of an innocent." Legna reached out to smooth a loving hand through her brother's hair as she continued to murmur soothingly to him. "Combine these, and the smallest perceived offense becomes like stepping into a Vampire's territory without invitation." The comparison made the Demon King lift his brows in understanding. The burn of battle faded from his jade eyes and he flicked a less aggressive gaze in Jacob's direction.

Magdelegna stepped around Noah and moved in between the two powerful men fearlessly. "Jacob," she said, again her voice pitched like honey, reaching to calm the inadvertently triggered beast within Jacob. "No one will harm Isabella. We would never do that. We could never do that when you are her protector."

"You cannot keep me away from her."

Isabella drew in a sudden breath when he spoke. It was the first civilized thing he had done in what seemed like ages, even though his voice was rough and devoid of all civility.

"We will not. Not unless you are going to truly harm her, as you know we are bound to do."

Isabella peeked around Jacob's tightly flexed biceps so she could see his expression. His tanned features were still drawn and dark, still aggressive, but there was reason entering his glistening black eyes. She felt his mind and emotions settling further down under Legna's subtle power to coax and soothe. Isabella suddenly realized that Demon females did indeed have power that was not to be underestimated. Legna could potentially be a very dangerous woman.

"I will never harm her. I will lay down my life before I will allow myself"—his eyes glanced acidly at Noah—"or anyone else to cause Bella hurt."

"When did I cause her hurt?" Noah protested with indignation. "I never even looked at her."

"But she looked at you."

Isabella gasped and ducked back behind Jacob's back. She winced hard as her face blossomed with mortifying heat. She buried her face against his back and prayed for a sudden sinkhole to open beneath her.

Comprehension dawned on Noah's face like a brilliant sunrise. He opened his mouth to speak but was too flabbergasted to form the words. Isabella could hear the step of his bare feet on stone as he came up to Jacob. Jacob was forced to take a step forward for balance because she was trying so hard to bury herself in his spine.

"I see," Noah said at last, "that this is my fault after all. Isabella, you will forgive me, but you are the first human ever to be an extended guest in my home, and I was not thinking of common courtesies."

"I never meant for this to become such a big deal," she muttered.

"I will be more careful in the future. I hope you can forgive Jacob and me for our aggressions. We . . . we are . . . There is a great deal of responsibility and control that must come with powers of such potential volatility as the males of my people are created with. But in the end, we are still elemental beings. I made the mistake of underestimating the true sense of guardianship Jacob felt where you are concerned."

Noah exchanged a silent, intense look with Jacob that went further than that politely explained apology. Jacob had deemed Isabella his property, a female under his protection and possession. When the King had inadvertently embarrassed Isabella by his lack of proper clothing, it had made Jacob aware that she had been looking at him, another powerful male, and that had been absolutely unacceptable to Jacob in his unsteady state of mind. The Fire Demon had mistaken the following aggression as an attack on Bella, an attempt to kidnap her from their censured protection.

However, to be honest, Noah had no idea how to explain this peculiar connection the Enforcer seemed to have with the little human female. The entire situation was very disconcerting.

The Enforcer had not yet overcome his initial impulses to spirit Isabella away from Noah's presence. It was important to their relationship that he gave Jacob the opportunity to regain control of himself with dignity. He knew Jacob well enough to know how he must be smarting already in the wake of having had Elijah whip him back into line. Now there was this misunderstanding on top of that. No one could be harder on the Enforcer than he was on himself, and Noah was trusting that it was that part of Jacob that would regain control.

"Excuse me while I get dressed," Noah said politely. He glanced at his sister, knowing that she would not be afraid to be alone with them. Removing his presence was probably the best thing for him to do just then, though he would return quickly. He knew Legna understood that she was expected to gently extract Isabella from Jacob's embrace in order to help ease the tumultuous emotions her nearness intensified. If Noah dared try such a thing, he'd likely lose a limb.

The King swirled into a sudden cloud of smoke. The cloud moved toward the stairs and the upper rooms in the north wing of the castle.

Legna had already chosen an approach.

"Bella," she said, automatically using the nickname Jacob had given her, "how do you like the clothing I loaned you?"

Bella moved as far to one side of Jacob as the clamp of his hand on her hip and arm across her body would allow, so she could see the other woman.

"It's very comfortable," she said. "You must have had to hem everything a great deal."

"Nonsense," Legna brushed off the detail. "Clothing is easy to replace and I was glad to help." Her eyes sparkled with warm teasing. "Besides, if we let you run around naked there would have been vine swinging, chest beating, and maybe even some marking of territory." Legna wrinkled her nose and gave a little shudder.

"That's quite enough of that, Magdelegna."

Absolutely 100 percent *Jacob* filled that smart reprimand. It made Isabella's heart leap happily, the flood of relieved emotion washing out of her until Jacob chuckled softly. He exhaled a long, decompressing sigh, closing his eyes briefly as all irrational impulses eased with Noah's departure. What it left was a smarting conscience and sheen of regret as he recalled his primitive behavior. He looked at little Bella, her dark head tilted so she could see past his arm to talk with Legna. He worried what she must think of him by now. Her mind was focused solely on her relief and her amusement with Legna, so he had no hint.

Jacob's entrapping arm lowered to his side, but his long, elegant fingers twitched slightly, as if they wanted to touch Isabella in spite of his command of them. The Enforcer's jaw became grimly set and he swore softly in his native tongue before turning his back on Isabella and moving to put a safe distance between them. His mind working properly again, he knew Noah would be back just as quickly as he had left and that he needed to withdraw from her himself, make it his own decision, or there would be another confrontation. Even though this had been a misunderstanding, he had been unable to voice his feelings like a civilized, intelligent being, something that had never happened to him before.

This, he realized, was the wicked humor of the Hallowed moon. He had seen healthy glimpses of his more bestial half during intense battle or hunt, but even then he had maintained logic and cunning, that which ruled important skills like fighting tactics. Never had he felt such a complete shutdown of wisdom and consideration. He hardly felt any true regret for what had transpired. Prickling within his psyche was a sense of triumph, the feeling that he had defended what was his and that he wished to revel in the success. Jacob felt the surge of response within himself and he could not control the feeling, could not banish it from existence.

Isabella was still trading innocuous conversation with Legna, moving close enough so the taller beauty could reach out to gently rub Bella's arm. There was no rush of possessiveness inside him as he watched the empath radiate her quickly growing attachment to Isabella. He knew this quickening friendship was because Legna was the only other one beside him who had met Bella and known instantly every good and noble quality within her. The female Mind Demon, he understood, would come to love Bella one day.

That was when he realized he would never be able to move far enough away from Isabella. The thought heated up his entire consciousness, making his breath come deep and swift. She was following him everywhere. Her presence clung to him like a static charge. He slowly stroked his eyes along the curving length of her, his eyes resting on her with blatant hunger reflected in their depths. He could not have hidden it under any circumstances. Not even knowing he was being so closely monitored as he was could dissuade the surge in his appetite for her.

"Jacob . . ." Legna said suddenly. "Jacob, do not—"

Her eyes flicked anxiously to a point beyond his shoulder, and he realized that Noah had returned to the room. He did not need to look behind himself to know. All of his senses reflected the imposing presence of the Demon King: his smoky scent, the rustle of his now fully clothed body, and the authority that eddied off him even when he was at rest. Isabella looked at him when Legna spoke to him, the glisten of her purple eyes in the gaslight like an arrow straight through his heart. How was it possible? How could a human woman make him feel like he had sworn he was never destined to feel? She stirred him so deeply, and all she was doing, once again, was looking at him.

"Legna?" Noah queried cautiously.

"Jacob is—"

"Jacob," the Enforcer said sharply, his harsh eyes pinning the female Demon in place, his sensual mouth pressed into a severe frown, "is fine. Be aware, young one, that there is a large difference between what I feel and what I act on. My control is beyond anything any of you will ever be capable of, so do not think it is you who keeps me in line. Either of you."

Isabella did not miss the fact that Jacob's reference to Legna's age was some sort of purposeful insult. The lovely female's cheeks flared with color, her elegant hands closing into fists. Isabella sighed, rolled her eyes, and placed both of her hands on her round hips.

"All right, that's enough. Everyone go back to your corners. Heavens. If I thought I could be responsible for setting three perfectly intelligent friends at each other's throats, I would have never crossed that threshold." She pointed to the large entranceway far across the Great Hall for emphasis. "Or"—she hesitated, then looked at the opposite side of the room, which also had an exit—"that threshold."

Jacob felt a smile settle over his lips and he cleared his throat. The sound purposely drew her attention, and, again with great purpose, he looked up over his shoulder to one of the stained glass windows, which had a small hinged window in its bottom that was perpetually left open.

"That threshold?" she asked, her voice pitched high with surprise. He felt her heart miss a beat in her shock and he felt bad for the spike of laughter that tried to lance free of him. He had a feeling that if he laughed, she would be far more threatening to him than Noah had been.

Legna, however, had no such control. She giggled irrepressibly and then quickly laid a hand over her betraying smile when Bella whirled to glare at her indignantly.

"I am so very sorry," she said behind the muffle of her hand. "It is their fault."

The empath pointed to her brother and his Enforcer, and Bella could see that behind their forcibly stoic expressions, their eyes were bright with laughter at her expense. Isabella grinned, turning her eyes to study the pattern of the marble veins in the floor as they both began to laugh.

Jacob's tension of the past few hours dissolved instantly with his amusement. "Go on, Bella, let Legna take you to call your sister," he said after he had regained his composure. "But do not keep Legna out in the daylight too long. She is not so strong as I and her brother. I have a few things to do before I rest for the day." He looked at Noah for a long minute. "I trust you have things to do here as well?"

Noah realized that Jacob was warning him that the idea of him accompanying Isabella around was not a welcome one. The King had not intended on doing anything but returning to his interrupted sleep once all was settled. In spite of the recent altercation, he was still taken aback by the possessiveness behind the veiled threat.

True, Jacob's loyalty to him was deeply ingrained in everything he did, but Noah had no illusions to cover the fact that Jacob had somehow marked this woman in his mind as his possession. Noah knew it was inherently a dangerous and unhealthy attitude for Jacob to indulge in, simply because he had no right to do so. On the other hand, he could not escape a niggling sensation in the back of his brain that this provocation to be Isabella's defender meant something very important. It was too curious, too deeply grooved in the remarkable to not signify something of import. He would have to mull it over while he slept. Noah hoped that when he woke he would have clearer thoughts and perspectives on the matter. Madness, necromancers, and whatever it was that allowed Isabella Russ to turn all of Noah's most powerful friends and allies inside out in their efforts to protect her—Noah instinctively knew these were all connected. All he needed now was some sort of clarity as to why.

"I am returning to my chamber," Noah announced, more for Jacob's peace of mind than anything. "Legna, do not hesitate to call me if you or Isabella should need me." He paused for all of two seconds. "Also, should your safety be threatened in any way, I suggest you call out to Jacob as well. He may be able to reach you far faster than I can."

Noah was highly aware of the sudden release of tension from his Enforcer's body. Noah had wanted to put Jacob's protective instincts at ease, and he had succeeded with incredible diplomacy. The knowledge that he would not be left out of the loop seemed to relax the Earth Demon greatly. Noah used the rather boring convention of the stairs to exit the room this time.

Jacob decided that a quick exit would be the only way he could make himself put necessary distance between himself and Isabella. So, without so much as a wave, he turned in a burst of movement, becoming a shower of dust that streamed swiftly upward and out that high, narrow window of colored glass.

"That is extremely cool," Isabella sighed.

"I suppose it is," Magdelegna agreed with a laugh, smiling warmly as she reached to rub Bella's shoulder in a gesture of friendly comfort. "Shall I take you to a phone?"

"Why aren't there any phones here?" she thought to ask.

"Well, the best way I can explain it is that technologies like electricity and telephones do not always agree with Demons. We believe that because we are so rooted in nature, there is something about man-made technological objects that just does not work properly when we are too close to them. They . . . 'go haywire' I believe is the phrase. They develop glitches."

"Oh," Isabella said softly.

"Sometimes, nothing happens at all." Legna shrugged. "Other times, just our nearness makes things get . . . haywire. It is one of the reasons Demons do not integrate fully with humans. You are very dependent on your technologies. Many of us prefer to live in isolation . . . in rural settings like this one."

"In places where archaic methods of living are not so out of the ordinary," Bella mused. "I see." She paused for only a few beats. "One last question?"

"I doubt it will be your last," Legna laughed. "All your questions are welcome."

"How is it you are all awake? I thought you had a powerful compulsion to sleep in the daytime."

"Accomplished Elders such as Noah and Jacob can put off this compulsion for sleep with effort and a lifetime of power control. Younger Demons, such as myself, are far more susceptible. This morning has been taxing for us all." She held out her hands and Isabella noticed for the first time that they were shaking. "We do not like to show weakness. Jacob and Noah hide theirs well, although Noah may not be affected. I am never sure, but his ability to manipulate energy . . . I suspect he could remain awake nonstop for days if he desired it. He is of Fire, and few of us fully understand the abilities of male Fire Demons."

"I'm sorry. I had not meant to stir everybody up. Why don't we do this later when it becomes dark? A few hours will make no difference to me or to Corrine."

"Are you certain?"

"Positive. No sense putting you through such an effort for something that can so easily wait."

"I would be fine," Legna assured her. "Just a yawn here and there."

"Still. I'm going back to my books. Come get me when you wake up."

Chapter Four

It was daylight once more when Jacob floated down through Noah's manor until he was in the vault, one moment dust dancing through the incandescent light, the next coming to rest lightly on his feet. He looked around the well-lit catacomb, seeking his prey. He heard a rustling sound from the nearest stacks and moved toward it.

There was a soft curse, a grunt, and the sudden slam of something hitting the floor. Jacob came around just in time to find Isabella dangling from one of the many shelves, her feet swaying about ten feet above the floor as she searched with her toes for a foothold. On the ground below her was a rather ancient-looking tome, the splattered pattern of the dust that had shaken off it indicating it had been the object he had heard fall. Far to her left was the ladder she had apparently been using.

With a low sigh of exasperation, Jacob altered gravity for himself and floated himself up behind her. "You are going to break your neck."

Isabella was not expecting a voice at her ear, considering her peculiar circumstances, and she started with

a little scream. One hand lost hold and she swung right
into the hard wall of his chest. He gathered her up
against himself, his arm slipping beneath her knees so
she was safely cradled, his warmth infusing her with a
sense of safety and comfort as he brought her down to
the floor effortlessly. In spite of herself, she pressed her
cheek to his chest.

"Must you sneak up on me in midair like that? It's
very unnerving."

She had meant to sound angry, but the soft, breathless accusation was anything but. Anyway, how angry
would he think her to be if she was snuggling up to
him like a kitten? Damn it, Demon or not, he was still
a sinfully good-looking man. Jacob was elegant to a
fault, his movements and manner centered around an
efficiency of actions that drew the eye. He was dressed
again in well-tailored black slacks, and this time a midnight blue dress shirt with his cuffs turned back. She
could feel the rich quality of the silk beneath her
cheek, and when she breathed in, Jacob smelled like
the rich, heady Earth he claimed his abilities from.

Besides all the outwardly alluring physicality, Isabella
knew that he was extremely sensitive about all his inter-
actions with others. She could feel his moral impera-
tives tingling through her mind whenever he was near.
His heart, she knew, was made of incredibly honorable
stuff. How could she find it in herself to be afraid of
that? Especially when he had never once hurt her, even
though there had been plenty of influences compelling him to.

"Shall I put you back and let you plummet to your
death?" he asked, releasing her legs and letting her body
slide slowly down his until her feet touched the floor.

The whisper of the friction of their clothes hummed

across Jacob's skin, and he felt his senses focusing in on every nuance of sensation she provided for him. The swishing silk of her hair even in its present tangled state, the sweet warmth of her breath and body, the ivory perfection of her skin. He reached to wipe a smudge of dust from her delectable little nose. She was a mess. There was no arguing that. Head to toe covered in dust and grime, and she smelled like an old book, but those earthy scents would never be something unappealing to one of his kind. Jacob breathed deeply as the usual heat she inspired stirred in his cool blood. It was stronger with each passing moment, with each progressive day, and he never once became unaware of that fact. He tried to tell himself it was merely the effects of the growing moon, but that reasoning did not satisfy him. Hallowed madness would not allow for the unexpected compulsion toward tenderness he kept experiencing whenever he looked down into her angelic face. It would never allow him to enjoy these simple yet significant stirrings of his awareness without forcing him into overdrive. True, he was holding on to his control with a powerful leash of determination. He was tamping down the surges of want and lust that gripped him so hard sometimes it was nearly crippling, but somehow it was still different.

Then he had to also acknowledge the melding of their thoughts as something truly unique. Perhaps a human could initiate such a contact if they were a medium or psychic of noteworthy ability, but she made no claims to such special talents. Every day the images of her mind became clearer to him. She had even taken to consciously sending him visual impressions in response to some discussion they were having with Noah, Elijah, and Legna. He believed that, if things continued to progress in this manner, he and Bella would soon be engaging in actual discussions with each other without ever opening their mouths. He didn't have fact to base that assumption on, but it seemed the natural evolution to the growing silent communication between them.

He had seen Legna staring at them curiously on several occasions. Luckily, because she was a female Mind Demon, she was not a full telepath. If she had been a male she would have been privy to some pretty private exchanges between him and Isabella. Nothing racy, actually, but he found Isabella had such an irreverent sense of humor that he wasn't sure others would understand it as he seemed to.

It was a privacy of exchange he found himself coveting. It was the one way they could be together without Legna or Noah interfering. It was bad enough that the empath was constantly sniffing at his emotions, making sure he kept in careful control of his baser side. Since the King was not able to subject him to the usual punishment that was meted out for those who had crossed the line as he had with Isabella, he had been forced to be a little more creative. Setting Legna the empathic bloodhound on him had done the trick. It was also seriously pissing him off. He knew she was always there, and it burned his pride like nuclear fire.

What was more, he couldn't keep his mind away from Isabella. And since even the smallest thought of her had a way of sparking an onslaught of fantasies that brought his body to physical readiness—well, it was the very last thing he wanted an audience for.

It had taken quite a bit of planning, and the deceptive use of herbal tea mixtures, in order to slip out from under Legna's observation so he could sneak away to the vault. The empath slept as soundly as the dead, and she would stay that way until this evening.

"I wouldn't have fallen to my death," Bella was arguing, her stubborn streak prickling. "At the most, I would have fallen to my broken leg or my concussion or something. Boy, you Demons have this way of making everything seem so intense and pivotal."

"We are a very intense people, Bella."

"Tell me about it." She wriggled out of his embrace, putting distance between them with a single step back. Jacob was well aware of it being a very purposeful act. "I've been reading books and scrolls as far back as seven hundred years ago. You were just a gleam in your daddy's eye then, I imagine."

"Demons may have long gestation periods for their young, but not seventy-eight years' worth."

"Yes. I read about that. Is it true it takes thirteen months for a female to carry and give birth?"

"Minimum." He said it with such casual dismissal that Bella laughed.

"That's easy for you to say. You don't have to lug the kid around inside of you all that time. You, just like your human counterparts, have the fun part over with like that." She snapped her fingers in front of his face.

His dark eyes narrowed and he reached to enclose her hand in his, pulling her wrist up to the slow, purposeful brush of his lips even as he maintained a sensual eye contact that was far too full of promises. Isabella caught her breath as an insidious sensation of heated pins and needles stitched its way up her arm.

"I promise you, Bella, a male Demon's part in a mating is never over like this." He mimicked her snap, making her jump in time to her kick-starting heartbeat.

"Well"—she cleared her throat—"I guess I'll have to

take your word on that." Jacob did not respond in agreement, and that unnerved her even further. Instinctively, she changed tack. "So, what brings you down into the dusty atmosphere of the great Demon library?" she asked, knowing she sounded like a brightly animated cartoon.

"You."

Oh, how that singular word was pregnant with meaning, intent, and devastatingly blatant honesty. Isabella was forced to remind herself of the whole Demon-human mating taboo as the forbidden response of heat continued to writhe around beneath her skin, growing exponentially in intensity every moment he hovered close. She tried to picture all kinds of scary things that could happen if she did not quit egging him on like she was. How she was, she didn't know, but she was always certain she was egging him on.

"Why did you want to see me?" she asked, breaking away from him and bending to retrieve the book she had dropped. It was huge and heavy and she grunted softly under the weight of it. It landed with a slam and another puff of dust on the table she had made into her own private study station.

"Because I cannot seem to help myself, lovely little Bella."

The thick silk of his voice slithered down her neck and spine, making her shiver. She reached up and shoved back her dusty hair, refusing to make eye contact with him.

"Okay, umm . . . Demon plus human equals . . . big bad things, remember? Full moon? October? Any of this ringing a bell?"

"You think I do not know that?" The question was low, sounding dangerous. "Do I seem out of control to you, Bella? Do you really think, even for a moment, that I would hurt you?"

"No, I don't think so." She finally met his piercing gaze. "But you weren't exactly *you* yesterday, now were you? And the night we first met? Didn't you say yourself it can hit any of you at any time? No one is immune." Bella moved to face him, her arms crossing her tummy from hip to hip. "Do you forget that I've seen the worst of a Demon's lust? I close my eyes sometimes and see Saul looming over me. That scares me, Jacob. I don't want it to, but it does."

Jacob's fingers curled into themselves, forming tight fists that were a signal of his building upset. She sensed it bothered him greatly to know she was afraid of him, that she was comparing the possibilities between them to her encounter with a perverted monster. However, it was the truth of her feelings, or some of them, and he needed to know it. She may have been caught up into his world by Destiny or whatever, but that didn't mean she was going to disregard her personal safety. Nor would she put any of his friends at risk. She was coming to care for Legna already, the stunning empath's purity of soul so beautiful and guileless that she could not help her growing fondness for her. After yesterday morning's display of Noah's power, she refused to even think of putting Jacob into confrontation with him. She also had a very clear feeling that the Demon Enforcer did not have very many friends, that Noah held exclusive rights to such an exalted position in Jacob's esteem.

It bothered Bella that she disturbed Jacob so much. It was like being an incredibly mean tease, stirring him up and having no intention of following through. It didn't matter that she wasn't trying to do it, it just mattered that it was what happened.

"Maybe I should leave," she said faintly, turning to shuffle papers into innocuous positions on her desk. "Maybe someone else should do this research. Noah has so much more experience in this than I do. I can read the English texts, even the Latin ones, but I can't read the works that are in whatever language that is. You have Demon scholars, and I'm just a human . . ."

"No. We need you." His tone was as firm as stone.

"So you say. All I know is that I'm a distraction to you, Jacob. One you don't need right now, from what I've been reading."

"You will not leave." It was a command, deep and forceful, filled with his frustration. Then he seemed to realize what he was saying and sighed, shoving his hand through his long, loose hair in agitation. "If you were out of the realm of my . . . my *people's* protection, then you would see the meaning of the word *distraction*," he promised her.

"There you go again. Is everything so extreme for you people?"

"Yes." His hand came out to frame her face, turning her around to look up fully into his eyes, his fingertips moving in a soft, tantalizing massage at the spot in front of her ear where her hairline began. "I will tell you this, Isabella. In my very lengthy lifetime, I have been single-minded in my devotion to a great many things for a great many other people. But you . . . you are the first thing I feel compelled to be devoted to for myself and myself alone. Do not think it is the Hallowed moon that makes me talk this way. I assure you, it is something much deeper than that, something far more cogent than such astrological fickleness."

"Jacob . . ." Isabella was breathless. Why couldn't a normal male say things like that to her? *Finally someone romantic, fascinating, and intelligent comes along, and he turns out to be not even of the same species.* Just her luck.

Jacob smiled, a broad toothy grin.

"I am a normal male," he insisted.

"Hey! Stop doing that!" She covered her head with both hands. "Don't read my mind. That's not fair."

"Fair? What does fairness have to do with it? I do not know why I am able to sense your thoughts, but since I have the ability, it is practical to use it."

"Well, it isn't ethical!" Her hands popped onto her hips, making him smile. "Sometimes very private things go through my head, and you have no business snooping into them. Just because you can do something doesn't mean you should."

"I understand that. However, you are the one who keeps tossing images at me when we are in public. Some of them quite disrespectful of my King and Elijah, I might point out." His eyes were twinkling with suppressed amusement as she thrust up her chin stubbornly.

"Those were given, not taken. Do I take things out of your head without your permission?"

"I do wish you would," he said softly, the suggestiveness of the simple statement sending a shiver up the back of her neck.

"Well"—she cleared her throat—"I'll thank you to keep out of my head. And since you mention it, you are about as normal as a hurricane."

"Yes, but there is even a time when hurricanes are considered normal."

Jacob smiled when she released a frustrated little growl, the sound striking him more as sexy than petulant or dangerous, as she might have wished it to be. He reached out to touch her throat before he could curb the impulse, feeling it vibrate with the sound for all of a second before his touch startled her and made her gasp. He felt her swallow, felt her breathe. Such living, vital reflexes. He could feel her pulse. Felt it quicken. No sooner had her blood begun to rush than he was being filled with her scent again. It was toxic to him, like too much candy, making his world tilt just a little off its axis. That primitive part of him stirred, lifted its head out of its controlled slumber.

Isabella saw black fire leap into his dark chocolate eyes. She held her breath, momentarily entranced as hunger licked hotly through his irises, turning them completely black. Those lustrous eyes were skimming over her, devouring her without so much as a touch. She was acutely aware of his power, his strength, and all the things he could turn and bend to his will if he but concentrated hard enough. It was not lost on her that she was quickly becoming one of those things. Whenever he came near, she inevitably bowed to him like a flower seeking the sun.

"Like roots seeking nourishment from the soil," he corrected, plucking her mental simile from her and turning it into one that suited him and his nature better. "But perhaps that would better describe myself, little flower." His voice was as warm as sun-baked earth. "Whenever I see you, I am overcome with the urge to be rooted within you, to be buried deep so your body can nourish me."

The imagery was like lightning coursing through her. It left Isabella panting gently for breath and brought slivers of quicksilver heat through her veins. Her head was bending backward, tilting her face up to his to meet the fractional lowering of his head. His eyes targeted the parted swell of her mouth.

She swayed closer to him, her body so raptly in tune with his that, if he shifted a shoulder forward, she would match the movement. She did this in such a way that, should they make contact, she would fit into the line of his body perfectly. Hunger clawed through Jacob relentlessly, his nostrils flaring as they filled with that exotic scent that was 100 percent Bella.

This time, Jacob's mouth was infinitely tender when it contacted hers. So much so that if not for the sparkle of heat that flushed her lips, she would have felt no contact. He pressed himself onto her incrementally, smiling against her mouth when she made a little sound of frustration at his taunting pace. He let her decide when she was ready, held so still but for gentle, breathy rubs of his lips against hers. Her hands reached out and curled with unconscious longing into his shirt. She was trying to pull him closer, but he would not obey her.

Come to me, little flower, if you want me. Come to me.

Isabella's blood was roaring in her ears so loudly that she almost didn't hear the soft, beckoning voice in her mind. Either way, she had decided she was through with his toying. She surged up onto her toes, thrusting her body upward into his, her mouth capturing his greedily. He opened instantly for the aggressive sweep of her tongue, groaning low in his soul as she fluttered like a soft, sensual butterfly within his mouth.

Both of his hands swept up into her silky hair, capturing her delicate head, pulling her deeper into him. As aggression switched hands, Isabella's body bowed backward, curving, fitting to his, and soaking up the hard heat he was giving off in great, stunning waves. Jacob's hands flexed tight as she locked herself against him. His tongue swept over hers with obvious hunger. His breath rushed so hotly across her mouth and cheek that she felt scorched by it. Isabella returned the intensity by sliding her hands up the back of his neck and into the depths of his rich hair, holding him as tightly to the kiss as he was holding her.

Jacob felt the slight sharpness of her nails as they traveled up the sensitive length of his neck, and the recoil of response that sprang through his body was awesome in both heat and primitivity. They unfurled within him, flexing every muscle in anticipation until Isabella found herself clinging to a man made of granite. The contrasts to the soft workings of her beautifully seductive mouth were astounding. Clearly she didn't mind that his mouth was the only relaxed part of his body. That is, if he could call his aggressive hunger as he devoured her sweet taste an exhibition of relaxation. She let him crush her against his stone-hard body, and she bent willingly beneath his intensity as he kissed her.

Her mouth was warm and lush, like a Brazilian jungle, and equally full of wondrous surprises. She kissed with wickedly adept skill, improving on herself every second. Somehow she always knew just how to match him, how to tantalize him further until he was groaning against her lips. Bella herself was gasping into his mouth, her clutching fingers in his hair urgent and demanding. Her petite, luxuriant body squirmed against his like a desert snake fitting itself into a tight cubby of rocks.

Violent, urgent demand clawed through him; it moved with sharp fingers of ice in amongst the burning of his body, just to be sure he would feel it as acutely as possible, to secure his entire attention.

Jacob suddenly broke off, jerking Isabella back by the hair as if he would put her at a distance. She swayed in his grasp, suspended between his desires as a war raged in his obsidian eyes. His fingers were gripping her scalp in a desperate massage of conflicting needs. He was shaking, and she could feel it. So strong, so powerful, yet quaking as if conflicting plates of the Earth were rubbing each other raw.

The discord lasted all of a couple of heartbeats, and then wild nature took over. Isabella cried out as his arms circled her like bands of steel and jerked her relentlessly against his rock-hard body. His mouth returned to hers, devouring her deeply, tasting her as if she were a glutton's favorite delicacy. His arousal was a palatable thing, and she savored it against her tongue, the bouquet of it as intoxicating as strong wine. He tasted of all the spices of the Earth combined in a heady flavor that sang like sensual music through her senses. Isabella felt his strong fingers molding to the curve of her back, sliding slowly over each contour, heading with purpose toward the bow of her waist, the flare of her hips. She pulled back ever so slightly to draw a breath, her lips glistening with the honey of their mouths. Jacob couldn't bear the sight or the separation. It was too much like denial, and he was through with that. He reached to recapture her, his kiss punishing in power and dominance, a reprimand in passion for depriving him of her when she knew he couldn't bear it.

Jacob groaned, the sound boiling up from the deepest regions of his body. He was being strangled by the restriction of his clothing, more so by the press of her body and her hands as they began to move over him with sudden liberty. He cupped her sweetly rounded bottom in both hands and she eagerly leapt up as he lifted her feet from the floor. She was so light, so tiny, like a precious, delicate fairy flying up against his towering body.

But the pixie had bite, as he soon was reminded. She slung one knee over his hip and nipped playfully at his lower lip in distraction. He wasn't expecting her other leg to snake so quickly around him so that he was suddenly caught in the erotic vise of her legs. Her torso rose up high in his embrace, their mouths separating as she gripped the back of his head, pulling him toward the fullness of her breasts.

It was another scent, different and the same all at once. Pure, he thought hotly, as the sharp tang of musk drifted up from her skin. She shuddered violently in his hold. He felt her memories of their first encounter flitting through her mind, felt her yearn for a repeat of what it felt like to have his touch on her breasts. Her eager desire inundated him, and within seconds he had jerked her T-shirt up and over her head, flinging it aside carelessly.

She watched as he focused on her bare breasts, his gaze completely transfixed, his hand slowly skimming over the top of one, then traveling to the other. His touch was feather light and maddening. This curious exploration was nothing like the demand to claim her that had motivated him the last time, nothing like the more aggressive needs she could feel radiating from him now with every fiber of her being. She was not ignorant of the danger she was in. She couldn't be any longer. She could feel it as he insinuated himself around all of her thoughts and emotions, and she around his. Inside each other. The actual joining of their physical bodies would be necessary to perfect them. That knowledge left a bereft place within her, as if she were hollowed out and incomplete because he wasn't already within her.

Jacob's touch narrowed to a single fingertip that skied down the slope of her left breast until it was just a lone fingernail that scraped over her rigid nipple. Isabella jerked sharply, unprepared for the spear of heat the simple touch sent rocketing through her. His mouth caught up her nipple the very next second, drawing it deep into the warm, wet home of his playful tongue. He suckled her and she moaned loudly, wriggling with frustration and pleasure in his single-armed embrace. A pulse of heat seeped down the center of her so hot and so wet that it burst the confines of her body. She was flooded with moisture, the beckoning nectar pooling hotly at the juncture of her thighs.

Jacob released her from his mouth, her sensitive body suddenly endangered by the need roaring through him as her fragrance swept his extraordinary senses. He jerked her forward against himself, his face burrowing beneath her hair where her neck met her shoulder. His teeth latched onto her with no warning whatsoever. He couldn't help himself. She was his mate, and he had to make it known to her and all those who thought to come near her.

Isabella gasped loud and long as his teeth pierced her skin, serious enough to mark her but stopping before causing truly painful damage. His hand wrapped around her throat, holding her still as a bestial growl of possession boiled out of him. His thoughts, dark and primitive, swept fiercely through her.

I am Jacob the Enforcer, a Demon of the dominant Earth. I am every blade of grass, every song of life that is sung on the planet. I am what has been from the beginning of all time, both known and unknown. I am every predator, and like them, I make it known that this female is mine by leaving my mark upon her. My scent will bleed into hers, just as hers

*already becomes a part of mine. She will smell of my body, of
my essence, and it will also mark her as mine.*

Satisfied by this knowledge, Jacob released her, his
tongue sweeping the wound he'd made before continuing up the line of her throat with voracious hunger
for the taste of her skin and the scent of her body.
Every so often his tongue would leave the path and his
teeth would scrape her sensitive neck. Every time that
happened, her small body clenched and expectant
gooseflesh bubbled up all over her skin.

Then his hands were raising her up to his hungry
mouth as he found the hollow of her throat, her collarbone, and the track of her breastbone. He broke away
to chase a bead of perspiration that slipped down the
valley between her breasts, catching it with the tip of
his tongue. He dragged that velvet tool across her skin
until he was drawing a thrusting nipple into his mouth.

Isabella was already half mindless with arousal as
Jacob shifted his hold and footing. Still locked around
his waist, she felt him press her back against an uneven
surface. She realized they were leaning against the
spines of rows of books stacked tightly onto the shelf
that was behind her. Then his hands were at the snap
of her jeans, and all of her attention shifted in shock.

Instinctively, her hands flew to cover his, but his
mouth was devouring hers in that very second, making
her go weak from head to toe, kissing her relentlessly
until her hands dropped away nervelessly. All she
could do was fumble for a hold on his shoulders, mindlessly responding to the passion that made her burn to
kiss him with every ounce of her will and strength.

She felt his hand slide down over her bottom again,
but this time he was even closer to her skin, having
slipped his fingers past the loosened denim of her pants.

The material slid lower, lower still. The fabric set her sensitive skin to screaming as it slid down her thighs. Her legs went lax as he supported all of her weight in a single hand, pushing the jeans from her body effortlessly and then urging her legs back to their embrace around his waist, not realizing in his haste and passion that his nails scored her in bright, feral red lines along her upper thigh. All the while, his mouth never separated from hers, and she was engaged beyond caring.

Jacob was suddenly free to touch her anywhere he wanted to, the lace of her panties the only barrier remaining between him and his ability to experience her skin. He splayed his fingers over the shuddering muscles of her belly.

"You are so soft," he groaned, breaking from her mouth and burying his face into the side of her neck again. "Your scent, Bella. It intoxicates me."

His voice was coarse even to his own ears. He opened his mouth on the side of her neck, sliding his hot tongue up its delicate length, dipping it into the hollow below her earlobe. His breath blew hot into her hair, over her skin, the speed chilling the sensitive back of her neck in spite of its heated temperature.

Jacob's hand slid down her belly, and Isabella was inundated with sensation coming from so many different places all at once. She had never known her senses could be so aroused, so tormented. Then his fingertips slid past the border of her panties, sliding silkily into the collection of curls hidden beneath the lace.

Her reaction was like tinder suddenly catching a flame. She made a wild, mewling sound, her hands flying out to her sides to suddenly grip whatever she could get hold of. Her fingers curled tightly around spines and tightly packed pages. Her whole body clenched violently, her hands jerking the books clean off the shelves. They slammed to the floor, dual bangs that marked the slip of first one finger, and then another, into wet, silky flesh.

Isabella was filled with an unexpected, wild terror. No one had ever touched her in this manner. In fact, no one had ever done half of the things to her that Jacob had been doing. As she gasped hysterically for breath and looked down at her body in his embrace, she realized that her wanton reactions would have never given that particular fact away.

"Jacob!" she cried, her hands scraping frantically at his shoulders as her fear mounted, choking off her ability to breathe.

"Shh, little flower, I will not hurt you." The soothing tone of his voice washed over her, dulling every sharp edge of fear just slightly. "Just feel, Bella. Feel what my touch can create in you."

His voice was hypnotic and seductive, as if he had Legna's power to affect the will of others with it. She knew without a doubt that he spoke the truth. If she just relaxed, he would show her everything—every last thing she had dreamed of, and even things she could never have imagined. As she hesitated, as she was lured by that temptation, Jacob slid a long, seeking finger into the sheath of her body.

Bella gasped, the stuttering intake of sound reverberating loudly in the enormous library. Jacob exhaled a heated curse in his own language, the word clearly meant as an intense, expressive compliment. She laughed at him breathlessly, without knowing why. Probably because of the rise in sensation and frustration the intimate touch created.

Jacob felt her shudder, marveled at how tight she felt

around his finger, how her very insides quivered with delicious, eager little spasms. He could pleasure her, just like this, make her completely mad with sensation and passion until she had no choice but to explode with it. *Sweet Destiny, who would have thought she could be so responsive?* Never had a woman fired so hotly under his touch. Never had a woman set him to burn as his little Bella was so easily able to do. She had her legs wrapped around both the man and the no-longer-hidden beast that were his make-up, and no one could ever have touched him that profoundly before. He pressed his thumb against the swell of feminine flesh that he knew would fill her with sensation, rubbing in minute, slow circles, moving his touch with deft, compelling skill in a stroking mock of what he would soon be doing to her body for real. She moaned, writhing against him, her reactions making him burn hotter and harder for her until he thought he might explode under the erotic duress. He wanted to rip free of the confines of his clothing, slide the throbbing and painful hardness of his aching sex against her . . . toying at that tight entrance for a moment before plunging himself deep into that taut, honeyed prison he was positive was meant to capture him and hold him forever. He pushed his insistent finger a little deeper into her body, just a moment longer, wanting to be fully assured that she was ready for him . . .

Resistance.

Jacob went very, very still. Something extremely important was swimming on the outside of his awareness, but he was deeply consumed with his need for her, instincts created at the birth of the Earth chaining him to his course. He broke out in a terrible sweat as she wriggled mindlessly against his frustratingly, abruptly still touch. So wet, and hot . . . and so tight.

Unused.

The realization hit Jacob like ice water.

Suddenly, reality came washing back in on him. Everything. All of it. He closed his eyes, groaning with agony as his body rebelled against his impulses to follow his sense of moral right. The beast in him argued that he had already gone too far, that he had broken all threads with honor the moment he had plotted to come to her without monitoring. What was more, Isabella was protesting against his cruel touch that made contact but did not fulfill the promise of pleasures he now realized she didn't realistically comprehend. How had he missed this important truth all this time he had traveled as a shadow in her mind?

Jacob realized he had not missed it. He had simply chosen to ignore the clues on a subconscious level because it would have interfered, as it was now doing, with his selfish desires. So now, he found himself in a position that tore him in two conflicting directions. If he did not leave her immediately, he would damage her badly, perhaps beyond all repair, as the risk of his darker nature taking over plagued him. But on the other hand, leaving her would be damaging in another sense. It screamed at everything Jacob was to not leave her so tormented, so close to pleasure, but left with the pain of being unfulfilled.

Jacob made a choice, slipping his touch out of her body, cringing at the agony of her confused protest. *Better this than the alternative*. They had come far too close as it was.

Isabella felt tears springing into her eyes, her face turning away from him as he slid her gently down onto her feet. His gentility only served to make her want to shatter even more. Her hands opened and closed on his shirtfront as she swallowed the rushing urge to sob out loud.

"Why?" she choked out instead. "Why?"

The plaintive question sent a sensation of betrayal slicing through Jacob's midsection. He had come here, knowing he should not. He had been unable to resist the lure, had lied to them both when he'd said he was fully in control, and had almost robbed her of everything precious and innocent she possessed. But her state of naïveté wasn't even the issue. He had once again fallen prey to her unintentional lure, disregarded the laws that he, above all others, was sworn to uphold.

"Bella," he croaked, the damp of wild frustration wetting his dark eyes. Rage swirled through him. It was all he could do to speak. "Forgive me. I beg you. Forgive me."

Then he was launching away from her, hurtling into the air, disintegrating into a dust devil that escaped the room as rapidly as she blinked her eyes. The room shook with his departure, the floor shuddering and the shelves rocking slightly as a rumble roared through. The gaslights hanging from the ceiling swayed.

Isabella dropped to her knees, suddenly too weak to stand, too stunned to cry. With numb fingers, she redressed herself. She was half blind with anguish by the time the room settled. Fully clothed once more, she tried to pretend that every nerve of her body wasn't wishing it, too, could leap up into the night sky in order to chase after the Demon who had left her so bereft.

She had no recourse for her feelings. She felt a horrific sense of deprivation and loss, an emotion she could only describe as grief. She didn't understand, and she had no one she could speak with to help her figure things out. Logically, she knew why he had shut down, why he left without explanation. It was self-explanatory.

She was human. She was too weak to make love with him. She was considered a lesser being, like a clever pet, and a taboo resource for passion.

She reached up to rub the deeply sore mark he had branded her shoulder with. This mark had not been thoughtless. He had made it with purpose. She had felt every ounce of the intention that had gone into it. Jacob didn't think her below him. She wore the proof embedded in her skin. However primitive an act it had been, it had been a symbol of commitment from him, and it had meant as much to her.

She reached up and angrily fisted tears from her cheeks, sniffling as she turned to look around. It was these laws and words surrounding her that had dictated he leave. This was the history of a race of elitists. Snobs, part of her thought meanly. Their traditions were steeped in implacable beliefs, and the one she was facing, she believed, was a prejudice. Demons had a thing about purity. It wasn't just humans who earned titles below their almighty culture. She had read the law herself, the one that had given birth to Jacob's duties so long ago:

> . . . *it is therefore forbidden for any of Demonkind to mate with creatures who are not of their nature, not of their strength or power. Those lesser creatures are ours to protect from ourselves, not to be violated in impure sexual abomination. This is the law. The dog does not lie with the cat; the cat does not lie with the mouse. Whosoever breaks this sacred trust must suffer under the hand of the law . . .*

She wanted to believe there was logic to this. She was a logical person. But there was never logic in encompassing statements, especially those written thousands of years ago, which, as she understood it, this one had been.

She had seen Saul. He was proof of the danger within every Demon, and she could accept that they were a volatile species in spite of their many efforts to be otherwise. Nevertheless, if she were cat to Jacob's dog, then why did they feel this way? Why would two incompatible species find themselves so . . . so well made for each other's needs?

Noah believed her to be unique, that she had a purpose in the future of Demon society. At first, Isabella had gone along with the idea just so she could stay and find out everything she could about this world of beings living parallel to her own. She would have been content to die a pale old lady in this library. There was more than enough knowledge within it to keep her sated for an entire lifetime.

But now . . .

Now she was beginning to believe she truly did have a purpose for being there. Maybe she was meant to find a way to kick the supreme starch out of their shorts. Yes. Something in this library could perhaps explain why every time Jacob barked, she purred.

She laughed at herself weakly. She looked around herself and saw the books she had accidentally pulled down lying on the floor. She scooted over to them to gather them up. She handled them gingerly, apologetically, sorry she had so mistreated them for so unrealized a moment. She dusted the front cover of one of them, reading the title.

Destruction.

She shuddered, not liking the ominous title in the least. Once again she was given proof of the extremism of the Demon race. She stood to replace the book, but suddenly she stopped. She blinked slowly, and clearing her mind of the last of her disturbed feelings, she looked at the title again.

Destruction.

Unexpectedly, she felt faint, the world spinning around her as the book dropped from her nerveless fingers.

She had just read the title of a book that was written in a language she had not been able to read only twenty minutes earlier.

Noah's cat-green eyes followed Jacob's pacing across his receiving-room floor, a frown etched into his mouth as his Enforcer's disturbance rubbed his senses raw.

It was clear Jacob was not going to share his thoughts willingly, and Noah was left to speculate. Jacob was as honest, dutiful, and loyal a soul as he had ever encountered. He was, in fact, more devotedly Demon than many of the Elder Demons were. His belief in their ways, laws, and code of honor was so pure that Noah could not help but respect him for it. This was why it troubled Noah to see Jacob so embroiled in what was clearly a turmoil of conscience. He did not broach the Enforcer, though, no matter how powerful the urge to do so. Instead, he sat quietly as the other Demon wore a path in his floor.

Then, simultaneously, the males were jolted out of their ruminations and their heads swung toward the doorway leading into the Great Hall. Three heartbeats later, the doors burst open, allowing a flock of Demons and a dismayed servant entrance.

"Forgive me, Sire, but they would not let me

announce them. They just pushed past!" the servant panted, his consternation flushing his normally tanned face.

"That is alright, Ezekiel," Noah said, making a gentle sign of dismissal that absolved the other male of responsibility. Noah narrowed his attention on the nine Demons walking toward him, recognizing the remaining Elders of the Great Council, save the Warrior Captain, Elijah.

"Welcome to my home, Councillors." He nodded to them and then focused on their apparently self-declared leader. "Ruth, would you care to explain what it is that brings you in such an impromptu throng?"

"Noah, it has come to our attention that you are aware of some happenings that you have not shared with the Council," Ruth announced, her tone cool and bordering on reproachful. "Would you care to share them with us now?"

"If I did, I would have called you myself," Noah countered, unapologetic and reminding them all of their failure in protocol with the easy observation. "However, since you have gone to such trouble to gather and approach me, I will discuss recent developments with you."

Noah rose from his seat and moved from the Hall to the Great Council chamber, aware of Jacob falling into line at his back, all his personal disturbances put aside under the press of this potentially combustible development. Noah took his seat at the point of a large triangular table, Jacob at the second and all the others filling up the three sides in their usual places. Only the third point—other than Elijah's chair—remained conspicuously empty, as it had for eight years now.

"Very well, Ruth, what is it you wish to know that you

do not already?" Noah encouraged, his mildly patronizing tone making the female Demon bristle defensively.

"Is it true that one of us has been Summoned and destroyed?" Ruth had never been one to mince words, for all her persistently troublesome nature.

"Yes. It is. Saul is lost to us."

A murmur of breath and distress slid down the sides of the table. Noah flicked his eyes to Jacob, finding the Enforcer's brown-black gaze cold and unreadable.

"Enforcer," Ruth said, as always refusing to use his common name, "I take it you have hunted and destroyed the creature responsible for this?"

"The necromancer does not exactly wear a bell around his neck, Councillor Ruth. But yes, I hunt him."

"Hunt." She spat the present tense at him like a derisive curse. "Which means we are still vulnerable."

"That would be the logical conclusion," Jacob returned coolly. "Also, I might remind you that the carriage of justice to other supernatural beings falls within the warriors' realm. According to our laws and distinctions, the hunt for the necromancer falls under Elijah's jurisdiction. However, I am in close contact with Elijah on this matter, as I have been the only one to get close to this magic-user. I will continue to assist the Warrior Captain in the hunt for him."

Jacob's calm made Ruth realize how badly she was coming off, and her face flushed with her discomfort. She didn't apologize for herself, however. Jacob knew she never would.

"What are we to do in the meantime, Noah? Sit and wait for the next of us to be snatched from our lives?"

"We have little choice at the moment. As you all know, there is no known protection against Summoning spells. However, you can be assured that Elijah, Jacob, and I are working on the problem."

"And yet the Enforcer still has time for his other duties," spoke up Councillor Simon, his thin lips pressed into a deep frown. He was referring to the fact that, the night before, Jacob had been forced to track Simon's son down and snap him back into line.

"I have time for everything," Jacob agreed, a feral smile sliding over his lips.

"Noah! Jacob!"

The entire Council jerked in surprise as the chamber door burst open and gave entry to Isabella, her arms loaded with scrolls, her eyes bright lavender points of information that was bursting to be freed. She stopped short when she realized she had intruded on a meeting, and swept her eyes uneasily around the room as a dozen Demon eyes focused solely on her.

"A human!" Simon whispered.

"She has sacred scrolls!" cried another, lurching to his feet.

"Noah, what is the meaning of this?" Ruth exploded, forgetting exactly whom she was addressing. Or perhaps not. Ruth was always in search of a way to jockey with Noah for the authority of a moment.

"Uh-oh . . ." Isabella muttered under her breath.

"I did not even sense her presence," someone whispered.

"Neither did I."

Jacob rose to his feet, the sound of his chair scraping back slowly over the marble floor piercing through the room and drawing everyone's attention. All eyes were on him as he came around the table and reached to take the human woman's shoulder under his hand. He pulled her into the protective circle of his arm and then guided her to his chair and sat her down. Putting Isabella in what was recognized as one of the three most powerful positions of the Council table brought about a collective gasp.

"You *dare*, Enforcer?" Ruth hissed, moving to stand as if she would go around the table and yank the human female from the chair herself.

But the force of Jacob's cold stare made her still midaction.

"Our most sacred law is to harm no human who does not harm us, Councillor Ruth. Would you transgress right before the eyes of the Demon who would punish you?" he asked, the calm of his voice speaking deep levels of threat. In contrast to this steely warning, Jacob's hand slipped beneath Isabella's heavy hair and circled her neck protectively. Noah did not think the Enforcer was even aware he had made the possessive gesture.

"She has no right here," Ruth argued, the force of the statement well diminished by her shock as she watched the most ruthless man of their kind take the human female under his tender auspices.

"She has information vital to the very questions you have been asking," Jacob countered smoothly, having touched on this knowledge briefly in her mind.

"Jacob, I don't think this is a good time," Bella whispered.

"Nonsense, human. Speak, if you have knowledge," Simon demanded.

Isabella's eyes narrowed on the Councillor.

"My name is Isabella," she snapped.

Simon blinked, clearly not comprehending for a very long minute that a human had just slapped him down. When it came to him, color rushed up his neck.

Noah's chair being pushed back caught everyone's attention.

"You will all leave. I will hear Isabella out in private and we will reconvene tomorrow night."

Isabella instinctively reached up and pressed her fingers to the back of the hand circling her neck. She saw the roomful of Demons stirring in discontent, casting Jacob distrusting looks. She didn't like the way it felt. Even as they all rose to obey their monarch, Isabella could feel their displeasure.

That was when the first push slammed into her brain.

It began like cold, invading fingers crawling along the back of her scalp. Shards of ice pierced her skull, embedding themselves into her mind like dozens of needles, each strategically placed in her long- and short-term memory in order to suck the knowledge from the synapses that held it.

Isabella jerked in shock, alerting Jacob to the fact that she was in some kind of distress. As the Demons continued to rise, a second push slapped her back in her chair, causing her work to fall helter-skelter to the floor as she threw her hands up to her head. When this invasion failed, there was immediately a third. Bella became aware of the source in a frightening instant. They were trying to force from her the information that Noah would not share. It was causing her head to blossom in pain, and she keened softly in agony. Her thoughts became Jacob's, and he knew the moment she did what was causing her distress.

"You will stop!" he roared, his voice ricocheting off every surface in the chamber, forcing everyone to fall very still under his outraged threat. "You will obey Noah and wait for your information. You will cease trying to scan Isabella this instant or you will answer to me!"

There were three Mind Demons in the Elder Council, including Ruth, who could be responsible for the attack. All three of them looked utterly shocked, along with the rest of the Elders in the room. Jacob couldn't tell if it was from his awareness of their actions or merely the threats themselves. He was Enforcer, and there was nothing more frightening in their world than his sense of injustice. His threat was not an idle one, and everyone knew it. Feared it. Even the intractable Ruth. Isabella visibly relaxed as her pain receded and the Demons exited soundlessly.

Noah closed the door after them and instantly moved to Isabella's side, kneeling beside her chair and taking her chin in his hand so he could turn her head and meet her eyes. It was only then that she realized how angry the silent King had become for her sake. Though there was no outward facial sign, she could see it in the stormy clouds of gray concealing the green of his eyes.

"Bella, are you well?" he asked gently.

Isabella appreciated his concern, especially after facing so much hostility from the strangers who had just left, but there was something disturbing her brain again. This was not painful, but it was familiar. Her violet gaze shifted away from Noah's, turning to focus on the male standing on the other side of her chair just as his long fingers began to curl into a fist. Her heart began to pound in double-time as she watched Jacob close his eyes, his jaw clenching so tightly she could hear the creak of his teeth. She understood he was trying to force himself to behave with rational care, to not take such violent offense to Noah's hands being on her, to the King's zealous concern for her.

"I am fine," she said softly, forcing as amiable a smile as she could manage over her lips. In truth, she was confused and exhausted. Jacob's behaviors seemed to vacillate so strongly, so intensely in one direction and then another. She decided to simply focus on his needs of the moment.

Isabella gently extracted her chin from Noah's grasp under the guise of gathering her discarded work from the floor. The King reached to help her, taking on some of her burden before rising to his feet. He was a good man, Isabella thought, kind and intelligent, thinking of others before himself. Marks of a man meant to be a leader. When Noah was not crossing Bella's personal space, she could feel how very much Jacob respected him, how devoted he would always be to Noah's every cause. All he need do was ask, and Jacob would serve him without question and without regard for his own life or safety.

It upset her greatly that she had become a point of discord within that melodic relationship. She thought of the revelations she held cradled against her chest, of how they could potentially serve up more discord, more upset and controversy. Would she be doing this society any good by revealing her new knowledge?

"I . . ." She swallowed hard. "I'm sorry. I didn't mean to disturb you. Really, it's nothing that can't wait. Actually"—she stood up and extracted the scrolls from Noah's hold—"all I wanted was, uh . . . help with some interpretation. But you are busy . . ." She rounded the peculiar triangular table as casually as she could while she spoke, even turning to back out of the room while giving them a bright smile that she hoped did not look as fake as it felt. "You know, there are lots of books down there, and I bet there's a translation." She reached up to smack her palm into her forehead, chiding herself for not thinking properly.

Isabella reached for the door and closed it even faster than she had originally opened it.

Noah looked over at Jacob, one dark brow lifting toward his thick hairline.

"Does . . . ?" He raised a hand to point to the door, looking utterly perplexed. "Does she have *any* idea what a lousy liar she is?"

"Apparently not," Jacob said with a long, low sigh. "I think that was my fault," he speculated wryly.

"Your fault?"

"Yeah . . . it is . . . a long story. We better get her."

"Relax," Noah chuckled. "She's leaning against the other side of the door, trying to catch her breath."

"I know. I just thought it would be funny if we opened it behind her."

"I never knew you actually enjoyed being cruel," the King remarked, humor sparkling in his eyes as they both stepped up to the exit.

Noah opened the door, and Jacob reached out to catch her, scrolls and all.

CHAPTER FIVE

It was her first trip—that she actually remembered—traveling the way Demons did. It had begun with Jacob turning her into dust and guiding her through that little window. Once they were truly airborne, Jacob altered them both back into their normal forms, only he was holding her cradled to his chest protectively.

"It is not far. Let me know if you become too cold."

Cold? She was trying to find the courage to unbury her face from the concealing column of his neck; she did not have the presence of mind it would take to feel cold. She was also clutching him so tightly that she was sure she was tearing the expensive silk of his shirt. After a while, though, the steady feel of his firm shoulders beneath her fingertips allowed for her heartbeat to slow enough to stop choking her, and the indomitable strength of his arms holding her began to make her understand that she was safe with him.

This did not give her the courage to look around herself, but she did lift her head and focus with all of her concentration on his face. His dark brown and black eyes shifted to hers when he felt her looking at him.

"How are you doing?" he asked.

"I'll be fine," she assured him shakily. *Right up until I hit the ground.*

Jacob pulled her head back down to the security of his shoulder, burying his grin in her thick hair when her humorous sarcasm flitted through his mind. She tended to forget that he could read her mind, just as she forgot she could just as easily read his if she tried more often. But she had that quirky human penchant called privacy, a custom that was not all that prevalent in the Demon culture.

"Tell me where we're going," she murmured next to his ear.

Her soft lips moved against his neck with her speech, her breath hot against his skin, bathing him in sensitivity. Awareness instantly shuddered through him, his body clenching with instant need. He had already realized that his good intentions wouldn't matter before long. If he stayed near her, he would tear her apart with his harsh desire for her. It was this knowledge that had forced him to pace before Noah endlessly until the Council interrupted his self-obsessions.

The Enforcer knew, though, that he could not maintain his close connection to Noah's home so long as Isabella was residing there. She tempted him far too deeply. So, he had paced before Noah's desk, trying to find a way to tell the Demon King that he had to drag himself as far away from the center of Demon culture as he could. He also needed to do this without blaming it on this innocent woman. The problem was not hers. He was the one lacking in control. It had brought him very low, doing the very thing he had lectured Kane on. It had brought Jacob to the other side of the sidewalk. He now knew what it felt like to be driven to those depths of immoral action even though principles cried out to do the right thing.

"Jacob?"

His name on her lips made him realize he had not answered her question.

"To my home," he told her, using the response as a reason to lean his face closer to her, to bury himself in her hair. She was, he realized, taking on more of his scent every day. Though she had showered and gotten herself dusty all over again since their last clash of passion, she still oozed his essence from her skin and hair. He had known she was a mimic when it came to scents, but he had never encountered a chameleon that could keep a scent that had already been washed away. It filled him with a rush of possessive joy. It reminded him that, right beneath his chin, under the soft fabric of her shirt, lay the mark he had left upon her shoulder.

They came to rest on a wide cliff, and when Isabella lifted her head at Jacob's encouragement, the vista took her breath away. They were on the very rim of what looked to be the English coastline. The house he had taken her to originally was settled behind them grandly, with the exception of the boarded-up wall that was in need of repair. As Noah coalesced into his usual form beside them, they walked toward the house. They entered through a conventional door.

"One would think that with all you can do, you could snap your fingers and fix that wall," she said breathlessly.

"If it were that easy to do everything, we would be able to protect ourselves from those who insist on dabbling in dark arts," Jacob pointed out gently.

"Well, not that it is any excuse, but humans don't realize that your kind are an actual race of people with intelligence, families, customs, and culture." She frowned and sighed, realizing exactly how poor an excuse that was. "But that's been our excuse over history far too many times. I'm sorry."

Jacob reached to rest her chin on the tip of his fingers, her sweet compassion for his people, especially after the way the so-called best of them had just treated her, touching him deeply. Noah's presence in the room completely faded from his awareness and he reached to kiss her supple lips with aching tenderness, ignoring any pain it caused him to do so.

"I am sorry, little flower. The Elders should never have treated you so poorly when you have been laboring so hard to help us."

"They didn't know," she whispered forgivingly, causing his heart to tighten at her benevolence. "They are afraid, and rightly so." She reached up and slid a strand of his hair between two of her fingers, caringly tucking it behind his ear in a slow, silky movement. "Fear makes the best of us behave terribly."

Noah cleared his throat, an effort to remind the couple that he was in the room. They jumped apart, and he watched in amazement as the electricity only he could see sparking between them crackled in petulant blue arcs before thinning out and breaking the connection. Noah had never seen such a thing between a Demon and a human before, and rarely between Demons. It fascinated while it disturbed him. The lightning was the fire of complementary souls joining. A female Fire Demon like his sister Hannah would know more about this aspect of such elemental connection, for she understood the fire between two beings and saw it far more clearly than he could. But he knew enough to know it was significant, and exceedingly unusual.

"Isabella, you have something to tell us?" he reminded everyone.

"Yes."

Noah once again took note of her hesitation, her struggle so very clear in her tattletale face. It was refreshing to the King to see that such guilelessness could still exist in the world.

She grabbed Jacob's hand and hustled him over to the nearest table, dropping her bagful of scrolls onto it. Noah followed, watching closely as she slid the first out of its protective container and unwound it, using objects from the table to hold it open. She treated the scroll gingerly, with great care and respect, and Noah was once more impressed. This woman was a true scholar, perhaps more so than he would ever be.

Both men realized after a moment that the text she was displaying was in *their* ancient language. They exchanged perplexed looks over her dark head as she bent to her task of situating the scroll. This was the very type of writing Noah had been having difficulty translating on the night Jacob had first encountered Isabella.

"Okay, look here," she said, warming to her impending lecture as she indicated the middle body of writing. "This is the original *Scroll of Destruction*. Great name, by the way. Anyway, it was written centuries before the book I found with the same name. That book was a translation of this scroll. Look, see, 'Whosoever wishes to know the fate of Demonkind must consult these prophecies . . .' Yadda, yadda, yadda, right? It's kind of like your version of Revelation. Correct?"

Noah nodded slowly. It was one of their most sacred documents. It was the list of Special Destinies and the Original Laws. He watched as she gently peeled back the first pages of the scroll.

"You are familiar with these passages, no doubt. The ones that refer to the way the birth of Christianity among humans would affect the destiny of Demons for all time. See? This tells how Christianity will become a majority religion amongst humans, how magic will be shunned as a result, lessening the threat of the 'evil intenders,' which I assume means necromancers. It isn't all that specific, so I took an educated guess."

"Good guess, little flower," Jacob praised. "You are exactly right."

She seemed to accept this with a nod as she reached to peel back more pages. "Well, then follows pages of various prophecies. Now, in the modern book version of this scroll, the translation is only slightly flawed up to this point. But then you come to here . . ." She indicated a passage far into the scroll. "Here is where it goes completely haywire. Now, at first I couldn't understand why the translation would be so in error. I thought perhaps a change in translators. But then I remembered that with many great religious doctrines, the influences of those who ordered translations often dictated what was considered acceptable and uniform to general belief. Significant works, to this day, are not accepted in their true translated states because it would make too many waves in the foundations of those belief systems. When this is translated properly, I can see why they were reluctant to remain true to the form of the scroll. Here, I will read the passage:

'And so it will come to pass that in this great age things will return to the focus of purity that Demonkind must always strive for. Here will come the meaning and purpose of our strictest laws, that no uncorrupted

human shall be harmed, that peaceful coexistence between races shall become paramount . . .'"

"There is nothing different about that than what is commonly known," Noah remarked, struggling to follow her swift translation.

"Wait, I am getting to that." She turned the page. "Listen:

'We must enforce ourselves more strictly as the time approaches. In the age of the rebellion of the Earth and Sky, when Fire and Water break like havoc upon all the lands, the Eldest of the old will return, will take his mate, and the first child of the element of Space will be born, playmate to the first child of Time, born to the Enforcers. The Demon. The Druid. And all will be returned to the state in which it all began. Purity restored.'

"Now," Isabella went on, unaware of the men who were so still beside her, "I couldn't figure out why this would be left out. It seems pretty simple a prophecy. Why would it be so frightening? That was when I read through all of your laws and realized—"

"All of them?" Noah spoke up suddenly, his astonishment ringing clear. "You were only down there a few days."

"I read fast," she shrugged.

Noah gripped the back of a chair until his knuckles turned white, seeking solace in the Enforcer's dark eyes, only to find them equally troubled. He had no choice but to watch as the little woman plowed through her information like a freight train.

"Anyway," she continued, "this is where your laws of crossbreeding come into play. Now, all along I thought

maybe it was chemical incompatibility or because of
your more animalistic natures that you would cause
harm to a partner not of your race. You even have
books supporting those theories. *Purity*. That word is
key. It's used very often in this scroll and I can't tell you
how many laws. Okay, listen, further in the *Scroll of Destruction*. It says right here:

> *'An Enforcer will be born and reach maturity as
> magic once more threatens the time, as the peace of the
> Demon yaws toward insanity. The Enforcer will be born
> to hunt the Transformed, will have the power to destroy,
> to walk unscented, to track, to see the unseen, to fight
> with courage and instinct the most powerful and most
> corrupted. This Enforcer's thoughts will be sealed except
> to Kin and Mate, will walk the Demon path in body
> and soul, though never born to it.'*

"So there, you see? How can there be so-called
'purity' if an Enforcer will be appointed who is not a
Demon? Hmm? But that isn't all." She went on eagerly,
whipping a second scroll from its casing, "This scroll,
and my calculations make it to be even older than the
other, is going to blow your mind. Check this out. It
says here that:

> *'Demon and Druid walk as one, mated, fused, com-
> pleted souls. One without the other lost and bereft, one
> race without the other doomed to madness and despon-
> dency, impurity and destruction.'*

"Do you know what that means? Your so-called pure-
blooded race used to be only half of another race, the
combined race that was once Druids *and* Demons! If

that's true, then all this nonsense about racial purity is something some fanatic made up a zillion years ago. It's *propaganda*, gentlemen! With your historically fanatical views toward purity of race, the very idea of outsiders as saviors must have been appalling to the translators. Therefore, they omitted this from the newer translations. This means you *need* outsiders in order to survive. You were looking for your cure? Well, here it is! Written in black and white in your very own vaults! Druids are the cure for Hallowed madness!"

"Then our race is doomed," Noah said softly.

Isabella raised startled eyes to the King. Her heart jumped when she saw his drawn, whitened features and his eerie stillness.

"Why do you say that?" she protested. "I mean, you just have to find . . . but you said there were other Night-walker species in the world. I have read about so many of them in your archives. I admit I only started to find out about Druids when I went into the east vault . . ."

"Because the east vault is the Druid archive, Bella," Jacob said roughly.

Isabella blinked in confusion, turning to look over her shoulder at Jacob.

"I don't understand."

"Isabella, almost a millennium ago, the ruler of the Druid race went mad and murdered the ruler of the Demon race," Noah explained grimly. "We went to war. There aren't any more Druids, Bella. The Demons destroyed them all. All that is left of them is in that vault. We destroyed an entire culture, murdered every last breath that could ever speak on Druidic behalf, save those ancient recorded scraps."

"If what you say is true, then we destroyed ourselves in the process." Jacob ran a weary hand over his face and

through his hair, meeting Noah's eyes. "All these centuries, we have been told only that the Druids were our
enemies once upon a time because of the deed of their
King. We were never told that we once walked together,
lived together . . . made a common history together."

"Revisionist history," Noah interjected. "A history that
the leaders of the time obviously rewrote for their own
ends during and after the war. How arrogant I was to
think our dedicated historians were above such things."

"No . . . no, I think you're wrong," Bella burst out,
fear filling her voice as she struggled with the implications her innocent findings could mean for their kind.
"What about the prophecy? How can a doomed race
suddenly give birth to new elements? Children with
power over Space and Time will change the world forever! Surely when you see this happening right under
your nose you won't be able to deny that!"

"You assume that the time prophesied is now," Noah
remarked.

"Well, of course it is. I mean, look at what is happening all around you! *'The age of the rebellion of the Earth
and Sky, when Fire and Water break like havoc upon all the
lands.'* Your people are the elements, you said so yourself. Fire, Earth and the rest. *'Rebellion . . . breaking like
havoc on all the lands.'* You see, in many historical texts,
'lands' does not mean 'land' as continents. It means
cultures. This is saying that Demons will cause havoc in
other cultures. The Enforcer mentioned above is to
exist as *'peace yaws toward insanity.'* It's a marker linking
the two prophesies to the same time. You told me yourselves that every year the madness becomes worse for
your people. And with the necromancer's sudden appearance, wouldn't you say magic has returned?

"That's it!" she exclaimed suddenly. "You didn't kill all

the Druids! Just, maybe, forced them into dormancy. Maybe some escaped. Maybe, over time, under the sweep of science and civilization, their heritage and knowledge was lost to their descendents just as some of yours was lost to you. And maybe, sometime in the future, when you start to accept other races into the circle of your culture, it will allow for the arrival of a Druid that, in the near future . . . when Jacob is succeeded . . ." She paused, thinking as quickly as she could while twisting her hands together in her abrupt despair.

Noah understood. If she was right, and the time prophesied was near, it would mean Jacob's death and replacement was an imminent event. She had to explain away her own logic now in order to prevent that inevitability from happening too soon for her to bear. "Those are very extreme maybes," Noah consoled.

"Sweet, merciful Destiny."

Isabella and Noah both snapped their attention to Jacob, who wore an expression of total shock.

"What? What is it?" Noah asked.

"She said it, and I almost missed it. Noah, in the prophecy, just after the lead-in, she said: ' . . . *the first child of the element of Space will be born, playmate to the first child of Time, born to the Enforcers.*'"

"So?" Bella asked.

"Are you sure it said Enforcers? Are you certain it is plural?" he demanded.

"Of course I am sure. See, right there." She pointed to the passage.

"Bella, there has never been two Enforcers at once. There has only been one. Never two. It is not me this is talking about, nor some unknown Druid of the distant future, it is . . ." He blinked, shock washing over him. "It is *you*. Noah, it is her!"

"Can it be?" Noah whispered, looking over the tiny human woman with awe, following Jacob's thinking rapidly. "A human Enforcer?"

"Whoa! Hang on there, guys. Let's not go off the deep end," Isabella cried hastily, raising her hands defensively and backing up several steps out of their reach as if they were trying to attack her. Not that she would ever beat them in a foot race, but it gave her a minor comfort just the same. "I am not an Enforcer. I'm too tiny, too . . . I'm a bookworm! I'm weak! I'm *human*. Stop looking at me like that! You're out of your freaking skulls!"

"'*The Enforcer will be born to hunt the Transformed, will have the power to destroy.*' Saul, little flower. Remember? '. . . *to track, to see the unseen, to fight with courage and instinct the most powerful and most corrupted.*' You killed him."

"That was an accident!"

"'. . . *to walk unscented . . .*' The Elders did not even know she was in my home," Noah added, clearly astonished. "They could not smell her, could not sense her. '*This Enforcer's thoughts will be sealed except to Kin . . .*'"

"That's ridiculous! Jacob is constantly nosing around inside my head, and I assure you I am in no way related to him!"

"'. . . *and Mate . . .*'"

Isabella heard the fateful words fall from Jacob's lips as if they echoed.

She had known, on some level, that this connection to Jacob was beyond something so simple as a passing crush. Jacob had known it. He had taken her into his arms in spite of everything he stood for, because on some level he had known this was no mere Hallowed madness.

Only a few days ago she would never have been

capable of imagining any of this, no matter how creative she might have tried to be. Facts and fantasies blurred in her mind, hazing her vision over like a suffocating fog. All the blood rushed away from the top of her body, racing to fulfill the sudden demands of her organs as she ran both hot and cold with chills, dread, and, most of all, excitement at all of the dangerous possibilities.

She dropped to the floor like a stone.

"Do you have any idea how this is going to affect everyone?"

Jacob looked up from his seat beside Isabella, his hand stilling midstroke through her hair, the pads of his fingertips nestled in the softer-than-silk strands that so attracted him. He had not moved fast enough, and she had fallen hard. His opposite hand was pressing a cloth to a cut on her forehead, trying to stem the blood that continued to seep from it.

"I know how it is going to affect you," Noah responded from his position by the window, his gaze trained on the landscape of the ocean just outside. "I know it explains why you haven't been able to resist her."

"We could be wrong." Jacob picked up a thick strand of the sleek sable hair, rubbing it between his fingers. "She is so small and so young. How can she possibly be meant to do what I do?"

"She is not even trained, and yet she tracked Saul. Killed him," the monarch pointed out.

"More accident than anything," Jacob retorted.

"Then explain what happened with Elijah."

Jacob couldn't, and Noah knew it. Elijah was a centuries-old, seasoned warrior, leader of an army of

Demons who dedicated their lives to the art of war and defense. He was powerful, just as prevailing in his elected duties as Jacob was in his. And yet . . .

"I cannot explain it," he admitted reluctantly.

"She was protecting you," Noah pointed out with infuriatingly quiet wisdom and matter-of-fact calm. "Out of instinct. Just like a she-wolf will protect her mate."

"Noah, she is a *human being*! Everything I have been raised to believe for hundreds of years tells me that I cannot be her mate, and she cannot be mine! I will hurt her! Hell, I already have!" Jacob curled his long fingers into her velvety hair, clenching thick strands between his knuckles in anger. Speaking the understanding aloud shredded at his conscience and heart like hundreds of superfine blades.

"Have you . . . ?"

"No! Of course not! I already told you, I am terrified I will hurt her. Besides, if things had gone that far, don't you think Elijah, Legna, or you would have come crashing down on me?"

"No one interrupted your interlude in the vaults yesterday," Noah pointed out.

Jacob narrowed dangerous eyes on the Demon King. "You knew."

It was a statement, not a question. The question was unspoken, and they both knew what it was. "After the fact," he assured him. "I trust you did the right thing, Jacob. You are Enforcer, after all."

"I *barely* did the right thing, Noah." Jacob's voice was low and his eyes shot daggers of black fire. "I cannot explain to you the intensity . . ." Jacob had to clear his throat of a hoarse hitch. "When she is close, if she so much as looks at me from below her lashes, or if she smiles . . ." Noah could hear the distinct sound of the

Enforcer's back teeth grinding shortly against each other. "I no longer know myself. I no longer know what is right."

"Well, it happens that if we are interpreting this prophecy correctly, the right thing would have been to take her."

"Damn you, how can you be so casual about this!" Jacob roared, lurching to his feet and advancing on the King. "You would so easily use her for an experiment of such magnitude? Use me? Knowing it could very well kill her and damn me for the rest of my life?"

"Better the two of you than our entire race," Noah countered. Then quickly, before Jacob could speak, "I say that as the ruler of a great many people, Jacob. It is the kind of choice I have been destined to make. The welfare of the many, weighed against the welfare of the one—or in this case, two. And do not glare at me with your condemnation, Enforcer. You make the very same choices every time you punish one of us for straying. You made the same choice when you told Myrrh-Ann you would seek out Saul, knowing full well that no Demon has ever been rescued from a Summoning intact and that you would be forced to kill him."

Jacob knew Noah spoke the truth, but that didn't make it sit any better on his conscience. Somehow, Isabella's well-being was far more personal to him, as well as far more important. She was innocent, in so many ways, and had never asked to become a part of their politics, or their salvation.

"As well as you know our taboos, Jacob, you know our belief in Destiny. If this is hers, there is nothing any of us can do about it," Noah reminded him, lowering his voice to a soothing level. "You rebel, but I sense that in your heart, in your very soul, you already know that she is your match. She is your mate. She is the only woman of any race to ever inspire such loyalty in the Enforcer before me. She is the only human to ever tempt you, the Hallowed moon be damned. You have lived over half a millennium, Jacob, and now, in this moment, you are drawn for the first time, even to the point of going against everything you have been raised to believe in. She is yours, Jacob," Noah said vehemently. "It is her destiny, and she is yours."

"I will not hurt her. I will not force our prophecies on her." Jacob walked stiffly back to the couch, once more tending her wound and stroking his fingers through her beguiling hair.

"You have no choice. If she were not human, I would accuse you both of being in the first stages of the Imprinting. The telepathic connection, the undeniable temptation to mate—"

"She *is* a human, Noah, and the Imprinting does not apply to her. It barely applies to us! There has not been an Imprinting for over two centuries, and just as long again before that. No matter how much you try to mold her into our ways, no matter how you try to manipulate me into easing my conscience, I will not let you win me over to your thinking and I will not force her!"

"It may seem that you have a choice," Noah said patiently, "but you know Destiny finds a way. You will not force her, because you will not have to. No one is saying that you do. It will just happen."

"I should have never brought her to our world."

"You were meant to bring her."

"I should have . . . I could have . . ." Jacob choked on the frustration clawing at his throat, turning his head aside so Noah could not see the distress building smartly in his eyes.

"You are half in love with her already, are you not?" Noah quizzed gently, his sharp jade and gray eyes trained firmly on his friend.

"Do not presume to tell me how I feel! It is bad enough some ancient piece of paper attempts to do so," Jacob barked back.

"Very well, I will let it go. There are other things to focus on, in any event. The introduction of these prophecies and histories into our culture will have powerful ramifications. It will also meet with great resistance. Look how strongly *you* resist, even when you long to find solace in any excuse to be with her. Imagine what fanatic purists like Ruth will do."

The very idea sent a sensation of dread down Jacob's spine. He finally turned his eyes onto Noah. "You are telling me that my personal life is nothing compared to how this other business is about to affect me," he stated gravely.

"You are the Enforcer. There will be much chaos, Jacob. I will make it as easy on you as I can. I will start by telling the scholars, and then, in time, the Council."

Jacob saw the wisdom in this course and realized very acutely in that moment why Noah was destined to lead them, and the rest of them destined to do service for him. With the scholars to support him, Noah could not be logically refuted, even by the most influential of Elders. With this surety, Noah could call on the warriors and the Enforcer to back him up in the event of dissent. The idea of the potential for civil unrest made Jacob's stomach churn. He looked down at the pale little pixie next to him. Isabella had fallen from a window and had started a chain of events of impossible magnitude.

"Look at her carefully, old friend. That," Noah said

softly, "may very well be the face that launches a thousand ships."

Isabella's eyes fluttered open, the violet expanding as her pupils narrowed under the light. She blinked rapidly, trying to adjust. She lifted her head slightly and groaned when a sore muscle in her neck stretched and the blood in her head began to pound uncomfortably.

She felt gentle fingers slide over her cheek from behind her, a thumb rubbing her ear gently, a soothing voice shushing her.

"Hush. Easy, Bella. You are safe."

She felt safe. As she woke further, she was aware of being tucked up like a spoon along the length of a comforting body, a heavy leg insinuated between her own from behind, a strong arm pillowing her head. She had never woken up beside a man in all of her life, but this sense of fitting perfectly, of warmth and protection, was always the way she imagined it would feel. They were in bed together, but the realization didn't distress her. He hadn't left her alone. He had kept her as close as he could, no doubt watching her every moment until he'd seen her stir.

"Jacob," she murmured, turning her cheek into his touch, nuzzling affectionately.

"None other," he assured.

She slid her hand over the sheets until her fingers laced with his. He clasped her readily, squeezing her fingers warmly.

"I am surprised you are not beating the hell out of me," he observed.

"I'm still waking up. I'll kick your ass later."

Jacob buried his face in her hair, smiling. "Thank you for the warning."

"Actually"—she turned her body until she had scooted around to face him, brown-black eyes to violet—"I think I'll kick Noah's ass. That would make me feel better."

"Please do. It would make me feel better as well." Jacob's hand fell to her cheek again, his fingers drifting over the silky soft skin. His thumb reached to stroke her lower lip.

"Can you answer a question?"

"Why do we feel like we have known each other for ages, when in fact it has only been a few days?"

"Cheater," she accused.

"Sorry. You have too open a mind for me to resist."

"Is that an apology? It sounds more like a character assassination."

"Do you want me to answer the question or debate the semantics of who should have asked it?"

"Does the answer have anything to do with prophecies and Destiny? Because if it does, I think I'll have a very bad headache."

"Actually," he said, "I was going to lean toward the old-fashioned theory of chemistry."

"Oh. Well, that sounds normal. Practically human, in fact."

"Bite your tongue," he rejoined, a twinkle of mischief flashing in his eyes.

"You first."

He pulled his head back, a fudge-colored brow lifting in surprise. "Isabella, are you flirting with me?"

Isabella sighed dramatically. "Not too subtle, huh?"

Jacob laughed, unable to resist pulling her forehead to his lips and kissing her. He tucked her head under his chin and hugged her small body against his.

"I cannot figure you out, Bella. Just when you have every right to vigorously wash your hands of me and all of my kind, you do not. I cannot understand your reasoning, no matter how much I sneak into your mind."

"Well," she said thoughtfully, "I think it's because every time I get upset, my rational mind comes barreling to the forefront, banishing emotion to a back burner. I start to think. I make sense out of your motivations, and I see reason in them. It kinda takes the fight out of a person when you realize you are all just struggling for survival and peace of mind the best way you know how."

"Bella?"

"Mmm?"

"If you are destined to be for me, I would be the most fortunate creature on this planet." He paused; something unpleasant was crossing his thoughts. "I do not know if you could say the same."

Isabella lifted her head, drawing herself up on an elbow so she could look down into his face. She wondered if he realized that whenever she moved her head, his hands automatically followed, finding ways to touch her face and weave into her hair. "Why would you say such a terrible thing?"

An unreadable emotion shimmered across his pupils. She suspected he was filtering his response. She was beginning to realize he always thought very carefully before he spoke.

"I am just used to people feeling negatively toward me. I am considered a necessary evil."

"Noah doesn't see you that way at all," she argued.

He thought about that for a moment and then nodded. "True. But I have never had to enforce Noah or his immediate family. Over the past four hundred years, mostly recent years, there is hardly a family who has not been somehow touched by the actions of the Enforcer. Punishment is a pretty severe business, and it is never forgotten. And do not ask me to go into details about it, because I will not. Suffice it to say it does not stand me in good stead with anyone."

"And what about you? I mean, will someone punish you because . . . because of me?" It was clear by the worry in her wide eyes that the thought didn't sit well at all.

Jacob didn't answer right away. How could he? This was such new territory to everyone, how could he speak with conviction on anything? The realization disturbed him. He had lived his life with an undoubted clarity of purpose, even if that purpose caused him some discomforts. Now there was just confusion, mystery, and speculation.

"I honestly do not know, Bella," he said softly, his disturbance at that confession written in his eyes. "And the deeper we go into this entire situation, the more I realize how little I truly know about things I once saw with perfect conviction. It is a hard thing for a man to come to grips with."

"For a woman too," she added, reminding him of how much this had turned her life over as well. "One day I am a librarian, the next, I'm a Demon hunter. Go figure." He smiled when she rolled her eyes comically, but he knew there was a great deal of disturbance behind those flip words. "After hearing how your society looks on you and your position, I'm not sure I want to find out how they will react to a *human*"—she mocked Ruth perfectly on the word—"Enforcer."

"There will be shock and dissent, I will not lie to you about that, little flower." He stroked his thumb over her cheek soothingly as he spoke. "Nonetheless, I have faith in my community. We are intelligent, devoted to the idea of fate, and structured soundly on our philosophies and prophecies, however distasteful they can be to us. We will adapt."

It wasn't until he said it that he realized he meant it. Felt it. He also realized that he was now talking of the prophecy as a foregone conclusion. It startled him that it felt so much more natural to him to accept it than it had felt to argue it with Noah. The conviction must have come through, because he felt her relax. She unthinkingly rubbed her lips and nose into his palm as her brows drew down in thought. It was one of the things that he enjoyed about her, the way she mulled things over thoroughly and without prejudice. It was what made her so exceptional, and he didn't need a prophecy to tell him that.

"Why would your people need two Enforcers? From what I gather, you do a fine job all on your own. You don't need me."

"That is not entirely true," he remarked, his voice quiet and compelling. He did need her. He had needed her for a very long time. It was something he was only now beginning to understand. All the same, he couldn't say the words aloud, couldn't pressure her with his personal desires. If she chose this path, he didn't want to be the reason why. At least, not the only reason.

When he didn't elaborate any further, Isabella decided to let the matter drop for the moment. She didn't see it the way he did yet, but perhaps in time she would.

"Do you think it's true? Do you think I'm the one from the prophecy? And if so, can you tell me why you think it?"

"I thought I already did. It caused you to take a

header into the floor, as I recall." His voice was filled with regret over that fact, his fingertip touching the bandage that covered her cut.

Bella lifted her hand to the bandage and felt around. It was a little sore but not as painful as she would have expected. She tugged at the covering, not knowing how badly she had been cut. She pulled it off before Jacob's protest could stop her.

Instantly, the air around them changed. It started with Jacob going very, very still, tension pulling his previously relaxed body into a hard wall of muscle. His eyes were trained on her face, and he was clearly holding his breath.

"What? Is it bad?" She went to touch, instinctively.

"It was. It was a bad cut, Bella." He could barely speak. It was as if he could not say it aloud for fear it would make it untrue. "But it has healed. Except for a fresh scar and some bruising, your cut has healed."

"Really? Jeez, how long was I out for?"

"Only a few hours."

"Oh." She drew her bottom lip between her teeth, nibbling it for a long minute as she looked into his darkly unsettled eyes. "This is significant to you, isn't it?"

"Have you always healed this fast?"

"No, of course not. I heal like an average human being."

"No longer," he remarked. "Now you heal like one of us."

"I do?"

He didn't say another word. Instead, he reached for the buttons of her blouse, his long, dark fingers manipulating the soft satin with such ease that she was unbuttoned to just below her breasts before she could even blink. Then he reached for her collar, sliding the seams between his fingers as he pushed the material back and exposed the whole of her shoulder.

Jacob's eyes, so black and so clearly haunted by his feelings, fell to the place where he had so purposefully marked her the day before. His thumb reached to slide over her pale, perfect skin, seeking for even the slightest bruise or ragged irregularity in the place he made his brutish mark upon her body.

"Yes, you do," he observed at last, letting himself look back up into her expectant eyes.

"Why? How? Are you, like . . . contagious or something?"

"I do not think so," Jacob said, a small smile appearing. "We have spent prolonged periods of time around humans for centuries and this has never happened."

"Well, then maybe I'm not your average human."

"This much I can vouch for with all certainty," he said softly, reaching to kiss the newly healed spot on her shoulder.

"Flatterer," she said, closing her eyes as his lips touched and lingered on her bare skin. She felt the kiss all the way through her body, her skin flaming and her breasts instantly aching at his nearness. "What I mean is," she managed to say with a low and breathless voice she hardly recognized, "maybe I should do a genealogy chart and see if I have any Druid ancestors."

"It would not be something you would find advertised, considering that your ancestors were probably hiding from us. This was not one of our more glorious moments in history, to punish and make extinct an entire race." Jacob sighed, the sound reflecting the depth of his regret.

"Well, you didn't do it, your ancestors did. All you can do is repair the mistake to the best of your ability.

If your race is going to overcome the moon madness, you have to find Druids, however watered down they may be by now, and reintroduce them into your lives and culture. At least, that's how I read it."

"Noah sees it the same way," Jacob agreed. "But that will mean bringing humans into our world, because it was apparently the humans they hid behind. That they bred with. If you are any example, I mean. If indeed you are a Druidic descendant." Jacob closed his eyes then and groaned. He rolled back away from her, lying back on his pillow and reaching to rub the bridge of his nose as if he suddenly had a bad headache.

"What?"

"Bella, when this gets out . . . if the need for Druids is true and accepted . . . if humans are where the Druids hid, it is going to be like an open season on your race. Sweet Destiny, I can see it now. 'But, Jacob, I thought she was a Druid.' How the hell am I supposed to handle this?"

"Oh dear," Isabella murmured, catching his drift quite clearly. Her heart ached to see him in distress. She could feel his alarm and concern for the future well-being of her race. "But, Jacob, what if nature has already compensated for that? With me." Jacob turned his head to look at her, his fathomless eyes training on her with a mixture of slow understanding, as well as hope. "I have"—she cleared her throat of the emotions that she felt in response to those in his eyes—"I've come to help you, Jacob."

Isabella felt within her spirit the powerful reaction he had to her words, to the understanding that such a truth could change him forever. She broke into a part of him she had never fully touched before, feeling the canyon of loneliness that had come with his long life.

It stretched behind him, littered with the deaths of friends and family who couldn't survive the enemies of their world, who had left him alone to the cold acceptance of being a pariah for his people. What was more, he had never fully shared his feelings about the depths of his isolation with anyone.

Isabella realized that no one knew. No one knew how lonely the Enforcer truly was, save herself, and she only because she could touch his mind. And now, as he faced what she was suggesting, he was devastated with fear for her. He did not want her to live the life he lived.

But Bella saw it differently. She felt a rush of delight and smiled at him brightly.

"Wow. I'm like . . . Wonder Woman!" She scrambled up onto her knees in the bed, bouncing on the mattress a little in her excitement. She placed her hands on her hips and struck a pose. "You know, fighting for truth, justice and the . . . the Demon way."

"I thought that was Superman," he noted dryly.

"Shut up." She dismissed him with a crooked grin. "I'm having a moment here. You know, I could lose the whole hunting and killing part of this, what with the yuck factor that comes with that." She shuddered from head to toe theatrically. "But I'm totally digging the special powers. I wonder how come they're only showing up now?"

"I wish I could answer that. I am as baffled as you are," he said.

"Well, the first time I noticed anything was in the library after—" She made an awkward dodge, clearly to spare him his guilt, but Jacob felt it like a smarting slap all the more. "When I could suddenly read your language."

"No, earlier than that," he said quietly. "Just after you

fell out of the window, you were assaulted by your empathy with Saul. Remember?"

"Oh yes. Then that was the first time. Right after you caught me." She gave a wry little laugh. "Maybe it's you after all. Maybe you *are* contagious." Isabella noticed his brow shoot up in sudden contemplation. "Oh no, you don't. It was just a joke," she said hastily. "I won't listen to you say what you're thinking."

"It would only be guesswork," he reminded her with a troublemaking grin tripping across his lips.

"Well, stop guessing," she commanded, punctuating the demand by leaning across him so she could punch his shoulder.

"You certainly are a bossy little thing," he observed, purposely reaching out to cup her shoulder in his hand, preventing her from leaving her position across his body before he wanted her to. He ached to feel her, in any way possible. There could be no harm in a little innocent exchange of body heat.

"Yeah, well, I'm regretting ever letting you catch me that night," she huffed, taking no notice of his machinations as she blew back her hair in that charming habit she had. It was an invitation he could not resist. His hands crept into her gorgeous hair, the luxuriant strands settling between his fingers.

"Hey, sweetheart, it was either me or the concrete. One of us had to do it."

"At this point I'm thinking the concrete would've been less painful . . . and less complicated."

Jacob knew she was being a brat, trying to tease and be funny, but her comment struck a sore chord in him. "Has it been?" he asked, seriousness flooding his voice. "Have we been painful for you? Have . . . have *I* hurt you, Bella?"

Isabella quieted, looking down into those solemn dark eyes from her position atop him, knowing that her answer would be vital to him. As was her way, she thought carefully for a long minute about her response. He would get the truth, as he always had.

"Only once," she admitted softly. She felt his fingers curl tightly into fists in her hair. It touched her that he was so concerned for her. "But not the way you're thinking, Jacob. It was that time, in the library . . ."

"Then it is what I am thinking. Damn, Isabella, I am so sorry."

"Jacob, listen to me. It wasn't what you did." She turned her head away, a flush staining her cheeks. Unable to look in his eyes, she confessed to him, "It was what you didn't do. It was . . . when you stopped."

Her face was so hot by that point that she could imagine she was as red as a ruby, but she had needed to answer him honestly. Jacob was motionless beneath her, but she couldn't bring herself to look at him, not having the first idea of how her bold declaration would be received. She was outspoken when it came to the things she was certain of, but this was all new territory for her. She couldn't even feel him breathing.

Then, just as suddenly, he was hurtling himself off the bed, dumping her off his body, leaving her to bounce on the mattress. Perplexed, Isabella scooped up the hair that had fallen over her face and threw it back behind her. Her sight restored, she saw Jacob pacing the length of the room, his hands running raggedly through his own hair.

"Jacob?"

"Isabella. Do not speak," he barked.

Isabella's feathers ruffled. She crashed both hands onto her hips. "Well, I'm sorry you find what I have to say so damn offensive! Excuse the hell out of me! I promise it *won't* happen again!"

Fighting back tears, unwilling to make any more of a fool of herself, Isabella scrambled off the bed and marched for the door. She grabbed the knob and jerked, but nothing happened. She checked the lock, all too aware this was ruining an excellent exit, and tried again. The door remained stuck. Isabella couldn't suppress the sob aching to escape her chest much longer and she stomped her foot in frustration. If she hadn't been so furious, she might have realized Jacob had come up behind her. As it was, she jumped nearly a foot into the air when he touched her shoulder.

"What?" she demanded, whirling around.

Very slowly, Jacob stepped closer to her, herding her backward into the door before resting first one palm, and then the other, flat against the door on either side of her shoulders. Then, in purposeful increments, he leaned his body closer to hers. By the time he had made full and secure eye contact with her, the barest of spaces separated their bodies. He was bathing her in the dangerous heat of his potent body, and her heart was pounding in double-time.

"Bella," he began slowly, her name rumbling out of his throat as if it were a rough purr, "you mistake me. Do not ever, *ever* make the error of thinking that I do not want you, little flower." He leaned even closer, his chest moving so near that she had to turn her head. His husky tone fell to a whisper as he engaged her ear, bathing her neck with a hot exhalation of unsteady breath. "On the contrary. If I pull away from you, you must know that it is because I want you so badly that when you say things like you just did, I am so plagued by my reactions that I am fearful of losing control.

"Bella, there is no safe haven inside me when it comes to this consuming desire to take you as my mate. My sense of morality has abandoned me as well. Even my safest, surest thoughts have joined in the clamor burning through my body as it demands yours. Do you understand? Mistake me not, little flower. I do want you. So badly it hurts. It hurt me too, as it hurt you, that day in the library."

"If so much of you is feeling the way you say," she said quietly, "then why are you ignoring it still? Especially now, knowing the prophecy and all?"

He pulled back slightly.

"I do not want you coming to me in a headlong rush because ancient scribbles, whose truths and purposes are merely theory at this point, dictate to you how you should feel about me. How few hours has it been since you told me how much I terrify you? You are frightened still, despite what you say. I can feel it and read it in your thoughts. Consider how that makes me feel!

"You are an innocent, Isabella. You cannot even say the word *sex*, and you blush when I say it." Jacob inclined his head with a purposeful glance, making her cover her telltale cheeks with her hands. "However much your body responds to mine, and believe me, it does so in beautiful magnitude, your mind is not yet truly made up. I will not force that decision on you. Not mentally or emotionally, and certainly not physically." His dark pupils searched her face so thoroughly she felt as if she couldn't possibly have a single secret left. "But do not mistake my need to put distance between us as anything but what it is, merely an effort to keep myself under control until such time as you do make up your mind, of your own free will, prophecy or no."

"But, Jacob," she said, her hand coming up to toy

with the open lapel of his shirt, "when we were in the library, and before that, even, we didn't know there *was* a prophecy."

So simple. So logical. So true. Jacob's hands curled into fists against the door, his longing and emotions straining at the very ends of their overtaut tethers. His senses clamored for her input. Even the warmth of her scent filling his nostrils couldn't begin to soothe the cravings of those other senses left destitute.

Jacob clenched his teeth for a brief, tight moment.

"Isabella, you must be careful what you say to me," he warned her roughly. "I am holding on to my control by the thinnest of threads. Understand, the consequences of that control snapping will be something you cannot take back, cannot change. Do you understand?"

"Yes. I do. And I want you to understand something as well," she countered quickly. "I may be a virgin, but that's only because no one got my attention long enough to change it, not because it's so all-fired important to me. I admit, I have always hoped I would have a special first experience, but when I think about it, I can't help but decide that I already have. Jacob, I could never have dreamed up the way you make me feel. I have never felt so much like a woman as I have when you have put your hands on me, when you have touched your mouth to me.

"No one has ever seen me with the passion that you do," she breathed with silky intensity, her sensual whisper driving over his every last nerve like eager fingertips slipping up his spine. "It's such an amazing feeling, to be craved like that. Some women have sex all their lives and never feel that. So, my innocence is now just a matter of physicality. Emotionally, I became very much a woman in your arms the very first night we were together."

Jacob sighed, an indulgent exhalation of breath that stirred her hair against her cheek.

"The naïveté in that statement alone serves to remind me of how innocent you truly are, Bella."

The blunt putdown, whether intentional or not, had Bella resisting the urge to slap him. His condescension was really beginning to irritate her. Inexperienced she might be, but at least she knew she had stumbled on something extraordinary with him. Different worlds, even so much as being species apart, and yet she understood this was a precious connection. An opportunity.

Even though it intimidated her, even though it was clearly cloaked in danger and good reasons to feel more than a little fear, she wasn't about to let it flutter away like a fickle butterfly. Perhaps the whole of her life had been a lead-in to this encounter with Jacob and all the rapid changes that were accompanying him. Perhaps, all along, her hunger for knowledge had been a subconscious search for Jacob and his people. Maybe there was such a thing as destiny, and maybe he was hers. Isabella knew there was only one way to find out and that it was a discovery she craved beyond reason.

"Fine. I understand," she said with a little shrug, turning her head slightly so he couldn't see her eyes. "If it's really that important to you, I'll go have sex with a human male first. Then I'll know what I'm talking about before I broach the matter with you again."

Jacob felt the statement the same way he had felt the blast of Elijah's intervention the first night he had touched her. It slammed into him with breathtaking brutality, destroying his sense of direction and balance. Rage surged through him, turning his eyes into glistening black voids. The idea of another man touching that precious skin, kissing her sweet, delicious mouth, was more than he could stand. What she was suggesting this time was too much. Beyond too much.

"Over my dead body . . . over my *obliterated soul* will I ever allow such a thing." The declaration was a cross between a growl and a soft roar. Bella could see him shaking from head to toe, could feel it vibrating through the door behind her. In all of an instant, the cool, sophisticated Jacob disappeared and a possessive beast reared its head in his place.

Now that's more like it, Isabella mused, with a mental smile.

"But"—she blinked her wide eyes up at him in all innocence—"you just said—"

"I said forget it, Isabella!" the Enforcer exploded, the pressure of his hands on the door at her back making the wood pop and creak ominously. "No one is going to touch you, do you understand?"

Isabella thrust her fists onto her hips, her delicate jaw thrusting out stubbornly.

"Well I'm not going to stay a virgin for the rest of my life, Jacob!" she declared in frustration. "Eventually someone is going to have to touch me, because I have no intentions of being a nun! Especially not now that I know what it can feel like to be wanted by a man and to want him in return. And since you think I'm too fragile for you, it will have to be someone else!"

Isabella suddenly found her head enveloped in those enormous hands of his, her eyes forced to meet his, compelled to see the fire of jealousy she had stirred up in his black gaze. His emotions buffeted her like a wildly breaking wave; his sudden, desperate covetousness and gripping fear battered her psyche like a million piercing daggers. The idea of another man touching her ripped at his insides, physically and spiritually, the cruelty and poison of it stamping his soul like a tattoo. In all of a heartbeat she regretted her game. She had never meant to hurt him, only to motivate him past his conflicts.

Jacob knew he had no justification for feeling this way, especially in light of the hastily sketched rules of conduct he was trying to force on himself and her. Yet a savage need to sear her to his side, body and soul, was strangling him brutally. He would kill anyone who even thought about touching her. In that moment he swore it to himself, and with his desperation-charred eyes, he swore it to her.

"Never," he rasped, the word falling from him on hot, rapid breaths. "Do you hear me, Bella? Never will any other man be allowed to touch you."

"Then that leaves only two choices," she reminded him, just as breathless as he was with his incensed feelings battering at her from all sides. "You, or nobody." She took in a deep, steadying breath, forcing herself to push away his influence in her mind so she could purposely lower her voice and shift her body into her next whispered words. This, she decided, would be her apology for her selfishness, for her taunting ways. She would no longer do this just because *she* craved it so desperately, she would do this because *he* did. Despite all his battling for his self-preservation, he refused to take into account how much he truly needed her. And for the first time, Isabella was truly understanding how much that really was.

"Frankly, Jacob," she said softly, her eyes leading his to glance down the inviting length of her body, "I think it would be such a shame to waste a body like mine, so soft, so eager to know what lovemaking feels like and so responsive to the way you touch it. It would be a crime to waste it on celibacy. Don't you agree?"

On a distant level, Jacob knew she was trying to manipulate him, but the awareness of it did not make her ploy any less effective. Arousal boiled through him in volcanic punishment, burning him from blood to bones until he was locked and rigid with it.

"You tempt me on purpose without knowing what you are toying with," he accused tightly, his eyes once again drawn down over the lush curves of the body she had spoken of, the body she was now rubbing ever so lightly against the hard contours of his. "Why would you do such a foolish thing?"

"Perhaps because it's my destiny to be your undoing, Jacob," she murmured softly, her fingers reaching up to trace his sensuous mouth with a slow, searching touch. "Or perhaps it's yours to be mine. I don't know. All I know is that I want to be with you more than I ever thought I would ever want anything in my life."

Jacob's breath came faster, his mouth warming under her exploring touch, his pupils dilating before her eyes. He let go of her, his hands pressing to the door behind her once more. Isabella was aware of his fingers digging into the wood, aware that his internal struggles were not yet over. It touched her that he was so worried for her. It made her want to be with him even more. She knew he'd never treat her lightly, wouldn't consider being with her a casual act. It radiated from every pore in his body.

"I could never find anything about you light or casual," Jacob said fiercely, not even realizing in the intensity of the moment that he had actually heard the words in his head, in her voice. "But you are right, I am worried. And believe me when I say it is with good cause. Do you remember the first time I kissed you? Within the span of a quick breath I was out of control. I was acting solely on instinct, the animal in my blood at the surface; the civilized man vanished without even putting up a fight. If Elijah had not interrupted us, I would have been brutal to your body, inconsiderate and unthinking of your innocence. I would have hurt you, only the urge to mate paramount in my thoughts. Isabella, you do *not* want that. *I* do not want that for you. You deserve so much more."

"More? As in the more you were giving me the second time we kissed, in the library?" she asked soothingly. "There was no animal then, Jacob. At least, not in control. The way you touched me, the way you made me feel"—her hands drifted in a slow, purposeful caress down the length of his neck, her eyes trained on the travel of her own fingertips—"and the way you stopped. Those were the acts of a caring and concerned lover." Her fingers dipped into the hollow at the base of his throat, then slid into the warm, open neck of his shirt. "You were attentive, you made me feel so wanted. Jacob, I want to feel that again."

"You forget," he said hoarsely, his eyes falling on her bare shoulder under the gaping collar of her blouse. "*You* are now revising history."

"No, Jacob, I'm not. I know what that was . . . I'm not a fool. I've felt that part of you more than at just those times." She reached to brush tender lips across his jaw and ear as she whispered softly to him. "I feel it in the hunger of your eyes when you look at me. I feel it when your breath draws deep as you take my scent deeply into you. Yes," she assured him when he stiffened in her hold, "I was aware. I've always been aware. I've heard every growl of that beast you leash so tightly. I have felt his rough urgency in your elegant hands, his bite in the scrape of your teeth. Jacob, I've learned the depths at which that beast lives, and it no longer frightens me. In the library, I never feared you for the beast in you. My only hesitation came from fear of the woman in me, of how to deal with my own inexperience. But then you, fiend that you feel you are, found the way to guide me past that. It was natural, Jacob, and it was right. We were right."

Jacob swallowed hard past the surge of hope and desire clutching his chest and throat. She was touching his mind on purpose, forcing him to see and feel all the truth in her beliefs. She had such unshakable faith in him and in the way she felt about what was happening between them.

"You do not know the power you have," he uttered in a voice like rough sandpaper. "You are so beautiful." He reached to cup her face in his hand. "So soft and so warm." His fingers fanned out against her skin, sliding silkily over her cheek, chin, and throat. He inhaled through his nose, a long, purposeful breath. "And that. Your scent. It drives me mad."

"Tell me why," she urged him, her voice sounding distant and dreamy.

"You are"—he leaned forward and nuzzled the side of her neck, breathing deeply of her—"clean . . . and sweet, like nutmeg, and tart like apples. And then the change . . ." He pressed his mouth to her ear, rubbing his lips against her, dipping his tongue into the little hollow it made. "Yes, right there," he murmured, "when your blood stirs, when your arousal sharpens. The scent of musk and everything female."

"I see," she said breathlessly, feeling the change flush through her body more than scenting it as he did. Her hands rubbed over the play of muscles hidden beneath his silken shirt. He was so powerful, and she could feel it in every inch of him she'd ever touched. She had not even begun to touch him, she realized suddenly. She'd always been far too overwhelmed by his need for her, by his dominance. She wanted to touch him, more than anything, and to feel all the contours of the body he kept hidden beneath the sophistication of silk and tailored seams.

Jacob moved to the side of her neck, opening his mouth, touching his tongue to her pulse, sucking softly and making her shiver as her flesh exploded in goose bumps. He smiled against her skin, well aware of the tiny pearls of flesh blossoming under the caress of his tongue. He lifted his head, rubbing his nose and lips up her neck, over her cheek, until he could see her darkening eyes.

"Where is it, Jacob?" she asked softly, her breath coming quick against his nearby mouth. "That animal you are so afraid will hurt me, where is it now?"

"Closer than you realize," he assured her.

Chapter Six

I would be fearful if I thought for even a moment I had to be, Jacob.

This time Jacob did take notice of her voice lilting through his mind. The link between them was growing stronger, seemingly with every touch.

I am in your mind, Enforcer. I would know if I had anything to fear.

Jacob looked deeply into her intense violet eyes, seeing the confidence in them radiating at him like a warming light. It was the first time someone had called him Enforcer and had actually made it sound like a welcomed, affectionate term. He felt his heart constrict within his chest, his throat closing with emotional tension. Until that moment, he hadn't realized how much he'd longed for someone to like him with affection and warmth outside of the connection of his siblings and beyond the respectful acquaintance Noah provided.

The feeling was profound. He couldn't hope to hide it from her and he saw her eyes fill with moist compassion for his solitude, for all the abuse he'd withstood from the very race that needed him. Bella's kindness was a remarkable gift, one he would not squander. She was giving and trusting, always without thinking about what it would cost her. She was a sunshine that he could bask in without ill effect. He would be careful with her, or he would die trying.

It was that moment when he realized how easily he could lose his heart to her.

That perhaps he already had.

He guarded the thought from her, feeling that she was under enough pressure as it was. If she would be his, and Destiny knew he wanted her to be, he wouldn't have her doing so out of charity for his people or the pressure of his growing feelings for her. She had to make her choices free of those encumbrances. He could be satisfied no other way.

Isabella saw him working on heavy thoughts, but he was keeping them locked safely away from her. True, she shouldn't be nosing around in his head after the lecture she'd given him on privacy, but she'd grown used to sharing her feelings and impressions with him. It connected them, and she felt secure with that connection in place. She glanced at her hand, which was absently toying with the first closed button of his shirt, her knuckles snuggled warmly against the exposed skin above it. She had read that the natural body temperature of a Demon was five degrees cooler than a human's, but somehow he always seemed so warm to her.

She flicked one finger across the button deftly, opening his shirt another few inches. She slid her entire hand beneath the fabric, concentrating completely on the smooth texture of his skin and the way it warmed to her touch. He sighed, his lashes fluttering down to obscure his eyes. When he looked up again, that black flame that was becoming so familiar was flickering in his gaze.

Jacob took a hand from the door and let it fall with purpose to the gaping lapels of her silk blouse. He began running the tip of a single finger over her skin in a leisurely fashion, from one side of her collarbone to the other. *One little touch, Bella, and you turn me inside out. Can you feel it?*

She could. She closed her eyes and let her consciousness meld with his, feeling from his perspective the way his body stirred and his blood warmed. His muscles flexed and tightened in anticipation, and she felt the heavy weight, pulse, and ache of the erection that strained with discomfort within his clothing.

Isabella was instantly fascinated. She couldn't help herself. The moment she slipped back into her own mind and flushing body, she slid her hands down the length of his torso, traveling the landscape of clothing quickly and succinctly until her fingers were gliding past his belt and along the stitching of his fly. Jacob sucked in a fast, brutal breath as she eagerly sought for his hardness through the fabric of his slacks until she was boldly and intimately cupping him in her happily situated hand.

"You are going to drive me mad," Jacob uttered in a strangled, dark pitch, his voice rumbling across her senses like the purring of a massive lion.

"Perhaps it's my inexperience, then, because I wasn't trying to make you mad," she remarked, curling her fingers slightly so that her nails made the next brush over the fabric confining him.

He groaned, the sound stirring up from deep inside of him, his body leaning into hers as if the simple pleasure she was giving him had weakened his ability to stand up straight. Isabella found herself enjoying that idea. Pleased with his reactions but dissatisfied with their cumbersome clothing, she raised both hands to the task of unbuttoning his shirt the rest of the way. She leaned toward him to stroke his solid flesh boldly as she bared it, dipping deep beneath the gaping shirt, her touch spanning his entire chest, his sides, and his back. Jacob was so lost in sensation that he didn't seem to realize his hand had instinctively moved to cradle her breast, kneading it gently through her bra.

He shuddered as her nails scraped lightly down the entire length of his back, her fingertips fanning and fluttering over his skin with gossamer curiosity. So simple a touch, yet so profound, and he felt the painful bliss low in his body, throbbing hard with demand.

"Be sure," he gasped suddenly, his hand squeezing her supple flesh, his thumb rolling over her distended nipple. "Be absolutely sure, Bella."

I've never been so sure in my entire life. Come into my mind and you'll know that, just as I do.

He did as she beckoned and couldn't mistake the calm that was at the core of her stirring passion. She was, as she said, completely without doubt. Indeed, her curiosity was growing exponentially, and the desires and thoughts flitting through her mind about what she wanted to do, to try, to learn and know, pushed him well past any point of refusing her.

He removed his touch from her only long enough to wrap her slight body in his iron embrace, pulling her feet from the floor until her breasts rested high against his chest and her hair tumbled down over his shoulders, her mouth smiling just slightly before he captured it with a slight stretch of his neck.

As he kissed her breathless, he moved back across

the room with her. Then, reluctantly tapering off his kiss, he kneeled on the bed and settled her gently in the center. She stretched out, the sexy, sensual movement and her teasing smile reflecting her pure satisfaction of her sway over him. But she had barely tasted what she would be capable of, and Jacob's blood ran like fire through his veins as he eagerly welcomed the realization. When she truly learned what her influence over him could be, he had a feeling he was going to be extremely lucky to be her lover.

With one hand, he skimmed through the remaining buttons of her shirt. Jacob put his mouth on her freshly exposed skin. She took a deep breath and released it in a low, trilling sound of pleasure, her back curving up toward his skillful lips. He nuzzled her through the lace of her bra, his lips brushing the aroused peak of her nipple. Then his mouth was open on her, his teeth drawing her in with a gentle tug, the moisture of his now-suckling lips penetrating right through the lace. She convulsed in response to the pleasure tripping through her entire body, all from that one small point he attended to. She reached to touch his cheek, a silent summons, and he lifted his head a fraction of an inch as she slid the material of her bra aside for him, exposing the beautiful, dusky peak. His mouth returned to her with quick enthusiasm, his free hand skimming over her delicate ribs, the crescent of her waist, and the tender curve of her hip.

Her blouse and bra seemed to fall away from her in those next few minutes. She was suddenly bared from the waist up, her hands buried in his hair as he teased her aching breasts with his mouth. The exploring hands that roamed her body drove her equally mad with his artful combinations of caresses. She felt him find the inner leg seam of her jeans.

Jacob pressed his fingers up along the ridge of cloth slowly, enjoying how every inch upward was warmer than the last. He left her breasts and their now-raging sensitivity, finding her mouth hotly. He sucked and kissed the flavor of her kiss feverishly onto his tongue, making himself insane with the pleasure of it while reveling in her gasps and moans of wild pleasure as they filled his ears . . . filled his mouth.

Then she was pulling his shirt from his slacks, driven by the urge to feel his flesh against hers. Jacob satisfied the demand raging through her wild thoughts, lowering his hot skin into contact with hers, all the while continuing that leisurely path up the inseam of her jeans with his fingers. She was not even conscious of how she wriggled and writhed in attempts to make him speed up his journey. She was completely unaware of how every twist of her hot little body beneath his triggered desperately primal urges. Her scent permeated his every pore, making him growl, low and intense, as he finally cupped the core of all that wonderful heat in his fervent hand. His palm pushed against her mound and his fingers pressed tight to her. He groaned when he realized she was damp right through the denim.

Jacob was suddenly rising up on his knees, stripping off his shirt as he did so. His actions were torrid, punctuated by a feral, rough sound, but Isabella was far from intimidated. She urged him on in soft whispers of encouragement, raised her hips when he went to strip off her jeans and panties, unbuckled the thin belt at his waist eagerly. When he was finally completely nude, he crept back onto the bed, his hands moving her knees apart with the intent of lying directly up the center of her body. She had watched his approach with wide, anticipatory eyes, and Jacob was forced to hesitate when she inadvertently sent off an impression of anxiety. He reached for her mind, threading himself into her thoughts, seeking the cause of her apprehension quickly.

Is . . . is that normal?

Jacob tried not to smile, knowing there was a good chance he would get smacked for it. He followed her curious gaze at his body. *Quite normal,* he assured her. But then, unable to resist, he added: *For a Demon.*

She gasped, looking up into his eyes, taking only a second to see the amusement glittering through the flames of arousal.

"You are so mean!"

"You are so adorable," he countered, chuckling softly as he nuzzled the sensitive spot he had found on the side of her neck with his lips. This distracted her just long enough for him to close his hand around hers and guide her touch to him. "And now, you can choose to get me back . . . or not."

Her hand curled open, that irrepressible tactile curiosity of hers leaping to the forefront as the heavy weight of his arousal rested in her palm. He slipped back into her mind, feeling her wonder as she discovered what it was like to touch a male so intimately for the first time. The first thing she noticed was that he was a contradiction of sensations, as hard as the iron his kind so feared, and yet that hardness was covered in velvety, hot skin. Soft and smooth at a surface touch, rigid and powerful with a stronger touch.

Her curious exploration went on, and Jacob broke out in a sweat as his entire frame shuddered. Her caress was pure ecstasy, forcing pulses of heat and incredible stretches of increasing hardness to the shaft between her curious fingers. She discovered the wetness her touch had milked from him, nuzzling it with her palm in such a way that a soulful groan was torn out of him. He rocketed into her mind, making her feel what he was feeling, causing her to cry out in delighted shock.

Feel this, Bella. Feel how you burn me.

He wrenched the command into her mind, and she obeyed him. She could feel the painful pleasure she caused him, could feel the impulses that raged through him because of every stroke, every embrace. She was panting out soft, excited sounds, totally unaware she was doing so, as she slid her palm along him from tip to base and back again. Need, stark with the howl of nature's wild soul, exploded into Jacob's mind and spirit. She felt it slam into her mind, scorching her psyche with its ferocious demands. She absorbed the brunt of it equally with him, and when they looked back into each other's eyes, the beast was at the ready in both of them.

Isabella heard the rumbling of a soft, beckoning growl. She realized the low, seductive call was her own, seeking the response of her mate. She vocalized again, the rolling sound a static-filled purr that sought to lure him closer. Jacob replied, the rumbling sound deepening and reverberating as it was expelled. He grabbed her toying hand by the wrist, his mighty grip painful as he pinned the torturous appendage to the pillow near her head. His eyes bored into hers, a midnight sheen that was reflecting the wild urgency scouring through his every vessel.

He lowered his head to the rise of her breast, baring his teeth as he did so. She was breathing so hard that her chest rose to meet him and she saw the satisfaction that rushed into his turbulent eyes. His teeth scraped over her and she felt them dotting across her skin. Again, he moved to the curve of her collarbone, up to the slope of her shoulder.

Then his hands were on her, flipping her over roughly, pressing her into the bed as his mouth pressed hard against her shoulder blade. His hands were at her hips, holding her in place as he used his thighs to push her up onto her knees, to seat himself against her with a savage dragging of her body over the rigid, hot length of his sex. Isabella was breathing in sharp gasps of pleasure as she felt his dominant stroke along the outer edges of her feminine folds. She felt her body flowering with craving, seeking and begging to be filled. The clamp of his teeth into the skin of her shoulder and the bruising force of his hands did nothing but intensify those desires.

Jacob felt the raging of his body, so close now as it was to the depths of the haven awaiting him, the slick welcome of her anticipation bathing him in invitation. Then she writhed back against him, demanding him with savage provocation, her wild little body seeking the fulfillment the throbbing hardness against her promised so hotly.

Jacob could not withhold.

He gripped her hips even harder, adding more bruises of intensity, and dragged her to the very tip of his rigid shaft. She cried out his name with wild demand and he felt her instantly pushing back against him, trying to force what his hold on her prevented. But even the beast within him had waited too long for this to not savor it. While he taunted her, he enjoyed her little noises and desperate movements. He rubbed against her again and again, causing her to buck with mindless pleasure as he stimulated her every expectant sense. Then he was at that precious threshold, sweat dripping from his hair and onto the small of her back as the restraint punished him as badly as it tortured her.

Finally, he released.

Jacob plunged into her in one brutal clash of their pelvises. He had not meant to. He had meant to absorb every second of pleasure he could from the progression of entering her. However, a moment before his erotic dive into her body, she had called to him.

"Jacob . . ." she had gasped, her head thrashing wildly from side to side, her very flesh trembling against him. "Please! Come into me. Please . . ."

This had been the blade that had sliced through his last thread of control. Fast or slow, she was so tight, so blindingly hot and wet, so perfectly crafted for him that it was the most tremendous experience of his lifetime, to finally be matched deep within her.

Isabella was so filled by Jacob she wondered why she did not burst. There was a flash of pain, but no more or less than the few bruises she'd already forgotten. She could not be bothered with it. There was far too much calling for her attention, calling for her pleasure. Jacob was calling for her, a low-seated rumble in his breast boiling up and over her shoulders as he bent over her small frame, letting them both absorb his first invasion.

She was not patient enough to wait for him. She tilted her hips and pulled herself forward, reveling in the hard slide of granite moving within her body, instinctively flexing feminine muscles to keep him seated within herself. Jacob's reaction was explosive in both sound and action. He cursed, again an impassioned compliment taken in context, and then released a soul-rending groan. He reached for her neck, his long, powerful fingers grasping and curling around the delicate column. His opposite hand drove up from her hip to her waist, the perspiration coating her skin making it a slick movement. Jacob reseated himself again, a thrust so profound and rough that it actually lifted her knees off the bed. A rowdy, primal sound erupted from his lips as she squirmed eagerly in compliance, her rough breath rasping beneath the press of his index finger on her throat.

The room trembled, the Earth reflecting his loss of control, the glass chimneys of gaslights and the panes of stained-glass windows jingling as the tremor increased. Jacob surged into her again, rooting himself as deeply in the sacred ground of her body as was possible. All the while, the bed was vibrating with the quaking of the house's foundations.

She was scorching heat, captivating wetness, the impossible tightness of her first sexual experience.

Jacob . . . don't . . . please . . . don't stop. Never stop.

Jacob groaned softly, moving with a slow, punctuated rhythm within her. He rode into her tight, wonderful body and reeled from the fervent high that resulted. Her passion was a sparkling prism of light and want, guiding him closer to her in the ways beyond the physical. He had no thought of controlling the vibrating world outside of the sphere of their awareness. Jacob understood only that he now shared space with the relentless, feral creature that vocalized, felt the need to mark her with teeth and the lengthening of nails that scored her soft body in long red lines. But at the same time she was too beautiful not to drag his heart and soul into the mixture. For that moment, he truly felt as though everything about and within him was coming together cohesively.

"Jacob," Bella purred in encouragement. "Oh, yes . . ."

He smiled with sly pleasure when his name passed her lips in that sultry manner, that spur of beckoning need that she could not cloak. He pulled back, reveling in the slick sensation for a second. Isabella gasped out, overwhelmed with a sense of grasping loss, her hips writhing back toward his instinctively.

It is not enough, little flower.

She didn't have time to ask. He left her, making her whimper in her shock and dismay. But then he was turning her over again, this time with amazing gentleness, drawing up her legs, coaxing them around his hips as he lay over her stretched-out body.

I must taste your mouth, little flower, while I am inside you. I must look into your eyes and see your pleasure.

So he seized her mouth with great need, devouring the delicacy she provided for him as he breached deeply into her eager body.

"Bella," he groaned against her mouth, repeating the depth of the thrust and being rewarded with amazingly increased feedback. Heat. Embrace. Eager, excited moisture. Everything about her drawing him in. She was perfect. He had never known such perfection—had never, in all his centuries, come anywhere close. This was a meshing of body, mind, and soul. It was enough to make him curse himself for waiting so long to be with her, even though he'd only known her for a few days. For possibly allowing her to get away, although he knew he could never have held her if she had been forced to his embrace.

Her scent, her textures, and her thoughts, they all surrounded him and filled him as he was filling her. He knew in that second, as he moved energetically within her body and felt the matching rhythm coming to her so naturally, that he was indeed fulfilling Destiny. He slipped into Isabella's mind, feeling the build of pleasure climbing hot and tense within her. He slid his hands over her, sought sensitive spots, purposely fanning the focused flame. It was incredible to feel it from her perspective, the growth of her first taste of release, of ultimate ecstasy. He guided his movements within her by following the sharp flutters of pleasure that whirled through her awareness at first one thrust and then the next. He learned the best way to cause her the keenest delight.

She began to gasp with each successive movement he made inside her, her hands clutching his shoulders violently, her thoughts screaming her euphoria into his soul. And suddenly Isabella exploded, a screaming starburst of rapture that flashed hot and bright, the purity of her bliss forcing him to join her in the cataclysmic release.

"Isabella!" Jacob had to claim her by name as he felt the detonation of climax raking through him. He came with violent, lurching spasms of pleasure that went on and on until he was pulsing the deepest parts of his soul into her. The intensity was so profound, he was certain that by the time it ended, she would know his every secret dream, need, and hope.

Every window in the house exploded, the tension of the conflicting twists of their casements finally reaching the breaking point. Jacob jerked Isabella's head to his chest, his broad back and shoulders protecting her from the shower of colorful glass that rained down from the stained glass picture window above the headboard of the bed.

It was several long, breathless minutes before either of them could move. Isabella suddenly realized the room beyond them was in chaos, and she wriggled her head out of his protective hold to view the destruction. Furniture was toppled and glass was strewn everywhere, including the bed they were lying in.

Finally, she looked up into his eyes, ignoring the concern so clearly reflected in them and smiling like a cat that had just discovered the birdcage was unlocked.

"It's a good thing you don't live in California," she remarked.

"Are you kidding? With all those active fault lines?"

Jacob touched her nose with a fingertip a moment before their bodies faded to dust. The next she knew, she was solid again and all the surrounding glass had been swept away.

"Neat. I bet you make a fabulous houseguest," she laughed, allowing him to draw her up over his body as he rolled onto his back.

"I am an excellent duster," he said.

"So I noticed." Isabella slid a knee on either side of his hips and slowly sat up, pressing her hands on his chest as leverage, still feeling a little weak after their tumultuous activities.

Jacob smiled, drinking in the incredible vision she made straddling him, her bare breasts and body marked with the branding of his mouth and hands, her tumble of hair curling like silky black smoke all around her, one stray tendril of it hooking around her left nipple. He stacked his hands behind his head and basked, not caring if she knew how self-satisfied he was.

"Well, you look very pleased with yourself," she noted, her hands going to her hips in that familiar gesture. Jacob wondered if she realized how it made her breasts thrust out in an all-too-fetching manner. Unable to resist, he removed a hand from behind his head and followed that curl of hair hooked stubbornly around her nipple.

Isabella held her breath and then sighed at how the simple touch stirred her so deeply. Just when she thought she was completely exhausted, she found she wanted him all over again. She was beset with the sense of having a lot to catch up on. It made her lips twitch and her eyes sparkle with renewed hunger.

"Oh boy," Jacob groaned. "I know that look."

"Do you?" she asked archly, reaching to trace the muscles of his chest with a fingertip.

"Even if I could not share your thoughts, little flower, I would know. It is the look of a young person who has just discovered their libido."

"Is that right?" She splayed her hands over his ribs, leaning forward on them until she could touch his nipple with her tongue, all the while maintaining her lock on his eyes.

"Did I mention," he groaned, "that I am probably too old for this?"

She rolled her eyes, apparently not impressed by his perspective. She scraped her teeth over the little nub her attentions had created.

"Aren't you sore?" he attempted.

What's your point?

Isabella opened her eyes, drawing in a sharp breath as a chill washed over her. She was staring into darkness, the cloud-covered moon outside the only light, and even that barely made it past the empty casements of the windows. Jacob was lying heavily over her body, an arm curled possessively around her midsection, a thigh trapping one of hers beneath his, his face buried so deeply into her neck that she could feel the touch of his lips on her skin. She would have enjoyed the sensation of waking up in such a way, should have enjoyed it, in fact, but there was something not quite right. She shuddered, and not because she was cold, although she was just about freezing wherever she was not in contact with Jacob. Bella was suddenly overcome with a creepy feeling about the night, a foreboding sensation crawling up her spine. She knew that she didn't want to be lying down or naked just then, nor did she want Jacob to be asleep. She acted on the instinct, pinching his shoulder firmly, making him start out of sleep rudely, but as the sensation of dread continued to fill her she knew there was no time for niceties.

"Ow. What the hell . . . ?"

"Get off me."

Jacob responded immediately, the tone of her voice compelling him to obey without question. She slid out of bed, the low, quick movements she made to retrieve her clothes putting Jacob on full alert. He stretched out his instincts even as he too got out of bed and crouched low to the ground. He drew on his pants as Bella, several moves ahead of him, crept up into the narrow frame of the window that had been above the headboard, balancing on the balls of her feet on the sill.

Wait for me, he commanded.

Can you feel it?

No. Tell me what you are feeling.

I don't know. It's . . . dark. It feels . . . evil.

He watched as she touched her fingers to her tongue and peered at them in the dark. He sensed what she was looking for. She was tasting the unmistakable tang of blood in her mouth, but it wasn't her own.

It is an illusion. Remember that. Your empathy is real to

someone else, not yourself. Jacob was behind her, peering out over her shoulder, still trying to find what she had such a powerful hold on.

Suddenly, Bella gasped and whirled around.

But she was a moment too late.

The intruder in the room swung something out into the darkness, connecting with the back of Jacob's head and sending him crashing into the dresser beside the bed. Bella cried out, leaping into the shadowy room from the sill she was perched on and making unerring contact with the malevolence that had struck Jacob down. Her hands slammed into its chest, grabbed fistfuls of fabric, and yanked forward as she brought her knee up into its vulnerable belly. Then she shoved back and snapped the hard flat of her palm into the attacker's nose.

The invader reeled back, but only slightly. The recovery was swift considering the force of her assault. The intruder swung out, fisting her so hard across the face that her head snapped back. Bella was stunned, but in some part of her mind she was aware that she wasn't even a fraction as injured as she should be. It swung at her again and she blocked with her forearm; it punched and she leaned swiftly out of range, then she shot the edge of her hand hard up into its vulnerable throat.

Its cry of pain was male and short lived. He reached up and grabbed her by the hair, yanking her so hard by it that she did a complete 180 on the heel of her foot. She was falling back, off balance, into her foe, even as a queer blue light suddenly erupted into the room, highlighting the raised hand it was coming from as he reached for her throat. "Demon bitch!" he hissed at her, coughing for her satisfaction from her last strike.

The blue bolt of magic that shot from his fingertips lanced through her with shocking pain, causing her entire body to convulse, every hair on her standing at attention from the electrical charge.

"His name! Tell me his name!" He had released her hair, his arm locking around her throat and choking her as he sent another bolt of energy through her body. She seized for a long minute before he cut the bolt off from her and let her fall slack in his grasp. "Give me his name, or I will kill you."

"Never," she croaked, without even knowing why she should be protecting Jacob's name from this monster. All she knew was that if she didn't break free soon, she was going to pass out from lack of oxygen or he was going to fry her from the inside out.

He loosened his hold so he could draw a knife from his sleeve and hold it to her throat. "Feel that, demon whore?" He pressed the blade into her flesh. "It's made of iron. I assure you, it has all the spells necessary to cut your head from your shoulders."

That's when Isabella finally absorbed the fact that he thought she was a Demon. She suddenly saw an advantage to it, screaming out as if the iron was causing her pain.

"Yeah, that's right. Hurts, doesn't it? Now give me his name or I'll kill you! Then after I kill you, I'll kill your lover. Look!"

He jerked her around so she could see Jacob lying on the floor. He even caused the room to brighten with his magic so she could see the blood pooling around Jacob's body. The vast emptiness of thought from him terrified her far more than the sight of his blood. Panic welled up in a distant corner of her mind, her heart aching in response, but she angrily pushed it all aside and focused.

"I bet you're wondering how I took him out so easy.

Well, you'll find out if you don't open that mouth of yours and *give me his name*!"

"His name . . ." she croaked.

"Yes, tell me," he said eagerly.

"Bond. James Bond."

Isabella slammed her head back, crashing into his face with her skull. She saw brilliant stars at the impact, but still she grabbed the hand with the knife in it and bit him as hard as she could. He shrieked, but she locked her jaw until the knife dropped from his fingers. Then she whirled around and sent her knee up into his groin with every last ounce of her newfound strength. He fell to the floor with another screech, writhing in pain, cupping his abused privates. Isabella tossed her hair back and glared down at her victim.

"Have a nice sex change, you son of a bitch."

With that, she swung out her foot and kicked him in the head. He lost consciousness with a little whimper, his head snapping and then lolling back in her direction. She nudged him hard with her toe in his pained parts, knowing it would take impossible control for him to fake unconsciousness under the circumstances.

Satisfied, she dropped to Jacob's side, oblivious to the fact that she was kneeling in his blood. She searched in the dim light for the wound it was coming from. At first all she found was the blood in his mouth, apparently from biting his tongue after striking his head on the dresser during his fall. It wasn't until she turned him over that she discovered a deep gash in his shoulder and the back of his head. They were in line with one another, so whatever he had been hit with had been long as well as sharp. Probably another cursed blade of some kind. Probably made of iron.

Isabella began to feel the tight grip of fear locking

around her chest. She remembered from her reading that iron in the hands of a necromancer could kill a Demon. The vital, magnificent being who had been making such incredible love to her only a short while ago could very well be dying in her arms.

"Oh, please," she prayed on a sob, "please let Legna hear me!"

LEGNA! Her mind screamed the Demon empath's name, the pain of her heart howling behind it. *LEGNA! HELP ME!*

Legna jolted in her seat, making Noah look up from the chessboard between them. Her face drained of color and Noah knew instantly something was exceedingly wrong.

"Legna?"

"Isabella . . ."

Noah lurched to his feet, coming around the table and drawing Legna up.

"Tell me!"

"She's terrified . . . Jacob. Something terrible has happened to Jacob. She needs us."

Isabella was sobbing by the time Noah and Legna materialized dramatically in the middle of the room. Noah's first act was to toss a ball of fire up at the ceiling, letting it hang harmlessly suspended as it cast light on the scene. Legna went directly to Isabella's side, crying out softly when she saw Jacob and all of the blood spreading around. Noah immediately noticed the other male lying unconscious on the floor. The smell of the necromancer struck Noah physically, turning his stomach with its malevolent stench.

"Legna," he commanded, "call Elijah." Then he looked at Jacob, his lips pressing into a grim line. "And Gideon."

Legna gasped, looking up at her brother in shock.

"Surely there is another medic, Noah. Gideon despises Jacob."

"There is none older, wiser, and more skilled than Gideon. Call him."

"He will not answer."

"He will. Call him. Obey me now."

Legna swallowed and moved away from the others, finding a distant spot so she could concentrate on her task. Noah knelt beside Isabella, who was rocking slightly in her grief, her small hands pressing to the wounds on Jacob's body in an attempt to stem the flow of blood.

"How did this happen?"

"I don't know," she hiccupped. "He didn't even sense the necromancer. I did, but he didn't. I don't understand. Jacob can sense anything."

"That is one of many questions, Isabella. Right now we are going to focus on getting Jacob a medic and then taking that monster into custody. I promise you, I will not rest until I have answers."

"He kept asking for Jacob's name," she murmured numbly. "Why? Why would he want his name?"

"I will explain later," Noah promised. He lifted his head as a violent breeze rushed into the room, swirled, and connected into Elijah. The warrior took a quick glance around and shot Noah a look.

"Elijah," Noah warned, holding up his hand. "Just take the necromancer safely away from here."

Elijah nodded and with a flick of his wrist, he and the necromancer vanished into a rushing gust of wind.

No sooner had Elijah left than a Demon Isabella had never seen before appeared in the burst of smoke and sulfur created whenever Legna departed and arrived.

Isabella's eyes widened when she saw the silver-haired male for the first time. The thick, shoulder-length hair was belied by the features of a male no more than forty and a vital physique to boot. She realized that this was the one called Gideon, and she also sensed that he was far older than the others in the room. It was in his carriage and the way he looked around at the chaos of the room with serene, cool eyes. Those eerie eyes matched his silver hair perfectly. Even if she had not heard Noah say so, she would have known he had tremendous power. He reeked of it.

His eyes trained on her, his pupils contracting slightly.

"A human."

"Oh, for Pete's sake," Isabella snapped, having had her fill of Demons making that distinction as if she carried some kind of plague. "Yes, it's human. It's also going to get pissed off if it doesn't get some help for Jacob damn quick!"

"From New York," Gideon noted, his eyes flicking over Jacob's inert form. "He has been struck with an iron blade. Ensorcelled. Until the spell is removed, it will leave the wound open and bleeding. Your attempts to stanch the bleeding with your hands are useless."

"Noah," Isabella said quietly, her words hissing out from between clenched teeth. "Tell this jackass that if he doesn't heal Jacob ASAP I'm going to kick his holier-than-thou ass all over the continent."

A silver brow lifted in curiosity.

"She is rather irreverent for a Druid," Gideon remarked.

Noah's head snapped up, his eyes widening in obvious shock.

"You know she is a Druid? How can you tell?"

"Quite easily, I assure you." Gideon forestalled the enraged woman's next verbal threat with a raised hand and knelt beside the Enforcer. "It is better he is not conscious. I do not imagine he would enjoy knowing it is I who will heal him."

"He holds no ill will toward you, Gideon," Noah said quietly. "In fact, your self-exile has weighed heavily on him."

Gideon didn't respond. He touched Jacob's pale face in a caress that could almost be considered affectionate. The Ancient's eyes closed and he released a long exhalation of breath. Isabella gasped when the wound beneath her hand began to knit together. She made a small sound of relief, mixed with a sob.

"He needs blood. Noah, come."

Noah moved to kneel beside Gideon without hesitation. He extended his arm, and Gideon grasped his forearm just above the wrist with one hand, his other reaching for a similar hold on Jacob's left arm. Color suddenly flared into Jacob's complexion, even as it drained slightly from Noah's. Isabella was aware she was witnessing some kind of transfusion, one without needles or threat of outside contamination. It was incredible, and she was grateful beyond words when Jacob finally stirred.

"The scar will remain forever. That I cannot heal," Gideon admitted regretfully.

"It doesn't matter," Isabella whispered, stroking Jacob's hair and face tenderly. He groaned softly, and she bent to press her lips to his. "Jacob. Jacob . . ." she whispered, kissing his mouth again and again.

Gideon cast a pregnant glance at Noah but didn't speak aloud at the incredible irony of the Enforcer having a human female touching and kissing him with obvious intimacy and affection.

"He will not wake just now. He needs to rest." Gideon passed a hand over Jacob, who promptly relaxed and began to sleep. "I suggest you take him somewhere safe. If one necromancer can find him here, it is likely that another can as well."

"I will bring him to my home," Noah assured the medic.

"Another? You mean there are more than just the one?" Isabella demanded. "I thought it was only one necromancer."

"It is never only one. However, you . . . you are a sin-gular curiosity. A human and Druid hybrid." He reached as if to touch her and was rewarded with a flash of movement that found his wrist caught and twisted in her hold. He didn't react with pain, however, just that lifted brow of curiosity. In an equally swift motion, he broke her hold and caught her wrist.

Isabella gasped as white light rocketed up her arm and through her body.

"The necromancer tried to electrocute you, yet you survived," Gideon murmured. "You heal rapidly. Your blood is most peculiar and—" Gideon stopped speak-ing and for the first time his expression registered clear surprise. "You are not mortal."

"*What*?"

"Gideon . . . " Noah warned.

Gideon looked at Noah sharply. "You knew," he said directly.

"He *what*?" Isabella spluttered. "He knew no such

thing! There is no such thing. I'm human and therefore mortal. You got your wires crossed or something, pal."

"That is impossible," Gideon said simply. Isabella had a sudden urge to slap him. She settled for jerking her wrist out of his hold.

"Noah, take us out of here," Isabella begged. "I want Jacob safe. Now."

"Of course. There will be time to talk when Jacob is stronger."

With that statement, Noah leaned over to touch Isabella and Jacob, and the three of them disappeared into a column of smoke that promptly slipped out of the room.

Gideon rose up to his full height, watching their progress as they faded into the night. He then turned his diamondlike eyes until they narrowed on the female Demon who had remained so still and quiet that she had gone unremembered. An interesting feat, considering the remarkable presence of the beauty.

"You have grown strong, Legna," he remarked quietly.

"In only a decade? I am sure it has not made much of a difference."

"To teleport me from such a great distance took respectful skill and strength. You well know it."

"Thank you. I shall have to remember to feel weak and fluttery inside now that you complimented me."

Gideon narrowed his eyes coldly on her. "You sound like that acerbic little human. It does not become you."

"I sound like myself," Legna countered, her irritation crackling through his thoughts as the emotion overflowed her control. "Or have you forgotten that I am far too immature for your tastes?"

"I never said such a thing."

"You did. You said I was too young to even begin to

understand you." She lifted her chin, so lost in her wounded pride that she spoke before she thought. "At least I was never so immature that Jacob had to punish me for stalking a human."

Gideon's spine went extremely straight, his eyes glittering with warning as she hit home on the still-raw wound. "Maturity had nothing to do with that, and you well know it. It is below you to be so petty, Magdelegna."

"I see, so I am groveling around in the gutter now? How childish of me. However can you bear it? I shall leave immediately."

Before Gideon could speak, Legna burst into smoke and sulfur, disappearing but for her laughter that rang through his mind. Gideon sighed, easily acknowledging that her laughter was a taunt meant to remind him that with her departure, so too went his easy transportation home. Nevertheless, he was more perturbed to realize that he'd once again managed to say all the wrong things to her. Perhaps someday he would manage to speak with her without irritating her.

However, he didn't think that was likely to happen this millennium.

CHAPTER SEVEN

Jacob woke to the sensation of being touched lightly across his belly, delicately and unhurriedly. He smiled, smelling her perfume even before he turned to look at her. He curled the arm she lay on up around her shoulders, drawing her warm, essential body closer to his, his face burrowing in the silky nest of her hair.

"Jacob," she whispered.

He heard the sob she tried to muffle under her hand and went very still. The tears that dripped onto him confirmed what his senses had already hinted at and he moved to put enough distance between them so he could see her face.

"Why are you crying, little flower?" he asked, his voice soothing as his fingertips caught first one salty drop and then another.

That was when he saw the bruises on her face.

Everything came rushing back to him. He jerked into an upright position, drawing her protectively to his back as he looked wildly around. He recognized the room immediately, the stone walls unmistakable as belonging to Noah's home. It allowed the tension to loosen slightly from his rigid body. He next turned to see Isabella, prying her from her clinging grasp on his back.

"Are you all right?" he asked, inspecting her for himself.

It was when she nodded that she exposed the bruising on her neck. There was only a faint red mark now where the knife had bitten into her skin in a three-inch line, but it was unmistakable all the same.

Jacob was awash with so many emotions at the sight of her that he couldn't immediately identify a single one. All he could do was wordlessly drag her up against his chest, crushing her in his fervent embrace, his breath shuddering from him in delayed fear and outrage that she'd been harmed. Worse, right under his nose. As a matter of logic, he was also entertaining the thought that it most likely had been she who had saved him, yet again, from the threat in the dark.

The realization did not leave his ego unscathed, but he was far more relieved that they were safe in Noah's home, all in one piece, together. Jacob dragged Isabella across his lap, folding his legs beneath her bottom as he did so, and cradled her closer still, rocking her gently and soothingly.

"Good girl," he said, praising her quietly. "Shh, it is okay. That magic-using bastard never had a chance against my little Enforcer. Hush, Bella, we are safe now."

"I thought he'd killed you. There was so much blood. It was all over the place. All over me."

Jacob winced, his chest constricting as if he had received a blow to his sternum. He felt her pain, her anguish, and her numbing shock over seeing him as she had. The entire incident was replaying in her memory and he was forced to watch it unfurl in their joined minds, once again helpless to come to her aid. His self-contempt spiked even as his pride in her resourceful actions did. She'd done everything right, saving his life, and he knew it would soothe her to remind her of that.

He did so, whispering softly into her ear as he rocked her, flattering her quietly, his words turning her perspective away from the sole focus of seeing him wounded and close to death. He knew that he'd been very close indeed for Noah to call on Gideon.

Isabella was calming in his hold, her weeping reduced to the intermittent sniffle. As her grief subsided, her hands began to move over him, touching him, taking in his body temperature, his vitality, the very fact that he was breathing and alive and once again as strong and potent as he'd always been. Jacob saw incredible irony in that, seeing as how both times she'd seen him in combat he'd ended up knocked senseless. Three times, if he counted Elijah getting the drop on him, but even he had to admit he hadn't exactly been focused at that moment.

"You're being too hard on yourself."

Her voice drifted up to him quietly, her lips pressing affectionate kisses into his neck. He sighed deeply, rubbing his hands over her in a way that communicated he didn't need consoling. It was she who needed comfort.

"I can accept you being born to fight by my side, Bella, but it is difficult to accept you fending for yourself when I am the stronger, more experienced partner."

She lifted her head away from her task of nuzzling his neck and looked for his eyes. "Jacob, the guy coldcocked you. That isn't your fault."

"I should have sensed something. Smelled him, heard him. When I think of what could have happened to you—"

"Stop it!" The command was followed by her sliding up onto her knees and pushing him back until she was looming over him, staring him down as he lay beneath her. "I see you more clearly than you see yourself. The almighty Enforcer." She made an indelicate sound. "You're nothing more than a Demon cop. And cops, despite all their training, all their experience, sometimes meet up with the wrong guy, on the wrong day, at the wrong time, and he gets the drop on them. It happens, Jacob."

"That is no excuse."

"Who needs excuses? It's just the way it is. Do you think I'd be alive now if you hadn't been in that warehouse with me?"

"If I had not encouraged you to go there, you mean?"

"Damn it, Jacob, cut it out! I'm so sick of this! I'm sick of you trashing yourself, and I'm doubly sick of others trashing you! You enforce the laws, you punish those who break them, and you destroy criminals that need destroying. Sometimes you win, sometimes you need help, sometimes . . . oh, I am so glad I was there to prevent the 'sometimes you lose' part, Jacob, because I don't know what I'd do if—" She broke off, rubbing the heel of her palm briskly over each eye to stem the moisture welling up once more.

"And, let me tell you this, Jacob. If I end up one of these Demon cops, some attitudes around here are going to change. You understand? It's called public relations, and if the public doesn't start to relate to you with the proper respect real damn quick, they're going to have to answer to me. I'm fed up with the way they treat you, just as I'm fed up with being referred to as 'the human,' as someone might refer to 'the smallpox.'

Your people are stuck up, snobby, prejudiced dorks, and they need some serious lessons in manners."

"I see," he said quietly, hints of amusement in his voice.

"*What* do you see?" she asked, sitting back on her heels and crossing her arms beneath her breasts defensively.

"I see," he repeated, sitting up to come nose to nose with her, "what they mean when they say: 'You are beautiful when you are angry.'" He punctuated the observation by weaving a hand into her thick hair at the back of her head and pulling her forward against his mouth. He kissed her gently but thoroughly, leaving her breathless and flushed by the time he pulled back to look at her.

"Oh. That," she murmured breathily.

"And this."

He pulled her mouth to his again, this time sliding his tongue past her lush lips and teasing the tiny mate she withheld, coaxing her into playing with him inside her mouth. She sighed softly, her sweet breath skidding delightfully over his taste buds. She responded to him so easily, so fully, as usual holding nothing back and showing no hesitation. Her trust in him was implicit.

He pulled away from her tempting lips reluctantly, his hands flexing around fistfuls of her silky hair. He pressed his mouth to her forehead, her cheeks, the brooms of her eyelashes, all the while listening to how she breathed, then how her breath would stop in little anticipatory hitches as he moved to a new target.

That fairylike touch of her fingers was drifting over his skin once more, tracing the curves and ridges of his muscles on his bare chest, making each and every one twitch in stimulation. Jacob released her hair, drawing his fingertips along either side of the supple curve of her jaw until they met up on her chin. Then he moved down to her throat, gently stroking the fresh bruises and thin red line where the knife had cut her. He didn't know how many hours he'd been unconscious, how many hours she'd had to heal before he could see the wound. He didn't want to think about how deep it might have been to start.

Stop. Please.

Did he hurt you badly, sweetheart? Are you all right?

I'm fine. Strangely, it didn't hurt half so much as it probably should've. Pretty funny considering how I used to wail over a paper cut.

Hey, I have had paper cuts. They hurt like a bitch.

She laughed, the bright burst cutting away at his distress, leaving him smiling just for the sound of it.

"You know what?"

"What?" he asked.

I think I'm beginning to really like having you here, in my head.

Just in your head? He followed the question up with a tug that sat her deeper into the well of his lap, matching heat to heat, making her aware of how she stirred him without even trying and probably always would.

"Jacob," she scolded, giggling in spite of her attempt to admonish him. "We aren't in your home anymore."

"Your point?" he asked, dipping his head to kiss her breastbone with a lazy play of his lips and tongue.

"Well, for one thing, Legna can read our emotions."

"Your point?" he quizzed again, pausing just long enough in his attentions to show off the mischief sparkling in his dark eyes.

"You suck," she laughed, wanting to smack him in

the head, but somehow ending up with her fingers deep in his rich hair.

"Your wish is my command," he noted, just as he nuzzled her shirt aside and caught her nipple up against his tongue.

Isabella exhaled a sharp sigh of pleasure, wriggling slightly to assist his access.

"Okay, so you suck in a good way," she said breathlessly. "Jacob . . . mmm . . . what about Noah?"

"Let him find his own woman. I am not sharing." With that statement, he swung her around and under his body, sprawling her out across the bed and eyeing her as if she were a buffet chock full of delicacies. "Such a tiny body, but you fit so much into it. So full and soft where it should be, and so tasty."

He kissed her belly through her shirt, then drew the fabric up with the sweep of a broad palm and kissed her again. He enjoyed the way her stomach clenched and quivered, rose and danced as he teased with mouth, lips, and tongue, painting erotic designs with the press of each. His mouth touched the waistband of her jeans and he stopped and sighed.

Do you never wear skirts?

Well, excuse me, but I haven't exactly been home for my wardrobe of late. I'm lucky enough that Legna got these for me or I guarantee you, you wouldn't be enjoying anything about the state of my laundry. Now stop bugging me and go on with that whole kissing thing.

Jacob laughed, muffling the burst of delight in the softness of her stomach, making her squirm under the interesting vibration it caused.

You have been trying to boss me around from the moment I met you!

Well, if you'd just listen, I wouldn't have to get bossy about it.

He reached up and slowly freed the fly of her pants, parting it to reveal more of her delightful belly and the beginnings of black, springy curls.

Ah, this is better. No panties.

Isabella giggled as his hands came under her and cupped her bottom, holding her hips still as he traveled the line from her belly button to those curls with his mouth.

Jacob, what are you doing?

Trying to figure out exactly what it is going to take to get you to stop laughing.

In the next second, he had shucked her jeans off completely, ignoring the fact that she was so overwhelmed with laughter that she was flushed a rosy red and gasping for breath.

Well, stop tickling me, then!

Oh, is that what I am doing? Then I will stop.

He kept his word. The next place his mouth touched her didn't tickle in the least. Isabella gasped in utter shock, her laughter dying sharply and her body jerking. Jacob paused, his long lashes flicking up to reveal his black eyes, clearly watching her as he teased her with a gentle tasting.

"Jacob," she said, her voice a tangle of trepidation and curiosity.

His large hands slid over her thighs, making her feel so vulnerable and so small as he eased her tense legs a little farther apart, exposing the flowering core of her to his mouth and his caressing fingertips. Isabella felt the room suddenly spinning out from under her as she was dragged into an entirely new vortex of sensation and pleasure.

It was a profound moment when she realized the depth of artistry there was to be found in lovemaking.

Or was it just lovemaking with Jacob? He was so sure of himself, so intent on the smallest touch, the simplest detail, increasing the magnitude, adding layers to create complexity. As he touched her one way, he tasted her in another. If she made the slightest sound of pleasure, he followed it, increased it, turning up the volume until she was close to screaming.

The surge of need in his thoughts and his reaction to her response washed over her as she reached for his perspective. She was in his mind, and so she knew how the taste of her on his tongue sharpened the needs of the beast within. She drifted off into the miasma that was her coherent thoughts as tides of new sensation washed up on her body. Such pleasure—close to what she'd already learned, yet different. Her nerveless fingers flexed where they were buried in his hair, the euphoria crouching inside of her like a hunting cat lying in wait, half of her wanting to scream at him to stop, that she couldn't bear it, the other half writhing and reaching for more.

She was wild beneath his hands and mouth. She couldn't hold still, constantly arching and twisting, the sounds bursting from her as primal as the arousal clawing through his body. He wanted her to burst free, to soar. She pushed him to his limits, her capacity for back-building before her release astounding. He leapt into her torrid mind, adding mental to physical, flooding her with image after erotic image of his memories of their initial joining, of what his release into her had felt like, sensation that nothing else in the world could come close to.

Isabella ignited. Her back arched and locked in one long, inconceivable spasm. She shrieked on a breath that went on and on, just as her release rode the top of the world in one endless shattering of time. She'd barely come to the drop off her crest when Jacob covered her with himself, his mouth engaging hers wildly, sharing the taste of her pleasure even as he thrust into her body with a brutality of urgency.

His hands gripped the bed violently, his nails tearing through the fabric audibly as he drove into her hot, reaching body. Still she cried out, every sound tearing him apart, reducing his world to nothing but her wildness and his response to it—nothing but the intense thrusting rhythm of his passion, which she matched with not only acceptance, but urgent bodily requests of her own. The sweet, hot flesh that surrounded him clasped at him in an insistent embrace, so eager and wild, doubling the sensation of every movement he made into her.

When she suddenly locked up once more, her hoarse wail of ecstasy snapping every last thread of sanity he had, he became ground zero, a cataclysm of excess that turned him completely inside out and back again.

He collapsed on top of her even as her limbs dropped weakly away from him and onto the bed. They lay together, gasping violently for breath, their hearts slamming into the press of the other's chest, their perspiration pooling onto her body one drop at a time.

Jacob turned his face into the curve of her neck, which had become like home to him, and knew what it meant to be complete. He wanted to laugh, to shout, to cry and dance, to sing and swear in every language he knew. The mishmash of impulses was so ludicrous that he did laugh, albeit breathlessly. But after a minute or two, the laughter came easier and stronger, until he was scooping her up and rolling her on top of himself so he could sprawl across the entire width of the bed, throw back his head, and laugh until the rafters shook.

Noah glanced up at the stone ceiling above him, smiling and chuckling. He had known something was up when Legna had hightailed it out of the house as if her shoes were on fire and the nearest water miles away. His suspicion had been confirmed when his home became the epicenter of a minor earthquake. And now, listening to Jacob laugh in a way he could not recall having heard before, he felt a calm settle over him. Destiny, as was Her wont, had been satisfied.

The Enforcer, the unloved, the undesirable . . . no longer existed.

"Amen," Noah whispered.

CHAPTER EIGHT

The ground shook beneath Elijah's booted feet, the only warning of Jacob's arrival. He looked at the necromancer chained spread-eagle to the wall and smiled wolfishly.

"Uh-oh," he offered as the ground shook more violently.

The necromancer's eyes widened slightly as plaster dust dribbled down onto his head. Elijah sat down, his wicked grin widening as he lifted his feet onto the table in front of him, crossing them at the ankles and rocking back onto the rear legs of his chair.

Elijah gave major kudos to Jacob for his subsequent dramatic entrance. The dirt floor of the cellar erupted like a volcano, spouting up soil and one mightily ticked-off Earth Demon. Then every last particle of earth sucked back into the hole Jacob had made, packed as tightly as it had been before he had disrupted it.

Jacob floated two feet off the ground, his blackened pupils flaring with menace and rage, the sheer power of his presence pressing at the air in the room. Jacob finally touched down on the ground, still saying nothing as he looked the necromancer over from head to toe. He gave Elijah a look over his shoulder, a silent message to the warrior that he had noted something significant already. Elijah could make an educated guess. This necromancer wasn't the one Jacob had been expecting to see, wasn't the one from the warehouse.

That didn't change the fact that this necromancer was in deep trouble.

"Is this the creature that dared to put his hands on my mate?"

Of course it was, but Elijah appreciated good theatrics. He nodded to Jacob, his expression suitably grave. "I haven't harmed him, knowing that it would be your due."

Jacob turned back to the necromancer. "Did you find the weapon he struck me with?"

"No. Not yet."

"You won't find it," the necromancer blurted out, his tone far too cocky for an idiot chained to a wall at the mercy of two incredibly powerful Demons, one of which was clearly in the mood to bash his head in.

"It does not matter. You will never again have the opportunity to use it," Jacob noted smoothly.

"Brave words coming from a coward too scared to meet me on even ground," the necromancer hissed.

In the blink of an eye Jacob had closed the distance between them, snarling in the magic-user's face, displaying a rare show of normally retracted fangs.

"Brave stupidity coming from a coward who tried to use a female to trap me," Jacob growled with clearly suppressed rage. "Do you know what my kind does to your kind when they threaten something so precious to them?"

"Whatever it is monsters do. I wouldn't know," the

necromancer spat. "You make yourselves appear like us, but you're fooling no one. I've seen what you really look like when you're stripped of your disguises!"

Again, Jacob shot that brief look at Elijah. The warrior dropped his feet to the floor, standing up so suddenly the necromancer jolted in fear. When the Warrior Captain rose to his full height in anger, it had an effect that could quell any man alive. The blond behemoth looked as if he could crush the world between his hands, and his bright emerald eyes held the rage it would take to do it.

"Would you care to explain how you have seen that?" Jacob asked, his slick voice clearly hiding menace behind the politely phrased question.

"I've seen a lot of things," the necromancer boasted. "I've seen vampires conflagrate in the sun, I've seen a werewolf implode from being shot by a silver bullet. I've seen your kind slavering and drooling entombed in a simple pentagram marked on the floor. This human make-up you wear starts to dissolve very rapidly after you're summoned."

"Actually, now that we are going to kill you, it does not matter what you know. It will die with you," he stated, shrugging his shoulders and smiling with obvious enjoyment over the idea.

"Fine, but you'll never get all of us. We've been prepared for getting caught."

"I see. So we are some kind of association, are we?" Jacob smiled that slightly fanged smile again. "I am six hundred years old, necromancer. Do you have any idea how long that really is? I have seen your kind come and go. The Demon not a foot away from you has forgotten more ways of defeating your kind than you can ever imagine." Jacob leaned so close to the necromancer's face that the magic-user could see the grain of his irises.

He'd been told these demonic creatures had awesome power. All he'd needed was a name. It would've given him more power than any of the others had captured, the necromancer thought as he looked at his intended target. He knew the possibilities of power the vessel held, and his failure screamed with rage in his head.

"And yet, with all this longevity and all of our power," Jacob continued, his tone deceptively intellectual, as if he were teaching a class, "we do not threaten other races. Unless an individual or society acting as a whole against us gives us cause. But your kind, attempting to pervert our powers for yourselves . . . to what end, I do not even wish to imagine. From what you say, ours is not the only race you hunt, destroy with malice and without justification. Tell me now, necromancer, which of us is the monster?"

"You want justification? Just look at yourselves! Look at how I found you!"

Jacob lifted a brow casually, not betraying in any way how much he wanted that particular bit of information.

"You say you don't destroy—well, what about the earthquake in Dover that led me to you? Yeah, we know what things you are capable of, so we know that sometimes natural disasters aren't all natural. Whenever there's an earthquake, a tsunami, an unusually violent storm, a plague, or wildfire, we know there's a likelihood one of you animals is at its epicenter. You're so easy to track and you don't even know it!" The necromancer barked out a laugh. "This isn't six hundred years ago, pal. Technology has caught up with you. You can't hide anymore. How much property damage did you rack up in that little quake you caused, demon?

How many injuries? Deaths? That one was minor,
but how many weren't so minor? Why'd you even do
it? Were you playing around? Showing off to your
she-bitch?"

Elijah moved literally with the speed of the wind to
place a restraining hand on Jacob's shoulder when the
necromancer's reference to Isabella struck the Enforcer hard. Elijah was certain that normally the other
Demon wouldn't have been so sensitive to mere insults,
but Elijah suspected the slim truths behind the necromancer's conjecture were throwing Jacob off balance.

"That is so like a human," Jacob said quietly, his
voice low and wintry, "to pass judgment on a people
just because they are different. You cannot take the
time to understand them, viewing them as a threat just
because they were born somehow a little stronger or a
little smarter. Ignorance and fear, the age-old call signs
of the oppressors of your species. You will not succeed
this time. Not with us. And I will see to it not with any
other race in the night world.

"From this day forward, your kind will no longer feel
safe. You think we are so easy to track? Your stench carries for miles. Did you know that? *We* can smell you,
necromancer. When you are shopping, playing, con-
niving, or rutting, you will always be vulnerable to us
simply by your stink, something you will never be able
to hide or get rid of. How many times have you caught
one of us with these so-called technologies and wondrous tracking skills? Once? Twice? Because, somehow,
by accident, one of us made the oh-so-rare mistake of
losing focus, or one of our young has not yet learned
total control over that which nature saw fit to give us?"

"You keep thinking that. It's not the only way, and I
know it as well as you, demon. A minute more and that

soft-necked mate of yours would've been screaming your name from the rooftops, making you prey to any necromancer for the rest of your days . . . which I promise you could be as short or as long as we want it to be."

This time Elijah had no hope of restraining Jacob. The Demon turned to dust in order to pass over him, rematerializing with a roar of outrage and a hand slamming into the necromancer's throat, smacking his head into the unforgiving stone wall behind him.

"She does not know my name, necromancer! Our mates never do, for this reason in specific. And I swear to you, you will answer for the harm you have visited upon her. In ways you could never imagine no matter how long I leave your pathetic carcass chained to this wall. Mark me, magic-user. The next breath you take, and every one after that, is yours only because *I* decide you should have it. Remember that the next time you think to speak of my woman."

With that, Jacob released the gasping necromancer, burst into dust, and left with a shattering of tectonic plates that nearly brought the cellar and the house above it down on the prisoner.

Isabella sighed softly, stirring between the sheets, enjoying the coming-awake feel of the warm and cold spots as she slid her limbs over the fabric. She stretched, yawning ferociously, feeling blindly for the warm male body that for some reason was not draped over her. When her search turned up empty air, she lifted her head from under the pillow and blinked against the sunlight pouring into the room. She groaned, covering her eyes with a slack hand.

"I see you have already become adjusted to the night."

Isabella gasped, sitting up and twisting around at the same time to face the voice that had addressed her. A second later she remembered how she was dressed, or rather, not dressed, and yanked the sheet up over her breasts as she glared at Gideon.

"What are you doing in here?"

"A Demon of the Body can go anywhere he chooses." He flicked that crystal gaze over her slowly. "And do not continue to try to sense me as you do others of my kind. I am too far away."

Isabella blinked, trying to figure out how sitting in a chair at the end of the bed could be considered too far away.

"It is called astral projection," Gideon explained. "It is how we of the Body travel. The separation of the soul from the body, existing in two places at once. But, unlike the human conceptions of the insubstantiality of astral projection, I can touch, see, smell, hear, and taste anything I want to in this form."

"That doesn't explain why you're seeing . . . I mean . . . sitting in my bedroom."

"I needed to meet with you."

"Says who?"

"No one. Yet. But it is only a matter of time before Noah and the others come to me and ask me to assess you."

"And I repeat, you felt you needed to do this in the privacy of my room while I slept? Improperly clothed, I might add? This won't go very far toward mending the rift between you and Jacob."

The Demon's eyes narrowed on her, and she suppressed a smug smile.

"What, exactly, has he told you about that?"

"Actually," she confessed, "he didn't. You did."

"I?" That irritating lift of one silvery brow.

"Yeah. Remember, you said it was a good thing he was unconscious because he probably wouldn't like you healing him? Which, by the way, he didn't even think about when he learned of it."

"No?"

"No. If I had to put a word to his feelings on the matter . . . he seemed accepting."

"I see."

Gideon's eyes roamed over her slowly. She was far too small for a Druid. But he could see the mark on her clear as day; there was no mistaking it. And her power was growing stronger by the minute. Even in these few hours she had changed, become more potent in the ways she already knew and in ways she hadn't yet discovered.

Gideon could also see Jacob's brand on her, could smell him on her body, imbedded in her pores and her chemistry for all time. He hadn't had time to notice earlier, but it was clear they were mated. The Enforcer had broken the very taboos he was sworn to protect. The ones he'd once upheld above his friendship with the Ancient. Not that Gideon hadn't known, that painful eight years ago, that Jacob had been in the right in the actions he'd taken against him. The Enforcer had done what his duty called for. He'd put respect and friendship aside, had even faced incredible peril to his life, all to protect the human female who had become the target of Gideon's momentarily warped reality. Gideon held no ill will toward the Enforcer, but his pride had been bruised and, for the first time in a millennium, he had discovered a fear of something.

It had brought him low to realize that one could have ultimate power, a millennium's worth of knowledge and experience, and still succumb to the basest of behaviors. He had thought himself forever above such things. Now he feared himself like he never had before. His isolation had been to protect others, not to punish Jacob. It was calming to know that Jacob held no apparent grudges. What was disturbing was that the intuitive little hybrid woman had somehow known he'd needed to know that.

"I am here to speak of the matter of your existence. I apologize for what you clearly perceive as rudeness. I ask that you remember my culture is not yours. Privacy, though valued in our culture, is expected to be disrupted. You see, we do not use the technologies of your species, such as telephones and cars and the like. I am sure you have noticed."

"I had noticed," she said.

"So we come and go with a different convention in this culture. Most of us are born with our own inherent means of long-distance travel and communication." Gideon indicated his presence. "You could call our lack of protocol for privacy a cultural weakness if you wish. Which brings me to you. You, apparently, are a sign of new weakness."

"I beg your pardon?" *Not only does he invade my privacy, now he insults me?*

"Yes. It has always been foretold that a Demon mating with a human would bring about repercussions."

"Those were fables," Isabella countered. "I discovered a prophecy—"

"Yes, I know all about that. They are not fables. Not entirely. There is always a grain of truth in everything. You may take that wisdom with you as fact, from one who would know."

Isabella nodded. The one thing she could not argue

was that he knew a hell of a lot more than she did. "So tell me, what is so terrible about all of this? Will it hurt Jacob?"

It didn't escape Gideon that she didn't even think to ask about herself, even in the face of all the drastic changes and discoveries she'd been undergoing.

"Before we can discuss this, you must be willing to accept what I am saying to you as truth. As fact. Not as conjecture or guesswork. What I tell you, I know. Otherwise, I will not speak of it. It is my way."

"Well, I suppose in the fifteen minutes total that I've been in the same room with you, I've found you to be an apparently candid person. Smart. Wise, if you prefer. Certainly old enough to know. Say, how old are you anyway?"

"That is irrelevant."

"Oh." Isabella rolled her eyes. "Okay, let's just speed this up so you can go back to your own body or whatever. I'll take what you say as fact until I hear otherwise."

"No one can refute me."

"We'll see."

It would have to do, Gideon realized. She was incredibly stubborn. Willful. It was a wonder Jacob tolerated her. He decided to test her mettle right off.

"You are immortal."

Isabella opened her mouth to argue, thought better of it, and then pursed her lips together briefly in irritation. "How?" she countered.

"Druids are immortal. You are half Druid. Therefore, you are immortal."

"I almost died as a child, when they were taking my tonsils out."

"I did not say you could not be killed. Immortal, to us, means long lived. Not indestructible. Although I promise you, it will not be so easy to destroy you now."

"And you know this so certainly how?"

"I thought we agreed you would not question me," Gideon sighed, sounding very put upon.

"Humor me," she parried.

"Immortals have a specific genetic code. As a Demon of the Body, I can sense that code on you. Just as I know that it is the waking of dormant DNA that is the cause of the changes you are experiencing."

"It is?" Isabella asked, her surprise clear in her tone. "But why did it wake up?"

"An excellent question," Gideon complimented, honestly pleased with her quickness of mind. "It woke the moment you came into contact with Jacob."

"How?"

Isabella and Gideon both looked up at the deep-voiced question, seeing Jacob standing just inside the open window, feet braced apart, his expression tense.

"Jacob!" Isabella reacted explosively, bursting off the bed in a flurry of sheet fabric, catapulting herself at Jacob, who opened his arms to catch her. He wrapped her up in his embrace, lifting her feet up off the floor and swinging her slightly as he chuckled over her enthusiastic greeting. She reached for his mouth eagerly, banishing the other Demon from her thoughts completely.

Jacob couldn't resist her, even though he was well aware of the ice-colored gaze studying him intently. He received her buss happily and returned it, but was very consciously wrapping fabric around her bare back, protecting her body from Gideon's unwelcome eyes. For a moment, he basked in the feel of warm bare skin under loose, thin cotton. Then he scooped her dangling legs up into his arms and moved her back to the bed, seating himself on it, Isabella on his lap, and pulling a quilt from the foot of the bed to wrap her up in. She rested her cheek contentedly on his shoulder, snuggling into his ministering touch. Once they were settled, his hand went to her hair, stroking it in an absently affectionate manner.

Gideon watched all of this with no little surprise. He remembered having one or two discussions over the centuries with Jacob about how neither of them felt the desire for a female companion. Even if they had been so inclined, relationships between those who were immortal were complicated and taxing. If one loved and lived with a mate for centuries, the loss of that mate was devastating. Gideon and Jacob both had lost large families, living to see parents and siblings and their siblings' children all perish. Wars, Summonings, and hunts. Demons who'd survived the wars with the Vampires and the Lycanthropes, endured the strange trickery of the Shadowdwellers with its morbid outcomes and the most devastating obliteration of the war with the Druids, had to now face lives completely empty of those they loved. After so many centuries, it just became too difficult to take risks again. Why enter relationships and invest one's emotions? Marriage was rare and sexual relationships sometimes limited only to the weeks of the Hallowed moons, when they were so compelled.

Love was left to the young and foolish . . .

And the Imprinted.

In light of the fact that it was a half-Druid female sitting in Jacob's lap, Gideon shouldn't have been so surprised. Still, she was completely outside of a culture that defined every part of who Jacob was. But there was no help for it. Forces far beyond even the power of Demons had made the match.

Jacob was looking up at Gideon now that he had settled his woman comfortably in the protection of his embrace. Gideon knew he was waiting for a response to his query as certainly as he knew Jacob was displeased at finding him in a room with his mate while she was unclothed. Gideon was unrepentant. He had his reasons, and he didn't need to defend himself.

"You asked how it is that you awoke her latent abilities? Without going into too complex a list of details, there is a code written on your DNA that, when in proximity to hers, triggers massive systemic alterations in her DNA and similar ones in yours, though on a smaller scale."

"In mine? I am no different," Jacob insisted.

"You have noticed no new abilities?"

"No. I would recognize if something had changed."

Jacob, you've forgotten something.

What, little flower?

You do have a new ability. You're using it right now.

Jacob went still, his fingers flexing in her hair as he looked down into her face. Her eyes were full of encouragement, brimming with acceptance.

"Isabella has just reminded me of a power that is new to me," Jacob said quietly.

Gideon leaned forward in his chair a little. "Telepathy," he stated. "That would suit not only what I know, but the prophecy as well. This is one of the first signs."

"I also seem to have an empathy where enemies are concerned," Bella noted.

"No, you do not."

"Oh, I am *so* going to hit him," Isabella growled to Jacob, her eyes flashing with violet anger. "How would you know?" she snapped.

"You clearly do not recall our agreement about accepting what I say as fact," Gideon noted calmly.

"Bella, love," Jacob said gently, "a Demon of the

Body of Gideon's age and abilities can simply look at you and see your powers." He turned dark eyes on Gideon, knowing a look of warning would be lost on the Ancient. "Gideon is merely stating facts as he sees them; he does not mean to be insulting. He is an extremely literal being. Unlike your culture, ours does not subvert meaning behind words. We are a very direct species, and though many of us have adapted our language tendencies to suit human sensibilities, Gideon is the oldest among us, as well as one of the most isolative. Because of this, he is far less diplomatic than what you are used to from the rest of us."

"Yeah, sure," Isabella acquiesced, but she wasn't feeling too warmly about it.

"For my part, Isabella, I will make an effort to remember there are nuances to your language that I am not skilled with. I am hoping you will bear with me." Gideon's largesse apparently served him well. Isabella truly did relax then, nodding with honest acceptance this time. Gideon sat back once more before continuing. "Tell me about the latest incident with the necromancer. In detail."

Isabella and Jacob did, jointly, with Isabella giving the more in-depth account and Jacob adding the impressions he had gleaned off the imprisoned necromancer.

"You say you tasted blood in your mouth, but there was none?"

"Yes," Isabella confirmed.

"Do you not see a parallel?"

"No." Bella felt the telltale flex of Jacob's hand and shot into his mind. "Your injuries? You struck your mouth on the dresser," she read from him. "But that happened afterward."

"Premonition. It is not empathy . . . it is premonition! You sense the future, Bella," Jacob realized in a rush. "Of course! You smelled smoke, sulfur; you were choking on it that night before we even got to the warehouse, but the smoke did not occur until my attack on the necromancer broke his concentration and Saul broke free of the spell."

"So last night, I was feeling the tension of our encounter with the necromancer a few minutes before it actually happened?"

"Something along those lines, yes. And the wound in my mouth. You tasted what I was going to taste in just a few minutes."

"Eww. Yuck. What a sucky power! What good is premonition so soon before it actually happens?"

"Increased time between premonition and occurrence, as well as understanding of what you are seeing, comes with time, training, and experience," Gideon informed her.

"Terrific. And after all that time I spent thinking turning twenty-one was the biggest milestone of my life. Thanks." She indulged in her infamous eye roll, making Jacob chuckle.

"Premonition is an anomaly for a Druid, but I noticed the genetic disposition for it when I took your hand. You see, Druids had . . ." He corrected himself. "Druids *have* specific abilities, just as any race inherently does. It is written on us all in code for all time, unchanged, with the exceptions of evolution and mutation, of course. Now, it is possible that the centuries of human and Druid breeding that led to who and what you are now has caused some unexpected mutations, a supposition supported by your unusual ability of premonition.

"Like ourselves, Druids draw strength from nature.

For example, your increased senses, the ability to heal rapidly, and extraordinary endurance. Your new instinctual fighting skills are an anomaly as well, but it is purely from nature that you borrow the ability to sense the presence of power, especially of evil. It is an intuition not too unlike that of any prey sensing the proximity of the predator."

"The necromancer. She sensed him when I could not because of premonition?" Jacob frowned. "I still do not entirely understand how I was unable to track him before his initial strike, though."

"You lacked nothing, Jacob, except information. There are many Demons who live in isolation. If they were Summoned, no one would be the wiser. It was only a matter of time before the necromancers seized someone closer to your attention."

"So how does this indicate I was not lacking something?"

"I recently discovered that Lucas, the Elder, is missing. I presume Summoned."

Jacob sucked in his breath, his body going so tight that Isabella was compelled to hug him in comfort. He absently returned the gesture as he looked down into her eyes. "Lucas is an Elder Demon of the Mind. If they have him imprisoned, he will teleport them anywhere they desire, allowing them to pop up without warning."

"But there was no smoke or that sulfuric smell like when Legna teleports."

"Elders do not leave that display behind. Their skills are such that they can transport themselves and others quite cleanly. As long as Lucas is under their sway, he can transport anyone who forces him to with no warning, and this is another reason why our safety is terribly imperiled. Especially anyone Lucas is or was closely acquainted with."

"Let us focus on the question of Bella's powers," Jacob said hastily. "Is there anything else we can expect?"

"Unfortunately, yes."

"*Unfortunately*?" she repeated.

"I am, of course, speaking from the perspective of a Demon who was once a part of the war with the Druids. I will attempt to refrain from casting any further bias on the matter."

"You do that," Isabella encouraged dryly.

"I am not the only one who will reflect that bias when knowledge of this power becomes widespread. You may meet with some prejudice."

Again her eyes went heavenward. "As opposed to what I got for just being the *human*?"

"Perhaps I am understating. You could be considered enough of a threat to renew the hostilities that set Demon and Druid at odds in the first place. Your life could be in danger."

"Wait a minute, I thought harming humans was bad," Bella said, wriggling when Jacob's grip on her arm became uncomfortably tight. She didn't have to read his mind to know what he was feeling.

"You are not entirely human. Do not mistake me; we have evolved a great deal since those times. But we have our fanatics just as any other society does. Though we like to think ourselves evolved beyond certain behaviors, fear can be a powerful motivator."

"Just tell us," Jacob demanded quietly.

"She can dampen power. It works on any supernatural being. Necromancer, Vampire, Lycanthrope . . ."

"Demon."

"Yes," Gideon confirmed. "And it will not just be a

dulling, unless the mix of her heritage has changed this. She can literally render them temporarily powerless. You see, when the ability comes to life in you, Isabella, it will always be on. The skill will be for you to shut it off. It was this capability that allowed the Druid monarch to kill the Demon King. They met under peaceful pretenses. When they were alone, the Druid dampened the Demon's power and murdered him."

"Oh my God. How did you ever trust each other? Knowing they had such superiority over you, how could you share a culture with them? And how did you ever eradicate a race of people you couldn't even get close to without becoming totally powerless?"

Gideon hesitated, for the first time showing a very human compulsion to be subversive. Isabella felt Jacob drawing to even sharper attention. ·

"Firstly, it was not a matter of trust so much as it was a matter of necessity. Druids and Demons were meant to have a symbiotic relationship. A Druid needs a Demon to bring its power to life. A Demon needs a Druid to dampen its power."

"Why would a Demon want to willingly have . . . ? Oh my. The moon madness," Isabella answered herself.

"Yes, this is a large part of it, though our ancestors dealt with a different degree of this. However, if we review the warnings about the risks involving mating with humans, you might find an equally compelling reason." Gideon's eerie eyes flicked from Isabella to Jacob. "Evidence to the fact was littered across your home last evening, Jacob. Had she been merely human, the loss of control you experienced could have been deadly not only for her, but also for others in the vicinity. Luckily, your power is already coming awake, Isabella. Considering the quiet degree of it and the circumstances of those . . . less focused moments . . . you have not noticed it.

"As for the eradication of the Druids, it was not an easy task. War never is. However, Druids have their weaknesses just as Demons do and, suffice it to say, they were thoroughly exploited." Gideon held up a staying hand when Jacob would have questioned him. "It comes to this," he said at last, "and this is what I must reveal to the Council: Demons were never meant to find their mates entirely amongst one another. They were meant to find the majority of them in the Druids. In destroying the Druids, we sacrificed knowing what it meant to find the perfect complementary spirit. I believe humans refer to it as a soul mate. We refer to it as Imprinting. It is why so many of us are so solitary, and why so many of us cannot find comfort in a member of the opposite sex . . . why there has not been an Imprinting in centuries . . .

"Until now," he countered himself with reverence in his tone. "Jacob, you find yourself providential among all Demons. It is why from the moment you met, the two of you have been unable to resist being a part of the other. Imprinting is a glorious and compelling intensity and it cannot be forestalled. When a Demon and Druid meant to be Imprinted come into contact, it immediately triggers the DNA alterations I mentioned. So you see, you are destined to meet for this purpose before you are even born, prophecy notwithstanding."

Isabella was staring at the Ancient with wide eyes, but what she was focused on was Jacob's emotional reaction. He had turned his face completely into her hair and a sensation of euphoria that was equal parts agony washed through him.

"This brings us to your weaknesses, Isabella," the

medic continued, oblivious to the emotions crashing through the couple he lectured. "Once a Druid comes into power after being triggered by a Demon, they must have a regular dose of exposure to that Demon from that moment on, somewhat like a human who must absorb sunlight for their health."

"You mean, Jacob is sort of like . . . a vitamin for me?" Bella asked numbly.

"It would be more accurate to say he is like an energy source. His presence recharges you, especially after large expenditures of your abilities. Without that recharge . . . well, you are aware of what happens to a battery that loses its charge."

"It dies," Isabella whispered, a sensation of dreadful trepidation washing over her. "Did you . . . do you mean to say that . . . Did you defeat the Druids by depriving them of their energy sources? You"—she swallowed hard—"you starved them to death?"

"It is worse than that, Bella," Jacob rasped, his voice rough and airless as horror dawned in his eyes. "It means they starved their *Imprinted soul mates* to death. Sweet Destiny, Gideon, how could you destroy the creatures you needed and loved the most?"

"Few did so willingly. Almost none, in fact. It was left to those of us without mates to impress the dictate upon them."

"Jacob . . ." Isabella gasped, trembling in his hold and shuddering with her thoughts.

"I am not proud of this history, Druid," Gideon said quietly. "I was a member of the forces delegated to imprisoning reluctant members of my own species, thereby forcing them to kill their beloved mates. It is no excuse to say I was a mere fledgling at the time, either. I can only beg you to forgive us for our barbarism as anyone might forgive a society for the mistakes it made when it was young. And though I ask no pity for it, we have suffered equally for our folly. After the war, the rash of suicides that followed almost destroyed us in populace. Today, we live loveless, incomplete lives with madness dogging our heels. Just deserts, one might say."

Isabella could not conceive of what she was hearing. Her head filled with images of Demons imprisoned by their own kind, their souls screaming for the mates they knew were starving to death without them. She herself, even after only these few days, couldn't imagine what it would be like to be forced away from Jacob.

"You have kept all of this to yourself all these centuries, Gideon?" Jacob asked hoarsely. "Do you know the implications of Isabella's existence?"

"Yes. I am aware of it."

Isabella turned questioning eyes to Jacob. His lips were white at the edges with his tension. "It means, Bella, that Druids have existed all of this time, and however watered down they may be, some of them very likely could have crossed paths with their Demon counterparts. And since neither would be aware of it, the Druid would have died inexplicably from the deprivation that ensued afterward. It also means . . ." Isabella felt him shudder with revulsion. "It means that all of these centuries as Enforcer, I may have been depriving Demons instinctually drawn to other human-Druid hybrids of their one true mate. Gideon, how could you keep such a thing to yourself?" he demanded.

"I did not know until my encounter with you, Isabella, that such a thing existed. As far as I knew, I had seen my last Druid a thousand years ago. Believe me, Enforcer, I am potently aware of what the ramifications of my silence about our history may have caused. I do

not need your condemnation to supplement my own."
The Body Demon at last rose to his feet, looking very
much as though he moved under the weight of his
information. "I will have Noah convene the Council
this evening. I will repeat all I have told you there. Mark
me well, Enforcer. Your mate will potentially be in
danger once I do this. It is because I owed you a great
debt that I came to warn you first. You must also take
measures that see to your own safety. Isabella will not
survive long if something should happen to you."

With that statement and a sharp wink of silver light,
Gideon left.

CHAPTER NINE

Jacob was beset by a sensation of weight pressing into his chest. There was no easy way to take in the thousands of ramifications that came with the knowledge Gideon had imparted. However, being that it was his culture and his world, he imagined he was far better equipped to deal with it than the silent woman who sat with her knees tucked up close to her chest as she leaned back against the headboard.

What could he possibly say to her in that moment? He had been responsible for everything that had been happening to her, for the complete upheaval of a life she was now realizing she could never completely return to. If she was going to live, she was going to have to remain associated with him for the rest of her now considerably extended lifetime, whether she wanted to or not. It wasn't how Jacob had wanted her to feel compelled to remain close to his side, and it sat very ill with him.

"Isabella," he whispered, his remorse heavy on the word.

She looked up, her pretty violet eyes seeming so large, vulnerable, and forlorn.

"I know your mind, Enforcer. Don't make this into yet another reason for you to abuse yourself." She reached to push back the heavy fall of that incredible hair of hers and gave him a wan smile. "You pick the strangest times to respect the privacy of my mind. If you were in here now, you'd know that I don't hold you responsible for all of this."

"How can you not? If we had never met—"

"If we'd never met," she interrupted him, "I'd have gone on living half of a life instead of a complete one. Jacob, what is it you think I'm leaving behind?" She stretched a moment, then climbed off the bed to walk up to him. Her nearness comforted him automatically, filling him with a sensation of peace that was in contradiction with his thoughts.

"All of my life I've never quite fit in. I lived on the fringes of human society, Jacob, a very solitary person with the exception of my sister and her few friends for company. The night I met you I was looking out at the moon, as I had thousands of nights before, and even then I knew there was something about it and the night that held important secrets for me. I spent years reading voraciously, in search of information. I think it was these answers I searched for all of that time. I think it was you I longed for, Jacob."

"I wonder if you would feel that way if you had a choice in the matter," he responded stiffly.

"I do have a choice, Jacob." She reached out and picked up his hand between hers. "I could choose to go back to where I was and slowly waste away. But it would have nothing to do with being deprived of necessary energy, Jacob, and everything to do with being deprived of all the things I have finally discovered with you. Do you have any idea the gift your presence in my life has given me?"

He could imagine that if it was anything like what she had brought to him, it was a very profound one.

"That's right, Jacob," she encouraged softly. "Everything in life is part of some greater plan of fate that none of us knows about until it actually happens."

"I always believed that Destiny gave us free will, Bella. That we all have a choice." He paused, toying with her soft fingers for a moment before bringing them up to the press of his lips. "Yes, I believe in special destinies, but . . . I wanted you to come to me because you chose it, not because you had to."

"Jacob, you aren't listening to me."

"I am! And I do not think you know what you are saying. How can you, in light of all the overwhelming things that have been happening to you?"

She jerked her hand out of his, curling it into a fist that promptly ended up on her hip. "I'm a full-grown woman with a mind of her own, Jacob, that's how! You keep expecting all of this to piss me off, to make me feel trapped, and when I don't, you're disappointed somehow and make every effort to see that I do! Perhaps it isn't me who's having a problem adjusting, Enforcer. I'm beginning to think that you're the one who doesn't want to commit to the implications of having me here."

"That is not true!"

"Then prove it to me. Not with your thoughts, but with your actions and your words. Tell me you want me here, tell me you want me to be part of your life the way I want you to be a part of mine." Her voice trembled and Jacob felt her hurt rush over his skin like little pinpricks. "Tell me I'm not the only one who's learning what it means to love someone else so totally that they finally feel they have a chance at being complete!"

Jacob was speechless for a long minute, his dark eyes wide with his realization. His gaze encompassed her from head to toe, drinking in every minute detail of her and finding nothing that he didn't already adore. He had known that long before this argument. He had very likely fallen in love with her the moment he had felt a passing impression of irreverent thought floating down to him from a window five stories up.

Destiny couldn't have chosen better for him.

Actually, it wasn't his feelings for her that he had ever really doubted. It was himself. Would he be what she needed him to be? Could a male who had lived such a solitary lifestyle, who had spent so much time embedded in work and responsibility have any idea how to treat so vital and loving a woman as she was?

"Isabella, I have never doubted my capacity to love you." He reached under the heavy fall of her hair to wrap a large hand around the back of her neck, drawing her closer to his body so he could feel her warmth. "I am afraid that, in spite of how much I love you, I will not know how to be worthy of it."

"That's because you've never had anyone to tell you how worthy you really are, Jacob. All you've known for these past four hundred years is censure and hostility." Isabella slid her arms around his waist, hugging her body to his with fervent affection. "But I'm here now, and I won't let that happen to you anymore. I'm going to give you so much positive feedback you're going to want to scream. I swear it," she said fiercely, hugging him tighter still. "If you stay with me, I will show you everything I always thought love should be. Stay with me, Jacob."

Jacob pressed his face into her hair, reflecting the

press of profound emotion constricting him as tightly as her arms were. "Gideon was wrong, little flower," he said hoarsely. "Your ability to render me powerless is already living a bright and potent life in you. I can barely speak."

Then don't speak.

She tilted her head back as she filled him with the thought and intense impressions of emotion and desire that floored him. He caught her mouth up against his and kissed her deeply.

I love you, little flower.

The silence in the Council chamber was so heavy, Jacob wondered if gravity had shifted. All were speechless, each barely breathing. Even Ruth, always the one with something quick to say in riposte, was subdued.

Gideon's presence had had a profound impact to begin with, the information revealed to them not withstanding. Jacob imagined it couldn't be easy to hear that the race that was so proud of its purity of breed was actually dooming itself with its ignorant prejudices of both the past and present. When it came down to it, the Demon race was proud of its intelligence and knowledge, as well as its culture and its power. Learning that their ancestors had been capable of atrocities similar to those they had often condemned the "less evolved" human race for was nothing short of painfully horrifying, in as much as it was enlightening.

"It would seem," Noah said, at last breaking the hush, "that our future as a race is going to change dramatically. The Council will need to discuss the ramifications of this in detail. I want it made clear that at this time no one is to approach any human being under any circumstances. The laws that have governed us toward them will remain in place until we can revise them. The Enforcer will still punish those who cannot control that impulse. Is this clear?"

"Clear, and wise," Elijah agreed. "I will loan my warriors to Jacob at a moment's notice should there be any need for it."

"Actually, that brings up something that must be addressed immediately," Noah said. "The Druid, Isabella."

Jacob stiffened in his seat, his fingertips tensing on the tabletop. Noah had not discussed bringing up Isabella to the Council with him. He had been prepared for all Gideon had imparted, but he had no idea what the King was thinking.

"It will be the duty of every person in this room to see to it that Isabella's safety and security amongst our race is paramount. This woman has brought salvation to us. We must recognize that and afford her the respect her actions on our behalf have garnered. It was she who discovered the prophecy, and for no other reason than having our best interest in her heart. We who have not treated her so kindly to date." Noah's eyes flicked to Ruth and a couple of the others, and each had the grace to lower their eyes.

"The prophecy has mapped out her future, and it is our responsibility to see that she fulfills it in good health and spirits." Noah paused long enough to look at his Enforcer. "The role of the Enforcer will change for all time. His responsibilities, already vast, will no doubt triple. Gideon and I have discussed this in great depth, and we feel that Isabella's training as Enforcer should begin immediately."

There was a communal indrawn breath from all sectors of the room, and Noah was highly aware of Jacob's eyes narrowing on him dangerously. Jacob was concerned with Isabella's safety, and Noah didn't blame him. But there was a method to his actions.

"So young? What can she possibly—" Ruth began.

"I do not recall opening the subject to debate," Noah said stonily, the look in his smoky eyes sending a bolt of alarm down Jacob's spine. He could only imagine how Ruth felt being on the receiving end of it. "This is a momentous day in the history of our race," the King continued, instantly shaking off the power he had used to quell Ruth. "This is the day we return all the wrongs we have committed to rights. Isabella will be the first to join our brethren, but she will not be the last. Think of the gift we have been given. At last we have the solution to a peaceful existence." He caught Jacob's gaze and held it intently. "Jacob and Isabella will be the gateway leading us to that future. They will guide us to the Druids we so desperately need. Jacob's blessing has unlocked the future for us all."

If it could have been, the silence in response was even heavier than that of earlier. Jacob swallowed thickly, looking away from Noah as gratitude swam through him. The King had just made a statement that would change the way the Enforcer was viewed for all time.

Enforcers, Jacob corrected himself.

Enforcers.

Isabella threw her head back, releasing a spray of perspiration from her brow. She was drawing in large amounts of air, her body crouching down low to the ground as she caught a telltale movement in her adversary's posture. A moment later, Elijah turned to air and rushed at her violently.

"No fair, you cheating bastard!" she shouted, taking two steps and springing into his attack, diving through the force of his approach as she might dive into water, completely streamlining her small body and allowing him to pass over her without buffeting her in the slightest. She hit the ground in a somersault, rolling up onto her feet with a triumphant cry.

Elijah materialized instantly, his laughter coming a moment earlier than his solidification.

"Damn me, Jacob, but she thinks fast!"

Isabella was jumping up and down, laughing and taunting Elijah. She posed, flexing her tiny biceps as if she were as powerful in shape and musculature as the warrior was.

"Super Druid wins again!"

Jacob was chuckling at her antics, giving Elijah a shrug that asked the warrior what else he might expect from the mate of the Enforcer. Isabella loped across the lawn and sprang into Jacob's waiting arms, her arms winding around his neck as her legs kicked up into his cradling embrace.

"Tell him to stop cheating!" she demanded, kissing him until he was too breathless to do anything but obey.

"Stop cheating," he commanded the warrior before he caught her flighty mouth tightly onto his.

"Oh, brother. Get a room," Elijah barked dryly. "Are we going to train, or are you two going to have public sex?"

Jacob laughed and dropped his eager burden back onto her feet. "When her dampening power kicks in, you are not going to be able to use yours, and neither will anyone else. That's why what she needs to learn is better hand-to-hand combat."

"And diplomacy," she reminded Jacob quickly. "I'm only going to fight if I absolutely have to."

"That is exactly how I approach it," Jacob agreed.

"Just remember, Isabella, fun and games with me and Jacob is one thing. Being forced to cause harm to someone else is a very difficult position to be in."

"Don't patronize me," Isabella snapped suddenly, all humor instantly dismissed as her hands went to her hips and her eyes flashed with indignant irritation. "Or do I have to break your nose again to remind you how, in the moment, I can be very serious about hurting someone else?"

Damn, but she knows how to go straight for a man's ego, Jacob thought with amazement as the warrior flinched visibly. It wouldn't surprise him if her ability to ferret out an adversary's mental weakness wouldn't end up being one of her best talents.

"All right, that is enough training for one day," Jacob announced, circling her hips with an arm and drawing her close to his side.

"Jacob, you promised you'd take me on patrol with you soon. I want to learn how to track properly. I want to watch you work."

"Not yet, little flower."

"When?" she demanded.

"Soon," he promised.

"You don't want me to go with you," she stated suddenly.

Damn this mental connection anyway, Jacob thought irritably.

"It is not that exactly . . ." he started cautiously.

"It's exactly that," she insisted.

Uh-oh, there go the fists on her hips, Jacob thought wryly.

"You're damn right I'm getting my back up," she

responded sharply, making him curse the errant thought. "You don't trust me."

"That is absolutely wrong. Our communication mentally is not perfect as of yet, Bella, so do not think you are reading that right. It is not that I do not trust you, it is just that . . . I am afraid that if I should happen to be threatened, you would not keep a safe distance no matter how much you promised otherwise and you would jump into the fray without any regard for your own safety. Until you have the natural protection you are intended to have for these types of encounters, I will not risk your safety."

"Jacob." Her eyes narrowed on him and he read her impending words from her thoughts before they passed her lips on the way to his ego.

"And do *not* bring up the fact that you have already done battle twice for my benefit if you want to make it through the night without a bruised backside," he warned.

Isabella's temper subsided as she realized what a low blow that would've been, especially knowing how hard Jacob had been on himself as it was. She lowered her eyes, glancing to the right to see if Elijah had made a discreet exit. Of course he hadn't, the big oaf. He was standing there hanging on the entire exchange with far too much amusement in his eyes. For once she wished she were the one who could turn them to dust and spirit them away to a quiet place.

No sooner had the thought crossed her mind than that eerie lightness washed through her. She looked up at Jacob, smiling that he'd so thoughtfully anticipated her need.

But the look on Jacob's face was one of total shock. Suddenly they shot back into their solid forms and

Isabella staggered under the clumsy return of her weight. That was so unlike Jacob. Usually these transitions went quite smoothly.

"It was not me," he said hoarsely.

His dark eyes were wide with unease. He was pushing away from her, spreading out his arms until he was literally touching the surrounding energy. She recognized him extending his senses in a wide blanket, riding the currents of nature, testing its natural rhythms and harmonies for the disturbance of an intruder. Of course, another Earth Demon could easily mask these telltale signs, but it would take an Elder to do so. He was currently one of the only three Elders with the skill, and he knew their energy signatures well enough to recognize that they weren't there.

"Jacob?" Elijah asked, tension radiating from his huge frame in great waves.

Jacob glanced at Elijah and a second later they both transmutated into dust and wind respectively, taking to the sky with blinding speed.

Stay where you are, Jacob demanded.

What's wrong? What's happening, Jacob?

I do not know. Someone just tried to turn you into dust, and it sure as hell was not me.

Isabella felt the ramifications of that possibility keenly. She sat down, her knees suddenly too weak to support her. Was this what Gideon had been afraid of? Was some other Demon trying to hurt her just because of some old hostility toward a race their ancestors had so unjustly persecuted?

No, Bella, this is something else, Jacob assured her gently. *I think it is safe to say that my people have become very accepting of you, and the ramifications you represent, these past days.*

Then who . . . ?

That is what I am trying to figure out. Do you think you can safely reach Noah?

Yes. Of course. It's only across the lawn, Jacob.

Believe me, when it comes to powers such as this, little flower, across the lawn might as well be across the world. Go. Go quickly. He will protect you.

Isabella wasted no time. She stood up and broke into a flat run. Her new strength had turned her into an incredible sprinter and she crossed the acre of lawn to Noah's home in the span of half a minute.

Noah looked up from the discussion over a scroll he was having with two of his scholars when she burst through the door, flushed and breathless. He didn't need to have Jacob's connection with her to know something had rattled her. She looked terribly frightened, an expression he'd never seen on her before.

Even when she had thought Jacob might bleed to death, she'd only shown anger and determination to stop it. This was honest terror in her eyes, and out of instinct Noah's protective magic flared into existence. His house was made from stone and steel along the outside for a reason. It was so nothing could melt when he heated up the outer walls with violent speed as he was doing just then. Anything that touched them would singe itself badly just by nearing the outside of the structure.

"Tell me," he commanded of the little Enforcer.

She did, spilling out everything that had happened in those brief moments. Noah suddenly didn't blame her for her fear. To have some unknown source picking apart the very molecules of her body had to be incredibly disconcerting for her.

"Fetch Legna, Isabella. She should be in her room. Do not worry. You will be safe here with us."

After she hurried off, Noah nodded to the two scholars curtly. The one on his left, of the Body, sat down abruptly, and in a second his astral self launched out of his body. The Mind Demon on his right closed his eyes and disappeared with a soft sucking of displaced air. Noah was proud of how quickly the scholars jumped to obey the task he had set upon every Demon to protect the Druid amongst them.

Isabella wasn't entering a traditional role of Enforcer, with all the apprehension and hostility it came with. His people were practical if nothing else. She represented a change in the one thing they feared the most. The madness of the Hallowed moons, and the insulting punishment that followed, could be a thing of the past. This was a powerful motivator for his people when it came to welcoming the little hybrid into the fold.

Once Isabella returned with Legna, brother and sister took seats opposite one another and slowly began to erect further protections around Noah's stronghold, working in a fluid, tandem dance of one-word instructions. Legna opened herself to the thoughts and intentions of everything within a mile. Noah set up a perimeter of energy-draining force. Legna circled that perimeter with one of dread. Anyone crossing this barrier would be overcome with the urge to run away.

Isabella felt all the hairs on her body tingling as power filled the room. She rubbed at her arms, chilled in spite of the heat Noah was radiating. Legna's upper lip misted with perspiration, very likely because of her proximity to her brother—or perhaps because she was concentrating so hard, extending herself to the very edges of her ability.

Just to protect her.

Isabella was humbled by the thought. She instinctively

moved closer to her protectors, her chilled skin welcoming Noah's ambient heat.

Suddenly, the world flared into her awareness. Isabella's brain was bombarded by a thousand feelings and instincts that weren't her own, each rocketing through her with furious speed. She felt the fear of dozens of animals as the tension in the surrounding area sent them running. She felt arguments, lovemaking, humor, and reverence from people living not too far away, the clamor forcing her to cover her ears in an effort to protect them from the cacophony of emotions. She sensed Jacob's tension, Elijah's outrage. In a moment she discovered the giant warrior Demon had grown fond of her despite everything he showed otherwise to taunt her.

Overwhelmed, Isabella sat down hard on the marble floor, her eyes wide and staring blankly as she tried to push it all away. Self-preservation flared violently to life in her . . .

. . . and then out of her.

A conflagration of flames burst to life all around her, radiating outward in a rapid circular wave of which she was the central focus. Legna screamed. Noah shouted.

And then everything stopped.

CHAPTER TEN

From their patrolling position in the sky, Jacob and Elijah felt the eddy of a tremendous blast of heat. They both solidified, whirling around to seek the source. They were horrified to see a circle of flames bursting out of Noah's home, racing across the lawn, and scorching it instantly to the soil.

Both Demons reacted in an instant. Jacob stretched out his arms and walls of earth shot up to meet the advancing fires. Elijah reached upward to the clouds, and as if throwing a spear, tossed a force of incredible wind at the back of the firewall to make sure it kept going in its present direction, and subsequently its demise, instead of possibly doubling back. The earth closed over the flames, dousing them instantly as it deprived them of oxygen. For good measure, Elijah stirred up a heavy rainfall, dampening everything in a matter of moments.

A heartbeat later they were soaring for Noah's home at top speed.

Jacob noticed immediately that there were no safeguards protecting the home. He knew that if Isabella had begged Noah for shelter and protection it should have been nearly impossible for him to approach. He sought his connection with Isabella, fear clutching at his throat. He'd felt a powerful burst of terror from her a moment before the explosion. But now there was nothing but vacant silence where her warm thoughts should be.

Elijah and Jacob shot through the high windows as arrows of dust and wind, becoming solid again in half a millisecond as they touched the ground.

Horrified, Jacob realized that every last surface in the Great Hall had been scorched black.

And in the center of the blackness lay three bodies.

"Bella!" Jacob yelled, stumbling and skidding over the blackened marble in his haste to gather her unconscious form up in his arms. Through eyes blinded by moist terror, he began to assess her for damage. She was raw and blistered, clearly burned as if she'd been in the sun for hours. Her hair was singed and her clothes melted to her skin, the scent of both choking her mate with outrage.

"It's Noah and Legna!" Elijah knelt beside the King and his sister. They were barely recognizable, their skin and clothes burnt nearly black, Legna's beautiful hair long gone. Jacob looked up from his burden, seeing tears shimmering in Elijah's eyes as he gingerly felt for a pulse in the throat of his monarch.

"Impossible," Jacob said hoarsely. "Noah is immune to fire!"

"We need Gideon. Now!"

Jacob watched as Elijah stood up, his fists clenching, his consciousness reaching out with the most incredible display of power Jacob had ever seen the other Demon use.

* * *

Gideon sensed the disturbance approaching seconds before it struck with wailing hurricane force at the windows of his home. He put aside the book he had been reading and stood up, cocking his head thoughtfully. He was being summoned, and by the power of it he suspected he knew by whom. His brow furrowed at the peculiar prospect, but he wasted no time in opening his door and stepping out into the maelstrom of wind. A moment later he was transformed into a part of it and was hurtling through the atmosphere.

Ashes stirred up in a wild fog of remnants of destruction as Elijah dragged Gideon into the room with incredible force, rematerializing him in a heartbeat. The minute the Ancient Demon was solid, Elijah staggered backward and dropped weakly to the floor. It had taken every ounce of his strength to perform such an incredible feat from such a distance.

Then silver eyes were encompassing the trauma in the room around him. In a rare show of emotion, Gideon swore softly. "What happened?"

"We do not know," Jacob responded. He quickly related what he and Elijah had seen as the Demon knelt by Noah and Legna's inert forms.

He reached for the King first, touching the charred flesh of his wrist, sinking his consciousness into Noah's body. His lungs were scorched from inhaling incredible heat, but other than that it was his skin and hair that had suffered the most. For a human that could have proved fatal, but it was a simple enough repair for Gideon to make. He started by shutting down all the pain receptors in the injured Demon's body. He healed the lungs first and then urged them to work a little quicker, a little differently, so as to flood the King with a high concentration of oxygen. Then Gideon meticulously began to rejuvenate patches of skin, one cell at a time. It took fifteen minutes before healthy flesh became visible to the two Demons waiting with anxiously held breath nearby. Once Gideon had repaired 50 percent of Noah's damaged skin, he broke away and turned to Legna. If he waited until Noah was completely healed, he would lose Legna. His fingers reached out to touch the female Demon's formerly beautiful cheek.

He was unaware that he was whispering under his breath in tandem to the mental processes of reconstruction. Jacob watched with fascination as Gideon repeated the list of mental processes required in his reconstruction procedure. It was rapid and flawless. Legna's natural skin tone began to flush over her limbs, her throat and her elegant face. She was once more pink and tan, soft and beautiful.

But still Gideon did not turn back to the King. He rested Legna across his thighs and reached to strip off his shirt. He gingerly slid it over her arms, covering her bare body carefully, smoothing long fingers down her thighs so that the tails went straight to her knees. Then he lifted the unconscious female higher into his arms, and brushing tender fingertips over the baldness of her newly repaired scalp, lowered his mouth so close to her skin that his whispered chant seemed like a kiss. In a minute, soft coffee-colored curls began to grow over the bare skin. In five minutes, they had lengthened to shoulder-length hanks. Gideon didn't stop until Legna's hair was pooling in its usual dramatic lengths over his arms and thighs.

Finally, he disentangled himself from the growth he'd created. He carefully laid her back along the floor, his fingertips lingering for a moment on the curve of her neck. Then, releasing a sigh, Gideon turned back to Noah. The powerful Body Demon was taxing himself with such an enormous undertaking, but there was no sign of that in the icy chips of his eyes.

When the replacement of Noah's hair was the only task left to him, Gideon paused once more in his care of the King to cast assessing eyes over Isabella. Gideon rose, stepped over the sleeping bodies of the recently healed Demons, and then crouched down across from Jacob. Even though he knew Gideon would do everything in his power to help Isabella, Jacob couldn't control the urgent request for help in his eyes. Gideon reached for Isabella, but hesitated before touching her skin.

"Jacob, I have to touch her to heal her."

"I know that. Why do you hesitate?" The Enforcer couldn't help the sharp impatience in his tone.

"It has been my experience that sometimes Imprinted mates do not respond well to members of the opposite sex touching their partners, no matter how innocently or well meant."

Jacob frowned, his first instinct to deny the ridiculousness of him allowing some petty jealousy to get in the way of Isabella's care. But he was reminded of the hostile surges of emotion he'd been struggling with whenever Noah had shown affection to her, or how when Elijah and Isabella had trained together these past few days, he'd sometimes been forced to leave so he couldn't see him lay hands on her pretending to harm her.

He felt a humorless laugh bubbling past his lips.

"Heal her," he whispered to Gideon, his voice hoarse with emotion.

Gideon nodded once, sharply, in acceptance. He concentrated on reducing the instinctive tenderness of his touch, making certain that nothing he did could be misinterpreted by the possessive Enforcer. There was no inner damage to Isabella at all, and she was by far the least damaged of the three. It was confusing and completely illogical. If anyone should have come through unscathed from this conflagration, it should have been Noah. The damage to Isabella's skin was swiftly repaired, and Gideon searched over and through her for any clue as to why she was the least harmed.

It took only a passing thought for him to brush away the scorched ends of her hair and regrow the raven mass back to its original length and health. He cast a heavy healing sleep inducement on her, reinforcing it twice so she wouldn't be able to wake herself from it. Then he straightened and walked away from the circle of Demons on the floor. He went over to a fourth body that neither the Earth nor Wind Demon had even noticed was there.

"Samson." Gideon answered the unasked question that was pending.

Elijah had regained a small amount of strength, and with it he moved to assist Jacob in bringing their charges to a safer, cleaner place.

"No. You rest. I will take them to my home . . ." Jacob began.

"No. You can't. We still don't know if other necromancers got a fix on your home because of that night."

"Not the one in Dover. I am not an idiot," he barked. Then he realized how his tone sounded and apologized.

"No"—Elijah raised a forgiving hand—"you're right. You aren't an idiot and you sure as hell don't need me pointing out things to you that even the rawest fledgling would know. I'm sorry. I'm just tired and this whole business has terrified the hell out of me."

"Follow me. I have plenty of room and you need to rest where it is safe," Jacob urged, rising to his feet with Isabella's limp body in his arms.

When Gideon entered the room, Jacob was seated in a chair beside Isabella's bed, both of his hands clasped around one of her smaller ones. He was rubbing the tips of her fingers against his lips, speaking softly to her even though she wouldn't hear him.

"When will you wake her?" Jacob asked, the question strained with his poorly suppressed emotions.

"I do not think she should be awakened for at least a couple of days," Gideon informed him. "Jacob, what you are feeling is normal for an Imprinted mate. It is . . . difficult for you to bear the loss of her thoughts within your mind. It was just as difficult for her when you were unconscious." Then Gideon ventured further. "Just as it would be deadly to her to lose you, it is often just as deadly for the Demon. Remember, we are the few that we are because of this. This is what it means to be Imprinted, and as time goes on, the connection will only grow stronger."

"I know," Jacob murmured, his face turned away, his eyes on the moon outside that loomed nearly full in the window.

Jacob would never have to fear the luring temptations of that Hallowed condition again, Gideon thought. Even now the medic felt the persistent clawing of talons of compulsion along the pathways of his mind. He wondered, for a brief moment, what it would feel like to live free of that disorienting threat to one's sanity. The Ancient had spent the past years studying ways to keep his inner peace during these holy times. It could be pushed aside, averted, ignored even, but it would never fully be expelled.

The Imprinting was the only cure.

But there was a catch. On the nights of the Samhain and Beltane full moons, an Imprinted pair would be driven to each other in single-minded sexual need, a desperation that wouldn't be ignored. This was why, historically, an Enforcer was forced to retire if he or she ever became Imprinted. How could they be vigilant on the two worst nights of the year for Demon madness when they were obsessed with their mate on those same nights? Even now Jacob sat and didn't move to go from his mate's side.

Gideon had maintained his silence on this matter, keeping it from the Council, thinking that by having a mated pair both as Enforcers, this might somehow work to their advantage instead, hoping that he'd not have to be the cause of robbing Jacob of everything that he'd lived for these last four centuries of his life.

"Jacob, you must leave here." Jacob looked at the Ancient so quickly that Gideon heard his neck crack loudly. He met the level of censure that was instantly in the Enforcer's blackening eyes. "She does not need your constant nearness this night. She is already completely healed, and natural sleep will suffice to replenish her energy stores until you return at the showing of the sun."

The Enforcer didn't respond. Instead he turned away again to simply gaze at Isabella's prettily resting face.

"Jacob . . ." Gideon tried again. "Jacob, you cannot sit here until she wakes. You have other duties to perform this night."

"The night is over," Jacob said coldly.

"Three hours hence. You must make sure—"

"Do not presume to tell me what I must and must not do!" Jacob roared, lurching to his feet with fisted hands, kicking away his chair so violently that it was crushed against the far wall, splintering into little bits. "Do not dare tell me how and when I must perform my duties! You know well enough how I excel at my obligations, Ancient!"

Gideon's chilled eyes didn't even blink at the violent slapdown. The metallic gleam of his pupils drifted to the tattered remains of Jacob's chair and then back again to its former occupant.

"You do not yet comprehend the intensity of the joining you have entered, Jacob. Fairy tales and long-ago memories of Noah's parents cannot prepare you for knowing what it truly means to be Imprinted."

"Really? Would you care to tell Noah that?" Jacob smiled, all teeth and no humor or friendliness. It was the smile of a predator snapping at its prey, distracting it until it frightened it into making a mistake.

"Noah knows all too well the fortunes and misfortunes of the Imprinting. Living with Imprinted parents is far different than watching it from afar. And yet, you now know more than he does, more than he may ever know, about what it feels like to be so entwined into the presence and the need of another's existence. It is imperative that you remember I know more about the history of this than you do and that you must trust my advice. Isabella can never become more important to you than your work."

Jacob responded with an ancient slur, one that told the Ancient medic quite clearly what he thought of his observations. "This of course coming from one who was so sensitive to this connection a millennium ago," Jacob hissed.

This time the Enforcer's strike made a deep impact. It was only then that it occurred to Gideon that only one so diplomatic as Jacob could possibly be so equally and adeptly cruel with words.

"There is a law, Jacob, that removes the Enforcer from his duties once he becomes Imprinted."

Though more direct than cruel, Gideon's information made measurable impact on the other male.

"I have never—" Jacob choked.

"Yes, and you have never heard of Druids being mated to Demons either," Gideon said impatiently. "Jacob, we were once companions, and so I say this as one who regrets that ever had to change. I am not saying that this law will still be put into effect, nor am I saying that anyone will even discover it exists. I am hoping that it will not until enough time has passed for you . . . for you to prove that it no longer applies as a necessary thing."

Jacob's left fist uncurled, his fingers flexing and stretching in agitation.

"But if only one Demon slips past your guard now, if only one human is harmed, especially in the wake of the fast-spreading news about Druids, the ramifications will be swift and painful. Law or no, I do not think you could live with the guilt of such a thing. You have never failed, just as your brother before you never failed. Do not risk damnation when happiness is so close for you."

"I never should have left her," Jacob confessed in a sudden rush, his hand picking Isabella's up blindly, clutching it against his outer thigh. "She should have been my first priority."

"She was. Or were you and Elijah just joyriding up in the clouds when you left her?"

"Damn it, Gideon! You are really beginning to piss me off."

"What an eloquent human phrase," Gideon remarked. "I can see it has not taken long for her to influence you."

"Influence me? Gideon, she is me. And every part of myself is her. But you do not get that, do you? If you had, you would have never been a part of the atrocity our people visited on the Druids." Finally Jacob turned his eyes on Isabella, the moonlight striking his profile with power. "I pray I live to see the moment when you discover what it means to find the other half of your essence in a delicate and beautiful creature like my Isabella. I live for the moment you learn to regret the platitudes you so sanctimoniously try to inflict upon me." Jacob tore his bottomless black eyes from his sleeping soul and looked at the medic. "Do you know what makes me Enforcer, and no other?"

"You were elected so by Noah."

"As my brother before me was. Elected, as my grandfathers and a dozen ancestors before me were. It is said that this is the only throne in the Demon world which carries a direct biological ascension. There is something in the blood of my family that predestines us as Enforcers. When Adam was elected, I thought I would never be called. I was quite . . . quite different back when he lived."

"It was a long time ago, Jacob. We were all quite different then."

"I was two hundred years old or so." Jacob laughed once, very softly, as he remembered that. "I was my mother's youngest, her baby no matter how old I grew. I was spoiled, bordering on indolent, and I believe I rather had a knack for practical jokes at the time." The recollection made him smile with a one-sided grin that took the ages out of his eyes.

"We were at war with the Vampires," Gideon added solemnly. "You became quite an impressive bounty hunter."

"Thrills and glory," Jacob explained. He smiled again, looking suddenly sly. "And women," he whispered, as if Bella might hear him. "I was not yet tired of women then." He sighed, his humor fading. "Then Adam was suddenly gone, without explanation, and we understood that he had died . . . and I understood that I would be asked to take his place." Jacob came to his point and looked at the Ancient to make it. "I have never once missed a catch. I will never, as long as I live, let a Demon transgress against another species, and I will never allow one of us who has transgressed upon another of our own race to escape justice. This is my calling. It is all I know and all I will ever be suited for. Neither law nor love can take it away. Only death. My law, current law as we know it, says only death will separate this Enforcer from his anointed position. If you ever speak of this other law to another, it will give those who hate me on the Council, which is definitely a majority, cause to remove me. Kane is not ready, Gideon. Only he has those special instincts born into our family that make us succeed as Enforcers."

"A genetic anomaly," Gideon mused, instantly looking into the Enforcer for the mark he spoke of.

"Yes. One that sends a sensation through my mind the instant a Demon begins to step over the line of reason in his thoughts. It is like a broadcast, and I am the only one alive who can hear it . . . feel it. Why do you think it is that I always know? I only use my elemental skills in the tracking and halting of the transgression. This is not commonly known, Gideon. Even you are having difficulty finding what you seek within me, though there is hardly a gene in the universe safe from your detection. If this were known, how long do you think I would live? How long do you think Bella would live, now that we have seen the same ability in her? What protects us is the idea that if one Enforcer dies, another will simply take his place. That the next will be no different than the last. There are those who would gladly assassinate me, and then my brother, to be freed of this, for we are the end of our line.

"So if I sit here for endless hours, it is because I feel no sense that I need to leave. If I stay, it is to protect the future of Demons, protect them from themselves. This woman . . ." He again rubbed the hand he held against his hip. "This woman will one day give birth to my heir. The heir of my blood, the heir of my duty. So if I sit here and will her to live, to breathe, and to love me, it is because of my duty that I do so." Jacob blinked eyes of flat, unemotional onyx at the medic. "And I do not think we will ever need to discuss this again, Gideon."

There was no threat, and there was nothing but. Gideon understood. Jacob would feel none of the guilt he was often plagued with if he had to protect his family.

"I am grateful that you saved my life and those of the others whom I hold most dear, Gideon. I will owe you a great debt if there ever comes a time you would ask for it."

"There is no question that I would always come to serve you, should you need me," Gideon said quietly.

"I understand that. But"—Jacob's mouth became grim—"I no longer understand *you*, my old friend. You have become a stranger to me. I always thought you a man of wisdom and benevolence, one who, like myself, could never bear to see an innocent harmed. I cannot believe that in all these years you never thought to tell Noah, who was searching unceasingly for a cure to our madness, that the cure had been obliterated with the Druids. Instead you let him hope, let us all hope. It was cruel and arrogant. Thoughtless. Unworthy of one so Ancient and revered." Jacob shook his head in bafflement. "We have nothing in common anymore, Gideon, and I am sorry for that."

Noah was the first to throw off Gideon's formidable sleep suggestion, a testimony to the King's awesome power. Still, it was a surprise to Jacob to see his monarch sitting in the quiet dark when he roused himself for the evening. Jacob went to Noah's side, sitting himself across from the Fire Demon on top of the low coffee table.

"I did not expect to see you for another day," he remarked, his voice clearly reflecting his relief.

"It is not in me to remain idle for long. My entire being is about manipulating energy. I would be a sorry example of our most powerful element if I could not draw energy from outside sources to replenish that which I have lost." Noah's expression remained bleak in spite of the effort to make the remark flippant. "Where is my sister?"

"She is here. Sleeping. Isabella as well."

Noah seemed to stiffen suddenly, and Jacob felt a sensation of trepidation rush up under the skin of his belly.

"How long will she sleep?"

"Legna? Gideon says another day or two."

"I meant the Druid."

Now that definitely put Jacob on edge. Noah had

always been the only one outside of himself to frequently give Isabella the respect of using her name, rather than referring to her in colder terms such as "the human" or "the Druid."

"Noah, what happened?" Jacob asked, but suddenly he was not so eager for answers as he had been.

"I can give you no specifics. The speed at which the incident occurred was blinding. But I will tell you one thing I am positive of. Isabella nearly killed my sister and me."

"What?" Jacob asked, his voice low and dangerous as his eyes narrowed defensively.

"We were setting up protective barriers, Legna and I. Isabella was spooked by what was happening. Naturally, she moved closer to those who were attempting to protect her. The moment she did . . ." Noah paused, shaking his head in mute astonishment. "The drain on my energy was like nothing I have experienced in all of my life. It was as though someone had flicked off a light switch inside of me, shunting away every last molecule of my energy. I was . . . vacant, dead . . . blind and deaf and paralyzed toward a power I have commanded since the moment it first woke in me when I was eight years old."

"Her dampening power awoke?"

"With a vengeance, my friend."

"But if you and Legna were drained, how did you generate such a massive firewall?"

"I did not. Jacob, Isabella did not just dampen our abilities, she *stole* them from us. It was Isabella who generated the firewall. It was my energy and power she used to do it."

"That's impossible," Jacob said hoarsely. He didn't want to believe what Noah was telling him.

"Imagine, for a moment, the terror Isabella must have been feeling. I heard her cry out, saw her reacting with some kind of pain, pressing her hands to her head, and then suddenly every essence of power was sucked out of me and sent out in a massive explosion, of which she was the epicenter. I remember nothing after that. Clearly I should be thankful for it. Anything that can leave me healing for an entire day afterward should not be an experience I would enjoy remembering."

"Gideon said nothing about this! Noah, I beg you not to blame her for this. Surely you see it was unintentional. How was she supposed to know? None of us knew. And if Gideon did and is concealing it, I will kill him myself."

"I do not think he does know. Before she came into the house, I was reading a scroll with two of the scholars that outlined the nature of a Druid in great detail. Nowhere in what I read was anything mentioned outside of what Gideon had already told us. No, Jacob, this is something different, something no one could have expected." The King sighed deeply. "I do not blame her. But I will be honest and say that in light of this new development, I now know what it means to fear something. Someone. And I am certain you can understand when I say the idea of being under the same roof as her is a terrifying one."

"That would mean it was not an outside source who tried to disassemble Isabella into dust." The other two Demons looked to the side to rest eyes on the Ancient medic who had appeared in astral form without sound or warning. "It was Isabella herself. Taking power from you, Jacob, and using it to satisfy what was probably a strong desire in her mind at the moment."

"Yes. I remember her thoughts were of wanting privacy, of wishing she had my abilities so she could be the one to sweep us away somewhere. It lasted a moment. It was awkward, clumsy, but never once did I suspect it was Isabella herself. But how? You never mentioned such an ability!"

"An aberration. Perhaps a mutation due to the cross-breeding of Druids and humans. I do not know precisely. It is an abnormality centuries in the making. I did make allowances that some things may have changed. However, I admit I had expected them to be weaknesses, a watering down of ability due to the unlikely genetic combination. I never suspected a Druid would become more powerful once mixed with the human genetic soup. I am realizing also that, if Bella is not unique in existence, these aberrations will be present in others. No two Druids will be alike. It is very likely that it will depend upon their mates what their power will be. Bella is practically a mirror for Jacob, absorbing his image, his power, and becoming his reflection. This is perhaps why they are so perfect for us, why they help to corral our power and our baser nature."

Gideon turned his cold, mercury eyes onto Noah. "Isabella is no different than you or I were at the earliest stages of development. If I had an ounce of power for every time the young of our race had accidents from the use of their untried abilities, I would be able to heal the world with a simple snap of my fingers. What makes this so difficult for you, Noah, is that it is very humbling to be taken so unawares. Especially by the backlash of something that has been yours to command with such ease for so many centuries. These mishaps are easily controlled with practice and training. The one who will be most endangered is the one who trains her." Gideon flicked his gaze to the Enforcer.

"I agree," Noah said with a grave nod. "And I understand. But can she do this to all Nightwalkers? To necromancers? Do you have any idea how powerful and how dangerous this makes an individual?"

"An individual who has a hell of a hard time finding justification in swatting a fly," Jacob reminded him harshly. "Isabella is a gentle, diplomatic soul. It will be our responsibility to see that she builds on the respect and consideration that is already heavily embedded in her morals. I remind you that she would lay down her life for any of you, that is how much she has come to care for you. It is bad enough I will have to tell her what has happened. I have to go into her room when she wakes and tell her that something she had no control over nearly cost the lives of the two Demons she has come to look on as family as well as friends. Knowing Isabella as you do, Noah, you tell me how you think she is going to feel about that."

That said, Jacob pushed himself up onto his feet and left the other two Demons behind as he began to climb the stairs.

Chapter Eleven

"I think I'm going to throw up."

Jacob frowned, switching from his seat on a new chair to a location beside her on the bed where he could touch her, bring her into the comfort of his embrace.

"No. Don't. I don't want to feel better yet," she said tightly, turning her face away from him as sharp tears stung her eyes. Jacob pulled back, respecting her request as best he could when every fiber of his being wanted to do just the opposite.

"Bella, everyone is okay now. It was an accident."

"An accident? Honey, rear-ending a cop is an accident. This is a catastrophe."

Jacob had never heard her sound so bitter, so defeated, and it tugged hard at his soul to feel her so wounded.

"I should've realized. It was my body, my thoughts. Why didn't I make the connection? Oh God, when I think of what could've happened . . . what did happen . . ."

"What has happened, for over a millennium, to every fledgling gifted with remarkable powers in this race and probably every other race of Nightwalkers.

No one, not even Noah or Legna, holds you responsible for something none of us could have expected. If I could tell you how many times Noah lost his temper as a kid and set his parents' house on fire—they were uncountable." He shook his head. "Hell, Bella, the first time I shape-shifted it took me a week to figure out how to switch back."

That made her release a soft, watery laugh.

"Oh, it gets better. Ask me what my first choice of animal was."

"Nooo . . ."

"A pig. Not just any pig, mind you," he said, talking over her startled laugh. "A huge, slobbery, grunting warthog. I had seen one at the zoo, and the next I knew . . ." Bella was laughing against her fists, trying to smother it with her fingers. "My father loved to tell the story for *years* about how he had to kidnap his own son from the zoo, a son who was so upset he squealed loudly the entire time his father was trying to smuggle him out. My father was a Demon of the Body, so he had no way of transforming me into a less conspicuous form of matter. He never let me live it down. Can you imagine? Centuries of being reminded of the most ridiculous moment of my life."

By then Bella was laughing so hard she had rolled back onto the bed, chortling up at the ceiling and clutching her cramping side.

"Stop it," she begged, nudging him in the side with the toes of one foot. "I told you I didn't want to feel better about this!"

"Of course, I think Legna tops this particular cake. You see, when Mind Demons teleport, they have to *remember* to teleport their clothes with them."

"Oh no . . ."

"Oh, yes. Noah's coronation anniversary. There is an incredible celebration every ten years, and everyone goes, even the most solitary of us. Legna was sixteen years old, and she was running late just like any typical teenager. She exploded into the room. Mind you, the display of a teleport in someone so young is ten times what you see her cause now, so she had everyone's attention. That youngling blushed bright red in places I never thought a woman could blush. It was a most enlightening moment."

"I'll bet!" Isabella giggled, her skin flushing in sympathetic embarrassment. "The poor thing!"

"Well, Noah responded very fast, so I assure you she only had time for a quick blush before he covered her in smoke, blocking her from a multitude of very astonished eyes. We do not tease her about it, however. Noah actually passed a law saying we could not. It was the only way he could get her to go out in public again. I am risking my peace of mind by telling you this. One chuckle in front of her, little flower, and you will doom me. So please . . ."

"Of course I won't," she giggled, sitting up once more and resting her cheek on the back crest of his shoulder. "Jacob," she sighed softly, nuzzling her nose against him. "What did I do to deserve you?"

"No doubt it was something very, very bad," he teased, turning to take her under his arm and draw her close to his chest.

She followed his urging quite willingly, straddling his thighs as she faced him, sitting back on her heels and letting her bright violet eyes scan every detail of his handsome face. He looked tired and a little mussed from what was no doubt the intensely repetitive act of running his hands through his hair. She reached out thoughtfully, taking a long dark ribbon of his hair between her fingers, fondling the consistency affectionately.

"No doubt," she agreed softly. "I find it funny, though, how good you are at keeping me from feeling overly guilty about something so terrible, and yet you can't do the same for yourself."

"Well," he said softly, reaching to mimic her caress of his hair with a finger coiling around a raven lock, "I suppose that is why I am lucky to have you. You are quite successful at distracting me from such things."

"I'll have you well trained in no time," she assured him.

"Yes, little flower. And we also will have you trained just as quickly. It will mean a great deal of hard work, a lot of experimentation, and no doubt a few more accidents, but you have always struck me as a very eager study. A quick one as well. You are less than a decade beyond the age of Fostering, so you have lost little ground as a fledgling and your power has already grown beyond that of most young Demons."

Bella sighed, her eyes taking a trip towards heaven.

"Okay, you lost me again. Fostering? And just what is the difference between fledgling and adult and Elder?"

"The Fostering is a very important tradition in our culture. When a child's power maturates to the point where they begin to have . . . accidents"—he lifted a pointed brow at her—"usually anywhere from early adolescence to about twenty years of age, the child is fostered out to their *Siddah*. Umm"—he searched for the comparative a moment—"godparents? Yes? Two chosen at birth to apprentice and discipline the child."

"You give your children away?" Bella looked as horrified as she sounded.

"Shh," he soothed quickly, his hands slipping deep into her hair and massaging the back of her scalp to calm her. "You would consider them adults in your society by the time the majority do this. It is more like college."

"What of the early starters? The early adolescents?"

Jacob sighed, knowing she wasn't going to respond well.

"It is the same as for humans. As early as nine, sometimes eight . . . though all before sixteen are extremely rare," he added quickly.

"Why can't you train your own children? I don't understand! How horrible it must be to be packed up and thrown out of their parents' house!"

"First of all," Jacob said firmly, forcing her to look into his eyes, though seeing her purple eyes swimming with tears was more than he could stand, "first of all, children are never allowed to feel abandoned. Weekends are reserved for rest and birth family, and *Siddah* love their fosterlings like their own. They are a part of the child's life from the moment it is born and named. They are family, just another branch."

"But—"

"Let me finish," he scolded softly. "Parents do not raise their own children past a certain point for one reason. It is often problematic for a parent to exert the stoicism and the influence necessary to control a child of power. Demons tend to love and cherish their child to the point of . . . well, if too much love is poor parenting, then so be it. So, a long time ago it was found that discipline was far easier for aunts, uncles, and family friends. I know this is true in human society too. Children will listen to others, behave for others, and perform for others far easier than they will for their parents. This is why the Fostering came about. Children grow up quicker this way, with a better sense of control, knowledge, and structure. We give them morals, Bella, the *Siddah* give them focus, and both give love and patience. My Fostering was one of my favorite memories of growing up. Share my mind, little love, and my memories. You will see that I loved my *Siddah* very much, and that my love for my parents never diminished because of it. I know your fears. It will not happen."

"How old were you?" she asked, even as she reached for the offered memories.

"I was almost twelve."

"Eleven! Eleven years old?"

"Bella, you forget . . . I am an Earth Demon. We, like Fire Demons, are both rare and powerful. You have seen what happens when we make love, Bella, and I am an Elder with control, training, and centuries of life experience to draw on. The same way I was not prepared for you is the same way a burgeoning power in an adolescent feels. Too much power, too many hormones," he said more pointedly, "and not the first clue as to how to control either. My male *Siddah* was the first and only person I talked to about things like sex. I could never have talked to my mother. She would have run screaming and crying from the room. 'My baby! My baby!'" He imitated her in voice pitch and a wild mock of pulling out his hair.

"Okay, okay . . . but surely your dad—"

"I loved my father, but I did not see much of him on a daily basis. Of course, there was a war at the time . . ."

"Another war?" She sighed. "Wait. Don't go on 'til my heart gets over the shock," she said with dry sarcasm.

"Nightwalkers are aggressive species," he relented. "Lycanthropes are the worst of them. They truly are mostly animal and they are extremely territorial. We warred steadily with them for the past three hundred years."

"Three hundred!" she was aghast.

"A long story with a very sick man at its center," he said dismissively. "His daughter is Queen now, and she has demanded peace these fifteen years. We were relieved to comply. Now. Back to the second part of your question. Fledglings are puberty to one hundred years, adults one hundred years to three hundred, Elders three hundred to seven hundred, and Ancients are the subsequent years."

"Why, you're almost an Ancient," she laughed. "You really are too old for me."

"And I will be the only Earth Demon to have ever become one," he told her.

"Oh." He felt her understanding that it meant none had ever survived as long as he had.

"Times are different now," he assured her, giving her a warm hug of strength and reassurance. "We are at peace or at least safely coexisting with all other Nightwalkers. There are no wars now."

She flicked her lashes to half mast, and he heard her thoughts loud and clear.

Yes, there is. And I fear for you.

Necromancers. Damn it, he had almost forgotten about that.

"They are Elijah's domain. As are all interspecies issues that we have. He will quell this as he has in centuries past. Trust him, he does not defeat easily. And I have domestic duties that will hopefully not cross paths with his too often."

"I see. And he'll just find these necromancers by . . . asking them to show themselves? Don't treat me like an idiot."

She pushed away from him angrily, gaining her feet

and pacing away from him. Her hands rested securely on her hips.

"Bella," he exclaimed, getting to his feet. "I would never do that. Your intelligence is one of the things I respect most about you."

"I see. Well, tell me something, bright eyes, how exactly did you discover there was a necromancer in existence in the first place?"

Her point hit him and he winced. She was right; the only way they would be able to ferret out magic-users would be by tracking down the Summoned. Which was his job, and which would inevitably lead him into battle with the necromancers.

"It's *our* job, Jacob," she reminded him firmly. "*Our* job to enforce. *Our* job to hunt the Transformed and destroy them, and *our* job to battle necromancers that get in our way. And Jacob"—she stepped up until she was chest to chest with him, as in his face as she could possibly get—"the more you mollycoddle me and shield me and get freaking chivalrous with me, the faster I'm going to get my damned head blown off! Is that what you want? 'Cause I can easily—"

"Of course not!" he exploded, the horror of the very thought shuddering through his dark eyes.

"Then stop it!"

"Okay! I am sorry!"

"Don't be sorry. Be smart. Be a partner, not just a protector. I'm going to be at your back, Jacob. Do you want me walking around looking at the pretty birdies when I should be prepared and . . . and whatever it is I need to be? Because I don't want that. I don't want to die . . . and I don't want *you* to die even more." She exhaled in a hard huff, her hair flying upward like a geyser. "Anyway, they kinda go together now, you know?"

"Yes, I know." Jacob reached for her face, his finger-tips seeking refuge in her hairline, his thumbs at the corners of her frowning lips. "Would it help if I told you I am a little rusty when it comes to having a relationship?"

"A little? They can hear your hinges squeaking all the way on Mars," she said irreverently.

He laughed, lowering his head to kiss the frown from her lips and the wry look from her upturned eyes. His lips had barely drifted away from her butterfly lashes when his affections were interrupted by a sudden yawn. He shook his head, blinking his eyes to refocus.

"You're tired."

"I have not slept well these past few days."

"Jacob, I'm having that urge to smack you again," she warned. "I'm draining you, aren't I? I'm . . . I'm sucking the energy right out of you."

"Yes, well, this is true," he admitted. "But it is like you said, little flower. You suck in a good way." He chuckled when she made a face at him. "I am serious. Do you realize that we can make love now without causing England to drop into the ocean?"

She hadn't thought about that. A sly smile drifted over her sexy little mouth.

"This too is true," she agreed, sliding her hands up his chest, over his shoulders and into the soft hair at the back of his neck. "I'd noticed you were avoiding the more physical side of this relationship."

"Only for your protection, Bella," he murmured softly, his eyes devouring the warm invitation that was blossoming over the way she held her body. With a modification of a single thought, she changed from being reproachful and righteous to silky and sensual. He would never get over that. "I did not want to end all of our lovemaking with fighting the latest necromancer

to ferret us out because my desire for you is so powerful, so uncontrollable that . . . that . . ."

"The Earth moves?" she asked archly.

"Cute. Yes, brat." He reached to pinch her bottom
and she giggled.

"Um, I do have to remind you, though . . ." She bit
her bottom lip, pausing to sweep obviously hungry eyes
over his entire torso. "I could very well be the one who
makes the Earth move now."

"Oh. Oh, damn, I forgot about that." She felt his hands
flex at her waist. He leaned a little closer to her, clearly
drawing in her scent, which he truly seemed to enjoy so
very much. He sighed deeply, reaching to nuzzle her
neck with his face. "To stay away from you takes a monu-
mental effort, little flower. I cannot even express to you
how difficult these past days have been for me."

"Nor can I express it to you," she murmured. "I was
beginning to think all you were interested in doing to
my body was work it to death in training with Elijah
and you. Of course, I picked up some fairly graphic
thoughts from you that assured me otherwise." Isabella
moved toward his lips with a soft feint of her mouth,
watching him move in natural preparation for the kiss
that did not come. She smiled teasingly into his eyes.

"And those were the ones I was not trying to hide," he
returned, touching his fingers to her cheek, skimming
her throat and collarbone, down the swell of her breast,
but pulling away before reaching the sensitive tip. She
swayed forward a little, her body wanting to chase after
the hand that had made the unfulfilled promise. She
recovered quickly, mischief and sultry intent flaming
sharply in the deepening purple of her eyes.

"Regardless," she said, continuing the mild conversation, "it doesn't change the fact that we've seen what

trouble I can cause with this power at my untrained fingertips. And if I were to describe how utterly mindless I become under your touch, it would be very clear that making love with you could be an even more dangerous prospect for us."

"Utterly mindless?" he asked, watching and feeling as she swept her fingers gently over the expanse of his chest, a teasing, barely there touch that drew his every nerve ending into rapt attention.

"Mmm," she affirmed. "Especially when you put your mouth on me." She leaned in to put her lips against the strong column of his neck. She felt him swallow convulsively. "I love what you do to me with your mouth," she whispered against his skin.

Jacob drew in a sharp breath, desire curling stridently through his entire body and soul.

"Bella," he whispered, his throat tight with the heat she sent flushing through him.

"I've been wondering," she remarked in an offhanded manner as her fingers began to slip the buttons of his shirt out of their closures. She finished her thought by pushing him back onto the bed, her mouth touching the skin she was exposing. He felt her curious little tongue sweep over him. He might have gasped under the sensation the simple touch caused, but she beat him to it. She sat up, looking down at him with an expression of shock and wonder. "Jacob, I can—" She broke off, closed her eyes, and took a slow searching breath in through her nose. "Is this what you mean?" she asked, her voice filled with erotic delight. "When you say you love my scent?"

Jacob could barely breathe, never mind respond, as he watched her use his abilities to arouse herself.

"Yes, honey," he managed at last.

She made a delighted sound, her hands eagerly

pulling his shirt farther open so she could bend her mouth to him once more, this time adding his acute senses to her natural tactile curiosity. She tasted him eagerly, thoroughly, instantly finding the best places to stimulate him on his neck, collarbone, and chest. She wriggled down his body, her industrious mouth sliding over his belly. Jacob could do nothing but weave his fingers into her silky hair, clutching it in his flexed fists.

"Bella . . ." he groaned as she nuzzled him torturously with her sweet, soft face, sexy lips, and hot tongue. Her nimble fingers were at his fly, freeing the closures before she lifted away from him and helped him remove the garments blocking her enthusiastic exploration. He lay back once more and she was immediately above him, kissing his mouth, reflecting the pleasure she was experiencing.

Then her mouth was back on his skin, inexhaustibly seeking his taste, his gratification. Her fingertips skimmed over his hips and thighs, scouting ahead of her inquisitive lips. Her hair was falling wildly all around him, and he reached to sweep it aside, unable to resist the lure of watching her exploration of his body. He felt her breath coasting over his arousal, his body twitching with his anticipation. She touched her tongue to him, her lips following, her incredible mouth drawing him into its wet warmth. Watching her do this had to be the most erotic thing Jacob had ever experienced in all the centuries of his life. She was perfect. Even as she ministered to him, she was becoming heavily aroused herself. He felt it in the tremble of her body, in the soft, intriguing sounds that vibrated out of her throat and against his aroused flesh. He could see it in the heated violet gaze she turned up to him.

With mutual action, Jacob and Isabella drew her up

the length of his body. She straddled his hips boldly, rising up and stripping off the nightshirt she was wearing. She flung it aside and quickly brought both hands to rub fiercely over his chest and belly and under herself to where he thrust hard and hot against the juncture of her thighs. Jacob made a low sound, half arousal and half satisfaction at her bold sexual behavior. He'd known she'd be like this. He'd told himself several times. But nothing could have prepared him for how it would make him feel, how it would burn him like a brand for all time.

She was in his mind, reading his every thought and desire. Anything he wanted to feel, to experience, she provided it a second after he thought of it. She was wickedly thorough, driving him completely insane. And just as the thought that he couldn't bear her sweet erotic torture for one moment longer crossed his mind, she slid herself up the length of him, tilted her hips just right, and took him into her eager body in one swift movement.

Her delighted cry drowned out his, the sound a rich, operatic note of staggering pleasure.

"Jacob," she groaned. "You feel so wonderful!"

Jacob reached for her hips, trying to anchor himself in the middle of the storm of sensation she was bombarding him with. She flexed herself around him and an expletive erupted past his lips.

"What does that mean?" she demanded, punctuating the request with a forward and back rock of her body that thrust him even deeper into her.

"It means . . ." he gasped, trying very hard to be coherent as she moved on him once more, trapping him as deeply in her hungry body as she possibly could. "It means you have stolen my thoughts and my soul and put them at the mercy of your pleasure."

"Mmm, I think I like the sound of that," she purred softly, moving in beautiful, torturous ways that assured her the theft was utterly complete. He watched her creamy skin flush with perspiration and her own climbing arousal. In her mind he felt how much pleasure every reaction she drew from him gave her. Her eyes closed, her hips riding him in a decadent writhing rhythm, she flushed hotter and hotter around him, coating him with the slick nectar of her body. He felt her driving herself up to her own peak, using the fit of his body with as much glorious skill as she could muster.

"Bella, you will be my death," Jacob gasped, his hips instinctively matching her wicked movements, his thoughts reaching for what she was feeling.

She was so close, every molecule vibrating with the pent-up fervor within her. Then he felt the flash of trepidation that shot through her. She was almost lost and suddenly afraid to let go. He knew why, but he'd be damned if she would deny herself her own pleasure while he took his. He reached for her sensitive body, shocking her as his thumb came to caress her intimately. He found the pleasure spot unerringly, and the combination of the touch and the hard thrust of his sheathed flesh was too much to resist.

She threw her head back, crying out at the top of her voice as every muscle in her body convulsed. In that moment he was overwhelmed by a vise of muscles that embraced him, by the honeyed heat that was beyond any conceivable temperature as it poured over him. His release was violent, explosive, and perfect. It seemed to last an eon, and then too short of a moment.

Bella collapsed on top of him, every muscle in her body feeling like rubber, unable to take any further commands from her. Jacob wrapped her up in his embrace, his face burrowing into her rich hair and his harsh breath still far from being regulated. He remained connected to her, and he was positive she wouldn't have relinquished him in any event. She was panting heavily from her exertion, her face burrowing into his strong neck, all of her trembling with the delightful aftershocks of passion.

"I will never feel anything like that again," she told him breathlessly.

"Baby," he murmured in her delicate ear, "give me a few minutes and that wicked mouth of yours and I promise you, you will feel it again."

"Jacob!" She laughed, trying to scold him unsuccessfully. Then her head popped up so she could see his eyes. "The Earth didn't move!"

"Damn, I must be losing my touch," he teased, reaching to flick an impudent tongue over one pert nipple.

"Jacob, you know what I mean." She giggled. "Stop that!"

"Stop what? Stop this?"

Isabella gasped, surprised to realize she wasn't as exhausted as she'd previously thought. And neither was he. The evidence of that was stirring within her very own body.

"And you make fun of my libido?" she demanded.

"Perish the thought. I adore your libido."

"Somehow I'm—Jacob, I'm trying to talk here!"

"And I am trying to shut you up," he taunted, repeating the sly touch again.

"Have better uses for my mouth, do you?" she queried impishly, her eyes sparkling with humor.

"Dozens of them. Shall I list them?"

"Oh no. Let me."

* * *

"Tell me something?"

"What?" Jacob asked, enjoying the feel of her hair beneath his hand as she nuzzled her cheek against his chest in a warm, kittenish way.

"No one ever explained to me why the necromancer wanted to know your name."

Jacob went very still, and Isabella allowed him a moment to gather his thoughts. She knew it was a very significant question, even if she didn't exactly know why.

"In many cultures it is believed that to give your name to someone is to give them power over you. For a Demon, it is a literal truth. A Demon's name is the key ingredient in a Summoning. Without it, a necromancer cannot Summon him, cannot control him, and has no means of gaining power over him."

Isabella lifted her cheek from his chest so she could look into his dark eyes.

"But everyone knows your name, Jacob. Any of the captured Demons could tell the necromancers your name."

"No. I am the only one who knows my name."

"I don't understand."

Jacob sat up, sliding back to lean against the headboard of the bed while she shifted position, curling herself around his raised knee, setting her chin on it and maintaining eye contact with him.

"When a Demon child is born, there is a naming ceremony," he began. "There are only four people present. The mother, the father, and the *Siddah*. These four people are the only ones who ever know a Demon's true name." Jacob paused a minute, reaching out to stroke a thumb over the rise of her soft cheek. "Think of it like . . . riot control?" He shook his head, knowing it was an inadequate explanation. "Though it is not a crime to come into power, the methods we must use to keep control of newly fledged Demons require both parents and *Siddah* to know the young Demon's name. It is a tool that allows one to quell power, to soothe and to settle the young one's mind. It helps them focus enough to gain control themselves. It is also handy when they get a little too *seneta yu va*." He tried to think of the equivalent and laughed. "Too big for their britches."

"So your name is not Jacob?"

"Of course it is. You may actually find this a little ironic, but after we are given our power names, parents choose a call name, like Jacob and Noah and Elijah, and they usually select the name from—"

"The Bible!"

"Yes." Jacob grinned. "You see, Demons have a great respect for the Christian religions. As you know, they gifted us with a peace and freedom that will never be matched. Choosing our children's call names from the Bible is to us an act of tribute."

"I think that's wonderful."

"It is an intimate tradition for expecting parents to spend an entire day selecting a call name. This is done with just the mother and the father, closed away from all the world. It begins with them recalling the first time they saw one another, the story of how each fell in love with the other, the foundation on which the child was conceived."

"It sounds positively beautiful, Jacob," Isabella whispered. She turned her eyes away from his briefly, and Jacob realized she was hiding a thought from him.

"What is it, little flower?"

She looked back, drawing her lower lip between her teeth in a telltale sign of apprehension.

"Jacob, according to the prophecy, you and I will have a child one day."

Jacob went very still, his breath locking in his chest as he was overcome with an inexplicable sensation of fear.

"Does this disturb you?" he asked as levelly as he could manage.

Isabella wondered if he realized how transparent he was in that moment. Sometimes Jacob seemed to forget that she was always a part of his thoughts. He was practically terrified that she disliked the idea of having a child with him.

"Well, frankly it does," she began, turning her face away so she could conceal her smile of mischief.

"I see."

"I'm glad that you do. It's unthinkable and I expect you to remedy the situation."

Jacob was speechless. He felt his heart turning over painfully in his breast.

Then she turned back, her eyes bright with merriment. "So how do Demons get married anyway?"

Jacob sucked in a breath at last, his skin flushing with the sensation of rapid-fire emotional tidal waves.

"Isabella . . ." he said, his tone dangerously full of reprimand. "Isabella Russ, are you teasing me?"

"Why no, Jacob," she declared, all innocence. "I was asking you to make an honest woman of me. If you think that's some kind of a joke, then I think it's time I went home."

She made as if to get off the bed, but he grabbed hold of her and tossed her back down into the softness of the comforter, looming over her dangerously.

"I am going to thrash you," he hissed, giving her a shake by the shoulders. "You delight in torturing me!"

"No more or less than you have delighted in torturing me!"

"Isabella!" He growled her name but ended it with a laugh he couldn't hope to contain.

"So are you going to answer me or not?"

"Did you ask me a question?" he rejoined.

"I believe I asked you to marry me."

"Ah . . . well, I do not recall you getting down on one knee or anything," he retorted.

"Look, I may be a modern woman, but that's going too far. Next you'll be wanting a diamond ring."

"Actually, I look better in emeralds," he chuckled.

"I'm sure. Listen, Enforcer, I don't have all night."

"In that case, Enforcer," he returned, "I should tell you that Demons do not have a marriage ceremony like you would expect."

"Of course not," she said dryly, rolling her eyes. "I'm sure whatever it is, it's pretentious and full of intensity. That is, after all, the Demon way."

"Yes, very droll of us." His expression changed, his dark eyes swimming with seriousness. "So much has happened to you in so short a time, Bella. How is it you seem so sure of this?"

"Jacob," she said softly, "how can I be anything but sure? You're my special destiny. I don't need a prophecy or anything else to dictate that to me." She reached up, running her searching fingers lightly over the shape and planes of his face. "My soul belongs with yours. Your heart belongs with mine. I feel this with every molecule of my being. I felt it the moment I saw some idiot walking down a dark street in the Bronx during the scariest hours of the night."

"Mmm. I love you too," he murmured, smiling against her mouth and kissing her until she was too breathless to tease him anymore. He settled into her body, fitting himself to her with unerring ease. She was made for him, and it could be felt in every place she came into contact with him. "I have lived a life that has seen and experienced a great many things," he whispered, his voice hoarse with the intensity of his emotion, "but until I met you I never knew what it meant to love a woman the way I know I love you. I cannot promise that to stay with me will be an easy thing. There is much uncertainty in both of our futures."

"I know, Jacob. I know this is no fairy tale. Happily ever after, while an appealing idea, is too much pressure for me anyway. We'll still argue, I'll still be too stubborn for words, and I'll no doubt drive you completely insane. But I'll make up for it by loving you to the best of my ability."

"I will continue to be hard on myself and I will get your back up on a regular basis, no doubt. I will most likely foul up with you with horrifying regularity because I am not very experienced in how to have a love relationship. I have been alone for so long, little flower, and I am afraid it will serve to trip me up quite often. But I will make up for it, Isabella, because I love you beyond even the best of my ability." Jacob smiled slightly, reaching to catch her sudden tears with his thumb. "I did not intend to make you cry, Bella."

"I can't help it. My heart"—she rubbed her palm hard over the spot where the mentioned organ was housed—"I feel like it will burst."

"How odd, little flower. Since I met you, my heart has done nothing but grow to make very certain it can accommodate you." He bent his head to her, kissing her gently, and then moved away, standing up and taking her hands to pull her from the bed. "Come, there is something we must do."

"What?"

"You will see."

Noah looked up when he heard footsteps on the stairs. He felt an alien sensation of anxiety when he saw his Enforcers descending toward him. Immediately he pushed it away, reminding himself that Isabella would never intentionally harm him or anyone else. Still, he stood up out of some deep-seated instinct, a need to meet her on his feet.

As soon as they came within his reach, Isabella dropped to her knees in front of him, her lovely violet eyes brimming with remorse as she took hold of his hand and pressed it to her cheek with great emotion.

"Forgive me, Noah," she begged in a whisper.

Noah felt his heart turn over and instantly regretted all the feelings his fear had engendered within him. He dropped to one knee and turned her eyes up to his.

"There is nothing to forgive, little Enforcer," he told her gently. He glanced up to look at Jacob, reading the gratitude in his expression quite clearly. "All you need do to repay me, Isabella, is continue to make this Demon, who is so like a brother to me, as happy as I have never seen him until your arrival."

Jacob drew in a soft, quick breath. He'd never thought he meant that much to Noah.

"There is no repentance in doing something that gives me so much pleasure, Noah," she said to Jacob's King. Her fingers circled his wrist affectionately, the touch meant to replace her natural impulse to hug him, which she knew would be upsetting to her possessive mate. "But I can swear to you that I will always be yours to call on for anything you need. I'll always be completely loyal to you, second only to Jacob and my sister."

"Come." Noah regained his feet, drawing her up to hers. "You have said enough. I am content. I will not stand for you to concern yourself over this accident a moment longer."

Jacob then stepped up, taking his mate's free hand and glancing at her. The Enforcers simultaneously lowered themselves to kneel before the King once more. Side by side, hand in hand, they looked up at Noah in perfect unison. Noah felt his chest constrict with overwhelming pleasure.

"My King," Jacob began, his voice low but passionate as he spoke the words of a ritual more ancient than time, "we ask your blessing. Give your loyal servants permission to be joined on the night of the full moon, as my parents were joined, as yours were joined, so that as a completed pair, our power and our loyalty can serve you and all of our kind for all of our lives."

"My King," Isabella echoed softly, her beautiful eyes brimming with tears, "we ask your blessing. Give your loyal servants permission to be joined on the night of the full moon, so that as a completed pair, we can provide Demonkind with its future generation. I swear they will be as loyal to you as I am, as their father is, for that is how we will raise them."

Noah stood silently before them, trying to work past the emotions that held him in thrall. He'd never thought to see this day, this day when Jacob would kneel before him, his dark head bowed close to that of the woman who would be his wife. Though she wasn't

Demon, Jacob had fed her the ritual words, and Isabella had spoken them with all of her heart behind them.

"Enforcers," he said at last, his hands reaching to settle warmly on their bent heads, "my blessing is yours. I only ask one thing."

They looked up simultaneously.

"Allow your King to perform the ceremony, for I could not tolerate it if anyone else tended to the union."

Jacob was rendered completely speechless. Noah had only joined one other couple in his reign, and that had been his sister Hannah and her mate. The honor he was giving them was an astounding one. Isabella read Jacob's reaction loud and clear, understood immediately the significance of Noah's offer, and sobbed softly under the magnitude of her gratitude. Uncaring of any further protocols, Isabella gained her feet and literally threw herself into Noah's embrace.

"Thank you! Noah, thank you so much!" she wept, kissing his cheek soundly. The King, looking quite baffled as he flushed under her exuberant affection, instinctively hugged his new Enforcer. After her tight clutch went on a minute more, he chuckled and looked at Jacob, who'd also risen to his feet.

"Enforcer, peel your bride off of me before she drowns me in her tears," he laughed.

Jacob stepped up and did so, taking his emotional Isabella into his arms, securing her against his body.

"You honor me, Noah. We accept wholeheartedly," Jacob said.

"I got that impression," Noah chuckled. "So, Isabella, you have two days to plan a wedding." He paused to yawn, and he saw Bella go suddenly rigid in Jacob's arms.

"More importantly," she said bitterly, "I have two days to learn how to keep from making my guests pass out."

"Well," Noah responded easily, "it seems that the effect is limited to those standing very close to you, at the moment. So I would imagine you need to worry more about keeping your groom conscious."

"Come, little flower, let us seek Elijah out. I wish for him to attend the wedding as well."

"Not yet." She stayed him with a hand on his chest. "I have one other apology to make."

She reached to kiss his cheek lightly, then broke from his hold and headed up the stairs, turning at the landing to head for Legna's room.

CHAPTER TWELVE

Isabella and Jacob walked down the street, passing under the window where they had first met. She stopped, looking up at the window she had tumbled out of, landing in the arms of her future.

"I hope my sister is home. She didn't answer the phone, but it's not like her to be out so late."

"Maybe she is getting lucky," Jacob teased, running a hand over the swell of her bottom as he pulled her close to his body.

"Jacob!"

"Come. Let us get this invitation over with so I can be alone with you," he murmured invitingly, nuzzling her neck with his lips.

Isabella giggled, swatting his hands away from her body.

She was laughing uncontrollably by the time she got her key in the door and burst into the apartment. She was so full of energy and joy that she didn't wait for Jacob to come in before she dashed madly for her sister's bedroom.

"Hey, sleepyhead! It's 2 a.m. Time to get up!" she

announced, leaping onto her sister's bed and bouncing on it enthusiastically. Corrine groaned softly but didn't seem to have any intention of being woken by Isabella. "I'm home! Wake up!" Isabella bounced and jiggled the mattress incessantly, knowing Corrine would have to surrender to wakefulness eventually. She grabbed away the pillow settled over her sister's head and whacked her on the butt with it.

"Corr, come on." Isabella frowned, reaching to push back the masses of auburn covering her sister's face.

Jacob jolted when Isabella screamed from the back of the apartment. He rushed to her side in a heartbeat, finding her dragging at the woman he presumed was her sister, pulling her torso into her arms.

"Jacob, she's ill! I can't wake her!"

Jacob hurried around his mate, easing her sister between his calmer hands, turning her over and laying her in the cradle of both of their arms. The bushel of red hair concealing her face tumbled aside, revealing a gray complexion, dark-circled eyes, and a face that Jacob had the strange sensation he'd seen before.

"You know her?" Isabella asked in shock, reading the faint recognition in his thoughts.

"Yes. I do not know how, but I have seen her before. Recently."

"Jacob"—Isabella was practically hyperventilating with her distress—"Jacob, there's only one reason why you come into contact with humans at this time of year!"

Jacob sucked in a harsh breath as his memory opened up with chilling recollection. "No! Damn it! *No!*" His rage was shuddering so violently through his body that Bella could feel the bed shaking.

Jacob grabbed Bella's sister up and dragged her away

from her, striding across the room. Bella rose up in hurt and distress.

"Give her back to me!" she cried, holding her arms out, sobbing. "Give her back!"

"I cannot. You must stay far away, Bella."

"She's my sister!" Bella scrambled over the bed, launching at Jacob's back when he turned to lower Corrine to the ground. He released her, lurching up to catch Bella's violent, headlong flight with the only power he had, the power of his strong body and sharp words.

"Bella! Focus!"

The command was roared in her face, shocking her into stillness between his grasping hands. At once she felt the vibration shuddering through the building, settling as her awareness of it settled her emotions down. Jacob began to walk her backward out of the room. The farther from her sister that they went, the more she and the building began to tremble again. Jacob drew her close the moment they were outside of the room, pressing fierce lips to her forehead, murmuring soothing sounds and facts to her on a soft breath.

"Listen, little flower, listen." He picked up her head between his hands, tilting eyes of wild violet up to his. "She is alive. She is extremely weak, and the labor of her breathing is hard."

"I need to be in there. Please!" She pressed urgently against him, leaning toward the room where her sister lay helplessly on the floor.

"No! You need to calm down and you need to trust me." Again he forced her to look at him. "If you go into that room while she is so weak, Bella, you will only be a liability."

"How can you say that? I'm her sister!"

"Yes!" he shouted back. "Your *family*! Who met *my*

family! Kane, Bella. Kane was the Demon who was seeking your sister this past week." He paused to close his eyes, kicking himself for missing something so obvious.

"Who?" she asked dumbly.

"Kane. My youngest brother. The night I met you, I had to hunt him and enforce him after he tried to enthrall a pretty redheaded woman. Your sister was that redhead."

"My sister . . . Kane . . . oh God, Jacob . . . she's my *sister.* She's a *Druid.*"

"So it would seem," he said tightly. "And, damn it, I let him touch her to prove to myself . . ." He shook his head. "However brief her contact with Kane, it was clearly enough. She is drained, starving to death."

The understanding seemed to weaken Isabella. Her knees collapsed and Jacob was forced to scoop her up and carry her to the couch by the window.

"Why won't you bring me to her?" Bella wept piteously. "Why are you doing this?"

"Shh . . ." he soothed as the floor and building lurched around him. Little objects floated off their surfaces, and he hoped the effect was limited to this apartment or that a lot of people were very asleep. "My sweet love," he whispered against her ear. "Look around this room. Tell me why I cannot let you go to her."

It made her focus on something other than her pain, and Jacob was able to settle them into the couch. He could tell when she began to comprehend. One thing after another landed back on its home territory, some safely, some shattering from the impact if they were too delicate. Comprehension didn't ease her pain, though. She was lanced through with it, shaking with it and crying her heart out.

"I can't go in there," she gasped tearfully, the sound

tearing at his heart and soul, "because I will steal her power. I will kill her. Oh God! Jacob, what if I—"

"No, no, no, no, no," he murmured quickly. "I can hear her breathing, I can feel her life. Some of my abilities are purely physical, little love, and you cannot steal them."

"You have to go to her," she said desperately, pushing at him, trying to force him to leave her. "Don't leave her alone like that! Jacob, I'm begging you!"

"Bella, listen!" The entire room crashed with sound as heavier objects were raised and let go. "Focus! If you keep this up, New York will end up in the ocean, killing you, me, and your sister!" It was harsh, but he had to appeal to her logic. He'd never seen her so much a slave to her emotions.

Except when she made love with him.

"Look at me!" he commanded her, grasping her head and making her look. "I need my power back, Bella, and I know you have it in you to give it to me. I need to call Gideon to us. It will take too long if I just try to replenish my energy, and it would never be enough to reach across oceans and continents in time to help Corrine." He took a breath, looking at her tear-streaked face and the huge eyes welling with new ones. "I know you can do this, little love. Remember when we made love earlier?" He kissed away tears gently, felt her nodding. "I felt you hold back. I felt your fear that if you released, you would blow up half of England."

Her hands reached to hug him close, her forehead falling on his shoulder.

"I refused to let you do that." He rubbed whispering lips against her ear. "But you said it yourself. The Earth did not move. Remember?"

"Yes," she said, nodding against his shoulder.

"Where did it go, little flower?"

She lifted her head after hesitation. "What do you mean?"

"I mean it just like I said it. While you continued to live and love, what did you do with my power? I know it was not in me. You pretty much were robbing me of everything in that moment," he teased ever so softly.

"Jacob," she chided, her face going hot.

"You stole it, little thief, and socked it away inside you. I know you remember where it is, too. If you remember to that moment of hesitation, just before I touched that sweet spot that excites you so much . . ." He brushed a thumb over her flushing cheek. "You made a conscious decision to block that power off so you could safely feel pleasure, Bella. Where is it, love? That place you keep it locked away. Look inside yourself."

She closed her eyes and he could feel her thinking, searching for what he was speaking of. He'd softened her and cajoled her with talk of lovemaking, drawing her out of her pain of the moment so she could focus.

In the next instant Jacob was blown back off the couch, landing hard on the wood floor and sliding a good three feet over its slick surface. He felt the resurgence of his power like the impact of a bomb. He struggled to pick himself up, motioning her off when she scrambled to help, concern and shock in her eyes.

"That teaches me not to pay attention," he groaned wryly. "I am fine. Better than fine. Phew!" He shook his head as surges and rushes flowed through him. She was a storehouse. As his body had struggled to bring him back to power hour after hour, she had kept siphoning it away and storing it. That was when he realized he was very lucky she hadn't blown him up by returning it. As it was, he could hardly focus. It was

actually an erotic sensation, so much life and energy
seething through him, all of it imbued with her presence and her scent because it had lived deep inside of
her for so long.

Isabella watched with fascination as Jacob staggered
under the weight of his returned power. She'd be
damned if she knew how she'd done it, but she had.
Still, she could already feel it inside her again, feeling
so much like him, hot and earthy, spilling into her like
thousands of kernels of grain . . . slowly . . . then more
rapidly, the door to the silo still open and she with no
way to close it down. Jacob flashed his dark eyes at her,
and she could feel the eroticism of what he was feeling
through his mind. She could see his eyes sparking with
facets of indigo, felt every muscle in his body clenching and hardening with power as it overflowed him.
She watched him, how magnificent he was, as he
reached out his arms to touch the natural energy of
the world around him. She watched his eyes slide
closed with a sensual drift of his lashes.

He expelled power, sending his urgent summons to
those who needed to come to them.

Kane lifted his head, feeling his brother's presence
in his mind, feeling his power and familiarity. He
didn't want to answer the summons, so he ignored it.
He hadn't been able to face Jacob since that terrible
night, and with his punishment still impending, he
didn't think he could. Anyway, he was under house
arrest, he thought bitterly, glaring at the Elder Mind
Demon he'd once called *Siddah*. He was pissed and
didn't care who knew it.

"You are behaving like a child," Abram scolded him,

turning the page of the human magazine he was reading called *Cosmopolitan.* "Answer the summons."

"What do you care?" Kane stormed, pacing the rooms of his living area with frustration. "I'm a damned criminal. What could Jacob possibly need from me? To sit and watch now that he's found his woman? Imprinted, no less! I know! I can be their best man. I'll stand there jealously hating my own brother. More so after I'm punished, for all the good punishment will do! I cannot get that woman out of my head, and her face is burned in my memory. I can feel her skin on my hand. I ache from head to toe with need for a beautiful creature who is . . . is . . . ."

"Human," Abram provided gently, his face full of compassionate understanding.

"Sweet Destiny, why doesn't he get this over with already? Let the punishment drive her out of my brain. I deserve it."

"Kane . . ." Abram sat up, dropping his feet to the floor as he reached out to sense the repeated summons, this one smacking into them both with obliterating force. Abram grabbed his ringing head as the wave passed. He'd only sensed it through Kane, who had gotten the brunt of it.

Kane was flat on his back, his head drumming with pain.

"Whoa." Kane sat up and shook his brain back into place. "Jeez, all he had to do was say it was important," Kane said dryly.

"I believe he just did. I never knew your connection to him was that powerful, Kane. Well done."

"You think I had anything to do with that? No. No, that was all Jacob." That gave Kane pause. "Cool," he chuckled. "Glad I didn't put up a fight," he said irreverently, joking about the enforcing incident for the first time since it had happened.

"You best go," Abram said.

"Consider me—" There was an explosion of smoke and sulfur that left the Elder waving his magazine frantically.

"Gone," Abram finished with an amused sigh.

Isabella scented the telltale odor of sulfur about thirty minutes later. She cocked her head, and Jacob looked up at her from his position on the bed near her sister. Bella was hovering in the doorway, unable to bear being out of sight of Corrine. Gideon had decided it would be safe enough where she stood for now.

She was confused, though, and she crinkled her eyes and shook her head at Jacob.

"Incoming," he informed her, identifying her premonition for what it was.

Still, she wasn't prepared for the mighty burst of smoke and sulfur that took place right behind her, suffocating her in a cloud so that she waved her hands frantically. She saw a handsome young male she'd never met before in the epicenter of the disturbance, but instantly recognized how much he looked like Jacob.

"Isabella, back away from him this instant," Gideon said. "You are too strong for Kane. He needs his power at full strength in order to most quickly aid your sister."

Isabella nodded, swallowing hard and feeling so terribly cold as she obeyed. To think that she was a hindrance in any way to her sister's well-being left her chest feeling heavy with dread. She was loath to leave Corrine's side but knew she had no choice. She allowed Jacob to take her under his arm and lead her from the room. He led her to a couch in the living room, seating himself and drawing her down into his lap. He cradled her and whispered soft, comforting thoughts into her mind. She clung to him, weeping quietly.

"Stop, Bella. I know you're blaming yourself. I hear it."

"I can't help it. For so many days I've known the greatest happiness of my life, and while I was so self-ishly enjoying it, my sister lay here alone . . . dying. I can't bear it."

"You could not have known."

"I should've realized! I'm supposed to be so smart! I should've realized that anyone related to me was probably as much Druid as I was! How could I be so stupid?"

"All of us who heard you talk of her dozens of times over these past days ought to have realized it as well. It was an understandable oversight, Bella. How were you to know she had met a Demon the very same night that you did? Sweetheart, I was there. As soon as I realized the implications of all Gideon had told us, I should have hunted down every human I had 'saved' from Demons this month and made sure none were Druids. I could do nothing for those in the past, but I certainly could save those in this recent season."

"How many, Jacob? How many are out there now, withering away like Corrine?"

"There could be none, or there could be at least a dozen." He unexpectedly put her aside, unable to be still all of a sudden, standing up and pacing the room. "And I dread to say I hardly ever pay attention to the humans I protect. I am usually far more focused on the Demon involved. I do not know if I would even know how to go about finding them."

Isabella stood up, reaching for his arm, stilling his frustrated pace.

"You don't, but I bet the Demons involved in the enforcing won't have forgotten who they had broken such sacred laws for."

Jacob looked down into her serious violet eyes, a sensation of relief washing over him. He pulled her palm up to his lips, kissing it with the intensity of his relief.

You must go, my love, and make these things right.

You need me.

"Please, Jacob, find them and be certain no one is suffering like my sister is. They're sisters and brothers of other people. Please, go and find them."

He could only nod. He was so overwhelmed by her selflessness, and yet she saw herself as having been entirely selfish. He cradled the back of her head with one broad hand, pulling her to his mouth and kissing her soft and deep.

"I love you, little flower," he whispered fiercely. "I will make this right for you."

"I know you will," she agreed confidently.

Kane didn't understand what was happening as he stepped into the strange bedroom. He didn't see his surroundings at first because his bemused eyes had followed his brother's back out of the room. Jacob hadn't said so much as hello but had merely pushed past him to drag a small, dark-haired woman into his arms. Kane turned to look at Gideon and took an unsteady breath. He'd never been within five feet of the Ancient before, and he couldn't understand what he could possibly want from him. Normally, he'd have been reading minds left and right, taking the shortcut to the answers he wanted, but he had no hope of getting past the Ancient's defenses. The dark-haired woman was a negative space, as if she weren't even there, and Jacob would have smacked him upside his head for even thinking about trying to use his power on him.

Kane laughed softly to himself. It was strange but, despite his apprehension at meeting the Ancient Demon who stood there looking all stern and implacable, it was the most relaxed he'd felt in days. That feeling, like he was crawling to escape his own skin, was easing by quick degrees, and he sighed with the relief. "So what is it?" Kane asked at last.

"The next time you are called," the Ancient said in a low, flat voice, his mercury eyes glittering with disapproval, "I suggest you make more haste."

"I know, but there was this little house-arrest thing I had to deal with," he said dryly.

Gideon's response was to lift a brow and then take a very purposeful step to his left, revealing the woman who was lying in the bed.

Kane sucked in a stuttering breath, making himself cough. She was pale as death, even a little gray, clearly emaciated of life and energy, but there was no mistaking the wild coils of long, red hair and the shape of the face that would be burned on him forever.

"What the hell is this?" he asked hoarsely, his dark blue eyes so much like Jacob's when glittering with outrage. His heart began to pound violently from just being in the same room with her.

"This," Gideon introduced with a sweep of his hand, "is Corrine."

"I know her name," Kane snapped. He tore his eyes away from Corrine's heart-shaped face, still beautiful in spite of her obvious illness.

"She is Isabella's sister," Gideon explained for his

confusion. "And she will one day become your family. However, not because Isabella will wed your brother."

Kane opened his mouth to ask for a clarification, but suddenly he knew.

He just knew.

He stepped closer to the bed, part of him still expecting Jacob to appear, to set him back on his ass as he had the first time. He could hardly breathe as he reached with shaking fingers to pick up the frail hand lying above the covers. Her fingers were long, graceful, her nails lengthy and manicured to perfection. He could see the outline of her bones through her translucent skin and his face contorted with pain to see it; his throat closed up with a rush of emotion like he was sure he'd never felt before.

"She still has a choice to make. This is not a foregone conclusion, you understand, Kane?" The lecture was soft and serious in his ear. "She will not love you until you win her. But before that can happen, my young friend, you must help her to become well. Come. Sit. Be patient. All will be revealed in time."

Kane obeyed the great Ancient without a word.

Isabella was pacing the floor when a sudden rush of wind blew past her. There was a loud thump behind her, and she whirled around to see Elijah lying in an indignant heap on the floor.

"Damn it, that was stupid," he muttered.

Despite her worry, Isabella could not help the giggle that escaped her as the giant gained his feet and dusted off his backside.

"I am sorry, Elijah."

"Yeah, yeah. It's not your fault. I got too close." He

gave her a sheepish grin. "Are you okay? Jacob told me to come to you. What's going on?"

She gave him a quick rundown of the situation. To her surprise, Elijah came closer to her and draped an arm over her shoulders.

"Don't you worry about a thing, Bella. Gideon prides himself on having never lost a patient."

"Elijah, how old are you?" she asked suddenly. "You don't act like any of the other Demons I have come to know. I don't mean this as an insult, but you act practically human. I mean, the only time I see you act with the same air of formality and reverence as the others has been during Council."

"Actually, I am five hundred and seventy-six years old. Outside of Gideon, Jacob, Noah, and I are the eldest Demons alive."

"What happened to your parents? Jacob's parents?" Isabella wondered why the question had never occurred to her before. And watching the way Elijah lowered his eyes and went a little pale, she realized it was a significant query.

"Well, let's just say that the last time there were necromancers existing en masse, they did a fair share of damage. My parents, Noah's father, and Jacob's father were Summoned at various stages over the past few hundred years. Jacob's mother didn't live very long after giving birth to Kane. I know I'm not much like the others. I guess after my parents were taken, I got a little fast and loose with all the seriousness of our culture."

"I suppose I can understand that. Thank you for sharing this with me. I can imagine it isn't an easy thing to talk about."

"Made more difficult by knowing necromancers have returned. But it is my hope that having you here is a good portent. Maybe this time we won't be so easily victimized, if we're blessed with Druids as good in their hearts and intentions as you are."

"I hope that is true, Elijah. But knowing humans as I do, I realize being a Druid won't necessarily make them a good person."

"This is true of any race, Bella. You only need to look at those like Ruth to see that," he said with a wink.

"You're incorrigible, Elijah." Isabella paused for a long moment. "Elijah, tell me something. How do necromancers learn what your true names are if so few people are privy to the information?"

"Well, I'm ashamed to say that it could be considered our own fault. Before we kept the ritual secret, we used to record names and births. Somewhere along the line, the necromancers procured a list of births. The devastation won't soon be forgotten. Gideon was the only Ancient to survive the slaughter. Jacob, Noah, and I are three out of only three dozen remaining Elders.

"I have no idea how the necromancers obtained the first Demon's name this time around. I suspect it was Lucas, because he was *Siddah* to Saul and the others who are missing. No doubt in his torment he revealed their names. You see, a *Siddah*—"

"Jacob told me. I know what *Siddah* are. Was Lucas *Siddah* to anyone else? Did he have children whose names he might reveal?"

"Lucas has two blood daughters." Elijah looked away, tugging at a loose thread of the couch's fabric. "And he was considered a great teacher among us. He was *Siddah* to a great many others."

"Oh no. Elijah," Isabella breathed, "how can you possibly protect them?"

"We can't. Each one of them realizes they may be the next to go."

"This is horrible," Isabella choked. "All of this time you've known this? Why didn't anyone tell me?"

"To what end, Bella? There's nothing you can do. All we can do is begin to hunt for the bastards."

Isabella absorbed his words quietly, gazing at the pattern of the wooden floor for a long minute while he watched her.

"I'm sorry," she said quietly. "I just feel so useless. I'm an enormous hindrance to anyone I come close to. I don't like it."

"It's a frustration we all go through, Bella. I know exactly how you're feeling. All of us do."

"Elijah." She contemplated him for a long minute, mischief lighting up her eyes. "You know, I'm forced to wonder if there isn't a smart-mouthed Druid female out there somewhere with your name tattooed on her genes."

She laughed when he gave her a horrified expression.

"There's no reason to be mean," he retorted. "I promise you this, little Enforcer, there isn't a Demon or Druid woman anywhere on this planet who could convince me I'd be better off with her. You'd be wasting your time trying to play matchmaker for me."

Any response Isabella would have made was cut off by the sound of the bedroom door finally opening. She hurried to broach Gideon.

"Is she okay?"

"She will be after a few days of constant exposure to Kane," he responded. "I do not expect she will awaken until then, but she is out of danger. She has displayed a remarkable fortitude, Enforcer. Usually it takes far less time to cause this level of damage. Perhaps it is because her contact with Kane was so brief."

Isabella bit her lip, chewing it apprehensively for a moment. "I suppose this means she and Kane . . . are . . . like Jacob and me?"

"It is no great curiosity, Druid. Jacob and Kane are of a similar genetic make-up, just as you and your sister are. It stands to reason that if Jacob and you are complementary, then your siblings are very likely complementary to one another as well."

"She will miss the ceremony," Isabella said regretfully.

"But she will live to see her own."

Isabella nodded. She could very easily live with that.

Jacob filtered softly into the room, entering by the window that had spit Isabella out, tossing her into his life like a shower of precious gold. He coalesced into his natural form, looking around the sunlit room slowly until he found her. She was curled up on the couch, shivering a little in her sleep because the cold October day was seeping in through the open window just as he had. Tonight the moon would be full at last. It would be the first Hallowed moon he would be spending as an Imprinted mate and an end to the hundreds of vacant, lonely nights beforehand. Tonight he would take his mate to wife.

He moved to her side quietly, kneeling down beside her makeshift bed, reaching to tuck an afghan around her trembling body. He brushed her hair from one cool cheek, slowly drinking in the curves of her beautiful face. He didn't need to, really, for it was burned into his memory and his heart for all time already.

I love you too, Jacob.

Her lashes fluttered up as the thought filled his head and heart. He smiled down into her eyes.

"I did not mean to wake you," he murmured.

"Then you'd have to become someone else, Jacob, because I'm fairly certain I'm always aware of your presence when you're close to me."

"Not for the wide world, little flower. I am quite content to be exactly who I am and to be greatly blessed with exactly who you are."

He touched his mouth to hers reverently. She smiled beneath his lips, waiting for him to pull back again so she could search his face more thoroughly.

"You look exhausted."

"I am a Nightwalker, little flower. We were never meant to be out in the day."

"Did you find them all? Please, tell me."

"Yes. All from this month. Gideon said that just the past two weeks would be enough, but I would rather be thorough, considering what was at stake."

"Were there any Druids?"

"Just one, Bella."

She didn't need him to tell her what had happened, it was written all over his drawn face and crushing thoughts.

"Oh no . . ." Tears sprang into her eyes and she sat up and drew him into her arms as tightly as she could. "Oh, Jacob."

He was silent and still as he let her try to comfort him. The Druid they had lost was a male, and the Demon he had ignorantly punished for finding her mate was the young daughter of none other than Councillor Ruth.

Ruth had never been considered even a neutral acquaintance, but this incident had most certainly made her a powerful enemy. As a consequence, she would now be a powerful enemy for Isabella as well. Their future wouldn't be an easy one, and it weighed heavily on him. In his conscience he struggled with the wisdom of making her a part of his life, and thereby a target to his enemies, both abroad and domestic, but in his heart he knew that he could never deprive himself of her sweet closeness, and logically he couldn't deprive her of his. He'd seen proof of that this very day.

Jacob didn't often find himself afraid, but he was when he considered what would happen to Bella should something happen to him.

"Jacob," she whispered softly in his ear, her small fingers sliding silkily through the hair on the back of his neck. "Jacob, physiology aside, how could my heart ever survive the loss of you?"

Jacob swore softly.

"So much for respecting the privacy of my thoughts," he teased half-heartedly.

"You're projecting, just as we both do when something affects us deeply." She pulled her head back, seeking his dark, troubled eyes. "But you have to stop trying to hide frightening truths from me, Jacob. Don't you trust me to be able to handle it? To be able to help you come to grips with it? I don't just want to be your partner because it was chosen by Destiny that we be so. I want to be your other half no matter what happens, Jacob, and I will settle for nothing less. For good and evil, for joy and sadness. These are all part of life, and you can't think to protect me from it all."

"I can damn well try," he said stubbornly, touching his forehead to hers as he frowned deeply. "What mate in his right mind would willingly want to expose his other half to danger and threat?"

"One who learns to trust her abilities to fight by his side if need be, just as she trusts him to be strong and protective. You once said you could accept that I was born to fight by your side. Has that changed?"

"No, Bella. I can accept it. But you have to forgive me if I find it harder to accept in some moments than in others."

"Of course," she said softly, brushing her mouth over his comfortingly. "I understand that. But I began to live the moment I met you in all the ways I was meant to live; it's only fitting that this life ends the moment you leave me. I'm determined, Jacob, that this won't happen for many, many centuries." She smiled gently, her eyes lighting up with tender, bright humor. "It could very well be that, in those future centuries, you'll come to be completely bored with all the things that seem so charming right now. Quite frankly, I'm a pain in the ass."

"I assure you," Jacob responded with a chuckle as he gathered her tightly to his chest, "I am well aware of that."

Isabella giggled, hugging him tightly as she rubbed her face against the fabric of his shirt.

CHAPTER THIRTEEN

Isabella exhaled, her breath clouding on the chill of the night air. She fidgeted with the long ribbons Legna had wound down the length of her arm in a crisscross pattern, the ends at her wrist dangling in two long, silky coils.

"Stop fussing," Legna admonished her, tapping her finger against Isabella's absently energetic hand.

"I'm getting married in a few minutes, Legna, I think I've a right to fuss." Isabella felt her heart turn over as she spoke aloud, listening to herself talk about her impending marriage.

"Well, brides are supposed to be blushing, as I understand it. At the moment you are no less than five shades of gray." Legna continued with her interrupted weaving of more ribbons in Isabella's hair. "And as much as it matches the silver of your dress, I think you would look better with a little natural color." Legna reached to smooth down a portion of the shimmering silver fabric that draped off of the bride's shoulders in a Grecian fashion. "You know," she pressed, "there are only two nights in a year when Demons perform a joining ceremony. Samhain and Beltane. If you pass out tonight, you will have to wait until next spring."

"Thanks for the bulletin. You're too kind," Isabella retorted dryly.

"Actually, purely out of kindness, I will tell you that your future husband is just shy of tossing his cookies himself, so you can take comfort in knowing he is just as nervous as you are."

"Legna!" Bella laughed. "You're a wretch!" She turned to look at the female Demon, briefly admiring how pretty she looked in her soft white chiffon gown. "And how would you know? You're standing too close to me to be able to sense his emotions."

"Because when I went to fetch the ribbons, he was seated next to Noah with his head between his knees." Legna giggled. "I have never seen anything rattle Jacob before. I cannot help but find it amusing."

Isabella smiled wanly, rubbing at the ache in her forehead.

"Tell me something, Legna, how do you filter through all of this?"

"All of what?"

"All this emotion. I think I can feel everything anyone is feeling in a five-mile radius."

"Well, I am just used to it, I guess. I discard all the useless stuff and block out what disturbs me. Believe me, it took quite a few years for me to perfect the barriers I use to do so. Do you need me to move away? Will that help?"

"No, please. You are the only thing keeping me on my feet at present. It's . . . It's becoming sort of like a background music."

"I find it interesting that my empathy affects you without any effort on your part, but when you absorb

powers from the males you have to actually concentrate to use it."

"Or be panicked," Isabella reminded wryly. "But
you're right. Perhaps it's because, like my abilities, the
nature of yours isn't how to bring it on, but how to shut
it off. Jacob and Noah and the other males have to concentrate to use their abilities, you have to concentrate
to *not* use yours."

"Not all. Teleportation takes a great deal of
concentration."

"Well, then that explains why I'm still here, instead
of popping up in Peru all of a sudden."

Legna laughed at that, giving Isabella's hair a final
pat. Legna stepped back and made a sound of ap-
proval. "There, you are all finished. You look lovely,
Isabella."

"Thank you," she replied, nervously touching her
hair to feel Legna's intricate work. "And, Legna, thank
you so much for standing up with me. It should be Corrine's place, but she's so ill. And, anyway, you've always
been so kind and generous toward me. This means a
great deal to me."

"It means a great deal to me too," Legna insisted,
reaching to squeeze one of Isabella's hands. "I am hon-
ored you feel me worthy to take the place of your
sister."

"Oh, Legna, you are beyond worthy. I'm very happy
that we're becoming good friends. I was so afraid you'd
never want to get within a ten-foot radius of me after
what happened."

"Trust me, if I told you some of the goof-ups I made
as a youngster, you would laugh yourself silly." She
smiled warmly and gave Isabella's hand one last squeeze.
"Enough of this. Are you ready?"

"Yes. Now, tell me again why I'm freezing my ass off in the middle of the woods?"

Legna chuckled.

"Because it is tradition. Your mate must find you and then carry you to the altar. Seeking you out is symbolic of his desire to let nothing come between you. Bringing you to the altar is a reflection of how it is his duty to help you over obstacles so that you may reach moments of joy together."

"It's very romantic," Isabella said, "if a little chauvinistic."

"Not in the least. The sharing of responsibility within a joining is symbolized just as strongly. The bride must tie the handfasting ribbon around her mate's wrist. The white ribbon symbolizes honesty and love and fidelity, and by allowing himself to be so tied means the groom must provide for her at all times, as she will provide for him. The black is a promise that they will forever do all in their power to protect their union, their children, and the perpetuation of the essentials of our culture."

"But you've tied a red ribbon to the end of the black, Legna. What does that mean?"

"Actually"—the Demon woman smiled—"there is no precedent for the red ribbon. However, I felt it only fair to have a physical reminder that you have a culture of your own and will have just as much right to perpetuate that within your children as Jacob does."

"Legna," Isabella giggled, giving her an admonishing look, "that is positively rebellious and feminist of you."

"I never claimed to be an old-fashioned girl," Legna confided with a wink. "Now, I must go and tell Jacob that you are ready and awaiting his arrival." She bent to give Isabella an affectionate kiss on the cheek. "Good luck. I wish you joy."

"Thank you so much, Legna."

The Demon woman smiled, then turned and dashed off. After she was out of sight, the sound of her breaking through the brush disappeared altogether and a soft breeze carried the scent of sulfur to Isabella.

Relieved to be free of Legna's empathic abilities, Isabella sat back against the large boulder that rested near the tall pines closest to her. She fussed with her dress and ribbons for a moment and then wrapped her arms around herself to conserve body heat. It was an awfully cold night, and if it were not only October, she would swear she scented snow in the air. She exhaled, playing with her breath in the cold air, making clouds of various thickness and speed with it.

"Damn it, Jacob, I'm freezing my butt off."

"I came as fast as I could, considering I thought it would be wise to walk the last few yards."

Isabella whirled around, her smiling face lighting up the silvery night with more ease than the fullest of moons. She leapt up into his embrace, eagerly drinking in his body heat and affection.

"I can see it now. 'Daddy, tell me about your wedding day.' 'Well, son,'" she mocked, deepening her voice to his timbre and reflecting his accent uncannily, "'The first words out of your mother's mouth were *I'm freezing my butt off*!'"

"Very romantic, don't you think?" he teased. "So, you think it will be a boy, then? Our first child?"

"Well, I'm fifty percent sure," she laughed.

"Wise odds. Come, little flower, I intend to marry you before the hour is up." With that, he scooped her off her feet and carried her high against his chest. "Unfortunately, we are going to have to do this hike the hard way."

"As Legna tells it, that's what you're supposed to do."

"Yeah, well, I assure you a great many grooms have fudged that a little." He reached to tuck her chilled face into the warm crook of his neck.

"Surely the guests would know. It takes longer to walk than it does to fly . . . or whatever . . . out of the woods."

"This is true, little flower. But passing time in the solitude of the woods is not necessarily a difficult task for a man and woman about to be married."

"Jacob!" she gasped, laughing.

"Some traditions are not necessarily publicized," he teased.

"You people are outrageous."

"Mmm, and if I had the ability to turn to dust right now, would you tell me no if I asked to . . . pass time with you?"

Isabella shivered, but it was the warmth of his whisper and intent, not the cold, that made her do so.

"Have I ever said no to you?"

"No, but now would be a good time to start, or we will be late to our own wedding," he chuckled.

"How about no . . . for now?" she asked silkily, pressing her lips to the column of his neck beneath his long, loose hair.

His fingers flexed on her flesh, his arms drawing her tighter to himself. He tried to concentrate on where he was putting his feet.

"If that is going to be your response, Bella, then I suggest you stop teasing me with that wicked little mouth of yours before I trip and land us both in the dirt."

"Okay," she agreed, her tongue touching his pulse.

"Bella . . ."

"Jacob, I want to spend the entire night making love to you," she murmured.

Jacob stopped in his tracks, taking a moment to catch his breath.

"Okay, why is it I always thought it was the groom who was supposed to be having lewd thoughts about the wedding night while the bride took the ceremony more seriously?"

"You started it," she reminded him, laughing softly.

"I am begging you, Isabella, to allow me to leave these woods with a little of my dignity intact." He sighed deeply, turning his head to brush his face over her hair. "It does not take much effort from you to turn me inside out and rouse my hunger for you. If there is much more of your wanton taunting, you will be flushed warm and rosy by the time we reach that altar, and our guests will not have to be Mind Demons in order to figure out why."

"I'm sorry, you're right." She turned her face away from his neck.

Jacob resumed his ritual walk for all of thirty seconds before he stopped again.

"Bella . . ." he warned dangerously.

"I'm sorry! It just popped into my head!"

"What am I getting myself into?" he asked aloud, sighing dramatically as he resumed his pace.

"Well, in about an hour, I hope it will be *me*."

"What the hell is taking so long?" Elijah complained.

"Elijah, hush," Legna admonished. "It is their joining. Let them be."

Legna moved to snuggle up against her brother, allowing him to keep her warm as the three of them awaited the bride and her groom.

"*Jacob*! I swear if you don't put me down this very instant I'm going to marry someone else!"

Isabella's voice carried shrilly through the night, half annoyed, half laughing. The three waiting at the altar turned in unison to see the couple break from the tree line. Jacob had indeed carried his bride out of the woods, but he'd done so by slinging her over a shoulder, leaving her backside displayed prominently.

Elijah choked on a laugh and Legna released a horrified gasp. Noah reached to stay her from moving.

"Let it be, Legna. What did you expect from the two of them?"

Serves you right, you little tease.

Jacob, please! You're embarrassing me!

And having me walk out of the woods in a state of arousal would not have embarrassed me?

I said I was sorry!

Was that before or after the mental striptease you sent me?

Isabella sighed with exasperation, and then giggled.

"You know, Emily Post is having heart failure right about now."

"Good, then that makes two of us."

Jacob approached the amused gathering standing at the outdoor altar made of a huge tree stump. With a shrug of his shoulder, he set his bride onto her feet. Isabella turned to face them, pushing back her flyaway hair, acting for all she was worth as if she'd just arrived in a limo.

"Isabella, Jacob, stand before the altar," Noah instructed, his voice impressively official in spite of the humor dancing in his eyes. The couple did so quickly, all smiles and repressed laughter. "Isabella, take Jacob's right hand into yours."

Isabella extended her beribboned arm, sliding her palm warmly into her mate's.

"Now, wind the ribbons around his wrist."

As she did so, Isabella felt Legna step up behind her and rest both hands on her shoulders, and Elijah did the same to Jacob.

"At this point I am to ask you if you gained permission from your monarch, but . . . I believe that would be a little foolish, considering."

The small gathering laughed.

"The two Demons who stand behind you hold you now to indicate their support of your union. They will not release you until your joining is complete, after which you will hold and support one another for the rest of your lives." Noah turned to Jacob. "Jacob, the Enforcer, beloved of this female, father of her future children, guardian of her heart, her soul, and her life, kneel before her to show her your acceptance of her gift of becoming your mate, your wife, the joy and center of your destiny."

Jacob did so quickly, kneeling in the damp grass, locking his gaze with hers.

"Isabella, you are my destiny," he said softly, bringing their joined hands to his lips.

"Rise, Jacob." Noah turned to Isabella as Jacob obeyed. "Isabella, the Enforcer, beloved of this male, mother to his future children, guardian of his heart, his soul, and his life, kneel before him to show him your acceptance of his gift of becoming your mate, your husband, the joy and—"

Legna released a startled gasp, cutting Noah off, the unexpected sound in the quiet reverence of the moment gaining everyone's attention.

"Legna, you're hurting me," Bella complained when the female Demon's grip tightened violently.

Isabella turned to see what had disturbed her friend and found herself looking up into the Demon female's terror-filled eyes. Legna screamed. It was a horrific sound of fright that made the little hairs on Isabella's arms and neck stand straight up. Instinctively, Bella reached for her friend with startled distress, grasping the biceps of the female Demon's nearest arm with her free hand.

"Legna!"

It was the first time Bella had ever heard Noah raise his voice in such a way, and the absolute fear she heard in his shout was alarming. It occurred to her in that moment that there was very little that creatures as powerful as the three men behind her could claim to be truly afraid of.

Isabella choked when she suddenly realized that Legna's feet and lower legs were dissolving away. In that moment, she looked like some kind of wraith, a half-present woman floating above the ground. Legna screamed again, clearly in horrible agony, her clutch on the bride growing even tighter while at the same time Jacob tried to pull Isabella away by their joined hands.

Isabella rapidly realized what was happening, that there was a name to what she was seeing, and all the ramifications beat down upon her like a million brutal fists.

"No! *No!*" she cried, hurling herself at Legna, wrapping her free arm around the Demon's increasingly fading body.

"Bella! Let go of her!" Jacob shouted.

But because of Isabella's strength, her very presence, none of them had the power to stop her.

"Don't go, Legna! Fight it! Don't let them take you!" Bella cried, tears pouring down her pale, cold cheeks as Legna's screams began to come back to back, each more bloodcurdling than the last.

All of a sudden, Isabella was awash with pain, the most breathtaking agony she had ever known.

A bright burst of orange light struck her like an atomic shock wave, blowing her body to pieces, right down to her last molecule.

Jacob howled in outrage when Isabella's hand tore out of his, rending the ribbons that bound them into two parts, just before she and Legna disappeared completely.

"Bella!" Jacob bellowed, all of his utter joy converted into a sudden, paralyzing agony. He fell to his knees, grasping at the earth that still held the impression of where she had stood only a heartbeat ago. His fingers clawed relentlessly through the grass and loam of the sacred place. He roared out, his cry like that of a wild and tortured animal, the impossible weight of his grief echoing into the cold and the dark until all the woods ran from leaf to root with the sound. He wrenched his body aside, his fists slamming into the altar, a sharp crack resounding into the night as the wood split.

"Jacob . . ."

Jacob swung his arm out, striking Elijah's hands violently away from him when he moved to touch him.

"How?" he demanded viciously of no one in particular, his eyes wide and savage, but clearly seeing nothing—nothing but the pain and fear on Isabella's face the moment she had been torn away from him. "She is not Demon! She cannot be Summoned! Who would even know to do so, would know her value?"

No one could answer him.

Elijah started in surprise and stumbled off balance when the earth beneath his feet rumbled and rolled, billowing like a shaken blanket. The warrior grabbed the Enforcer.

"Jacob! Stop it!"

The Enforcer looked up at the Wind Demon blankly. The ground between Elijah's feet split apart. The warrior took to the air in reflex. He glanced down and saw steam burst from the ground. A moment later the ooze of superheated molten rock began to seep from the multitude of small fissures that had opened around them.

That was when Elijah realized he was reprimanding the wrong Demon.

He reached toward the sky, grasping at the heavens until clouds coalesced and exploded. Rain burst from their underbellies, drenching the magma that was trying to escape the depths to which it should have remained confined. The area exploded in steam as Elijah shot to the ground, landing behind his monarch.

Noah was standing with his feet braced hard apart and his hands clenched into fists so tight that blood was dripping from the cut of his own fingernails. Elijah could see the Demon was trembling hard, but it had nothing to do with the rumblings of the earth beneath their feet.

Elijah was at a loss for all of a heartbeat but then reached to grab the King by the arm and jerked him hard to get his attention.

"Time," he spat harshly. "Jacob. Noah. Time is of the essence. We three are the only ones who have a hope of correcting this. It will take all of our combined efforts, and it will need to start now. This very moment. There are no moments to waste on pain or rage or anything else, no matter how justified!"

Jacob dragged himself up to his feet, feeling as if his

heart had been sucked into the same vortex that had stolen his Isabella. He flicked a cold gaze up to Elijah and the King. He saw in Noah's hollow gaze the very same thing he was thinking. *Time is nothing.* No Demon, not *one*, had ever been saved from a Summoning intact. But Bella was not Demon, and Legna . . . none of them could ever give up Legna without a fight.

The trembling ground finally gave way to quiet, settling into peace, only crusted stripes of steaming rock left to pay reminder to Noah's outrage. The Demon King took a deep breath, as if cleansing himself of his wrath with oxygen.

"Four, Elijah," he corrected hoarsely. "We four. Go to Gideon and demand he come here this very instant." Noah's voice was completely unrecognizable, and Elijah could tell he was on some sort of autopilot. However, it was enough that the King was moving into action. "When we find her"—Noah looked into the eyes of his Enforcer, his cheek twitching with the clench of his jaw—"you better remember exactly who you are and what your duty is, Enforcer. If she suffers for even one second—"

"She will not suffer," Jacob swore, his voice reflecting the ice in his veins. "I would never fail your trust in me."

Then the Enforcer turned that rough, chilled voice to the Warrior Captain.

"Fetch Gideon. Now."

Elijah knew the hunter in the Enforcer when he saw it, felt it surging forward, and knew that whoever had stolen Jacob's bride was going to pay in violent, primal ways for their heartless transgressions. As for Legna . . . seasoned warrior such as he was, even Elijah would not contemplate that question until the reckoning of it was forced on him.

Elijah became part of the wind a fraction of a second after that thought. Jacob flicked cold, merciless eyes back to the King.

"There is hope. If Bella is with her, if she survived this magic . . ." Jacob had to pause and shake off the surge of rage that came with the obliterating concept that she might not have. "So long as there is breath in Bella, there is hope. She will do anything she can to protect Legna."

"And if there is no hope?" Noah asked with a stoicism that still seethed as the earth had moments ago. "Will your bride stand by and allow my baby sister to . . ." Noah closed his eyes, his teeth clenching with a rage that made him shake and breathe with violence enough to spew fire. "Will one so green, so soft in sensibilities, ever find it within herself to give peace to Legna if we cannot reach her? Will I find my sister a monster, rushing to murder and fornicate at her every demented whim? I have protected, cared for, and nurtured Legna from the day my mother died when she was not five years old," Noah said in a voice that must have been raked over the coals of hell. "You will forgive me if I do not trust one so callow with so precious a task. I will not stand by and allow this."

"I swear to you, Noah, I will not allow it either. And you must trust Bella. The softness you see hides a fierce little warrior and a moral code to rival mine. Rest easy in that."

"I will rest easy when Legna is safe. Safe from her captors . . . or safe from herself."

"I know. And I will rest easy when I am wed."

"Do everything in your power to provide me with the one, Enforcer, and I will do everything in mine to provide you with the other."

Jacob extended his hand and Noah clasped it to seal

the oath, neither realizing that Noah's touch was swiftly burning away the torn ribbons draping over Jacob's palm.

Isabella was falling fast and out of control.

Then in a blink, she hit the ground hard, knocking the breath from her body and sending a shower of stars across her vision.

"Holy cow, two for the price of one!" a distant male voice exclaimed.

"That's impossible," a second man returned.

"Well, you see it, don't you? So I guess it isn't all that impossible after all."

"You! Demon! What is the meaning of this?"

There was a long, soft, gurgling hiss and then, in a horrific voice Isabella had heard once before, it responded.

"It is . . . unprecedented, my master. But you have two. Two. Am I to be rewarded? Set me free, my master."

"No, Demon. I'm not satisfied yet." The speaker's voice changed, becoming soft, hypnotic. "But I promise you that as soon as my experiments are complete, I'll set you free."

Bella blinked her eyes halfway open, blinding herself with the enormous amounts of light that shone around her. The room was full of that eerie blue light she'd first seen in the warehouse after meeting Jacob. She sat up slowly, expecting every bone in her body to shatter under the motion. But after a quick internal assessment, she realized she was little more than bruised. Squinting against the light, she looked around herself.

She was lying in the center of a huge pentagram that had been chalked onto wooden floorboards. The blue light was quickly fading, allowing her sight to improve, and she saw Legna's crumpled form lying less than a foot away from her feet.

Everything suddenly rushed in on her and she remembered what had happened and understood exactly where she was. But how had this happened? She wasn't a Demon. From what she'd been told, when a Demon was Summoned, it caused no danger to anyone in the immediate vicinity; a Summoning was quite specific and limited to the power source connected with the name used in the imprisoning act.

So then how had she been caught up in it?

She realized the how and why could wait to be answered later. She turned onto her hands and knees and slid over to Legna. When she touched the other woman's cheek, it felt as though she were burning up with fever. What had Jacob said about a Summoning? Had he ever mentioned how much time it actually took for a transformation to take permanent hold? *Oh, why didn't I pay better attention?* How is it she had never found a book on the subject of Summoning, what with all the books and scrolls and prophecies and laws she'd consumed?

"Look, that one is awake."

"They're females. I didn't think there were females."

"Have you never heard of a succubus? Of course these creatures of hell have both sexes. Look at how beautiful they make themselves. Who wouldn't be tempted by that?"

Isabella finally looked up to see the faces of the people who were talking. There were two men standing relatively close to the pentagram in which she lay and a male and female seated on a table not too much farther away.

That was when she noticed the smell.

It was an awful stench, like burnt animal hair, gasoline, and rotten eggs combined. She felt her stomach turn over and her mouth water with nausea. She pressed her sleeve to her mouth and nose, hoping it would ease the disgusting odor.

"That one is a small one," the female laughed. "I think you should throw it back."

The men chuckled over her humor. The tallest one moved closer to the edge of the pentagram, crouching down on his haunches so he was eye level with Bella.

"What do you think, spawn? Should we throw you back?"

Isabella did not respond. Instead she moved to take Legna's torso into her lap, trying to make her unconscious friend as comfortable as she could, cradling her head to her breast protectively.

"Aww. How sweet. I think it actually cares for its friend."

"Give it up, Ingrid. In a few hours these two will look just as ugly and slobbery as the others. Then they will be spitting out names to save their own necks like this one does. These monsters don't know a thing about loyalty."

Isabella's eyes followed the careless hand gesture the tall necromancer made, and for the first time she noticed there was a second pentagram in the room, and in its center sat a completely Transformed Demon, looking exactly as Saul had before his death.

"You know, Kyle, I think that little one is stronger than she looks. It took hours before the male woke up initially. The other female's out cold, yet she's already conscious."

"You have a point," Kyle remarked. He picked up something off the floor and threw it at Isabella's head. She couldn't do anything more than duck with Legna burdening her lap. The object glanced off her shoulder. She recovered and glared at her captors.

"You made it mad," Ingrid chortled, grabbing her sides as she rocked with laughter.

"Aww, did I make you mad, little spawn?" Kyle taunted.

"I don't think it talks," remarked the more rotund necromancer who was seated next to the sorceress.

"I'm sure it does, it's just being stubborn. Isn't that right, spawn? Demon bitch?" Kyle grinned evilly at Isabella. "You want out, don't you, little spawn? If you behave, I'll let you go real soon. Come on. Say something. I know you want to."

Isabella just turned her head away, fighting back the sting of angry tears. She was fairly certain she was in no immediate danger, but Legna's life might hang on what she was able to accomplish in these next crucial minutes. She tried to calm her thoughts, tried to seek Jacob's mind, but he was mute to her. She had no idea how far they'd been transported, and she imagined the room was blanketed with spells to prevent her from calling for help.

But then again, she mused, if her dampening ability worked as Gideon claimed it would, she should be able to neutralize any magic. Still, it was a hidden card and she kept quiet and still as she tried to figure out how best to bet on her particular ace. She glanced at the chalk drawings beneath and around her. They were meant to hold a Demon. Would they hold a Druid? Or maybe she had disarmed them by her mere presence.

Her four captors were too busy being cocky and self-righteous. They likely would have never considered the possibility of the captives breaking such a foolproof power symbol. She glanced at the other Demon, who was at present chewing off one of the claws on its foot.

Why should they doubt the pentagram? It apparently had been working quite well with this other Demon.

Oh, Jacob, where are you? I don't know if I'm ready to do this all by myself.

But she might have to, she realized as nothing but silence answered her. She couldn't allow Legna to be their next victim. But it wasn't just a matter of escape. She had to see to it that all of those who could possibly know Legna's true name could never use it against her again. That would mean not only destroying the necromancers, but also destroying the perverted Demon who'd sacrificed Legna, revealing her name for the hope of freedom.

Isabella began to rock her burden softly, more for her own comfort than anything. She tried to think as clearly as she could, considering as many options and possibilities as she could. If indeed her dampening power was affecting her prison, it could just as easily affect her captors. However, she would be discovered if one came too close and became aware of something being amiss before she was ready to act.

Physically speaking, none of them presented an obvious challenge. In actuality, the group looked a lot like a collection of geeks. They sort of reminded her of the high school chess club. It was clear they were smart, probably extraordinarily so in order to become users of complex magics. Isabella realized she could sense other things about them, no doubt because she was still siphoning from Legna.

They were full of a strange false confidence. They knew they were powerful, knew they were smart, and knew they were doing incredible things, but in the end it didn't change the deep-seated feelings of inadequacy they were trying to push aside. Isabella knew that feeling.

She had been considered less than acceptable herself in her school days. But unlike the four before her, she had realized that none of that adolescent behavior counted out in the real world. She'd left those feelings behind the day she'd graduated into a world that praised intelligence and creativity and scrabbled to snap it up.

The four were trapped in their school mentality, although none of them could be a day less than thirty years old. It was no wonder they had turned to such a despicable crusade, with all its horrific consequences. It gave them a chance to be the bullies for a change, to set a group of creatures below themselves.

Isabella absorbed all this quietly, filing it away in an accessible place. She had a feeling it might come in handy.

The one called Kyle had finally moved away, having grown bored with her lack of rising to his bait. He was wearing a blue and gold cloak straight out of a Merlin fairy tale, and so were the others. Isabella had to keep herself from laughing at the theatrical absurdity of it.

"Why do you suppose we caught two?" the rotund necromancer asked.

"Maybe they have the same name. I don't know, Rick. But you know what they say, don't look a gift horse in the mouth. Santo is going to be very impressed. The more of these things we catch, the more magic he'll share with us. I'm dying to learn that fire spell he was telling us about."

"I want to learn the glamour spell," the sorceress said. "I would kill to look like a supermodel and go teach some guys I know a lesson in humility."

"You don't need any of that. You got me now," Rick reminded her, scooting closer to her to drape an arm over her shoulders.

Isabella turned her attention away from the exchange

and looked down at Legna. She was a little pale, still out
cold, but otherwise didn't seem changed in any way. As
much as it relieved Isabella, it perplexed her. Somehow
she'd gotten the impression that transformation began
immediately after a Summoning. But then again, she
couldn't tell if there were any internal troubles occur-
ring in Legna. She bit her lip worriedly, closed her eyes,
and once more tried to find Jacob in her thoughts.

CHAPTER FOURTEEN

Jacob sat crouched on the head of one of the many gargoyles decorating the old brick building. He turned his sense of smell into the brisk night breeze, trying to gather information, while at the same time he tried to ease the panic that caused his heart to race madly. He looked down to the pavement ten stories below him where Noah was leaning with seeming idleness against the brick exterior of the same building. In truth, Noah was tracking the ebb and flow of the energy around him. Every living thing in the universe had a unique energy signature.

What the necromancers didn't realize was that a Summoning didn't just pop a Demon out of one place and then drop it in another. Summoning converted the victim to a form of its purest energy, and then this energy was dragged through an extremely physical route over however many miles it took to get from the starting point to the end point. This could be tracked with a great deal of ease for those who were skilled.

The problem came at the end of the trail. The closer you got to a necromancer's hiding place, the more confusing the search became. Jacob had learned during the last rash of Summonings that necromancers were very good at cloaking themselves. They used spells and tokens and several other methods to make themselves invisible to even the strongest of Demon hunters.

It was at that point that Jacob would be forced to rely on instincts and logic rather than senses, the point when he had to try to think through the most sensible place a necromancer might choose to hole up in. Unfortunately, as in the case of Saul, highly populated areas such as the Bronx made the possibilities endless. There had been dozens of warehouses in the area of Isabella's apartment. If not for her premonition, it could've taken him far too long to search them all.

Necromancers, however, weren't very good at remaining inconspicuous. On many occasions, Jacob had rooted them out just by asking the question he'd posed to Isabella that night when they first met. Very often a necromancer's peculiar activities drew attention. And then there was the factor they couldn't hide: their scent. If they'd recently walked the street, Jacob could find them in a heartbeat.

Jacob leapt off the gargoyle, lofting down to street level with fractional increases in his weight and manipulations of gravity. He landed soundlessly beside Noah.

"My trail is cold. Are you having any luck?"

"No," Noah sighed, reaching to rub at the tension in his neck.

"They can't be too far from here."

"Can you sense Bella yet?"

"No, I cannot." Jacob clenched his teeth together.

Jacob suddenly caught a familiar scent in the air.

"Elijah," he and Noah said in unison.

Elijah swirled into form in front of them a moment later.

"What news?"

"Gideon thinks he can find them," Elijah said. "He's searching the area in astral form. He said something about Bella's genetic code being a neon beacon. I have no idea what it means, but it sure as hell sounded good to me."

Isabella was pacing a small arching path on the far side of the pentagram, having decided that putting some distance between her and Legna might help the female Demon regain consciousness.

Two of the necromancers had left the room. The third was busy in the makeshift kitchen a good distance away. The sorceress was still seated on her table, snapping a piece of gum incessantly as she read from a large book that looked as ancient as some of the books Isabella had read in the Demon library. It was clear, however, that the female's attention was divided between the page opened before her and Isabella's movements, which she watched with obvious curiosity.

After a few more minutes, the magic-user put her book down and hopped off the table. She shoved her hands in her pockets and strolled up to the pentagram.

"Hey, you," she addressed Isabella. "What's with the getup? The ribbons and the dress?"

Isabella stopped her pacing, tilting her head and contemplating the other woman.

"I was at a wedding," she said quietly.

It was clear Ingrid hadn't expected Isabella to actually respond, as her eyes went wide.

"A wedding? You guys have weddings?"

"Yes." Isabella stepped a little closer to the edge of the pentagram. "We have weddings, we have husbands and wives and children. We have artists, poets, doctors, and ministers, just like you do."

"Yeah, sure you do." Ingrid snorted with her laughter. "Why would I lie?"

"Because you're going to do anything you can to save your neck."

"And do our acts of self-preservation differ so much from what you would do if our places were exchanged?"

That remark seemed to make the sorceress uncomfortable. She shifted her weight from one foot to the other, snapped her gum, and burrowed her hands deeper into her pockets.

"Yeah, well, if our places were switched, I wouldn't end up looking like that." She indicated the Demon in the second pentagram.

"Are you so sure? The magic you use is full of poison and evil. It may be that it could make anyone look like that. Even a human."

"Yeah right." Ingrid laughed, a short barking sound. "The magic just strips away all this glamour magic you things use. Every Demon we summon is always impossibly good looking. It isn't natural. There's what's natural for you monsters."

"Monsters? What makes us more monstrous than you? You who enslave a living, breathing person and use them viciously, with no sense of mercy or compassion?"

"You aren't a person, you're a Demon from hell. I've read the stories of the mischief, cruelty, and seduction you all take so much delight in. It's what you do that's wrong. But unlike other humans, we aren't so blind to the existence of magic and the disgusting things that live

342 *Jacquelyn Frank*

at night, poisoning innocent people with vampirism, lycanthropy, and God knows what else."

"You sound so very sure of yourself."

"Because I know I'm right."

"I wonder," Isabella remarked quietly, "I wonder how you'd feel if our positions were reversed and someone believed that of you. You are, after all, using magic. People will be afraid of you for that."

"Don't be stupid. This isn't the same thing at all. And don't think your sly words are going to work, spawn. I know your tricks."

"You don't know half of my tricks," Isabella said, her eyes flashing dangerously.

"Go ahead," Ingrid taunted. "Try it. Try and use your spells and magic. I'd love to see you twisting in agony on the ground when the pentagram reflects it back on you. Would serve you right for trying to screw with me."

"You first," Isabella baited her. "Let's see some of this power you use so righteously. Surely it can cross the barrier. Come on, you know you want to fry my insides with that electrical charge you use. Oh, yes," Isabella informed her with a smile when Ingrid's eyes practically popped out of her head, "I've met your kind before. Oh! And look at that! I'm still alive and well. Imagine that," she hissed.

"You're a liar. You're a no-good, lying Demon bitch!"

"You probably knew him," Isabella continued matter-of-factly. "He did say you were some kind of society. I can't imagine it's a very large society. Tall, dark-haired fellow? A cross between a geek and an athlete? No?"

"Shut up," the woman hissed, her hands escaping her pockets and clenching in anger. Ghosts of blue energy began to snap through her aura. "You better shut up or you'll learn real fast how easily my magic crosses the pentagram."

Isabella took a step closer, allowing a taunting smile to play over her lips.

"Ingrid, get the hell away from there!" Kyle grabbed the woman's arm, jerking her back from the pentagram. "What're you, stupid?"

"Let go of me," Ingrid snapped, jerking her arm free of his grasp. "It can't cross the pentagram. I was perfectly safe."

Kyle glanced warily at Isabella. She gifted him with a sly smile and was rewarded with the shiver of discomfort that coasted through him.

"So," he said, "you do talk after all."

"I can't vouch for my diction, but yes, I talk."

"Kyle, she doesn't sound like the others," Ingrid whispered fiercely. "They all had that weird accent. She sounds like . . . I dunno . . . like she's from Brooklyn or something."

"What difference does that make?" Kyle snapped irritably. "She can sound like Scarlett O'Hara for all I care. She's still a Demon. They're all liars and actors, trying to trick us. Stop being so naïve, Ingrid."

"I'm not being naïve! I'm telling you, I've a bad feeling about that one. It's like she isn't even afraid. All the others were terrified of being trapped."

Kyle seemed to stop and think about that for a moment. He turned and walked over to the second pentagram.

"You! Do you know that one?" He pointed to Isabella.

"That one . . ." The Demon gurgled with contemplation, its clawed hands reaching to scrape and gouge the wood of the floor on either side of it.

Just then Legna made a soft sound from behind Isabella. Bella turned, torn between what the Demon was going to say and aiding Legna. She hoped that whoever the Demon was, he had not met her. However, it wouldn't matter in the end. He was going to say whatever it was he was going to say and she wasn't able to stop him. She turned to face Legna, watching her raise her head, then draw herself up to her hands and knees weakly. Bella didn't move toward her, afraid that she would affect Legna's regained energy.

"*Aine ya hulli caun*," Isabella said suddenly, only then realizing she could put her language skill to use for something besides interpreting prophecy.

Legna turned her head toward her, her eyes widening with shock and fear.

"Demon speak," the other trapped Demon chortled. "Demon that one is. Yes."

"What did she say?" Kyle demanded.

Damn it, Isabella thought fiercely.

"Demon speak. Yes . . . ." The Demon pulled an impressively large splinter out of the floor. "Afraid, be not. She says to be not afraid to Legna . . . Indirianna . . . pretty, tasty Indirianna."

Isabella swallowed hard, wrapping her arms around herself for warmth. She knew the Demon had just spoken Legna's power name, she could see it in the weakened woman's eyes as her expression turned to utter horror.

"Lucas," she said hoarsely.

"Indirianna!" Lucas chortled, suddenly leaping about his cage like an excited chimpanzee. "*Rentinon Siddah to Indirianna!*"

"Lucas!" Legna sobbed, scrabbling over to Isabella's side of the pentagram in order to get closer to Lucas.

"Legna," Isabella warned softly, taking the other woman by the arm and drawing her under her hold. "He isn't the Lucas you know," she whispered into the trembling woman's ear. "Don't provoke him, his reactions will only hurt your heart."

Legna swallowed loudly and Isabella could feel the nausea that washed through her friend.

"How long?" Legna managed to ask, suddenly sitting up and inspecting herself, running shaking hands over her body, raising limbs into her line of sight.

"A little over an hour. Legna, how much time do you have?"

"I do not know. None of us knows. We have only saved one Demon from Summoning in all these centuries."

"Only one?" Isabella repeated in shock.

"Yes, and he was never the same in spite of it. It was as if all of his civilization warred with an insane animal inside of him."

"What happened to him?"

Legna's eyes filled with tears and fear.

"Jacob killed him. He had to. He began to attack our females. When Jacob caught up to him, they had a terrible fight, and Jacob was forced to kill him to save his own life. Oh, Bella . . . I am so frightened. What will Jacob do when he finds me?"

"Legna . . . Legna, Jacob isn't going to kill you."

"Jacob the Enforcer! Enforcer comes! Kill me! Kill me, Enforcer!" the wild animal across from them started to taunt, laughing maniacally as he leapt and rolled around his prison wildly.

Legna gasped, and Isabella paled.

"Do you know Jacob's name?" Legna whispered fiercely.

"No. I don't."

Legna sighed with relief, relaxing for the first time since she regained consciousness.

"Good. Lucas is a male Mind Demon, meaning he is a full telepath. He could steal it from your thoughts."

"No, Legna. You forget. I'm immune to telepaths. No one can read me but Jacob."

"Yes, that is right. Yes, good," Legna agreed breathlessly, her chest rising and falling rapidly. "But . . . Destiny help me, without my power I cannot keep him from taking names from me."

"Move away from me, Legna, maybe that will help."

"No. Do not make me leave you," Legna begged fearfully.

"Okay. Shh. It's okay," Isabella whispered, hugging her close. "Let's try and figure something out. Do you know how long the rescued Demon was caught for?"

"I do not. But Jacob told me that it had taken him four hours to find Saul."

"It's okay. Don't be afraid. I won't let that happen to you."

"Hey, spawn. Quit chattering. If you're plotting an attempt to escape, you can forget it," Kyle barked, making Legna start in Isabella's embrace. "Your males couldn't escape no matter how much they tried, so you can bet you're far too weak to even try it."

"Great. A chauvinist necromancer. Just what the world needs," Isabella said dryly.

"You better watch your mouth," Kyle warned.

"Isabella, do not provoke them," Legna begged.

"It's all right. I won't." Isabella stroked Legna's coffee-colored tresses comfortingly.

She went silent, and the necromancer seemed pleased at her obedience. He crossed over to Ingrid again, a decidedly smug saunter in his step.

"You see? She's just as afraid as the rest. She's just trying to hide it, Ingrid."

"If you say so. When will we do the first spell? I want to see what kind they are. Especially the small one."

"Give me about a half hour. When the others get back."

Isabella looked up into Legna's eyes. She had heard Kyle as well, and it was clear she was putting her fear aside as she tried to think more logically. Bella almost wished she wouldn't. If Legna began to think about Bella's powers with the other Mind Demon close enough to read her thoughts . . .

"Pink elephants," Legna murmured. "Pink elephants."

Isabella smiled, allowing herself a small laugh. "Pink elephants in polka-dot dresses," she added.

"Pink elephants in polka-dot dresses with bright red parasols."

"Pink elephants! Pink pachyderms. Dots. Dots everywhere!" Lucas giggled happily.

Legna and Isabella exchanged victorious looks. As long as Legna kept the absurd image in her head, Isabella's identity and abilities were safe from theft. Bella had to admit she would not have had the discipline. She might inadvertently steal power, but she couldn't have stolen Legna's experience, her wisdom, and her centuries of training herself to remain in control of herself at all times.

So they were alone with only two magic-users. Isabella considered it would be a good time to try and escape, but that would leave two others out there who knew Legna's name. She also couldn't depend on Jacob reaching them in time, but it would really help if he were there.

"God, Jacob, where are you?" she muttered against Legna's hair.

Isabella was leaning her weight on her hand, her fingertips brushing the chalked circle that bound them. She noticed this and glanced to see if she was being watched at all. The necromancers were distracted. Using Legna's body as a block for her actions, she could test her ability to cross the outline. Slowly, biting her lip hard, she crept her fingers over the edge of their prison, and then quickly drew them back.

One test successfully completed, Bella thought, with a sigh of relief when there was no adverse reaction. She wasn't bound to the pentagram.

Suddenly, Legna shivered, her entire body locking up. The empath suddenly went lax, falling back onto the floor, blacking out. But then an eerie, soft breeze ruffled the unconscious woman's dress and hair. A moment later her eyes opened and she sat back up. She looked straight at Isabella.

"Greetings, little Enforcer," she said, her silver eyes flickering with experience of the ages.

"Gideon?" Bella whispered in shock.

"None other." Gideon stood up, his way of carrying himself radiating distinctively through Legna's figure. He looked around slowly, assessing everything he saw. Then he closed his eyes and concentrated.

After a long moment, the medic settled Legna's body across from her, sitting with one knee raised and her wrist resting leisurely on it. It was such a distinctly male position that Isabella had to turn down her eyes before she ended up laughing.

"Tell me what you know," he instructed with his usual lack of gentility.

"Four necromancers, three males and one female, and, as you see, Lucas." She indicated the Demon across the way. She paused. "Gideon, how is it that I'm here?"

"I do not know the truth of the matter. I have hypothesized, and when my research is complete, I will give you the fact of it."

"Gideon," she growled low between her teeth. "I'll settle for your best guess."

"Very well. A Demon's name is attached to the essence of that Demon's power. A power that you were absorbing at the moment of Legna's Summoning. My guess is that because of this, you were mistaken for the actual target and were drawn into the Summoning just as Legna was."

"Oh. I see."

"An act of providence, Enforcer. My internal diagnostic of Legna tells me that she is whole and well, unaffected by this trap. I suspect you are nullifying the energy that would cause her to transform."

"Hey! Didn't I tell you two to stop chattering?" Kyle barked from across the room.

Gideon glanced at the necromancer as if he were some sort of pesky fly.

She leaned in to whisper. "Where is Legna?"

"I sent her to sleep. She is safe in her subconscious."

"I didn't know you could do this."

"Have you never heard of Demonic possession?"

Isabella's spine straightened in surprise. If she didn't know better, she'd think Gideon had just cracked a joke. But his countenance was just as matter-of-fact as it had always been.

"That tears it. I'm going to teach you a lesson,

spawn," Kyle spat, marching up to the pentagram, his brown eyes full of indignant anger.

"What does it matter if we talk to each other, necromancer? Are you so afraid that you might not be able to hold us?" Bella countered, trying to toy with his psychology in order to keep him from doing anything that would reveal the truth of the matter.

"Hardly!" He snorted. "But you'll learn to obey me, you little bitch."

Kyle glanced around, clearly trying to decide on a form of punishment. Isabella's breath started to come a little faster and she sought the comfort of Gideon's silver eyes. Instead, she saw them close and a moment later Legna's body dropped lifelessly to the floor.

"You made that one faint," laughed Ingrid. "That's just too funny! Come on, Kyle. Teach that one a lesson. She's the one that deserves it."

Isabella suddenly rose up to her feet, bracing them apart and settling her closed fists on her hips. She wouldn't meet his threat sitting on the floor like some little weakling.

"Kyle, what's going on?"

The necromancer turned to see the other two had returned.

"Good. You're back. Let's start the spell. I can't wait to hear these two scream."

Isabella crossed the width of the large symbol, coming right to the edge closest to the magic-users. They ignored her as they began to join hands and form a crude standing circle. She heard Legna move somewhere behind her, just as Lucas started to screech. Monster or not, it was clear that he was very familiar with the ritual they were starting and that he was utterly terrified of it.

"Bella?"

"Stay back, gather your strength," she hissed to Legna.

Sparks of blue light began to sparkle like tiny fireworks around the chanting necromancers.

Hurry, Gideon, hurry! she prayed fiercely.

We are coming, little flower.

Isabella was so unbelievably relieved to hear that powerful, loving voice in her head that she felt like crying.

Jacob! Please, I can't do this alone! I can't protect Legna and fight necromancers and one of the Transformed all by myself. I know I'm not that strong!

Stay calm, Bella, you are capable of doing anything you will need to do to survive. You always have. We are almost there.

There are four of them, and they know how to combine their strength. They're starting a spell. Please be careful, Jacob. If you get too close to me you won't have your power!

I know, sweetheart. Relax, and trust us. When I tell you to, be ready to distract them. If you break their concentration it will backfire on them and knock the wind out of them.

I know just what to do.

That's my little Enforcer. Just remember, once you break the magic, you will set Lucas free. We will handle the necromancers. You must focus on Lucas.

Isabella nodded even though he couldn't see the gesture. She focused entirely on the foursome before her, her eyes narrowing into lavender slits of concentration and intent. Everything faded from her awareness, only the ribbons of blue light weaving between the necromancers holding her attention. If she'd seen her own smile in that moment, she would have realized she'd become the hunter she was destined to be.

Bella, do it now. Be careful.

She didn't even respond. She stepped over the edge

of the pentagram, clearing her throat loudly as she advanced quickly on them.

"Excuse me, but where can a girl get something to eat around here?"

Ingrid was the first to look at her.

"Kyle!" she screamed, her eyes practically bugging out of her head. "Kyle, it's out of the pentagram!"

Kyle jerked around to look at Bella, the blue energy flashing in wild twisting ropes as its flow was disturbed.

"That's because *it* isn't a Demon. Boy, for a bunch of geeks, you sure are stupid."

That cut it. Their concentration went to hell, and so did the magic they'd controlled. A huge explosion of crushing force blasted all five of them off their feet. Isabella's back slammed violently into a wall and her breath was forced from her lungs, the ominous sound of a bone snapping resounding in her subvocal hearing. She dropped to the floor like a stone, landing with a weak grunt. She tried to get up, scrabbling to her hands and knees, gasping for breath and then losing it all over again in a scream as pain blossomed brutally across her right side.

She gritted her teeth, determined to fight the pain and get to her feet. Jacob and the others needed her. She was the Enforcer, born to hunt the Transformed, and she needed to do her job. She staggered to her feet, shoving her wild hair away from her face, causing another spear of pain to drive into her side.

And then she saw Jacob.

He entered the room in a detonation of dark, vicious dust, coalescing into his tall, powerful form in the span of a breath. His rage radiated off him like a nimbus, every muscle in his body taut with deadly beauty, every handsome line of his face carved from marble vengeance.

Seeing him at last gave her a rush of strength and determination unlike anything she'd ever known before. She straightened up, full of pride in her mate, her hand falling away from her ribs as her pain was pushed back into oblivion. A blast of wind struck her, twisting her beribboned hair into a sleek black banner behind her head. She didn't even look to see Elijah become solid. Her full attention went to the second pentagram.

Lucas leapt into the air, his powerful wings finally free to carry him out of his prison. He was heading for a large window, clearly unperturbed by the glass in his way. Isabella gave chase, scrabbling over a series of crates that were stacked up to the window level. She couldn't have wished for better luck. If they took their battle outside, she wouldn't have to worry about disrupting the powers of the Demons who fought the necromancers behind her.

Bella! Not outside! If he gains the open, he will escape you!

Trust me, love, he won't want to. You told me yourself, the Transformed have only two thoughts. Now that the first, freedom and self-preservation, is satisfied, that leaves only the second, and the full moon that magnifies it a thousand times.

She felt the disquiet and doubt that twisted around inside of him, but he said nothing and thought nothing to gainsay her. She turned to her task, leaping headlong out of the window mere seconds after Lucas crashed through the glass.

Elijah turned on the nearest necromancer, a short, chubby fellow who looked as though he were going to soil himself with fear. He gave him a wicked smile and a low growl of greeting.

"Come, necromancer, at least make it interesting. You know . . . dying in a blaze of glory and all that."

Elijah received a vicious bolt of power in the center of his back in response. He staggered forward with the force of it, his flesh feeling as though it was being flayed apart. The warrior was able to ignore the pain that followed, having trained himself to remain on his feet through far worse injury, and regained his balance while turning to seek out his attacker.

"Leave him alone, you monstrous bastard!"

A female. And she was five times more powerful than the one she was protecting. Before Elijah could move, a streak of white and tan crashed into the woman, tackling her to the ground. Legna let out a cry of triumph as she grabbed the other female by the throat, forced her to hold still, and locked eyes with her.

"Spawn, am I? Straight from hell, yes?" she hissed viciously, a resonating, animalistic sound trebling out of her. The rush of her returned power made her giddy, just as the sharp influence of the moon encouraged her wildness. Her predator's gaze pushed past lens and retina, driving through the tunnel of black pupil as she thrust herself into the necromancer's mind. "See, sorceress. See yourself in hell."

Legna tore through every memory, every source of fear imagery her captive had ever had. She ravaged the female's mind as a strip miner ravages the earth, dragging from it precious minerals of sins and diabolical wrongs she'd committed.

Ingrid screamed at a bloodcurdling pitch as she felt herself being thrust into the bowels of her personal picture of hell, the one that had terrified her since she had learned of the concept at the age of six. She was cast down into a pit of flame and poison, feeling her flesh corrode away as hell began to scream her name, long and loud and full of punishing intent. Every person and creature she had ever wronged in her life began to well up from the poisonous pool she was bathing in, each clawing and scraping at her and howling for revenge.

She was very much alive when her accusers began to tear her to pieces.

And very much dead beneath Legna's hands by the time they finished.

"Hell is in your mind, necromancer," she whispered to her defeated foe, "and so is death, the very moment you believe in it."

Meanwhile, Gideon's astral form was hovering over the third male. The magic-user was considering his options, trying to figure out what to do, and Gideon could see it in the furtive shift of his eyes.

"An attack will be useless. You cannot harm me, infant," Gideon stated blankly.

Unfortunately, the necromancer didn't realize that Gideon was merely stating a fact.

The necromancer began to conjure up a cloud of poison, using the gesture of his hands to send it swirling around the Body Demon. He backed it with a push of force, trying to drive the poison into the Demon's cellular structure. Gideon watched the poison seep through him as if he were studying the marching pattern of a line of ants. However, since he was in the lightest corporeal adhesion of his astral form, there was nowhere for the poison to go, so it spilled away from him, scudding over the floor. The necromancer's eyes nearly bugged out of his head as he witnessed this.

Then he was being pinned in place by implacable silver eyes.

"How tragic, that so weak and pathetic a being has managed to cause such pain to my kind," Gideon observed coolly.

Then, with the speed of a thought, Gideon became fully corporeal, his astral form solidifying into the perfect manifestation of his fierce reflexes and hard muscle. He shot forward with savage grace, a hand shooting out to snag the necromancer around the throat. He pivoted in a single motion, slamming the nasty creature into a wall for added counterforce in his effort to strangle the life from the kicking, struggling sorcerer. With merely the pressure of his fingers and palm, he played the role of death closing in on the damn fool mortal. Powerful magics or no, he was as fragile as any human and no match for Demon strength. This was without making mention of the barely capped fury the normally controlled Ancient found himself struggling with.

"You will never again threaten Magdelegna, or any other Demon, with your ignorance and avarice. Your death is too easy a punishment, necromancer. Be grateful for that."

A last breath rattled out of the necromancer, and Gideon released him with an absent shaking of his hand, as if flinging off some vile contaminant as the body fell to the floor. He turned his back on it without the slightest regret.

His mercury gaze sought out Legna, settling on her just as she rose from her position over the female necromancer. She threw back her head and shoulders, taking the deep, cleansing breath of a female predator satisfied with her kill. She'd always been the most beautiful female he'd ever seen, but now, in this victorious moment, she was utterly stunning. Gideon felt a savage response within himself, an urge so vital that it took nearly every ounce of his formidable control to tamp it down and lock it out of his thoughts so she wouldn't become aware of it.

Chapter Fifteen

It was Jacob and Noah, side by side, who took on Kyle.

By far the most powerful of the four, he unleashed a barrage of electrical spears from his fingertips. Noah reached out one hand and every last bolt suddenly targeted it as if attracted by some sort of magnet. There was a sonic pop as Noah absorbed the fierce attack and literally sucked the energy into his own. Noah was impressed with how the necromancer remained unfazed, instantly dishing up a second attack.

Unexpectedly, the floor beneath Noah and Jacob splintered, sending them crashing through it. With a fast thought, Jacob altered their weight and the pull of gravity, allowing them to land on their feet in a gentle touchdown. They turned to launch themselves back to the necromancer's level, but the brash creature had followed them down, levitating above them as he unleashed a third offensive.

Out of nowhere, a hail of iron nails suddenly flew at the two Demons.

Jacob felt them sinking into his shoulder, hip, and thigh before he even realized they were coming at him.

Several more hit Noah, knocking the King back off his feet. Each nail felt as if someone were extinguishing a cigar deep in the tissue of his body. They burned, scorching his flesh, the pain driving him to his knees. Using every ounce of concentration he could gather, he reached for Noah and, grabbing his wrist, deconstructed their bodies into swirls of dark dust. The nails were left behind and dropped with a clatter onto the cement floor.

The Demons rematerialized, ignoring their pain as they finally opened a counterattack.

Noah released a ball of fire, catapulting it at the necromancer with shocking speed. The necromancer muttered a rapid spell and the fireball struck an invisible barrier not a foot away from its target. Noah swore under his breath even as Jacob focused his thoughts. Noah felt the room's atmosphere change and saw the necromancer shudder. Jacob narrowed his effect, not wishing to bring the entire building down on their heads as he manipulated gravity. The necromancer staggered under his own increasing weight, falling to his knees.

Then suddenly Jacob was struck with a powerful feedback of his own power. It crashed into him, sweeping him off his feet and slamming him to the ground with a cough of stolen breath. He'd never experienced this before. His exposure to the dealings with necromancers in history was limited to the hunt of the Transformed. It was Elijah who had the best experience in defeating these creatures. He found a new respect for the Warrior Captain as he realized the necromancer was far more dangerous than he and Noah were giving him credit for.

The necromancer was smiling toothily, clearly enjoying their frustrated attempts at attacking him. Then he flung out his hands as he muttered another spell. This time the hail of iron that swept toward them was a flock of blades like those of a circular saw, filling the room with a whining sound as they spun through the air toward them. Jacob and Noah uttered the exact same profanity as they burst into smoke and dust, barely escaping injury.

"That's right, spawn!" the necromancer mocked. "Get away while the getting's good. I have more ways of throwing iron at you then you can ever imagine!"

"We need to get out of here. We are hindering Jacob and Noah's battle. They can't go full bore with us in the building," Legna said quickly.

Gideon disappeared instantly and Elijah grabbed his imprisoned necromancer by the back of his neck and scattered himself to the wind. Legna hurried up the stairway of crates Isabella had taken to the window so she could see outside. She focused on a nearby street corner and then disappeared from the building with a silent pop, reappearing on her chosen corner.

She turned to face the males as they rematerialized next to her.

"Where's Isabella?"

"Pretty."

"Yeah, yeah, I know all about it," Isabella muttered as the altered Demon circled her in an obscene dance of lusting interest.

They weren't too far from the building they'd just left, down in a sloped pit of freshly hoed dirt, apparently a new construction site of some sort. Isabella was

aware of Jacob's struggles with the necromancer in the
building behind her, but she mostly concentrated on
the lewd contemplations of the Transformed Demon
before her. She glanced around, wondering if any
of the construction equipment would provide some
much-needed iron weaponry. But iron was an outdated
metal, steel long since being the choice for its strength
and resistance to corrosion.

The Demon's nostrils flared as it repeatedly took in
her scent, its forked tongue licking up and down one
of its longest fangs with obvious avarice.

"Come on, handsome, you know you want it," she invited silkily, tossing back her hair so she could flaunt
the lush curves of her body. She sounded pretty confident to herself, which was actually quite amazing considering her heart was about to beat right out of her
chest with her anxiety. Could she do this without an
iron weapon?

Remember, little flower . . .

Her mind was suddenly filled with image after image
of her training with Elijah, as well as the hand-to-hand
victories she had achieved with so little effort ever since
this adventure into her new life had begun. It had been
instinct that had carried her through, and it was instinct combined with training that would make her
even more easily victorious.

The Demon lunged for her, falling onto the ground
and scrabbling in the dirt when his target moved too fast
for him to comprehend. It rose up on all fours, snorting
and shaking off dust like a dog shakes off water, turning
to see where she had gone. She was standing exactly
where he had been when he'd started his attack, brushing invisible dirt from her silver dress's skirt.

The Transformed stared at her in confusion for a

moment, sniffing warily to see if she was the same
target he'd just tried to obtain. This time it was he who
moved too fast for her to distinguish, his claws rending
the silky fabric of her dress as she jumped away at the
last minute. She gasped in shock as her side blossomed
in pain once more, this time with the added injury of
dirty talons breaking through her fragile skin. The
Demon backhanded her across the face, knocking her
right off her feet and sending her down into the dirt
with a sprawling cough. He fumbled across to her,
clambering over her body, clutching and groping at
her with slimy, clawed hands.

"Bella!"

Noah's head jerked around when Jacob suddenly
snarled out his mate's name. It was clear the Enforcer's
focus was torn in that moment between two battles, and
Noah needed him to focus on only one. He grabbed
Jacob by the sleeve, jerking him out of range of the
necromancer's latest attack, slamming him physically
into a nearby wall in a way that got his full attention.

"Pay attention!" Noah growled at him.

Jacob's outrage served to treble Bella's, the two blending within her heart and soul and propelling her reaction. She reached up and raked her fingernails over the
foul creature's eyes. It reared back instantly, howling in
pain and anger. Isabella pivoted on the ground with her
hip, her legs flying with impressive force toward the
Demon's head. There was a satisfying crack when the
two met.

Once the Demon had fallen, the little Enforcer went

at him with both barrels. She fought like a wildcat, plotting each strike to its most vulnerable spots with predatory cunning. If anyone had seen her, they might have thought she was toying with the powerful creature, playing with him like a child plays with unpalatable food on its plate. The Demon yowled with hurting and frustration as the soft, pretty toy he'd wanted turned on him with the vengeance of twenty hells.

Bella muttered a swift plea to Jacob's Destiny before she launched herself full strength at the Demon, her hand clutching into a fierce fist as she targeted the distorted ribcage that protected its poisonous heart.

The cry of a wildcat wailed through the night.

Jacob and Noah tried to rush the necromancer in their insubstantial forms, but he'd thrown up another barrier to keep them at bay. The Enforcer and the King dropped to their feet in full form.

"How the hell do we get close to him?"

"The others are out of the structure. We do not need to get close to him any more," Jacob announced darkly. He threw his arms out wide and literally rocked the world.

The necromancer was unprepared for the earthquake and his instinctive human reaction of fear as the building started to fall down around him. It broke his concentration, and Noah took advantage of it in a heartbeat. He threw out an enormous ball of heat, causing everything burnable to combust. He only spared the area immediately around Jacob. The room exploded in flame. The necromancer screamed as his ridiculous cloak and all the rest of his clothing turned to instant ash. The scent of burning flesh filled the air.

And just like that, in an instant of time, the battle was over.

Jacob and Noah left the inferno. Noah was in no danger, but Jacob could only bear the heat for so long. They appeared on the sidewalk beside the others, dragging the scent of smoke and soot with them.

"Hmm, cozy campfire, brother dear," Legna laughed, throwing her arms around him and letting him hug her with the devastating relief in his heart.

"Are you okay? Tell me you are okay," he said fiercely, practically squeezing the breath out of her body.

"I am fine, Noah. Nothing happened to me. Gideon said it was because of Isabella."

"Thank Destiny," he said feverishly. "Thank Destiny for Isabella."

"Where is Isabella?"

Everyone went still and they all turned to face Jacob.

"Don't you know?" Elijah asked.

"No. I cannot . . . She is not with me . . ." He cocked his head as if listening for something. "Wait . . . she is close . . . and she is upset. Damn it, she is crying."

As if it had been choreographed, all but Elijah left the sidewalk, each in their own fashion, hustling after the dust devil that was Jacob.

Jacob whipped into solid form on the ground of the construction site, turning around sharply to seek out his Bella. Relief washed through him when he saw her sitting on a log several yards away. He ran over to her with the speed of a cheetah, skidding to a halt in the dusty dirt that surrounded her.

"Bella?"

She looked up when he spoke, and Jacob couldn't

help the choked gasp that escaped him. The sound was echoed several times as the others caught up to him. Isabella was covered in dirt, soot, and what could only be described as goo. The cleanest place on her was the two rivers of skin on her face that had been washed clean by her tears.

And then there was her hair. It stuck out in short, crispy spikes, little tendrils of smoke still curling up out of the charred mass.

Bella burst into fresh tears, sobbing with such wretched misery that Jacob dropped to his knees and gathered her up against himself.

"Aw, sweetheart, hush. It will be okay," he soothed, hugging her and comforting her as best he could. "What happened?" She smelled awful, looked awful, but for the most part appeared undamaged, and nothing could have relieved Jacob more. He welcomed the vitality and emotion of her tears. She was crying, embarrassed and mad as hell at herself for some reason he couldn't fathom in that moment, but she was alive and safe and in his arms where she belonged. Nothing else mattered.

"I . . . I forgot . . ." she hiccupped miserably. "It's so stupid." She shuddered with another sob. "I forgot that after you kill the thing it . . . it bursts into flames! Oh, Jacob . . . Jacob, I burned all my hair off!" she wailed piteously.

Jacob turned his face aside, trying for all he was worth to not even think about laughing. If she caught wind of an ounce of humor from him, she would no doubt murder him on the spot. It was difficult, though, because the flood of his relief backed the wash of humor that bubbled up in him.

Unfortunately, Noah didn't exercise the same amount

of control. He made a muffled sound of poorly repressed laughter, earning himself a backhanded smack in the head from his little sister.

"Noah! Do not dare!" Legna hissed.

"I am sorry, Bella," the King stammered around his escaping laughter, "but I cannot help it!"

"Fine," Isabella sniffled indignantly. "You go ahead and laugh. I deserve it." She turned her eyes up to Noah, the spark of temper in them too quick for Jacob to catch. "After all, I burned you *bald*, Noah, and I'm sure you looked twice as ridiculous as I do now!"

"Bella!" Legna gasped incredulously, popping out a laugh as her brother's humor instantly faded and he flushed red as a rose.

Then Bella laughed, a short sound that was half giggle and half sob.

"I suppose I look pretty funny. And I know how hard you're trying not to laugh, Jacob, so you might as well give up."

"No, I will not laugh at you, little flower. I am too relieved to have you back to laugh."

Bella swiped at her tears with dirty hands, causing a wild swirling pattern to appear in the dirt on her cheeks. She looked up at him with sheepish eyes.

"Can we go home? I need a shower."

"Of course we can," he told her, scooping her up against him as he regained his feet. "You had a hard night's work tonight, my little Enforcer. A shower is the least of what you deserve."

"Did you get them all? Oh, of course you did. You're you." She sniffed away the last of her tears. "I'm glad. That means"—she was hit with a yawn, finishing her thought around the distortion it caused "—no one can hurt Legna anymore."

"We were lucky that they were not very strong over-all. I have seen far more powerful necromancers, and they are not so easy to defeat," Noah said, his tone sounding a little more than grave.

"Thank you, Isabella." Legna reached to squeeze the little Enforcer's dirty hand affectionately. "And do not worry about your hair. Gideon can fix it. Right, Gideon?"

"If you desire it."

Legna paused and looked up into the Demon's steady silver eyes, wondering why he'd worded his response in such a way. Was it her imagination, or had he directed that to her and not to Bella? However, he seemed just as indifferent as always, and she shrugged it off.

"And do not forget," Legna said eagerly to Isabella. "Tonight is still your wedding night!"

"Provided we finish the ceremony before the moon drops," Noah remarked.

"Uh . . . not to spoil that idea," Isabella piped up, "but I think I broke a rib or something."

"Oh, hell!" Jacob exclaimed, gingerly setting her back on her feet. "Why didn't you say so? Carrying you like that must hurt!"

"This is a fact," Gideon agreed, "considering she has broken three ribs and suffered deep lacerations. Beneath all that charred fabric, she is bleeding quite extensively."

"Oh. Well, I guess that's why it hurts," Isabella noted with a wry little laugh.

"You think?" Legna said dryly.

"I cannot heal you in my astral body. I will await your return to Noah's home."

Gideon winked out in a sparkle of white light.

"That's easy for him to say."

"Not to worry, Bella," Legna called as she backpedaled

away from Isabella swiftly. "Legna's travel agency is at your service."

With a soft pop of displaced air, Legna swept the Druid away. The men waited until Legna lifted her head from her concentration.

"Safe and sound," she reported. Then, with a grin, she popped herself off.

Gideon was just getting to his feet when Bella and Legna materialized in Noah's home a moment later. Though a good deal of work to refurbish the King's home had already begun to take place, Isabella couldn't escape the feeling that the still-sooty surroundings matched perfectly how she looked and felt in that moment. She found a stone bench and lowered herself onto it with a sigh as Legna moved quickly to her side. The beauty took up her hand.

The Ancient medic moved close to the female Enforcer, crouching down before her while he slowly examined her with both his eyes and his senses. The medic's silver eyes focused on the stain of blood spreading beneath Isabella's right breast.

"You are fortunate not to have punctured a lung." He reached for a seam at the waist of her former bridal dress and gripped it in his free hand. With a swift jerk he tore a large swath away from the seam, exposing her brutal wound. Legna made a soft sound of pained sympathy when she saw the sharp fragment of bone jutting out through Bella's skin.

"You bear it well," Gideon remarked.

Bella looked at him in surprise.

"Gideon . . . did you actually just pay me a compliment?" she asked, making sure her shock was well magnified in her voice. Legna ruined it, though, by laughing in an irrepressible snort out her nose, making Bella first laugh, then gasp in pain.

"Perhaps now you will have a care respecting an Ancient," Gideon said with his usual, unshakable superiority.

Gideon's eyes slid half closed and his fingers began to slide down the deep neckline of her dress, along the line of her breastbone. Bella jerked harshly and Legna gasped.

"Can you not stop her pain?"

"That is what I am doing," Gideon said, his tone perplexed as he clearly tried to focus further. "You must relax, Bella," he instructed as he reached for the torn wound, seeking to begin with healing ribs beneath her breast.

"Wait!"

Isabella grabbed Gideon's hand and simultaneously held her other palm to her forehead as if suddenly bludgeoned by a very bad headache.

"Oh, boy," Legna said softly, releasing a giggle as she quickly perceived what Gideon couldn't. "Gideon, I suggest you wait a little while."

"Nonsense. The longer we wait, the more taxing it will be for her."

"Explain that to her future husband," Legna said pointedly, reaching out two fingertips to pluck the medic's wrist away from Bella as if he were going to contaminate her.

Apparently, in spite of his distance from his mate, Jacob was refusing to tolerate Gideon's hands on Isabella without being present himself. Gideon sighed but waited until the triad of powerful Demons all coalesced in the Great Hall some time later.

Jacob swore softly, raking a hand through his hair as he went to stand like a guard at Bella's side.

"Never," he said low on his breath, "let any other man touch you without warning me well in advance first. Better yet, never let any other man touch you."

"Jacob, you're being ridiculous," she scolded him.

"Just obey me on this one matter, Bella."

She looked like she wanted to argue, but she just wanted to get the healing over with, so she shrugged in half-hearted agreement.

"My apologies, Gideon," he said tightly to the medic. "Feel free to continue."

Gideon nodded, studying the Enforcer for a long minute before slowly returning his attention to Jacob's injured mate. He reached for a less overtly sexual place on her body this time, allowing his fingertips to skim over her forehead as he went to touch the charred remains of her formerly lovely hair.

The growl that erupted out of the Enforcer was so chilling that Gideon actually jerked away from Isabella as if something had just tried to bite off his hand. When his eyes darted to the feral expression in Jacob's eyes, he was surprised the Enforcer had not done exactly that. After a moment, Jacob seemed to recover himself, realizing with obvious horror that he'd just threatened the oldest of their kind.

"Ah hell," Jacob sighed, turning away from his mate and the medic. "I am going to . . . go somewhere else."

Jacob burst into a shower of dust, slipping away on the fastest breeze he could find.

Perplexed at this complete contradiction, Isabella looked at Gideon.

"The moon has effects even you cannot quell, Druid," he explained. "You can keep him from losing control and causing damage with his abilities, but your proximity can only affect the manifestations of his power, not of the beast within him, nor the instincts that come with it. Frankly, I am surprised that I do not find I am deprived of a limb right now."

Bella gasped suddenly, her eyes widening enormously.

"Fear not, Enforcer. I am certain Noah and Legna would have kept me safe."

"I don't care about that," she exclaimed, missing the mild consternation that flitted through the medic's silver eyes. "Jacob *left*!"

"He realized he could not control himself. It was a wise decision."

"I know that," she barked in more than mild irritation. "And you're supposed to be an almighty Ancient?" She rolled her eyes. "I mean he *left* when he was standing right *next* to me!" She sighed heftily when they continued to look at her for clarification. "Okay . . . try this. Jacob, here." She pointed to the sooty floor near her feet, which still held the imprint of his shoes. "Bella, here. Jacob . . . Bella . . . Demon . . . Druid . . . Power . . . power *dampener*!"

"Hey!" Legna exclaimed as she lit up with understanding. "How did you do that?"

"I . . . don't know?"

"Well you must have done something," Noah pointed out.

"She did," Gideon stated calmly. "She injured herself."

"I did," Isabella agreed. Then she frowned. "And that means what, exactly?"

"When pain receptors fire in such magnitude, it disrupts the flow of energy in your body. It is very similar to the way injury and great pain hinder a Demon's ability to concentrate. For you, however, it is all taking place on a subconscious level."

"Oh! I get it!" Isabella smiled triumphantly. "Um, you better heal me while the healing is good. I can hear Jacob grumbling in my head."

"I suggest you think of something other than my touch, Druid. I should not like you to inadvertently send him the very images he is attempting to distance himself from."

"Hey, Bella," Legna said with a giggle. "See any pink elephants lately?"

Isabella found Jacob sitting on the altar, his fist on his raised knee, his chin on his fist as he contemplated the clouds that ghosted over the moon. She bent to kiss his cheek, her newly grown hair coasting silkily over his nose and mouth. He lifted his chin, opening his palm to catch the soft ebony strands.

"You must be tired," he said quietly. "I know being healed wears a body out."

"So does beating the tar out of no-good necromancers," she said, her hand pressing against his thigh until he dropped his leg at its insistence. She turned and settled herself in his lap, her arms wrapping warmly around the back of his neck. He wondered if she had any idea how the hold affected him. There was something about holding her in this particular manner that made him feel like the king of her world. He drew her close to his chest, pressing his lips to her forehead.

"You *are* the king of my world," she said in a whisper, returning his kiss with one of her own. "Lucky me to have such a romantic and loving soul for my monarch."

"And you are the queen who rules over my heart.

Bella," he said fiercely, "I have never known such acceptance, such love. Sometimes I feel it is a wonder that I do not burst into flame with the intensity of it."

"Please, Jacob," she sighed, "if you love me, you will not use the phrase 'burst into flames' ever again."

He chuckled at that, kissing her cheek and her neck before tasting her lips gently.

"The night is over. There will not be time to finish the ceremony," he said with regret.

"I would imagine that means you and I have a date, come Beltane."

"I am sorry. I wanted this to be a special day for you. I even thought it might be normal . . . almost human," he said with regret.

"Everything that can possibly go wrong, going wrong on a bride's wedding day is as normal as it gets, Jacob."

"Yes, but how many brides get turned into toast after doing battle with a monster?" he asked bitterly.

"The ones who forget to duck fast enough. Come on Jacob. Don't do this. If you resent what I've become because of you, then you resent who I am . . . resent me."

"Never," he said fiercely. "I will never resent you." He was quiet for a long moment. "But I will never be glad to see you march into danger. You have to forgive me this chauvinistic part of my love for you, Bella, but I will never feel completely comfortable watching you risk your life."

"And do you think it's any easier for me, Enforcer? Don't you know how hard it was for me to leave you behind, leave you to fight with that prejudiced, evil son of a bitch? I know how powerful he was, I could feel it from head to toe." She rested her forehead in the crook of his neck. "But I'm glad you are who you are, if only because I have someone to turn to and ask . . . does it ever get easier?"

"Does what?"

"Killing, Jacob. I never . . . never intentionally . . . Is it always so hard?"

"Always," he assured her tightly. "It is the day it is no longer hard to take that you should begin to worry."

She nodded mutely as he gathered her even tighter against himself.

"Do you think, little flower, that there will ever come a day when you regret meeting me?" he asked quietly.

"Yes," she said simply.

"I see," he said tightly.

"Would you like a specific date?"

"You are teasing me," he realized suddenly.

"No, I'm dead serious. I have an exact date in mind."

Jacob pulled back to see her eyes, looking utterly perplexed as her pupils sparkled with mischief.

"What date is that? And why are you thinking of pink elephants?"

"The date is September 8, because, according to Gideon, that's possibly the day I will go into labor. I say 'possibly,' because combining all this human/Druid and Demon DNA 'may make for a longer period of gestation than usual for a human,' as the Ancient medic recently quoted. Now, as I understand it, women always regret ever letting a man touch them on that day."

Jacob lurched to his feet, dropping her onto her toes, grabbing her by the arms, and holding her still as he raked a wild, inspecting gaze over her body.

"You are pregnant?" he demanded, shaking her a little. "How long have you known? You went into battle with that monster while you are carrying *my* child?"

"*Our* child," she corrected indignantly, her fists landing firmly on her hips, "and Gideon only just told me, like, five seconds ago, so I didn't know I was pregnant when I was fighting that thing!"

"But . . . he healed you just a few days ago! Why not tell you then?"

"Because I wasn't pregnant then, Jacob. If you recall, we did make love between then and now."

"Oh . . . oh Bella . . ." he said, his breath rushing from him all of a sudden.

He looked as if he needed to sit down and put a paper bag over his head. She reached to steady him as he sat back awkwardly on the altar. He leaned his forearms on his thighs, bending over them as he tried to catch his breath. Bella had the strangest urge to giggle, but she bit her lower lip to repress the impulse.

So much for the calm, cool, collected Enforcer who struck terror into the hearts of Demons everywhere.

"That is not funny," he grumbled indignantly.

"Yeah? You should see what you look like from over here," she teased.

"If you laugh at me I swear I am going to take you over my knee."

"Promises, promises," she laughed, hugging him with delight. Finally, Jacob laughed as well, his arm snaking out to circle her waist and draw her back into his lap.

"Did you ask . . . I mean, does he know what it is?"

"It's a baby. I told him I didn't want to know what it is. And don't you dare find out, because you know the minute you do I'll know, and if you spoil the surprise I'll murder you."

"Damn . . . she kills a couple of Demons and suddenly thinks she can order all of us around," he taunted, pulling her close until he was nuzzling her

12376   *Jacquelyn Frank*

neck, wondering if it was possible for such an under-used heart as his to contain so much happiness. It felt as though his chest were going to explode.

"I'd love to see how happy you are changing diapers and getting spit up on."

"Are you kidding? That will no doubt be the best part," he chuckled.

"Are you sure?" She was suddenly very serious. "Jacob, you've been so solitary for so long. Adjusting to me is going to be difficult enough as it is, but a baby too?"

"Bella . . . my sweet little flower," he said softly, reverently as he took her head between his hands and pressed their foreheads together. "After over four hundred years of solitude, I think I am ready for you and an entire barrel full of children. Nothing could please me more."

"Oh, Jacob," she sighed with delight, kissing his lips eagerly. "How did I get so lucky?"

"Well, as I recall . . . you had the bad luck to fall out of a window."

"Ah, but that was good luck, because you caught me."

"No, little flower," he murmured, pausing to kiss her deeply and thoroughly. "I think it is safe to say that you are the one who caught me."

We don't think you will want to miss
Jacquelyn Frank's next novel in this great series.

GIDEON: The Nightwalkers

will be available in the summer of 2007.
Here's a sneak peek.

Gideon wore the habits of his lifetime like an unapologetic statement, and he wore them very well. He blended the male fashions of the millennium in a way that was nothing less than a perfect reflection of who he was and how he had lived. This only served to beautify his distinctive and powerful presence and his incidental confidence.

"Gideon," she said evenly, inclining her head in sparse respect. "What brings you to my chambers, so close to dawn?"

The riveting male before her remained silent, his silver eyes flicking over her slowly. Her heart nearly stopped with her sudden fear, and immediately she threw up every mental and physical barrier she could to prevent an unwelcome scan and analysis of her health.

"I would not scan you without your permission, Magdelegna. Body Demons who become healers have codes of ethics as well as any others."

"Funny," she remarked, "I would have thought you to believe yourself above such a trivial matter as permission."

His mercury gaze narrowed slightly, making Legna

wish that she had the courage to dare a piratical scan of her own. She was quite talented at masking her travels through the emotions and psyches of others, but Gideon was like no other. She was barely a fledgling to one such as he.

Gideon had noted her more recent acerbic tendencies aloud once before, irritating the young female even more than usual, so he resisted the urge in that moment to scold her again and instead let her attitude pass.

"I have come to check on your well-being, Magdelegna. I am concerned."

Legna cocked a brow, twisting her lips into a cold, mocking little smile, hiding the sudden, anxious beating of her heart.

"And what would give you the impression that you need be concerned for me?" she asked haughtily.

Gideon once more took his time before responding, giving her another of those implacable perusals in the interim. Legna exhaled with annoyance, crossing her arms beneath her breasts and coming just shy of tapping her foot in irritation.

"You are not at peace, young one," Gideon explained softly, the deep timbre of his voice resonating through her, once again giving her the feeling that she was but fragile crystal, awaiting the moment when he would strike the note of discord that would shatter her. Legna's breathing altered, quickening in spite of her effort to maintain an even keel. She did not want to give him the satisfaction of being right.

"You presume too much, Gideon. I have no need for your concern, nor have I ever solicited it. Now, if you don't mind, I should like to go to bed."

"For what purpose?"

Legna laughed, short and harsh.

"To sleep, why else?"

"You have not slept for many days together, Legna. Why do you assume you might have success today?"

Legna turned around sharply, driving her gaze and attention back out of the window, trying to use the sprawling lawn as a slate to fill her mind with. Mind Demon he was not, but she knew he was capable of seeing far enough into her emotional state by just monitoring her physiological reactions to his observations. Legna bit her lip hard, furious that she should feel like the child he always referred to her as in their conversations. Young one, indeed. How would he like it if she referred to him as a decrepit old buzzard?

The thought gave her a small, petty satisfaction. It did not matter that Gideon looked as vital and vibrant as any Demon male from thirty years to a thousand would look. Nor did it matter that his stunning coloring gave him a unique attractiveness and aura of power that no one else could equal. All that mattered was that he would never view her as an equal, and therefore, in her perspective, she had no responsibility to do so for him.

Gideon watched the young woman across from him closely, trying to make sense of the physiological changes that flashed through her rapidly, each as puzzling as the one before it. What was it about her, he wondered, that always kept him off his mark? She never reacted the way he logically expected her to, yet he knew her to be extraordinarily intelligent. She always treated him with a barely repressed contempt, though she never had a harsh word for anyone else. He had almost gotten used to that since their original falling-out, but this was different, far more complex than hard feelings. Gideon had not encountered a puzzle in a great many centuries, and perhaps that was why he was continually fascinated by her in spite of her marked disdain.

"It is not unusual," she said at last, "to have periods of insomnia in one's life. Surely that is not what has you rushing into my boudoir, oozing your high-handed version of concern."

"Magdelegna, I am continually puzzled by your insistence in treating me with hostility. Did Lucas teach you nothing about respecting your elders?"

Legna whirled around suddenly, outrage flaring off her so violently that Gideon felt the eddy of it push at him through the still air.

"Do not ever mention Lucas in such a disrespectful manner ever again! Do you understand me, Gideon? I will not tolerate it!" She moved to stand toe to toe with the medic, her emotions practically beating him back in their intensity. "You say respect my elders, but what you mean is respecting my betters, is that not right? Are you so full of your own arrogance that you need me to bow and kowtow to you like some throwback fledgling? Or perhaps we should reinstate the role of concubines in our society. Then you may have the pleasure of claiming me and forcing me to fall to my knees, bowing low in respect of your masculine eminence!"

Gideon watched as she did just that, her gown billowing around her as she gracefully kneeled before him, so close to him that her knees touched the tips of his boots. She swept her hands to her sides, bowing her head until her forehead brushed the leather, her hair spilling like reams of heavy silk around his ankles.

The Ancient found himself unusually speechless, the strangest sensation creeping through him as he looked down at the exposed nape of her neck, the elegant line of her back. Unable to curb the impulse, Gideon lowered himself into a crouch, reaching beneath the cloak of coffee-colored hair to touch her flushed cheek. The heat of her anger radiated against his touch and he recognized it long before she turned her face up to him.

"Does this satisfy you, my lord Gideon?" she whispered fiercely, her eyes flashing like flinted steel.

Gideon found himself searching her face intently, his eyes roaming over the high aristocratic curves of her cheekbones, the impossibly full sculpture of her lips, the wide, accusing eyes that lay behind extraordinarily thick lashes. He cupped her chin between the thumb and forefinger of his left hand, his fingertips fanning softly over an angrily flushed cheek.

"You do enjoy mocking me," he murmured softly to her, the breath of his words close enough to skim across her face.

"No more than you seem to enjoy condescending to me," she replied, her clipped words coming out on quick, heated breaths.

Gideon absorbed the latest venom directed toward him with a blink of lengthy black lashes. They kept their gazes locked, each seemingly waiting for the other to look away.

"You have never forgiven me," he said suddenly, softly.

"Forgiven you?" She laughed bitterly. "Gideon, you are not important enough to earn my forgiveness."

"Is your ego so fragile, Legna, that a small slight to it is irreparable?"

"Stop talking to me as if I were a temperamental child!" Legna hissed, moving to jerk her head back but finding his grip quite secure. "There was nothing slight about the way you treated me. I will never forget it, and I most certainly will never forgive it!"